Lox seemed to hes Let's talk a little about morality, since the human mind is capable of all kinds of self-delusion if it thinks itself to be uniquely in the right.

"You have a wife and children, do you not, Mr. Kulat?"

Kulat tensed, not answering. If these madmen didn't know about his family they would be safer.

"It was a rhetorical question, Mr. Kulat," Lox said. "We know you do. And we're not, for the moment, at least, interested in them. This could, of course, change."

Lox let the threat hang in the air for a few moments, then said, "I would like you to imagine whichever one it is in the world you most love, in the hands of your enemies. Put your best loved face to that image in your mind. Perhaps it's your wife, or your son. Maybe it's a father or mother.

"Now picture that best loved face, and the human being behind it, kidnapped, mistreated, tortured, dismembered. What would you not do to save them?

"If you didn't know how to save them, would it be wrong for you to hire someone who did?"

Lox gave a grim smile. "I ask you these things, Mr. Kulat, so that you will understand that you are the key to saving someone else's best beloved, and there is no limit to what we will do to you, on behalf of our principal, to get that person back, whole and safe."

Baen Books by Tom Kratman
★★★

COUNTDOWN
★ H HOUR ★

★ ★ ★

TOM KRATMAN

BAEN

COUNTDOWN: H HOUR

This is a work of fiction. All the characters and events portrayed in this book are fictional, and any resemblance to real people or incidents is purely coincidental.

A Baen Books Original

Baen Publishing Enterprises
P.O. Box 1403
Riverdale, NY 10471
www.baen.com

ISBN: 978-1-4516-3793-9

Cover art by Kurt Miller

First Baen paperback printing, August 2012

Distributed by Simon & Schuster
1230 Avenue of the Americas
New York, NY 10020

Printed in the United States of America

10 9 8 7 6 5 4 3 2 1

★★★

For Number Three Daughter,
Sarah, aka Smurfette, aka *Pitufina*

★★★

★★★

PART I:

Republic of the Philippines, Guyana, and at sea

★★★

★ CHAPTER ONE ★

The times they are a changin'
—Bob Dylan

Bonifacio Global City (ex-Fort William McKinley), Manila, Republic of the Philippines

Cool air from a wall vent bathing him, the second richest man in the Republic of the Philippines, Lucio Enrique Ayala, sat in a comfortable, fabric covered chair, legs spread, trousers undone, with a young stripped-to-the-waist girl's head bobbing rhythmically above him. Occasionally, she stole a glance at a small clock on the table beside the old man's chair. Ayala assumed she was timing herself, prolonging the festivities, the better to please him and secure her own position.

From outside and below, on the other side of the broad glass, curtain-framed wall, came the faint sound of very light traffic. Of *course* the traffic was light; not only could few afford a personal automobile anymore—not that all that many ever had in the Republic of the Philippines—but the building in which Ayala sat, and which he, in fact, owned, sat in an area that discouraged traffic in any case.

The girl, Marissa, was something above the local, theoretical age of consent, twelve. She was also somewhat below the more practical age of consent, eighteen. In theory, this meant that, given the totality of the circumstances—provision of an apartment and of a stipend—Ayala could have been charged. He could have been but, of course, he never was. That's what it meant, in real life, to be the second richest man in the Philippines.

Old Man Ayala wasn't far behind number one, either.

Of average height among his people—which is to say, short—commonly dark, and—despite the approximately Spanish-Basque naming conventions—highly mixed in his ancestry. He also had a rich—and old—man's tastes, especially in women. Or girls.

He had his hands in a little bit of everything; real estate, shipping and transport, insurance, brewing, mining, manufacturing, telecommunications, and—so it was alleged—a not inconsequential chunk of the estate of a former president of the republic . . . for safekeeping, as it were. Ayala owned banks. He also had an indirect interest in any number of bordellos. Some of that interest had developed when he'd been a young lieutenant in the Philippine Army.

"Banks? Bordellos?" he'd been known to observe, with a shrug; "What's the difference?"

Almost the only thing Ayala didn't have a hand in was piracy. This wasn't a matter of moral scruples so much as a *deep* loathing for the Moros and other Moslems who dominated the industry, coupled with a realization that it was a wasting game. Make money for a couple of years; then trade would decline to the point that you were stuck with some ships, boats, and aggressive young men who were good for nothing *but* piracy. And dangerous, to boot.

No, Ayala had no direct hand in piracy. He made a fair piece of change from maritime insurance, however, which paid almost as well and was much steadier and safer, both.

As befit his station in this predominantly—and where predominant, highly—Catholic country, Ayala kept several mistresses, usually young and, since he had, after all, gotten on in years, highly pneumatic. This, in more senses than one. It wasn't actually his preference but, since a vacuuming mouth could maintain an old man's erection better than a tight vagina, it would have to do.

His wife didn't mind; she was very old school. She'd been *picked*, many decades before, precisely because she was very old school. That, also, in more senses than one. In truth, she'd have been embarrassed if her husband hadn't kept up appearances by maintaining several women. In her small circle of friends, small because she and her family had few peers on the islands, she boasted of it.

A pearl beyond any possible price, was Lucio's opinion of his—his own little and open infidelities aside— much-beloved Paloma. Of his seven children, he was much less fond. *He* was a rich man. They were just the sons and daughters of a rich man.

Which thoughts—*wretched parasite children*— completely destroyed the mood. Ayala put his hand gently on the bobbing head of the girl and ordered, "Stop, Marissa. I'm just not"—he cleared his throat—"quite up to it."

The girl pulled her head away, her normally pretty face stricken. She had this apartment, something she could never have afforded on her own, plus a not ungenerous stipend, only from pleasing the boss. Chewing her lower lip nervously, she gave a quick glance to the clock on the wall.

"No, child, it's not your fault," the old man reassured her. "I'm just . . . well, never mind; it's not your fault. I'll see you next week, at the usual time."

The girl nodded, still looking quite worried. She rearranged his trousers, *very* carefully closed the zipper, and then stood up and away to allow Ayala to stand. He saw, after standing, that she was looking down, still gnawing her lower lip, still fearful. He patted her cheek, quite gently, and said, "I *told* you, girl, it's not your fault. Your position is still secure."

Only then did she smile and only after she had did he feel he could leave. Even so, he thought the smile forced.

Ayala's guards, two all-business veterans of the Philippine Army and one even more anal retentive former Philippine Marine, were waiting on the other side of the door to the girl's apartment. Before the apartment door even closed behind the old man, the guards had formed a loose ring which they maintained until entering the elevator. At that point they took station between their employer and the sliding doors. For their defense, and his, they wore fairly high-end body armor under their dark suits, and carried pistols concealed in either shoulder or small-of-the-back holsters. For that matter, Ayala wore a partial chest and back covering under his own dress shirt.

The wood-paneled elevator began its slow descent. It moved silently, evidence of a degree of careful maintenance that few spots in the world could boast anymore, but which was still available for the moneyed and their pets . . . and their pets' gilded cages.

Ayala pushed any remaining thoughts of the girl out of his mind. He did, after all, have more important things to worry about. And she, in the big scheme of things, was about as important as a functioning toilet, and considerably less so than his next bowel movement.

Looking upward, Ayala mused, *Glad I got out of oil before the bottom dropped out . . . but, dammit, I caught the rise in precious metals almost too late . . . and China needs rice, with Yunnan and Guizhou half in rebellion over the re-collectivization, which is to say, making the children of high party cadres de facto feudal lords . . . Maybe buy more agricultural land? Opium is way up, along with every other euphoric known to man; go figure? Weak and useless people always turn to drugs when times get tough. Worth it to pay the bribes and convert some land to the poppy? Possibly; the price of personal honor has dropped precipitously of late. Problem is, I know almost nothing about that trade and the people who do can't really be trusted.*

Ayala sighed, audibly. The guards paid no attention; they were used to the old man's few little quirks.

And Wang-Huntington is insisting on payment one third in precious metals or it's no deal. But with the inversion between fiat currency and metals, I don't know if I can afford to give up the gold and silver. And, of course, it's that inversion that's driving them to insist.

The world is becoming a very screwed up place. I'm not sure I understand it anymore. And if I don't, who the hell does? Would W-H take indentured girls in lieu of the gold? China's still got that female shortage. Maybe I should propose it? Hell, the girls may as well be turning tricks in brothels in Shanghai as here in Manila. Who knows; a few of them might even find husbands.

On the other hand, I wonder if I can get someone in the army to raid a couple of villages on Mindanao for some Moro girls. Only fair, given how many of our girls they kidnap. Better, that would be mixing business with pleasure . . .

The elevator began to slow. The guards stiffened to full alert. Forearms and hands, once relaxed, moved suit jacket tails backwards, not quite exposing their pistols, something the old man found distasteful, but slicing fractions of a second from the time required to deploy those pistols.

The elevator stopped with a shudder. Quietly, the doors began to slide to the sides. About the time they were halfway open, or a bit more, the air began to vibrate even as the guards started to fly apart in red mist and disassociated chunks of meat and bone.

Though he was a pure Moro for as far back as anyone could tell, in looks Janail Hapilon might have been any Christian Filipino, any resident of Manila, so many were the Christian slave girls in his ancestry. Certainly nothing in his epicanthic fold, his medium dark skin, or his straight hair, close cropped and tinged with gray, gave a hint that he was the leader of the Harrikat, one of the more vicious splinter groups purporting to fight for Moro independence from the Republic of the Philippines.

Janail had seen good times and bad in his nearly fifty years. He'd seen the movement for his people's independence wax and wane. He'd seen the core of the thing sell out for a place in the "legitimate" government. He hadn't seen most of his comrades being killed, but he had seen the results.

And, in the end, what did any of it matter? I fought, so I thought, for God . . . and now, as I near the end of my days, I find I don't even believe there is a God.

Apparently reading a newspaper while sitting on a creaking, unpainted bench in front of the apartment building, and slightly off to one side, Janail saw Ayala and his three—*Three . . . good, he's still a creature of habit*—guards debark from a limo and enter through the glass doors.

As they disappeared into the elevator, Janail made a cell phone call—those still worked, despite all the world's problems—to a team of his closest subordinates, waiting not too very far away. They'd arrived dressed as was Janail, himself: decent, lightweight suits, hidden firearms, body armor. They were, in fact, a near match in appearance to the three men escorting their target. None of Janail's men were veterans of the Philippine Armed Forces, of course, yet all were veterans.

Indeed, the concierge standing behind a semi-circular desk in the lobby found them totally unremarkable. He glanced up only to make sure the newcomers weren't street riffraff, but returned his gaze immediately to a folder laid out on the desk. He only looked up again when he sensed the suppressor of Janail's pistol peeking over the ledge of the desk. A single *phut*, and the concierge fell back. Janail moved him and folded the body more fully behind the desk, then fired again. The concierge's head exploded. Janail took his place, likewise standing, with the elevator doors at forty-five degrees to his left. He placed his cell phone on the desk, above the late concierge's papers. The screen on the phone showed a closed door, somewhere upstairs.

Given the building, the number of kept women inside it, and the number of well-to-do men visiting those women, Janail's team was the platonic essence of unremarkable. Indeed, shortly after the cell call and the arrival of Janail's crew, more executive sorts, with anywhere from one to three bodyguards, passed by with little more than politely exchanged nods. Janail carefully made his own greeting nods deeper. Anything else would have been out of character for the role he played. He wasn't worried that one of them, or anyone else, would leave before Ayala. He had a tiny camera he'd placed on the wall opposite the door to Ayala's mistress's apartment that fed an image directly to his cell phone. He knew when that door opened and when old man Ayala left.

Dammit, he's early. Stupid houri can't follow instructions.

Janail looked left and right at the four men who had joined him, spread out in two teams of two, each team forming one leg of a deep V facing the elevator. He barked a brief order. "Get ready. He's leaving before he was supposed to." With his cell he sent a previously prepared text to the other two members of the team, the two who had taken care of old man Ayala's driver and were now waiting with the teams' own transportation.

Their weapons were still hidden under suit jackets, hanging from shoulder straps. They were standardized for the team; Russian PP-90M1's. These had many disadvantages. Their sights were poor, though that didn't matter since Janail had had laser pointers mounted to them. Their charging handles, deep buttons set above the barrels and muzzles, were completely idiotic. Slow disassembly time—it took twenty to thirty seconds to unscrew the single screw that held everything together—made them unsuitable for military use.

But they had advantages, for this, which far outweighed the disadvantages. Their helical magazines carried a highly respectable sixty-four rounds. They also made the guns extremely concealable under a suit jacket. Best of all, they were strong and stout, capable of firing Russian armor-piercing ammunition—7N31, a seriously +P round—without exploding in their firers' faces.

There was a suppressor available for them but, since they couldn't use subsonic ammunition and still have a prayer of getting through the body armor, suppressors would have been somewhat superfluous.

Janail considered himself lucky to have acquired them. He also considered himself lucky in his followers, even though . . .

These fools; they believe. And I can make good use of that; I can use these morons to get what I still believe in, which is money, and the pleasures of this life. Better still, I can use a chunk of money to get my hands on some truly awesome weapons—nukes, gas, bio—and use those to blackmail entire countries. With that money . . . ahhh . . . the nonexistent Allah can go stew; I'll have paradise and all the houris I want, here and now.

Janail's narrow eyes returned to the lights above the elevator door that indicated the current floor and direction of travel. He'd reconnoitered the place long since, and knew to the second how long it would take for the doors to begin to open. Just as he knew that the target would be well back in the elevator. Even so, he'd drilled his band to the point of nausea to take out the central forward guard from the flanks, then turn their fire on the flankers. *The prime target must* not *be hit!*

"Make ready," he ordered again, lowering himself to take maximum cover behind the desk. His minions were expendable. He was not. The four followers present obeyed. On their own they shouldered and leveled their submachine guns at the elevator doors, tensing as they did so.

Ayala stood at the rear of the elevator, stock-still—but for some trembling—and wide-eyed, as his assailants stepped over the ruined bodies of his former guards. Two of them slammed his back to the wall, mostly to stun him, then twisted him down to the floor. The other two took care to make sure that all three guards were dead with single bursts: *brrrp . . . brrrp . . . brrrp.* Still more red mist arose, even as chunks of bone and bits of gray matter flew to ricochet off or stick to the elevator's walls and floor. One largish chunk of brain hit the wall, then began a slow, sliding descent, leaving a bright and thin red trace behind it.

The first two then spun Ayala to his belly, pressing his face into the blood, bone, and flesh. He felt his arms pulled back behind him, then crossed, then finally taped together at the wrists.

His brain barely registered the sight of the floor passing below him as the two took him by his arms, just under his armpits, and dragged him out. Then let him fall once he was out of the elevator, caring little that the old man's face smashed into the floor. The four then gathered around, taking either an arm or a leg each, and picked him up. They began a trot then, carrying him out of the lobby briskly.

Ayala barely noticed the shrieking of tires as two vehicles pulled up to the building's entrance. He did notice when he was propelled into the back of one of the vehicles. Rather, he noticed that his head struck something hard. After that he didn't notice much for a while, neither the changeover to a different vehicle, nor when he was bodily carried from that second vehicle to a small boat putt-putting in a deserted inlet along the coast, south-southwest of Manila.

★ CHAPTER TWO ★

Change and decay in all around I see . . .
—Henry Francis Lyte, "Abide With Me"

Bonifacio Global City, Manila, Republic of the Philippines

Blue lights flashed, whipping across concrete, shattered glass, and marble. Manila's police were on scene, as were several quite useless ambulances, and a medical examiner.

For the life of them, neither ambulance crew nor medical examiner could understand the rush. These guys, three guards in the elevator, a driver and another guard in a nearby limousine, and one now unfolded concierge in the lobby, were deader than chivalry, especially the former, they having done a numerically inexact but otherwise fair reenactment of Bonnie and Clyde at the ambush.

There were more guards there now, living ones. These belonged to Old Man Ayala's eldest son, Luis, sometimes called "Junior," despite not bearing the same given name. Surrounded by their close and tight cordon, Luis stood, hands clenched behind his back, head down, teeth clenched; a study in personal sorrow.

14

In a small gap on the cordon, yet kept outside of it, a police detective faced inward toward the younger Ayala. The detective's beige suit wasn't nearly the caliber of that worn by the younger Ayala. For that matter, it couldn't have matched those of his guards, nor of the dead guards, nor even the concierge, prior to their being ventilated. Generally speaking, police work didn't pay. In any sense.

"Who *did* this?" demanded the son and heir apparent.

"It's impossible to know at this point, sir," the policeman patiently explained to the younger, but infinitely wealthier, man. "The fact that your father wasn't killed suggests very strongly a kidnapping for ransom. The . . . thoroughness with which the others were killed suggests more than a criminal enterprise. You can expect a ransom demand, probably within the next couple of days. We will monitor—"

"You will *not!*" Luis exclaimed. "Maybe for western missionaries and journalists you can invoke the law to prevent payment of ransoms. My father and his family are above that. What they want, whoever took him, they shall have, and any interference that threatens my father's life, from any source whatsoever, will be crushed."

The policeman said nothing except, "As you and your family wish, sir." He thought, instead, *The golden rule . . . who has the gold makes the rules. That any money paid may be turned into the means of kidnapping or killing thousands means nothing . . . who has the gold makes the rules.*

Oh well, I didn't make the world; I just have to get by in it, as it turns to shit. I have to get by in it, for me and my own family, as well as I can.

Another police vehicle pulled up to the curb. With a short but polite bow, the police detective backed up, faced away from Luis, and walked to the newly arrived squad car, then around to the passenger door. There, from the rolled down window, with air conditioning turning to steam in the hot, moist air, a grandmotherly—in fact a grandmother's—face peered out.

"Six dead, Aida," the policeman said to the grandmother, who was also an inspector, once semi-retired and now called back from retirement. "And old man Ayala kidnapped. The eldest son has told me we're to keep our hands off."

Aida Farallon—something of a legend in the Philippines, though undeservedly obscure elsewhere— scowled, too much the lady to curse the storm she felt.

"Unusual circumstances?" she asked of the detective.

The plainclothesman shrugged. "Maybe not. They knew when he'd be here, but in itself that's no big deal. The old man was something of a creature of habit. His girl, up on the twenty-first floor is . . . well, frankly, not bright enough to lie well. She knows nothing."

"Who do you think did it?"

"Ten years ago I'd have instantly blamed the Moros," the detective answered. "Now? Now, it could be anyone out for a fast buck."

Aida, skilled in reading people, shook her head. "You don't believe that for a minute."

Shaking his head, the detective answered, "No. No, I don't. Moros or Huks. This thing reads the kind of organization and precision ruthlessness criminal gangs— besides maybe TCS—can rarely muster. It smells political. Moreover"—the cop held up a brass-washed steel casing between thumb and forefinger—"this is not your normal ammunition. Russian 7N31. Sure, it *looks* normal. But try to fire this from a normal pistol or submachine gun and the thing will likely blow up in your face; Plus P Plus Plus. Designed to pierce body armor."

Aida took a pencil from her pocket and held it, eraser end first, toward the detective. He placed the casing carefully over the rubber end. Aida then flicked on the dome light in the police car, and held the brass close to her eye, examining it closely.

"Looks normal enough," she said.

"Sure," the detective agreed. "But it isn't. Not only does it have *much* higher pressure, the bullet's a steel penetrator in a polymer frame. Weighs very little, a bit over half of a normal 9mm. It moves *fast*, hits armor, leaves the polymer behind, then the steel continues on.

"Fortunately, it's rare."

"Any chance of tracing it?" she asked, holding the pencil out for the other to retrieve his evidence.

The detective shook his head, taking the casing back and slipping it into a plastic bag. "Not really. This travelled only through black channels. The blackest. Even if the Russians could help, they won't.

"I'd wonder if it wasn't Victor Inning who put these into the stream of commerce. But he's been so out of the picture for the last several years that I seriously doubt his involvement."

The cop smiled, a bit ruefully. "Some ways, I wish Inning were still in business. *He*, at least, had *some* scruples."

"Some," Aida agreed, "but not all that much."

The old woman leaned back in her chair and flicked off the dome light. Staring upward, through the windshield, she rocked her head for several long moments.

"*Cui bono*?" she asked, of no one in particular. Then she sneered, saying to the detective, "To hell with what the boy wants. I want the Ayala mansion and its communications monitored twenty-four, seven. *And* everyone in the entire clan's cell phones."

Still sneering, Aida nodded in the direction of the cordon around young Ayala. "Silly rich-boy turd thinks he can intimidate *me*? I'm a grandmother. I've got more important things to worry about than a career.

"Besides," she added, "I know the boy's mother."

"Potentially a lot of trouble," the detective said, "and I don't just mean our efforts."

"Trouble?" she asked. "Let me tell you about trouble. Trouble, real trouble, happens when a bunch of ideological or religious lunatics get their hands on enough money to buy a nuke, or some new bug, or to set up a serious lab to make serious gas. *That's* trouble.

"I'll handle the mother."

Off Fort Drum (*El Fraile*), Manila Bay, Republic of the Philippines

It wasn't the mother of all coastal fortifications. Rather, it was the multi-great grandchild . . . on steroids, with two twin fourteen-inch turrets, topside, and reinforced concrete ranging up to thirty-six feet thick around the sides. As much as fifteen of those feet, though, had been blasted away by bombardment during the early and late stages of the Second World War.

From a distance, and if the light were poor, one might almost have thought the forward turret, Battery Marshall, still capable. The rearward one, though, Battery Wilson, gave that the lie; of its two guns, one had fallen back completely inside the turret while the other only stuck out a few feet from the glacis, and that at an angle that said, "ruin."

Fort Drum, the old concrete battleship with its wrecked and rusted steel turrets and casemates, passed to port doing its fairly routine three knots. That is to say, while the ruined fort never moved, never had, and never could have—at least short of a world class earthquake or asteroid strike—the flowing tide, pushing through the narrow entrance to Manila Bay, tended to give it a wake just as with any ship moving at about that speed, said wake having fooled sundry aviators into believing the thing was moving.

The little motor launch into which an unconscious Ayala had been laid *was* moving, and at rather more than three knots. It was also bobbing and weaving with its forward movement, the natural waves, and the somewhat unnatural ones caused by, among other things, Fort Drum and the tide. Between the rap on the head and the motion, the old man began to throw up into the shallow bilges of the launch.

"Pull his head out of it," Janail ordered. There was little sense in kidnapping the old tyrant only to lose him to drowning in his own vomit.

Dutifully, one of the team members grabbed Ayala's

thinning gray hair and held it up, forcing him into a purely face-down position to allow the puke to drain.

"Bastard stinks," the guard commented.

"So might you . . . or I, in the same circumstances," Janail countered.

"Wha . . . ?" whispered a frail old voice.

"Ah, he's coming to. Very good. If he's conscious, he's unlikely to die on us.

"How are you feeling, Mr. Ayala?" Janail asked, most politely.

"What . . . what do you pirates want of me?"

"Not pirates, old man," Janail answered, "freedom fighters." *As in the freedom I'll have when I have your ransom.* "And what we want is money to continue the struggle."

"Where are you taking me?"

"No reason for you not to know, I suppose," Janail answered. "We're going to rendezvous with a larger boat just west of Corregidor. To which destination"—Janail uttered something in Cebuano, which language Ayala didn't understand—"we're now turning."

The launch began a sharp turn to the right. Without being able to see anything, Ayala couldn't hope to place the direction. Still, he saw no reason to doubt that he was heading toward Corregidor.

"From there we'll sail to Mindanao. You'll be there a while, until we can finalize transportation to elsewhere."

"Why me?" Ayala asked. "Who put you up to this?"

Janail laughed. Then, relenting, he said, "Why . . . why *Allah* put us up to this, old man." *Whatever I do—or don't—believe, that's for the benefit of the troops.*

Malate, Manila, Republic of the Philippines

Under an early morning sun, Aida pulled her own automobile—a tiny red conveyance, none too new—up to the curb fronting a row of carefully trimmed hedges that almost completely concealed the stilted house set back from the street in this quiet neighborhood west of Taft Avenue. Magnificent palms grew from gaps in the sidewalks here, lining both sides of the street. The shade they provided was minimal, though the ambience was considerable.

Before stepping out of the vehicle, she considered flipping her sun visor down to reveal the police symbol that would let any patrolling cop know that hers was not a car to be ticketed.

"But . . . nah," she muttered. "Better a ticket than to reveal where I've been and who I came to see."

She stepped out, cursing softly that arthritis was finally catching up with her old bones. Walking the half dozen steps to the break in the hedges that led to the house, she stopped and announced, in Tagalog, "You know I'm armed, Pedro. Madame knows I'm armed. And you and she also know I'm not giving it up. So just forget about the search; open the gate, and get out of the way."

Aida thought she heard a faint snickering from the other side of the wooden gate slung between the hedges. If so, though, the man on the other side, Pedro, Madame Ayala's chief bodyguard, showed only his usual iron face as the gate swung wide.

"She's expecting you, Aida," Pedro said, also in

Tagalog. He swung his head backwards and over one shoulder indicating that Aida was to proceed on into the house. "She's also expecting you to be armed. 'Forget it, Pedro,' she told me; 'Aida's not giving up her pistol.'"

"Thanks, cousin," Aida said, brushing past Pedro and another man whose face she didn't know. The other guard carried a submachine gun. That this was strictly illegal bothered Aida not a whit. The old rules, after all, the manmade rules, weren't working anymore . . . and no one knew it better than she did.

Though she shouldn't have been, Aida was surprised to discover there were lights on in the sitting room in which Paloma Ayala awaited her. The surprise wasn't the daytime light, per se; Aida had grown up in a more civilized time when that was quite normal. No, the surprise was that, since worldwide mandates to stop the manufacture of old style incandescent bulbs had kicked in, most people in her country could no longer afford the green bulbs, a single unit of which cost between three and ten percent of a person's *annual* income. Thus, the old incandescents, cheap and reliable, were being hoarded because they could not be replaced.

Of course the cost of an LED bulb isn't even pocket change to the likes of the Ayalas, even if it's beyond the reach of everyday people. Well . . . maybe somebody will actually start making the old bulbs again and to hell with the Eurotrash and Kano *greenies. Maybe.*

Aida's eyes swept past the glowing bulbs. As they did, for a brief moment she felt contempt. That passed away with the thought, *We could take all the Ayala's money and pass it out. Then what? Apart from a couple of years of rampant inflation, the common people still wouldn't be able to afford the westerners' feel-good fantasies.*

If the lights surprised her, Aida was positively shocked when her eyes came to rest upon Paloma Ayala's face. *Damn! I didn't think she had a tear in her entire body, and here she looks like she's cried rivers of them.*

It was true enough. Madame Ayala, like many an Asian woman, showed her age but barely. And that bare little bit she had covered with expensive makeup by cheap but skilled local labor. The expensive makeup was runnelled and seamed by tear tracks. One false eyelash hung, half off. The woman's hair was frizzled, as if she had been tearing at it without cease. Her eyes were red and puffy in a way no amount of skill and no expense could fix.

Tears began to flow again as Paloma cried out, "Oh, Aida, what the hell am I going to *do*?"

It took quite some time—hours, it seemed like, to the policewoman—to calm the stricken Mrs. Ayala down.

"I can make a phone call," Aida said. "Our own people won't get your husband back alive; you know our track record with these things is very mixed. And you have to be prepared that the people who have Lucio are going to do some vile things to pressure you to pay when the time comes."

"I couldn't stand it," Paloma admitted, then asked, "A phone call to whom?"

Aida chewed her lower lip, answering, "A former . . . associate. He's with an . . . organization that specializes in these things. So far their track record is good. But they don't come cheaply. Fair, yes. Cheap? No."

"It can cost everything I—*we*—own, so long as it gets my husband back in my bed, healthy and safe."

"It's not quite that simple," Aida said. "You know it's possible one—maybe more than one—of your own children is in on this. You can't let them . . . "

"Why do you think I insisted on meeting *here*," Mrs. Ayala said. "I already *know* that much. Make your call."

"Okay," Aida agreed. "It will be a couple of days, though. I've got to gather some information first. Hopefully, too, the people who've grabbed Lucio will identify themselves and make an initial ransom demand. The more solid information on the threat that I can pass on to my contact the more likely they'll take the contract."

★ CHAPTER THREE ★

Happy, peaceful Philippines . . .
—Anonymous, "Damn, damn, damn the Filipinos"

"Lawyers, Guns, and Money" (SCIF), Camp Fulton, Guyana

Officially it was called "the SCIF," the Special Compartmentalized Information Facility. Despite the name, it never had seen and in all probability never would see anything officially classified as "Special Compartmentalized Information," since the regiment and corporation didn't use the designation and the combat units the United States rotated through Camp Fulton would never reveal anything that deeply classified in what amounted to a foreign installation.

Even so, it looked like a SCIF, with thick concrete roof and walls, half buried under ground, covered with jungle growth, and impervious to electronic penetration. It was also surrounded by barbed wire and permanently guarded, inside and out. And, if it never held any official special compartmented information, it held all the regiment's and corporation's secrets. These tended to fluctuate around legal work, procurement, sales, and contracting, which is to say, money. Hence the unofficial but common name, "Lawyers, Guns, and Money."

Before the visitor hit any of those offices, however, down a narrow side corridor leading from the wide central one, was the office of Ralph Boxer, retired Air Force two star, and de facto chief of staff for M Day, Incorporated.

In that office, on the wall behind Boxer's desk, was a poster, a copy of the famous painting by Leutze of "Washington Crossing the Delaware." The caption underneath said, "Americans. We will cross an icy river to kill you in your sleep. On Christmas." Beneath the poster, sitting at his desk, Boxer, an older man, grayed but not balding, spoke into a telephone.

"You finally ready to take me up on that offer, Aida?" asked Ralph Boxer, Executive Officer and practical Chief of Staff of M Day, Incorporated.

"Not hardly," answered the voice on the phone. The English was accented, but crisp and clear. "Ralph . . . I've got a problem . . . I think *we've* got a problem . . . that's pretty much in your line of work."

"Are you on a secure line?" Boxer asked.

"No, but I bought a throwaway cell phone and enough credits to call you. You'll have to call me back before we get cut off. No one's tracking this one, if that's your concern."

Boxer thought, *She's never been given to panic . . . but there's something that sounds a lot like panic in her voice.* "Your number's not showing on my caller ID," he said. "Give it to me; I'll call you back directly."

★ ★ ★

"I'll bring it to the boss and the regimental council," Boxer agreed, "but I've got to tell you, honey, that I'm going to recommend against. We've got a problem here—coming soon, too—that no amount of money can buy us out of. Frankly, we can't spare—at least we can't be sure of being able to spare—the force.

"And, no, I'm not just setting this up to drive a harder bargain."

The voice on the other end didn't answer for a minute. When Aida spoke, she said, "Well . . . ask your boss to consider the amount of trouble there'll be for you and everybody if the worst sort of barbarian—these are the *Harrikat*, Ralph! Even *Abu Sayyaf* considers them vile—gets hold of the kind of money Ayala's ransom would bring."

Abu Sayyaf was a different Moro group; and noted, itself, for extreme measures and inhuman ruthlessness.

"Doesn't really change anything, Aida," Boxer replied. "We've still got a major problem of our own, right here and now. Who did you say grabbed Ayala? And how much are they demanding?"

Terminal One, Ninoy Aquino International Airport, Republic of the Philippines

It was nearly the hottest part of the local day. Air conditioned or not, Terminal One was muggy, the air thick with dampness and the cloying aroma of a sea of sweaty humanity. One of three international terminals, and one of two that also served carriers other than the Philippines' own airline, the terminal was also the oldest of the lot and showed its age in ways both plain and subtle.

Terry Welch—ex-U.S. Army Special Forces and currently Major commanding Company A, Second Battalion, M Day, Inc.—passed customs, then moved to a fairly open spot in the jostling human sea to wait for Lox. Big, even for an American, Terry towered over the tide of Asiatics passing him to either side.

An elderly, gray-haired woman, lightweight business suit-clad, and sprightly for all of her gray, walked up and asked, "Terry?" Her mildly slanted, deep brown eyes looked both terribly inquisitive and also very intelligent. If she had any wrinkles on her café au lait skin, they were tolerably hard to see.

"Yes, ma'am," Terry answered, inclining his head respectfully. He already recognized Aida Farallon from his final briefing with Boxer. "I'm waiting for my—"

"Here, Terry," Lox announced. He'd started with the regiment as a sergeant, but now was rated and paid as a warrant officer. He handed Welch a cell phone purchased from one of the airport concessions. Then he turned to the woman, gave a short but polite bow of his head, and said, "*Magandang tanghali po.*"

Aida cocked her head and smiled, saying, "Ralph told me one of you would speak Filipino with an almost perfect accent."

"With all due respect, Ma'am," Lox answered, "my accent *is* perfect for certain parts of Luzon."

Aida considered that. Indeed, she seemed to be running through a cerebral file. At length, and not a very long length, she agreed, "Aurora, I think."

"Ooo, you're good," Lox admitted. Then he turned head and eyes away from Aida to focus on something in the middle distance.

"Eh?" Aida shrugged. "Been around. Cop for better'n twenty years, doncha know? Still keep my hand in a bit, too."

"Where now, ma'am?" Terry asked.

The old woman scowled. "Just call me 'Aida.' And now we go collect your bags. After that, I'm taking you to see the victim's wife. And *right* after that, I'm out of your lives. Because, at heart, I'm *still* a cop, and I don't want to have the first clue about what you're doing, lest I feel duty bound to interfere."

Aida's eyes locked on Lox who, instead of moving, was standing stock still with his eyes still focused in the distance. She followed his gaze to a suited man, his face ornately tattooed, apparently just off a plane and waiting impatiently for someone or something.

"TCS," she announced. "True Cinnamon Siblings. Use to be True Cinnamon Sisters, but then they took on men to add some muscle. And, yes, those titles are in English. There's a reason for that; the gang, just like the Salvadoran MS-13, didn't start here, but in the states, in TCS's case in San Diego, California. They got their start in the States, got deported, and set up in business here. Big in prostitution. Medium in drugs. Heavy into kidnapping. They *own* a chunk of the city; the police won't even go in there anymore and the politicians won't let the army loose to clean it up."

"Like parts of Europe, with the Muslims?" Lox asked.

"Sort of," Aida agreed. "But they're not Muslim. To

the extent they're anything, I suppose they're Catholic . . . or maybe Christian Animist. Or maybe some kind of heresy I've never heard of. But Muslim they definitely are not.

"What's bothering you?" she asked. "The tattoos? I'm not sure what they mean—can't read the code in any detail—but I'd guess he's pretty high up in their chain of command."

Lox shook his head. "It's not the tattoos," he whispered. "He's packing. He just got off a commercial *airplane* and he's packing."

Aida looked a bit below the tattooed face and shrugged. "Yeah, he's packing. Go figure: Filipino carrier and I'm sure he got himself enrolled as a reservist in our equivalent of the States' Sky Marshal program. No surprise. Maybe some money but no surprise.

"They call themselves a nation and they're serious about it," she said. "They're their own nation, in us but not of us. And why not? They judge. They tax. They police . . . in the area they control they police better than regular police did. But they recognize no obligations to the rest of us. Citizenship is something they use when they get caught outside their own area to try to keep out of jail, a pure one-way street. Beyond it, being a Filipino means nothing to them."

Lox sighed and said, "*Sic transit* Nussbaum?"

"Huh? Nussbaum?" Aida asked.

"An academic and cosmopolitan philosopher of a few years back," Lox explained. "Among other things, she insisted that the logic of nationalism and patriotism required the drawing of ever narrower circles of in and out groups. Seemed incapable of observing that, in the real world beyond her brainpan, it's the breakdown of nations that causes people to fall back to ever narrower circles, while nations have so far proven the only thing— besides religion—capable of creating larger circles of acceptance. Silly woman tried to reason with a mob once, during the Great Chicago Ipad-9 riots. They tore her limb from limb.

"He"—Lox pointed with his chin at the tattooed TCS leader—"is an affront to and refutation of her world view. Then, too, so was the mob that killed her."

Aida shrugged; the fantasies of the intellectual class interested her little. "I suppose," she said, "based on some things that Ralph Boxer told me, that they're a little like your organization that way."

"No, ma'am . . . Aida," Terry replied. "We're both symptoms of breakdown, yes. But M Day is only a symptom, not a cause of the breakdown. And even there, we're more like the fever that helps fight off disease. Large criminal gangs owing no duties to anybody outside of the gang? They're both symptom *and* cause."

"As are fuzzy minded intellectuals and academics," Lox added.

Aida's auto stopped on the same narrow, palm-lined street, not far from the gated gap in the hedges that led to Paloma's meeting house. Through iron gates Terry had caught glimpses of small, but well-kept bungalows, many of them raised on thick stilts.

"Through that one," Aida said, pointing with her chin as her hands were still tightly wrapped around the wheel.

"Expect armed men on the other side, maybe three or four of them. Maybe only one or two, too. Expect to be frisked."

Terry nodded, saying, "Thanks, ma . . . ummm . . . Aida." Lox added in a Tagalog farewell in the polite form. From a shirt pocket Terry took out a thick envelope, which he handed over to the woman.

"What's this?" she asked, a hint of indignation rising in her voice. Gnarled fingers bent the envelope a few times, then squeezed it experimentally. "I didn't strong arm Boxer for money!"

"Officially," Terry replied, "I don't know. Unofficially, Boxer told me it was airfare to our base—Swiss Francs because who knows where the dollar is going—plus some, if you cared to join us someday. He said, 'keep it, save it, use it when you feel the time is right.' He said, too, to consider it a tentative signing bonus and that it would be subtracted from your real bonus if you actually did sign on with us. He also said that if there were some close relatives you thought might need a safe haven, then maybe a place could be found for some of them, too. Might be in a line battalion. Might be cutting grass. Or anything in between. But a place."

Aida nodded somberly, thinking upon the benefits of having a secure bolt hole. "Well . . . maybe then," she agreed. "We'll see." She passed over a computer disk, explaining, "That is a bill of particulars for every at-large Abu Sayyaf and al Harrikat operative and sympathizer I was able to extract from police files. Both, because you never can tell when someone's going to switch over. There's also an intelligence summary from the army in there, but I wouldn't necessarily call it authoritative. There's no difference in the level of fighting, after all, between a province we've cleared of the enemy and one we've abandoned. In any case, it's free, not something Boxer paid me for."

Both exited the car from the curb side. Lox dragged his bag after himself, dropped it to the street, then reached in to pull Welch's out as well. The pair grabbed their bags, then walked to the gate. Aida's small sedan was screeching a turn around the next corner even before they reached it.

There had only been two guards, both of them on the gate, when Lox and Welch walked through. They'd been polite enough, but also firm. Nobody was getting in to see Madame until and unless they were thoroughly searched.

Terry shrugged, saying, "Well, do your jobs then."

As the guard squatted to finger Terry's ankles, the American thought, *Let me tell you about the very rich. They are different from you and me.*

Search completed, one of the bodyguards remained on the gate, securing it and likewise the bags. The other led them to the bungalow, up the broad wooden steps, and into a living room furnished in wicker and cooled—inadequately cooled—by a large overhead fan. Terry still had the disk given him by Aida safely stowed in one pocket.

"The two Kanos you were expecting, Madame," the guard announced.

An old woman, wearing a printed silk dress and with a string of pearls precisely sized for her age and station, was seated on one of the wicker chairs with her legs demurely crossed. Above the pearls, on a simple gold chain, was a crucifix. Quality told; behind the wrinkles—and there were surprisingly few of those—was a bone structure that boasted a past of rare beauty.

She nodded and said, "Thank you, Pedro, that will be all until I summon you." Her accent was pure New England. Her tone was pure command, as if by right.

"Yes, madame," the guard agreed, with a polite bow of his head. He withdrew backwards, then disappeared out the front door.

"Please, gentlemen, be seated," Mrs. Ayala said, indicating with a bejeweled hand a pair of wicker, padded chairs opposite her own. Terry thought the hand surprisingly youthful, if not precisely young. He also thought that the gold, rubies, emeralds and pearls detracted from that youthful appearance.

"Radcliffe?" Terry asked, as he took his seat.

"Mount Holyoke," the woman answered, serenely. Weeping and shrieking time was over; this was business.

Terry nodded. *Old money. They're different.*

"I have agreed," she said, "which is to say I have agreed, tentatively, to your . . . your *firm's* conditions. 'Double or nothing.' And 'all you find, all you keep.' I don't care about the latter and the former appeals to me. An agreement, however, is not my husband back in my bed. Tell me how you intend to get him back when the police and the army cannot."

Terry liked—no, he *admired*—that kind of directness, and said so. He then added, "I trust you will not be offended if I am equally direct, Madame?"

"Not at all," she answered.

"We believe," Terry began, "that one of your children—"

"Without proof of guilt," Mrs. Ayala interrupted, "I cannot allow you to interrogate any of my children."

Terry shook his head in negation. "We don't want to anyway, not as long as there's a chance one of them would inform the kidnappers that we're here, or if their disappearance would."

"On the other hand," Lox asked, "if we obtain that proof?"

"I'll heat up the irons for you myself," she said, old eyes flashing with young fire. The brief flash subsided; the eyes softened. "I have seven children, after all, but only one soul mate. There must, however, be proof before I will permit it."

"Fair enough," Terry agreed. "That said, if we have the proof we also, most likely, have the location where your husband is being held. So it may not be necessary, anyway."

"Necessary or not, if one of my children is responsible, I want that one dead."

"We don't have any problem with that," Terry agreed. He had to work to keep surprise out of his voice. In his, admittedly limited, experience it was the rare wife who preferred husband to offspring. *But, then again, she did use that word, "soul mate." This does not make her more trustworthy, however.*

"Do you have any idea which of your children might be responsible?" Terry asked.

"I do," Mrs. Ayala admitted. "I will not tell you my suspicions, however. That will be one of my checks on whether you identify the right one. Please continue."

Terry nodded and tapped a pocket. "I have what I believe is a fairly complete list of people who may know something about your husband's disappearance. Once the rest of my initial team flies in, we will analyze that and pick a list of likely lucrative targets."

"Your initial team will consist of?"

Terry almost said, "Fourteen," the true number coming in, including himself and Lox. He decided, all things considered, that it would be better to have some force available of which his employer was not aware. *Not like I have reason to trust her, after all.*

"Eight," he lied, adding another partial lie, "All intelligence specialists.

"Once we have a narrow list of likely targets, we'll kidnap, interrogate, and almost certainly kill them. We have to be a bit careful," he added, "because if we start too low it may warn off those who are higher placed, while if we start too high, it may alert those actually holding your husband that someone is on their trail. This could cause them to move him to someplace no one has any clue to."

"I don't see a solution to the problem," Mrs. Ayala said.

"We'll try to restrict ourselves to the peripherals, the journalists and politicians who are in bed with the Harrikat."

"And if that doesn't work?" she asked.

"Then it would be hopeless," Terry admitted, cautioning, "my organization never offered you more than a best chance.

"In any case," he continued, "we have to assume we have some success. So, assuming that we do, the better part of a battalion sets sail sometime in the next forty-eight hours from our base to here. They should be here in about five weeks. By then we should have Mr. Ayala's location pinned down with some specificity. We recon; we plan; we attack to free him."

"You will need some assistance before then." It was not a question.

"Yes, Madame," Terry agreed. "And we will do precisely nothing but analyze until the money is in escrow. Since you've accepted our offer of 'double or nothing,' that comes to seventy million USD. As for what we need; Mr. Lox?"

Lox began to reach into a pocket to produce a shopping list of sorts.

The Filipina put up that same bejeweled hand, palm forward, and said, "Don't give it to me. I am leaving Pedro with you for the duration of your contract. He can get you anything you need, within reason. Think of him as our . . . liaison. He is one of only two of my bodyguards that I absolutely trust. The other one is at the gate. That one will accompany me to my home when our business is finished. Pedro has a car, a taxi I had him purchase—yes, it's properly licensed; you never know—and will take you anywhere you need to go, or do anything you need done, that requires a degree of camouflage. In addition, there is an old estate in Hagonoy—Pedro will take you there— big enough to house the few of you coming initially in considerable secrecy. A small boat comes with the estate. It is also isolated enough—by which I mean *very* isolated, that no one is like to hear anything from a . . . . shall we say . . . 'rigorous' interrogation. There is also a very small airstrip."

Lox sent Welch a glance that as much as said, *I dunno about you, but* I'm *impressed.*

"Well, of *course* you're impressed," Paloma Ayala said. "My husband didn't marry me just for my bygone looks."

"Madame," Lox said, in Tagalog, "I assure you; you are just beautiful." He meant it. Even great age could permit and retain its own kind of beauty.

"And I didn't marry him because of his flattery," she snapped back.

★ CHAPTER FOUR ★

If the highest aim of a captain were to preserve
his ship, he would keep it in port forever.
—Saint Thomas Aquinas

MV *Richard Bland*, Georgetown, Guyana

M Day, Incorporated, owned a dozen freighters of varying sizes. Only two of those had really mattered, so far. These were the MV *Merciful* and the MV *Richard Bland*, the latter named for one of Biggus Dickus Thornton's boys, killed in action during a boarding mission. While the other ten had, typically, three members of the corporation (or members of the regiment, if they were alone among themselves) aboard; usually the skipper, his exec, and the engineering officer, the rest being hirelings from anywhere where manpower came cheap, *Merciful* and *Bland* were fully corporate crewed. They had to be for the kind of things they did.

The other ships might run the odd questionable cargo. They might, even, with a little switching of crews, support an underwater demolition team to, say, mine and sink a large number of boats and ships bringing fortification material, rockets, and mines to Gaza under the guise of humanitarian aid. Typically, *Bland* and *Merciful* launched armed attacks from ship to shore. Of course, they also carried innocent cargoes frequently enough to disguise their purpose.

Though about of a size, each carrying just under twenty-eight hundred TEU, and a bit over thirty thousand gross registered tons; where *Merciful* had a single gantry that moved fore and aft, *Bland* had three cranes, one forward to port, the other just abaft the beam, to starboard, and a third, centered, just behind the superstructure that housed the crew, overlooking the eighty-foot rear deck. It just wouldn't do to have to give up the use of one, once compromised, because it looked too much like the other.

The paint helped there. *Merciful* was painted up in a montage of clasping hands, olive wreaths, and doves, suitable for the purely fictive humanitarian organization that, so far as a records check would have showed, owned it. *Bland*'s hull above the waterline was a straight gray, though darker than Navy gray, with the superstructure painted white. Both hull and superstructure showed enough streaks of rust to ensure the ship didn't stand out as a combat vessel.

The rust bothered the crap out of *Bland*'s new skipper, Captain Tom Pearson, even if he understood and agreed with the purpose. Standing a couple of inches under six feet, broad in the shoulders, balding, Pearson looked at a minor rust stream marring his command's white super-structure and scowled.

Pearson, new to the ship, didn't know yet what the vessel's problems might be. He was *still* trying to locate all the property alleged to be there on the secret manifest. *Bland* hadn't been used as an assault carrier in some twenty-nine months; there just weren't that many missions that called for a complete naval invasion. It had gone through the number of skippers, and had had at least one complete crew change because of the Gaza flotilla mission.

Still sneering at the rust, Pearson thought, *Maybe it's necessary, but it's just not right. Ah, well, at night, at least, it doesn't show much. Which is . . . ah . . . important, what with the fucking* Army *showing up. Though if that were the only problem . . .*

Though the regiment was just the regiment, members of its air and naval squadrons still tended to think of themselves as "Air Force" or "Navy," and the ground components as "Army." The two exceptions were Cazz's Third Battalion, which thought of itself and was thought of as, "Marine," and Biggus Dickus Thornton's team of former SEALS, who were in the "Army" portion—Second Battalion—but generally worked with and for, and still thought of themselves as, "Navy."

Though, at least, we'll be getting Charlie Company, Third Batt, which ought to know its way around a ship.

"Ahoy de *Bland*," Mr. Drake called up from his small Guyanan Revenue Authority watercraft. The boat was, of course, intended to help him improve Guyanan revenue. Perhaps it did. From Drake's point of view, though, its major purpose was helping him do a pretty good side business on his own. This had gone way past turning a blind eye to M Day's activities for a little financial consideration. Since his daughter, Elizabeth, had married into the regiment, the customs officer had become an unindicted coconspirator.

Not dat de regiment don' pay fair for meh trouble, Drake mused, while waiting for an answer from the deck of the ship, looming above. *But it not so important as watchin' out for meh little girl . . . even indirect.*

A dozen people, none of them uniformed, sat the boat behind where Drake stood at the wheel. These were three each from the Aviation Squadron and Charlie Company, Third Battalion, plus four from Alpha Company, Second, and two from the regimental medical department. Drake's next lift was to bring out the first four cooks, a couple more each medics and nurses, two aviation maintenance crew, and A and C companies' armorers.

Still seated on a none-too-comfortable bench, A Company's exec, Captain Tracy P. Warrington, tall, slender, mustached, and graying, looked up at the *Bland* with distaste.

My whole fucking family, for about a dozen generations back, was Navy. I joined the Army to avoid it. So where am I? About to board a ship to sail to points not particularly well known. Fuck.

Bastard Welch, sticking me with this shit while he goes gallivanting to the Philippines to do something I'm better at—Human Terrain Analysis—and ducking what he's better at.

Still . . . I suppose politics intrudes and, given the client, we had to put highest rank forward. Oh, well; I didn't make the world—or make it start falling apart. I just have to live in it.

Warrington let out an audible sigh. *And with the people in it.*

"Stand by, Customs," called a voice from above. "We're lowering a ladder."

Warrington heard a scraping, followed by a splash. *When they say ladder; they mean ladder. Oh, my aching, weary bones.*

Glancing in the direction of the infantry company commander tasked to support the operation, Warrington asked, "Cazz brief you people on shipboard customs and courtesies?"

"Yes," answered Andrew Stocker, late of the Princess Patricia's Canadian Light Infantry, now commanding— pending an anticipated change in the personnel system—an A Team of C Company, Second Battalion, which team provided the leadership of C Company, Third Battalion, M Day, Inc. The team itself tended to be Commonwealth: Canadian, Brit, British Gurkha, Aussie, and Kiwi. Supposedly, that anticipated change would come sometime soon, with a break in the command relationship between the teams and Second Battalion, with the teams falling directly and permanently under the battalions of the companies they led. The current system had seemed promising, but had never quite worked out.

"Why?"

"Because I don't know shit about them," Warrington answered. He pointed his chin at the general direction of the splash. "That means you go first."

★ ★ ★

The ship had been modified in a couple of significant ways. For one thing, there were reinforcements built into the deck and gunwales to allow the crew to set up landing pads for helicopters. For another, the two bottom levels of containers contained nothing but food, cots, bedding, arms, ammunition—to include one container labeled "APERS mines"—and equipment for a strike force. Of those levels, the lowest was only partial, leaving a substantial open area—roughly nine hundred square meters—with containers held on steel beams above it, to allow for a mess and planning area for the embarked force. Since the area also served as a sort of recreation center, one wall—actually just the ends of forty-foot shipping containers—held a wide screen TV which was turned on only at night or at the commander's discretion. Currently, the television displayed one of the more attractive female talking heads from CNN, though the sound was turned all the way down.

"The message I got was cryptic, at best," Pearson said. "What are you bringing aboard and what's the mission, Major?"

There can be only one captain aboard ship.

Stocker smiled wickedly at Warrington, seated across the table in the expansive mess hall down near the bilges. *You can send me up the ladder first, but* you're *in charge and* you *get to brief.*

Warrington shrugged. To Pearson he answered, "The mission's a hostage rescue. Under the circumstances, we can't grab counterhostages which, frankly, blows. We don't know yet where the hostage is being held, except that he's probably still somewhere in the Philippines. We don't know what kind of force the people holding him can muster. Our advance party is trying to answer those questions, even as we speak.

"As for what's coming aboard . . . a lot less than I'd like. One infantry company; Stocker, what's your strength?"

"One hundred and eighty-six officers and men, including three armored car crews with vehicles, two mechanics, seven cooks, and a six man medical team," the Canadian answered. "Three armored cars and crews are what they gave us. But with only a single LCM, that can only carry two, one of them is probably useless."

Warrington had already known that; the answer was for Pearson's benefit.

"In addition," Warrington continued, "I've got thirty-eight from A Company, Second Battalion. The rest are already forward or moving there. We're also taking on one UAV, two helicopter gunships and two CH-750 STOL fixed wing aircraft—"

"So we'll need to assemble a flight deck?" Pearson interrupted. "Which means we'll need to practice it. A lot."

"Yeah," Warrington agreed. "The flyboys will include fourteen flight crew and eighteen ground, including for the UAV, which is something less than generous. We're getting one LCM-6, with a crew of five. Yeah, just one, so I hope your stash of rubber boats is adequate."

"I've got eighteen Zodiacs," Pearson replied. "Ought to be enough. Yes, with motors. At least I'm *supposed* to have eighteen. I've only found seven so far. My predecessor in command was possibly not as organized as one might have liked."

"Which possibly has something to do with why he got moved to staff," Warrington said. *I hope to hell all eighteen are there.*

"Lastly," Warrington continued, "regiment is sending us with a seven-man medical team, three more cooks, and a four-man intelligence cell. All told it comes to two hundred and seventy-five. You have space and rations for that many?"

"For twice that many," Pearson said, "though that *would* be a little cramped." A trace of doubt clouded his features. "I was hoping for a patrol boat to defend the *Bland*."

"Yeah, me, too," replied Warrington. "My boss asked for it. Regiment said, 'Fuck off.' Along with a couple of troop carrying helicopters. Also, 'Fuck off.' And one of the mini-subs. Likewise, 'Fuck off.' Be a bitch if it turns out we need them."

"Be a bitch if we had them and lose our home base because of it," Stocker said. "Eh?" *And my local boys are not even a little bit happy about being dragged out of their own country, which everyone suspects is about to be attacked, to sail to some other country about which they know nothing, to do something they really don't give a shit about.*

Through multiple decks, through the sound insulation provided by five to six layers of forty-foot containers, Warrington could still feel the vibrating whine of the central, starboard side, crane, lifting some cargo—*Probably one of the Elands*—aboard. *That, or maybe the troops' baggage. No matter, that's the "Navy's" problem so long as it all gets aboard. My problems, on the other hand . . .*

Warrington turned his attention to A Company's chief medic: Gary Cagle, short, very nearly as wide in the shoulders as tall, and with only one good remaining eye and a pronounced limp, both injuries the result of being shot down in a helicopter, somewhere over Chalatenango, El Salvador, in the late Eighties.

"Fuck . . . fuck . . . fuck," Cagle said, small drops of sweat flying from one quivering hand, said hand pointing at the contents of what was supposed to have been a twenty foot refrigerated container. "Fuck."

"It's *all* bad, Gary?"

Cagle's head and hand dropped simultaneously. His hand "silenced," the quiver moved to his voice. "It's been sitting there, in oven temperatures, for anywhere from two weeks to six months. I just can't tell. Would *you* want us to shoot you up with any painkillers or antibiotics that have been sitting in an oven for up to six months?"

Warrington shook his head. "Put that way, no. What do we do about it?"

"Incinerate it and get more," answered Cagle's wife, Beth, standing slightly behind Warrington in the passage formed by containers. She went by the handle of "TIC Chick," for Toxic Industrial Chemicals, and knew whereof she spoke. She was also chief doctor for the enterprise, and, where drugs and medicine were concerned, her word was law.

"That, and get a storage reefer that works. Or get this one fixed. I'll see if regimental medical has sufficient to spare, but I can tell you now that they really don't. Neither does Guyana, all things considered."

"Here's the really messed up part," Warrington said.

"Before I came here I checked up on the mess stores. Three dozen forty-foot reefers, every one of which is humming. We've got twice as much food as we need. And *this* one, the one *key* one, has gone tits up . . . ummm"— Warrington's face reddened—"pardon me, TIC Chick."

"I've heard the word before," she said.

"Yeah . . . I suppose. Anyway, *this* one, the one we really need, is fucked . . . ummm –"

"Heard *that* word before, too."

The bridge was lit only by a faint red glow as the first of two CH-750's allocated to the mission touched down on the temporary angled flight deck constructed atop the topmost layer of containers. The pilots and ground crew had had a lot of practice by this time. A light touchdown and two bounces and the thing was stopped, not more than a couple of feet past the flight deck's midpoint. Three minutes after the engine stopped, its wings were folded; its propeller oriented upper left to lower right; its tail was turned around; and a four-man ground crew was easing it, ass end first, into the container where it would reside until needed. Unseen, two of the ground crew tied it down to half-rings welded to the inside of the container.

The red glow of the bridge lights made the captain's scowl seem even more fierce than usual. Pearson still hadn't been able to remove that scowl from his face, nor to get over the embarrassment of one of *his* reefers—and the most important of the lot—failing. "Regiment says we can pick up a new supply at Capetown or, failing that, Tuticorin." He shrugged. "At least they're more or less on our way. I don't think they've thought that one through."

"I'd feel a lot better about it," said Warrington, "if they had some *other* ship make the pickup and deliver it to us at sea. We're supposed to be fucking *secret*, after all."

"None available," Pearson replied. "They're all either committed to home base defense, or too far out of the way."

"Yeah . . . well . . . I'm thinking we're going to have to retrieve them by air."

"That has its own problems," Pearson pointed out. "We'll not only have to erect the flight deck again, but we'd risk being spotted by ground-based radar. And neither the South African nor the Indian navies are organizations to be sneered at. Neither are the air forces. At least not when you're a big fat freighter."

Below, on the temporary flight deck, the first of the CH-750's had disappeared as the container doors were closed. Even as the crane whined the container into the air to move it to stowage, Number Two touched down.

★ CHAPTER FIVE ★

Neither dead nor alive, the hostage is
suspended by an incalculable outcome. It is not his
destiny that awaits for him, nor his own death,
but anonymous chance, which can only seem to him
something absolutely arbitrary. He is in a state
of radical emergency, of virtual extermination.
—Jean Baudrillard

Caban Island, Pilas Group, Basilan Province, Republic of the Philippines

Lucio Enrique Ayala scratched absentmindedly at something itching his leg. Insect or jungle fungus, he didn't know. His ancient back rested, if that was quite the word, against the center pole of the hut in which he'd been imprisoned. His posterior and the back of his ancient, skinny legs rested on dirt rapidly turning to mud. From one leg led a rusty iron chain, triple looped about his ankle and running off to a rock bigger and heavier than he could have lifted as a young man.

He'd tested the rock, shortly after being chained to it. *I sure as hell can't budge it now.*

Old Man Ayala didn't have a clue where he was, except that it was mostly jungle and not too far from the sea. *Big help, that is.* No *place in this part of the country is too far from the sea.* He recalled that his captors had said something about "Basilan," shortly after his capture, but whether he was actually on that island, or on one of the more than seven *thousand* islands, greater and lesser, that made up the province he couldn't know.

Probably not Basilan Island, though, he thought. *Too many very nervous Christians, there, too mixed in with the rest, and the army takes too much interest in the place for my "hosts" to be as comfortable as they plainly are . . . some one of the other islands completely owned by the Moros . . . probably one the army's given up on.*

He looked down at his tightly chained ankle and felt a surge of despair, thinking, *Not that it makes a lot of difference; the army could be half a mile away and they'd still not have a clue I was here. And they'd be as likely to bring down artillery on this hut as to make any effort to see what was inside, first. Can't say as I'd blame them.*

Ayala had done his military time as a young officer, long, long ago. A signals man, he'd been. And, like everything else in his life, he hadn't let the experience go to waste. Briefly, he mentally chalked off what he did know, even if he thought the knowledge useless. *I'm not all that far from the sea; I can smell the water and, when the wind's just right, hear the surf. I'm either in or near a major Moro base. I think I've seen as many as two hundred of the bastards at one time. And it is a major base; regular huts for barracks, rifle ranges, big kitchens and mess halls, a more or less regular hospital, though I didn't note any doctors. I saw that much, at least. And they've got some heavy weapons, too. Mortars certainly. And I thought I saw a recoilless rifle on someone's shoulder the last time they walked me like a dog for exercise, two days ago.*

So what's that mean? At least a big company, the way we'd think of it, or maybe a small battalion in Moro terms. I'd guess a small battalion. And that's just what I've seen. Could be five times as many within a half a mile. Shit.

The old man sighed. *Ah, Paloma, pearl of my heart. I wish you hadn't been such a stickler for appearances. I'd much rather have been in bed with you, comfortably, than with any number of young bimbos. And I'd sure as hell rather be in bed with you now than here, with this band of pirates.*

Smiling, Ayala thought, *Ah, my very dearest, what pirates we were, together, in our youth.*

Zamboanga International Airport, Mindanao, Republic of the Philippines

It was one of the world's amusing little incongruities that, no matter how much technological sophistication had grown in matters of communication, the most secure form of communication remained what it had been in Caesar's day and before, the human messenger. For what Janail needed, no mere message carrier would do; he had to go himself and he had to fly out of this nothing much airport.

The "International" part was usually more wish than reality. Oh, there'd been any number of international flights over the years—not even including American and Japanese fighters and bombers, circa 1942 to 1945—but the service never seemed to last. Zest Airways or South East Asian Airlines or Nocturnal Aviators would give it a whirl, then eliminate the service after a few months or years. It was simply a loser, and no one really seemed to know why. This, perhaps, helped explain why different air lines kept trying.

The sucker airline *du jour* was Royal Brunei, the sultan's finances being in a parlous state, what with the Allah-help-us, rock bottom price of oil in a world rapidly sliding into the poor house.

Not that the sultan was willing to bet a great deal of increasingly scarce money on the venture. No, no; not when he'd already had to add fifty percent to the number of Gurkhas he kept on hand, the Gurkhas being affordable where keeping up the oil welfare state was becoming increasingly unaffordable.

No, there was no money to spend on new aircraft for a new service. The sultan—or, rather, a cousin running the airline on the sultan's behalf—had brought a couple of Fokker 50's out of retirement and put them to work.

Which works out conveniently for me, thought Janail, trudging up the ladder to the Fokker's cabin, *because I really didn't want to go through Manila, even if I'm reasonably sure the authorities don't have a decent picture of me.*

'Course, I'd have preferred the complete anonymity of travel by sea. Sadly, too many pirates who answer to

nobody. *Too many pirates, too many* hungry *pirates, given how little trade there is lately. Especially down by Sulu.*

Kudat, Sabah, East Malaysia, Island of Borneo

Flight, airport, and civilization were all well behind Janail now. With the lights of Kudat glowing dimly to the west, aboard a narrow skiff, putt-putting between the overgrown green banks of the inlet jutting south from the Sulu Sea, Janail slapped absently at a buzzing mosquito. Maddeningly, the damned thing refused to stay in one place long enough to be killed, moving from ear to neck to face and back to ear, without ever once settling down for a meal.

"Fickle bastard," the kidnapper muttered. *Note to self: When I'm sultan, mosquito eradication program. High priority.*

Seated beside Janail, his companion, the Pakistani Mahmood Abdul Majeed, gave a victory grunt. He'd succeeded in killing one of the little winged Satans. "*Il hamdu l'illah,*" the Pakistani muttered, in a language not his own.

Odd, thought Janail, *that this fat little scientist retains all the faith I've long since cast aside. Not that he needs to know that, of course, but playing along with his religious carping since we met in Brunei is getting wearisome.*

Where Janail traveled on a single, not very large bag, tucked under his seat, the Pakistani's baggage took up most of the forward third of the skiff, from just ahead of their legs to just behind the man at the machine gun at the bow. Mahmood's assistant, Daoud al Helma, sat in the sodden bilges, just behind that.

First pointing his chin at the baggage, Janail then inclined his head toward his companion and asked, "And you're *certain* that you can tell if the devices work with your instruments?" He spoke in English, their only common tongue.

"Yes," Mahmood answered, eyes automatically trying to follow an unseen flying pest. "At least insofar as anyone can tell without actually detonating one. I can check the quality of the nuclear material, judge the serviceability of the conventional explosive, determine the quality and serviceability of the switches and detonators. All that."

"You're certain you can't be fooled?"

Mahmood shook his head. "No, another scientist with the right backing could perhaps fool me with a counterfeit. And the man we're going to see could easily buy that scientist and give him that backing. But you shouldn't worry, even so."

"Why not?"

"Because some things can't be counterfeited and, given the raw materials, I can make a bomb, or two of them, no matter what the pirate ahead may think."

Ahead loomed a massive yacht, well—even ostentatiously—lit and very, very unconcerned with the infestation of pirates in the area. If the light had been natural and external, the yacht's hull would have shown as blue. As was, it seemed a black to match the night.

Janail couldn't make out the details, despite the lights, but he was reasonably certain that the yacht was so thoroughly armed, and its occupants so willing to open fire on the slightest provocation, that the yacht's master considered pirates the least of his problems.

No more does the fully grown great white shark fear the hammerhead.

Yacht *Resurrection*, between the coast of Kudat and the island of Pulau Banggi, South China Sea

Physically unprepossessing, balding, very rich, and with the paunch that usually went with that, Valentin Prokopchenko sipped an almost incredibly ancient Dalmore from a chilled glass. He considered vodka a drink for peasants. *And* I *am not a peasant.*

Born into an hereditarily highly placed—one may as well say, "aristocratic"—Communist family, in the former Union of Soviet Socialist Republics, as a young man Prokopchenko had seen the writing on the walls. "Let others try to salvage this house of cards," he'd said to himself, back then, as Soviet communism had begun to crumble. "I'm looking out for me and mine."

And who could blame him? Even his parents— dedicated Communists, to be sure—hadn't been so dedicated as not to watch out for the futures of their ever-so-precious children just a little more than they tried to ameliorate the plight of long-suffering mankind. Their wisdom in this was amply shown when son Valentin had, indeed, taken care of them, keeping them from the grinding poverty of the collapsing Soviet Union's final and worst days.

At least we thought they were the worst,

Prokopchenko thought, then took another sip of his scotch. *We lacked imagination. The worst days are now, except for the days to come.*

Where Boxer, back at Camp Fulton, in Guyana, kept a map on his wall which could have been labeled, "Advance of Barbarism across the Globe"—it was actually labeled, "Marketing"—Prokopchenko had a very large plasma screen. His organization, moreover, was larger and considerably better funded, than M Day, Inc., if not quite so well armed, conventionally. Minions fed the computer that fed the plasma screen with data ranging from trade routes and volume, through corruption indices, through influence of the intelligentsia, through drought, through the rise in certain communicable diseases, through mass migrations, through per capita wages, taxation, life expectancy, the price of food, through inflation levels and the skyrocketed price of precious metals . . . through . . .

Suffice to say, if there was a phenomenon or trait of intelligence importance, Prokopchenko's screen showed it, both individually and in composite form. And in the composite?

We're fucked.

Everything, every indicator, is for a near total collapse of civilization within twenty years. A couple of relatively strong city states might survive the fall. Singapore has a chance. Maybe Panama, which might as well be a city state already. Maybe a couple of dozen others will make it. But every form of organization above the level of a city or, at best, a not too large province, is crumbling under the weight of corruption, deindustrialization, demonetization, breakdown in law, and every man or woman for him or herself. And the only cities I expect to survive are the ones that break away from their larger states soon; those, and the few that have no larger state to suck them dry.

And, yes, I had my shortsighted part in all that, not that my contributions were decisive and not that it would have made any but the slightest difference if I'd been a model of communist propriety throughout the old empire's collapse. I doubt if anything I did hastened the fall by five minutes. "There is a tide in the affairs of men," after all. And our tide is going out.

If I didn't expect the United States to break up I'd move my family there. But they've devolved into two big groups—and a whole bunch of little ones—that hate each other beyond words. Ripe for a breakup, that's what Panarin said, and though I didn't believe it then, I believe it now. So he was off by a few years? The essence of the thing he pegged perfectly. Beirut in the 1980s would have been safer than the United States in twenty years.

So why am I here, vending things that will surely hasten that fall and by rather more than five minutes?

Because in the days that are certainly coming, when no man can turn to or trust anyone but himself and his close blood relations, solid, material, universally recognized and accepted wealth will be all that will see one's family through, all that will buy the private armed force to keep unruly strangers away. Well . . . those and a large spot of the Earth's surface to call one's very own.

I can't save global civilization; no one can. So I have to do the next best thing and save some of it—a larger chunk than this boat—for me and mine.

★ ★ ★

"It's not the biggest yacht in the world," Janail said doubtfully as the skiff thumped against the *Resurrection*'s eighty meter hull.

Mahmood shook his head, visible now in the brighter light from the ship. "Most of Russia's nouveau riche went for more ostentation, yes. Prokopchenko, though, is old aristocracy and privilege. He doesn't need the display. He needs speed, security, a helipad, and a fair amount of computing power. This gives him that."

"And you trust him?" Janail asked, not for the first time.

"Not even remotely."

"You're the one who put me in contact with him," Janail accused.

Again Mahmood shook his head. "I trust me. I trust you. I trust him only to put his own interests first. Since we—you—have or will have something he badly wants, I trust that."

"Money? From the old man's ransom?" Janail scowled doubtfully and, again, not for the first time. "He *has* money. Lot's more than he can get from us."

"He has less than he used to," Mahmood answered. "Much less. And, of what he has, there is probably little that cannot be traced to him. What he will get from us will not be traceable, I think, and so he can use it for whatever purposes he has that he may think good, but that others would not.

"And, too," Mahmood added, "he is in his own way a pious man, like ourselves. I think he thinks to serve Allah, even if by another name.

"But I still don't trust him."

★ ★ ★

Valentin glanced up at the knock on his seaborne lounge's entrance. Automatically, he looked up to see a guard wearing the white tropical uniform he'd had issued to the company he kept aboard.

"Your guests are here, sir," the guard corporal announced.

Valentin's eyes glanced over the uniform, inspecting it from the shako, with its double-eagle and reversed swastika insignia, down to the shoes. He, himself, had never served. Family connections had seen him well out of the Soviet Union's draft. But, like other Russian boys, and girls, he'd had a healthy chunk of what the West would have called, "Basic Training," while still in elementary through high school. Thus, though never a soldier, he could hum the tune well enough to maintain the respect of the ex-soldiers he employed for security. He hummed an even better tune for the old orthodox priest he kept on retainer, half for the benefit of his guards and half for public image. And *that* was sheer hypocrisy.

"Very good, Corporal," Prokopchenko answered. "See that they're searched and brought down."

★ CHAPTER SIX ★

In war, the real enemy is always behind the lines. Never
in front of you, never among you. Always at your back.
　　　　　—Jean Raspail, *The Camp of the Saints*

Safe House Alpha, Hagonoy, Bulacan, Luzon,
Republic of the Philippines

"Search the house for bugs," Terry ordered Lox, a scant
three minutes after Pedro had left for the airport to pick
up a few more members of the advance party. He gave the
order as far from the house or any manmade feature as
possible. One just never knew.

Lox raised an eyebrow. "And if, rather *when,* I find
some?"

"Leave them for now. Put up standard markers to
warn off the rest. I just want to know where we can and
can't speak freely."

Lox turned to get his baggage, sitting on a concrete
pad just outside the entrance to the main house. He
turned and said, "I don't like having a single safe house

and that provided by an employer I am by no means sure we can trust."

Welch nodded. "As soon as Semmerlin, Graft, and Franceschi get here, you and one of them are going to go find us our own, along with a car that won't have a watcher attached." Then he changed his voice to just above a whisper. "Because, pleasantries aside, I don't trust the bitch, either."

"There's three more waiting at the airport," Pedro announced, half in, half out of his "taxi." Behind it, clustered at the open trunk, three more of Terry's advance party unloaded their limited baggage. These were Master Sergeant Graft, the team leader, medium height, stocky, and rather more than half gray; Semmerlin, maybe early thirties, tall, slender, and blond; and a new troop, Ferd Franceschi, who looked vaguely Balkan, if anything. Franceschi was fairly new, though his background had seemed to the regiment *most* promising.

"They'll probably be the last until the main force gets here," Welch answered. To one of the three newcomers, Graft, he said, "Let Semmerlin and Franceschi worry about the bags. I want you and Lox to go back to the airport with Pedro. Your escort. He has a lead he needs to check out in a not so good spot. You'll be gone two to three days. Stop at a tailor and get some suits made.

"Speaking of which, Pedro? Guns? Permits?"

"Guns tomorrow," the Filipino answered. "Permits . . . maybe three days. Criminals efficient, but even with bribery, bureaucrat only works so fast, ya know?"

★ ★ ★

Once the tail of Pedro's taxi had turned behind the main gate, Terry held up his hands to stop the remaining two in place. "The house is bugged," he said. "Presumably by our principal. We've shunted the furniture around a little, enough to place one flat surface by the right side of the door to any bugged room. Some already had tables. There're a couple of crossed pencils on the tables of any room that has a bug."

Semmerlin nodded, unsurprised. Franceschi, new to the regiment and the team, but formerly of Australian SAS, looked a little nonplussed. In a reasonably understandable accent, he asked, "Our own employers spy on us?"

"Usually," Terry replied, with a grin. "We tend to work for the very rich. They don't trust us peasants for beans. And with good reason. Hell, you're one of them, or you were. You should know that."

"Hey," the Aussie objected, "I'm trying to rise above my roots. Besides, 'Australia, as everyone knows, is inhabited entirely by criminals.'"

"Fuck. Next you'll be quoting Monty Python at us."

"I have a vewy good fwend in Wome . . . "

"Fuck."

EDSA, Pasay City, Manila Metro Area, Republic of the Philippines

The EDSA, the Epifanio de los Santos Avenue, was the major highway and ring road encircling Metro Manila. It was just off of there that Pedro let off his two passengers.

Lox waited until the taxi had disappeared into traffic

before asking, "First question; did any of you mention how many of us were coming?"

Graft thought for a moment, then shook his head. "No; we mentioned 'the team' but not how big it was."

"Good. Just FYI, we don't have a lead and, at the moment, I'm not looking for one. We're going to get another car, buy a dozen throwaway cells, contact a realtor, and buy or rent us a safe house for the other half of the team."

"Bad principal?" Graft asked.

"Let's just say a different class from us, and to her we'd be pretty expendable. Let's also say that Terry thinks better safe than sorry."

"Fair enough," Graft agreed. "Gotta love a paranoid CO. But it's going to be a bitch to find a safe house here. It's not like the old days, when this place was crawling with flyboys and squids. The other half of the team is going to stick out."

"Wouldn't help if they were still here; we'd stand out among them, too. And an expat suburb won't do for the same reason."

Graft shrugged. "Yeah, I suppose so. So we need a cover story for why there are half a dozen unusually well built gringos in one house in Manila."

"The whores?" Lox suggested.

"Nah. People who come here to run the hookers come singly or, at most, in trios. Six is just too many."

"Crime?"

Again, Graft thought not. "Our people even *look* like they're involved in any kind of crime and we'll attract the kind of attention we *really* don't need. Someone's going to want their cut, and we won't have any cut to give them."

"Well *what* then?" Lox asked, with exasperation.

"Dunno. Let's get a car and go find that real estate agent. Maybe something will suggest itself."

"Better make it an SUV," Lox said. "And we'd better make it quick, since the other six are coming in this evening."

South Green Heights Village, Muntinlupa City, Manila Metro Area, Republic of the Philippines

"It'll do," Graft agreed, once the realtor had stepped away to lock the place up.

Lox shook his head. "You're just tired because, after two and a half days of continuous house hunting, this is the first one we've seen that isn't awful."

"No," the master sergeant disagreed, "I'm serious. This one will do."

"This one" was a smallish mansion, on about a one and a half acre lot. White stuccoed and with square, fluted columns, the place boasted seven bedrooms, plus maid's quarters, a head-high surrounding wall, also white and stucco, plus sufficient messing facilities and a living room large enough for group planning. The furniture was sparse, but the house itself was pretty plush. A garage, tucked in underneath the bedroom level, had walls on three sides with the opening facing the perimeter wall. The gate was offset so that there was no easy direct view from the street of the parking space. No one would see anyone entering or leaving, not in any detail that wouldn't be obscured by the SUV's tinted windows.

"And we've got roads," Graft added, "that will do for a quick getaway. In fact, we've got a lot of roads, so it would be a quick and unpredictable getaway. If that turned out to be impossible, there's unbuilt wooded area"—he pointed to the northwest—"about three hundred meters thataway. And more, even closer, to the south. We've got the big lake, Laguna de Bay, a mile to the east, too, so a water exfiltration is, at least, a possibility. There are some expats around, so a few gringos, more or less, won't excite any excess curiosity."

Lox still looked skeptical. "Okay, so why are they here? Six Kanos in one house, even if it's a big house, is still freaking suspicious."

"That's one of the *beauties* of the place," Graft answered, grinning with enthusiasm. "It's fancy enough that an American or European businessman with an administrative assistant and four bodyguards wouldn't be out of place.

"By the way, how much did the realtor say the owners wanted?"

"Two hundred thirty-three thousand USD. I can get it for two hundred, if I slip the realtor ten under the table."

"Wouldn't happen in the States," Graft sneered.

With a chuckle, Lox replied, "No, in the States, these days, I'd have to slip the realtor twenty but I'd get it for a hundred and ninety. Speaking of which," he added, seeing the realtor coming back, "make yourself scarce for a bit. They're corrupt here, though maybe not as bad as we're becoming. Even so, they've enough sense of propriety not to want witnesses."

"And, speaking of witnesses," Graft said, leaving for the SUV, "it would be suspicious as all hell for an American businessman with an administrative assistant and four guards not to have a maid and/or cook."

"One thing at a time, Sergeant," Lox chided. "Now we go to the realtor's office and close on the property. Then we're going to see if an old acquaintance of mine can set this crew up with, at least, a few shotguns. Or whatever. *Then* we worry about a maid and a cook."

Samurai Arms, Inc., National Road, Bucal, Calamba City, Republic of the Philippines

"*Samurai* Arms?" Graft asked, seeing the business' name neatly painted on the plate glass window fronting the street. A spotless, apparently brand new, van sat in an alley next door.

Lox gave a half shrug. "The Filipinos can hold a grudge, just like anybody else, but they don't make a religion of it. And the war was a long time ago. In any case, this place exists in good part for 'gun tourism,' Japanese who can't have weapons come here—a few other places, too—and get to make a joyful sound unto the Lord."

"What's going to be available?"

"You never can tell," Lox answered. "Legally, he usually keeps around three hundred open and aboveboard guns on the premises. But he runs a little side business where it's catch of the day." Pointing with his chin at the glass door with the warning sign that absolutely no loaded weapons were allowed within, Lox said, "Come on."

As the door swung open, a guard—it was most unlikely that the proscription on loaded weapons applied to him—leveled a shotgun at the pair of Americans. Lox just stood there calmly while Graft began raising his hands.

"Knock it off, Manuel," commanded a fair skinned Filipina standing behind a glass case. "These are *clients*." Sheepishly, the young guard lowered the shotgun.

"Ben's in back, Peter," the woman said.

"Thanks, Gracie," Lox answered, starting forward toward a steel door to the right of the display case.

"Haven't seen you in—what is it? Five years?"

Without stopping he answered, "Closer to six, Gracie. Been busy."

"Hmmph," she grunted. Clearly "busy" was not an acceptable excuse. Careful of her well-shaped and painted nails, she reached a delicate finger, bearing a perfect almond nail, down to press a button. From the door came a loud buzz and the sound of a bolt being electronically thrown.

The office behind the door was nothing remarkable. A wooden desk held a computer, along with a pile of files, most quite thin. There were a couple of loose papers that looked like invoices. Behind the desk stood a couple of tall bookcases, holding titles like *Small Arms of the World* and *Jane's Infantry Weapons*, as well as three ring binders hand labeled with sundry titles and years for various gun magazines, almost entirely American. A few other binders bore official sounding names or numbers. Those were probably the local firearms laws and regulations.

On the wall above the desk were several graduation

certificates, ranging from Advanced Handgun to Submachine Gun (Distinguished Graduate) from Front Sight Firearms Training Institute in Las Vegas, Nevada. There was also a certificate for the Tactical Explosive Entry Course, from the Philippine National Police Special Action Force. Next to that was a BS degree in Criminology from the UPHSL, the University of Perpetual Help System Laguna. Lastly, though placed above them all, was a promotion certificate to the rank of Master Sergeant (Reserve) from the Philippine Army.

At the desk, and matching the names on the certificates, sat one Bayani—Ben—Arroyo. He looked very damned young to be a master sergeant, even in the reserves.

At the sound of the bolt retracting, Ben had swiveled his chair to face the door. As soon as he recognized Lox, he was out of the chair, pumping the American's fist and pounding his shoulder. "Dooode, where ya been?"

Before Lox could answer, or even introduce Graft, Ben directed both him and Graft to chairs against the wall opposite the bookcases.

"Ah, never mind. You won't tell me anyway. Whatcha need? Right . . . stupid question. What *kind* of guns do you need?"

"Depends on what you have, Ben."

"Right." The Filipino turned and walked the step and a half to the bookcase. He took from it a relatively thin binder, which he opened and handed to Lox. "These are what I have in stock right now."

Lox flipped a page, then another, and then a third. "Prices have gone up, I see. Police making life difficult?"

Ben shook his head. "No, dude, *demand* has skyrocketed.

Nobody's happy with just a shotgun and a revolver anymore. People, especially people who can afford better, are running scared. They want the real deal and fuck the law."

"Business must be good then," Lox said.

Ben put out a hand, palm down, and waved it a few times. "It is and it isn't. I'm tellin' ya, dude, crime has gotten a lot worse than the government will admit to. I lose customers all the time; kidnappings, robberies, murders, you name it."

Lox shrugged; times were tough all over. He handed the binder to Graft, saying, "Pick what you think the men will need."

Graft began to thumb it. "Right off, I want a half dozen sets of under the jacket, level three, partial body armor. These En Garde Executive vests look about right."

"What sizes . . . by the way, who are you?"

"My fa—" Lox started to say. "No, wait a minute; *your* fault. *You* never gave me a chance. Ben, this is my . . . co-worker, Michael. He knows what he needs better than I do."

"Okay. Anyway, Michael, what sizes?"

From a pocket Graft pulled out a small notebook in which he had the jacket sizes for each man in his team. He read off those of the six who would be going to the second safe house.

"I can handle everything except the really big guy," Ben said. "Just not a lot of demand for large sizes here. I can get you an old PASGT in extra large. It won't hold SAPI plates, of course, but I can get those and a harness to hold them. Will that do?"

"It'll have to," Graft agreed. "Now as for firearms; We

need half a dozen .45's with four mags and five hundred rounds each. Suppressed would be nice, but only if you can get us some subsonic ammunition . . ."

"No sweat."

"Good. Also, two AA-12 shotguns; those, or Akdals, or Saiga 12s. And I'd like to get a pair of these Russki PP-90M1's . . ."

"Can't help you with those," Ben said. "Sold the few I had a while back, maybe three months. I've got *Sterlings*, though," he added brightly.

★ CHAPTER SEVEN ★

O Curse of marriage,
—William Shakespeare, *Othello*

MV *Richard Bland, mid Atlantic*

I suppose it had to be something, thought Warrington, seated behind a built-in desk in the office that went with the ground force commander's quarters, within the *Bland*'s superstructure. *Why not this?*

"This" was an altercation, verbal only, between Captain Stocker and Sergeant Hallinan, on the mess deck, centered on proper safety procedures for a rifle but really about the very different kinds of personnel that tended to gravitate to, on the one hand, the special operations world and, on the other, the—more or less—"regular army." Strictly speaking, of course, there was precisely *no* segment of M Day, Inc. that was actually regular. Still, attitudes carried over. One of these attitudes was concerned with the technical; what, in fact, was safe and what wasn't. The other was legal and moral. Among the American and even

Commonwealth spec ops types, rank had long been a fairly fuzzy proposition: Captains cut grass and picked up cigarette butts, while, often enough, sergeants led missions. Let a PSYOP major show up to support a Special Forces A Team led by a captain? That captain was in charge. Conversely, among the regulars, rank and position were hard, fast, and even sacred. "If senior, I will take command . . . "

The regulars' position was, generally speaking, that the Special Forces community sacrificed long-term order, stability, and discipline for short-term tactical gain. SF generally thought the regulars had something up their butts, possibly a stick, but often enough, their heads.

They were both at least partially right.

And they're both basically right, here, too.

Warrington looked up at the tall, skinny, brown-eyed Hallinan, with distaste. "And your story, Sergeant?"

Standing just forward of his company's sergeant major and the first sergeant for A Company, a few feet from the seated Stocker, Hallinan braced to attention. Sure, special operations forces, to include 2nd Battalion, M Day, were pretty informal. But there's a time and place for everything. Since he didn't know how much, if any, trouble he was in, this seemed like it might be one of those times and places.

"Sir. It's like this. I'd just come off the sub-cal range, forward. I was heading to stow my rifle in the arms rooms. The galley was on my way—can't avoid it really—and it was lunchtime, so I got in line. Didn't bust the line or anything, just jumped in behind one of the Guyanans. Then Captain—"

"Major," Warrington corrected, even while thinking, *Silly damned custom.*

"Right, sir. Major Stocker came over and asked me about my safety, which was not, per SOP, engaged. I help up my hand, extended my—be it noted, sir—*trigger* finger, and said, 'This is my safety.' The captain—"

"Major."

Hallinan glanced down at the line officer, then returned to attention. "Right; the major told me to engage my mechanical safety. I said we didn't do that. He made it an order. I said my orders come from Lava, who's a colonel, and Terry, who's a *real* major. At that point . . . Cap . . . Major Stocker told me I was under arrest. Then the sergeant major showed up and marched me here."

Warrington nodded. "Is that substantially correct, Sergeant Major?"

Straight faced, Puerto Rican accent subdued but noticeable, Sergeant Major Pierantoni answered, "Yessir. Substantially, sir."

"First Sergeant Kiertzner?"

Kiertzner had actually retired from the British Army as a sergeant major, held the rank of master sergeant as the senior NCO of the team that was the cadre for C Company, and was a first sergeant by virtue of being the senior noncom in C Company. He wore his old British Army rank on a leather band around his wrist, since M day wasn't really all that touchy about such things. He also sported a Vandyke, since the Regiment wasn't especially anal about facial hair, either. The troops, in deference to his old rank, tended to call him "Sergeant Major" rather than "Top."

Like many of the senior noncoms in M Day, Kiertzner could have taken a commission if he'd wanted to. Instead, he'd *liked* being a noncom too much to give it up.

The Brit-born, if Danish extracted, first shirt ahemed and said, "Umm, yes. Substantially, sir. Sergeant Hallinan left off a few minor details."

"Like referring to my entire company as wannabes," offered Stocker, shooting Kiertzner a dirty look. "Like saying that if my men weren't competent enough to be trusted with loaded weapons maybe they should find another line of work? Like—"

Holding up a silencing hand, Warrington said, "I get the idea, Andrew. Sergeant Major?"

"Yessir, that kind of detail," Pierantoni agreed. *But you'll have to ask for it, Tracy; I'm not volunteering anything.*

"I see. Hallinan, you are dismissed to your quarters. Stay there until I send for you."

"Sir." The sergeant executed a sharp—unusually so for 2nd Battalion—salute, took a step back, faced about, smartly, and then departed through the hatch. Pierantoni closed the hatch behind him. Then Pierantoni took a seat, himself, opposite Stocker. Kiertzner leaned against the wall.

"This shit always happens," Warrington said, as soon as the hatchway clicked shut.

"Indiscipline and insubordination?" Stocker queried.

"It isn't, you know," Warrington countered, wagging one finger. "Or not exactly what you mean by it. Hallinan's a good man. I can trust him to do the right thing even if nobody's watching him. I can tell him to sit in a muddy hole for three days and watch X, and he will stay there, wide awake, watching X, if he has to prop his eyelids open with sharp twigs or wire his own balls to a field telephone. But it's a different kind of discipline and a different kind of subordination. And that's appropriate for the kind of soldier he is, which is a different kind of soldier than what you're used to.

"*But*, whenever we mix the two, regulars and spec ops, we have this kind of problem. Because the two outlooks just don't mix for shit.

"How loud was Hallinan?" Warrington asked of Pierantoni.

"The cap . . . the major's troops heard the exchange, sir, enough of them. At least the last part, once the two of them got heated."

Placing an elbow on the desk's Formica top, Warrington made a fist and rested his cheek on it. "Right. Of course. Wouldn't do to be subtle." He glanced at Stocker. "I don't suppose any of that was your fault."

"Might have been," the Canuck admitted. "I'm not used to being told to fuck off, for all practical purposes, by a noncom."

"Major Stocker," said Pierantoni, "screamed at Hallinan, 'Put your fucking safety on, you blockhead.'"

Stocker shrugged. "Yeah, okay. I suppose I did."

"And thereby made this much more complex and difficult than it needed to be. Shall I lay out the problems for you?" Warrington hadn't made an offer. He intended to lay out the problems, whether Stocker wanted to hear them or not. Fingers began to extend, one by one, as he ticked off the problems.

"One, and the one you probably care about most; I have to punish Hallinan, who did nothing wrong by our ethos, or you lose prestige and authority in your company.

"Two, assuming I do punish him, it's going to create bad blood between my people and yours.

"Three, if I don't punish him, your people are going to feel that their form of discipline has been spat on.

"Four, if I do punish him, *my* people are going to feel like their form of discipline has been spat on.

"Five—"

"I get the idea," Stocker said.

"Oh, no," Warrington corrected, "I've just begun to scratch the surface. Five, your people might or might not be needed. But we know my people will be. So because you had to butt in—"

That touched a nerve. Angry now, Stocker raised his voice. "Now wait a God damned minute. In case you didn't notice, this is a metal ship. An accidental discharge *was* going to ricochet until it hit somebody."

"There *wasn't* going to be one!"

"Six," said Pierantoni, over the officers' shouting, "it's got the two senior ground fighters aboard arguing like children."

"I fucking hate it when you're right," Warrington said, *sotto voce*. Stocker just glared, though the heat of the glare dissipated quickly.

"Which leaves us with what we're going to do about it," Pierantoni said. "Rule One is that we can't, on our own hook, change the SOP. Any of our people carrying arms will *not* have them on safe. With what we do, where and when we do it, it's a bad—a deadly bad—habit."

"Reconfigure the ship to separate out your people and mine?" Stocker suggested. "More than they already are, I mean. Maybe set up a different galley?"

"Doesn't buy us much," Warrington said, shaking his head. "And we do need to get used to each other, if we're going to end up fighting together. And, despite what I said before, we might.

"How about training your people to our firearms safety standards?"

Now Stocker shook his head. "Shoveling shit against the tide. That, or maybe starting a shit tsunami rolling downhill. You can't imagine the trouble we've had drilling them into something like fanaticism over putting their weapons on safe. They're good troops, but they're still from the Third World. Changing this, now, would toss into question everything we've drilled into them. Confusion to us, rather than the enemy."

"So what, then?" Warrington asked of Pierantoni.

"Three days bread and water for Hallinan, for mouthing off to an officer, then ignore it," the sergeant major said. He shot a glance at Kiertzner, who nodded silent agreement.

"It was just Emperor Mong," Kiertzner said.

Stocker snickered; the emperor was something of an inside joke to Commonwealth forces.

"Emperor Mong," Kiertzner sighed. "A malevolent celestial being. You never see him, but his unique talent is to encourage young folk to take the least sensible and most damaging course of action by making that seem like a splendid idea. He's the one who whispers into a young soldier's ear, 'I know it's Sunday evening and you have an early start tomorrow morning for a heavy week, but surely if you just go out drinking, stay out until 0400 and then *don't go to bed*, you'll be fine for PT at 0600,' or 'just go ahead and hook up your boogie box to the vehicle batteries using commo wire. What could *possibly* go wrong?'

"It is the emperor's proud duty to advise the young soldier that there's no need to use a condom with the girl he just met who is practically leaking on the floor with her unquenched desire. He, too, serves as a kind of Cupid, or matchmaker, who will assure the young soldier that the tart he's been seeing would make a fine wife. His Imperial Majesty will confidently assure the smallish infantryman that, why of course he'd be a match for that entire gun section of broad-shouldered gunners in the local tavern. His power is unfathomable, and his wickedness beyond measure.

"His power is particular impressive in Scotland. And at sea. And when that space shuttle blew up? That was Mong, whispering, 'Go on, see what pushing that red button does.'"

"Oh," said Pierantoni, "a relation of Murphy's."

"Distantly related, yes," Kiertzner said, "but they have different functions in the Divine Order. Murphy just fucks you. The emperor grows your dick so you fuck yourself. And one of the problems with the emperor is that perhaps one time in twenty his advice is sound. Which is, as it turns out, just enough for young troops to keep taking his advice."

"Ah. I can see that."

"Okay," agreed Warrington, "but what do we do?"

"Easy, sir. Major Stocker tells his people to ignore our rules; because the"—Pierantoni added the quotes through tone of voice and bracing his neck—"'Guyanans are real soldiers and us Second Battalion pukes are not.' We sit hard on our people to keep their overactive mouths shut and to minimize any differences."

Both the officers looked at him as if he were either crazy or stupid.

"Then you brilliant bastards come up with something better. That's what you get the big bucks for."

Way back in the dim mists of antiquity, when he'd first been thinking of going either U.S. Army Special Forces or to OCS, before eventually doing both, then Sergeant Warrington had had a company commander who had taken an interest in him, enough so to snag him as a driver, and use the opportunity to explain to him how to be a company commander. This included how to do nonjudicial punishment. Since the Corporation had adopted over U.S. military law pretty much in toto, the advice still held good.

That long-ago commander had given a number of rules, or guidelines. "Rule One: Nonjudicial punishment should be very rare, indeed. Most problems can and should be handled well before it gets to you. If you find you're having regular NJP sessions, there is something wrong with your command.

"Rule Two: Take the time to plan the event. That means write out the script and rehearse it, if only in your mind. If you're a decent human being, it's hard to be a bastard. Rehearsal helps.

"Rule Three: Use it as an opportunity to build your chain of command. Get input from the squad leader, platoon sergeant, and platoon leader. Ask the question: 'Is this soldier salvageable?'

"Rule Four: Always max out the guilty bastard, but then suspend any punishment you think is excessive, or likely to do more harm than good. Taking money or rank or both from a married man hurts his family, something you ought not want to do, if it's at all avoidable. Restricting him to the barracks hurts him, in fact, gives him a serious—possibly terminal—case of lackanookie. Tie that in to the recommendations from his chain of command. Remember, too; suspended punishment reduces the probability of appeal.

"Finally, Rule Five—and I cannot emphasize this enough: Always, always, *always* add to the punishment, *'and an oral reprimand.'* Once you invoke those words, you can give an ass chewing so abusive that it would get you court-martialed in other circumstances. There is no practical limit in what you can say and how you can say it, because you will have invoked the magic words. This also tends to partially cover up your excessively kind and generous nature in suspending a goodly portion of the more material punishment. That said, sometimes you will want to do the oral reprimand first. And, in any case, remember that a commander is always on stage."

Having somewhat skirted Rule Four, insofar as he lacked the legal authority to reduce Hallinan's rank—and didn't want to anyway; Warrington was on Rule Five at the moment: *"And* an oral reprimand."

Warrington began conversationally. "Just out of curiosity, Sergeant Hallinan, were you sleeping during the classes at

SWC"—that was the U.S. Army's Special Warfare Center at Fort Bragg, NC—"when they lectured you on the delicate nature of dealing with local forces and their chains of command?"

"Ummm, nosir," answered Hallinan, normally somewhat light skinned and now gone positively pale in anticipation of what was coming.

"Ah." That was still conversational. But then Warrington's voice rose a notch. "So you were too fucking stupid to pay attention? Or was it that in your incarnate ignorance and arrogance you figured that applied to everybody but you? Did you figure that your ever-so-fucking precious ego was so important that the mission didn't matter?"

"Sir, I—"

"Shut the fuck up," Warrington snarled. "If I ever thought your opinion was worth listening to, I don't think so right now." Elbows on desk, he began massaging his temples as if suffering from a terrible migraine. *Yes, boss, I remember that a commander is always on stage.*

"Now let me tell you what you've done," he continued, and proceeded to do just that in an echo of the problems he'd previously listed for Stocker and Pierantoni. He embellished as seemed fit.

When he was pretty sure all the color that could disappear from Hallinan's face was gone, Warrington added, "Maybe you don't think it's a such big deal, compromising the mission and such. Certainly nothing to match the bruise to your poor widdle ego. So what if over a hundred million dollars gets paid to terrorists to do Satan knows what with? Small change, right? No big fucking deal?"

Warrington stood then and sneered. "You stupid piece of dog shit. I ought to just have them weight your feet and toss you over the side. Maybe the frigging fish will get more use out of you then we're likely to."

He began pounding the desk. "What"—bang—"the"—bang—"fuck"—bang—"were"—bang—"you"—bang—"thinking? Oh, silly of me; you weren't thinking. You're too goddamned stupid for thought. You're a six-foot assemblage of *shit* masquerading as a soldier."

Warrington stopped the ass-chewing then, just glaring at Hallinan with feigned disgust. Then, turning to Pierantoni, he asked, "Recommendations., Sergeant Major?"

"Despite current appearances," the sergeant major answered, "he hasn't always been the worthless pile of used tampons he currently appears, sir. They say suffering is good for the soul. I'd recommend three days bread and water."

Again glaring at Hallinan, Warrington announced, "So be it. Sergeant Hallinan, commencing at—"

Whatever Warrington had been about to say was cut off by Pearson's voice, coming over the ship's intercom. "All hands and passengers, this is the captain speaking. Assembly on the mess deck in twenty minutes. Commanders of the ground force to my cabin immediately."

★ CHAPTER EIGHT ★

A world without nuclear weapons would be
less stable and more dangerous for all of us.
—Margaret Thatcher

**Yacht *Resurrection*, between the coast of Kudat
and the island of Pulau Banggi, South China Sea**

The corporal poured tea for Janail and Mahmood.
Valentin Prokopchenko had set his scotch aside and would
not, for politeness' sake, drink it while the Moslems were
in his presence. Daoud al Helma had been left above,
guarding Mahmood's testing equipment and the more
personal baggage.

"You can do an exterior test of both devices now," said
Prokopchenko. Here, too, English was the only common
tongue. "Upon deposit of half the agreed sum, in the escrow
account I have given you, you may partially disassemble and
evaluate *one* device, of your choosing. Upon full deposit, you
may take delivery. I trust this is acceptable to you."

Janail looked at Mahmood for confirmation. He knew
nothing about such things.

The scientist nodded. "It's all right, Janail. I can tell—to a better than ninety-five percent certainty—with the testing materials I have brought."

Turning back to Valentin, he asked, "Where and how did you come upon not one but *two* such warheads?"

"I had them built," answered the Russian. "More specifically, as the warheads on what the West calls the SS-27 rockets were changed out from single to MIRV—"

"MIRV?" Janail interrupted.

"Multiple Independently-targeted Reentry Vehicles," Mahmood supplied, patiently. In his own sphere, Janail was something of a master, but that sphere didn't include strategic weapons. "A warhead of separate warheads, each of which goes its own way after a certain point."

"Like a shotgun?" asked Janail.

"Yes," agreed Mahmood, "if you can imagine that each pellet from a shotgun targets—and hits—a separate organ, one for the left eye, one for the right, one for the heart, one for each lung, two for the kidneys . . . "

Valentin chuckled softly. The analogy was rather apt, in its way. "Quite. We—the Russian Federation; as if we could actually afford it—are switching out our older warheads for newer ones, MIRV's, mostly out of fear of the Chinese. The older warheads were broken down to their components and mostly sent for reprocessing.

"The inert casings, tritium reservoirs, and sparkplug tubes, I bought for scrap. The conventional explosives I had cast anew. The tritium, deuterium, and plutonium-239 were . . . harder. Note that the tritium cartridges are almost brand new.

"It's fortunate that our security procedures have not

improved noticeably since Lebed first discovered we were missing over one hundred devices. And security over the components is even worse. For example, the gold around the plutonium had been stripped off and disappeared before I got to it. How whoever did that managed it, no one seemed to know. That, I had to have newly plated on.

"Oddly, the really hard parts were the krytron switches. Fortunately, in a country that has not really fully overcome socialist principles of accounting, shoddy workmanship to meet an imposed plan, unpaid work days to overproduce, and which further accepts the need to write off a certain percentage of what is produced because it is junk, it was possible to obtain enough. I fear that, someday, one of my country's warheads will not work because it got the junk while I obtained the good material.

"Yes, of course a fair amount of money changed hands for each step and piece. Hence my price." *Actually, remarkably little money, in the big scheme of things, and what I spent has very little to do with my price.*

"What about the permissive action link?" Mahmood asked.

"There are none," Prokopchenko answered. "Since these are privately produced, I saw no need to add any. Moreover, the world being the way it is, how could any buyer be certain I gave the proper PAL codes?"

Never mind that I really do *want you to have and to use these things. I don't want you to know that for a certainty.*

The *Resurrection* had an elevator running right from Prokopchenko 's office down to an indoor pool, on the next to lowest deck. It only made sense to have had it placed there, Prokopchenko, spending as much time as he did in less than sunny climes. Now the pool was hidden by its mechanical covering, strong enough, in itself, to serve as a dance floor. An oval section of lead shielding had been thrown up around it. More lead plates covered the ceiling, as well as the floor where the water of the pool didn't provide its own considerable degree of shielding.

Prokopchenko's mistress, an extraordinary, utterly stunning, indeed breathtaking, six foot tall Ukrainian girl named Daria, was *most* put out by the loss of the pool. Worse, the guards wouldn't even let her off the elevator anymore, not at the pool deck. And all the hatches to the pool area were locked. *Inconsiderate bastard. I'd fuck a couple of the guards in revenge, but the religious fanatics would just as likely report me.*

Daria's mood wasn't improved by being locked in her quarters, with the guards bringing her her meals, since the day prior. "There are things about my business you are better off not knowing," Valentin had explained. *As if that's an explanation!*

The elevator bearing Valentin, Janail, Mahmood, and his assistant into the bowels of the ship opened its door upon three leveled muzzles, from three submachine guns, in the hands on three *very* serious looking guards. At the guards' sighting of their leader, the muzzles were raised, even as the men snapped to attention. The acoustics of the pool deck, which had often enough in the past served as a party room, were excellent; the motions made barely a sound.

Past the guards, bent over one of the bags, Daoud removed a couple of dark jumpsuits of an odd material, thick and slightly stiff. Various other implements were already unpacked and set up near the sole entrance to the lead oval.

Mahmood walked to one of the panels and felt it with bare fingertips. *Lead, and not thin,* was his judgment. *It would be an unusually elaborate hoax to set this up just to fool us.* He glanced around at the guards and saw one chewing his lip nervously. The others looked anything but calm. Prokopchenko, himself, likewise seemed a tad unsettled. *No, no hoax. This may or may not be a pair of functional bombs. But, if they're not, then more than likely the Russian himself was fooled and believes they are.*

Daoud walked over, bearing two of the jumpsuits and two masks.

Though much of Mahmood's testing equipment was old and obsolescent, he and Daoud helped each other into the very latest antiradiation suits—made of demron, a liquid metal—from Radiation Shield Technologies, in the United States. Since these had no offensive use, they were not on anyone's proscribed technologies list. In point of fact, even if those charged with developing such lists had foreseen this particular use, it would have made no difference. The oldest of old-fashioned lead suits would have worked as well; they'd just not have been as comfortable.

Suited up, they then loaded upon their bodies an Ortec Detective-EX, a portable X-ray digital imaging system from Scanna, the laptop that went with the Scanna machine, a Dewar's flask filled with liquid nitrogen, a handheld "pager"—which was a low-tech device for measuring gamma radiation, another handheld explosive sniffer, plus a couple of small bags not much larger than a laptop carrier. Under one arm Daoud tucked a flat screen, about two feet by four.

So laden, the pair more or less waddled to the exterior door, their equipment clanking. The door was mounted in a projection, an irregularity, from the main oval. Throwing a bolt and then turning a knob, Mahmood pulled the thing—*ugh, yes, real lead and no hoax*—then waddled through, followed by his assistant. The latter then closed the door, before Mahmood opened the interior one.

Il hamdu l'illah! was the scientist's immediate thought. He felt a wave of reverence wash over him at the Almighty's beneficence in providing this means to avenge the many wrongs done to his people, which included all the people of the *Ummah*, the entire community of Muslims in the world, to include the majority who probably had no interest in nuking anybody.

The devices, two cylinders of about two feet in diameter by four and a half in length, sat on wheeled cradles atop the pool cover. They shone a dull silver compared to the cover's matte black. The Russian hadn't bothered with painting them. Still, paint or no paint, they seemed to the Pakistani ripe with menace. The two unloaded most of their equipment on the floor.

Before wasting his time with the more elaborate tests, Mahmood held up the "pager." No sense in going further if there was *no* radiation, after all. That dutifully beeped. *Ah, good.*

He placed the pager on the floor, taking up the Ortec

Detective-EX. This he repositioned on the floor, pointed at the nearer of the two devices. He checked that its internal nitrogen tank was full, and that the thing was fully powered. Then, pressing buttons until "ID Mode" showed on the upper left corner of the small screen, he set the timer for sixty seconds and hit the search button. He watched for the full minute, as the device listed nuclides positively identified.

All consistent with plutonium-239. Now for the next step.

While Mahmood fiddled with buttons, Daoud set up the Scanna, connecting X-ray generator and digital imaging plate to the laptop, and mounting the emitter to a tripod. After marking certain points on the bomb casing with an X-ray blocking tape, to give common points of reference, Daoud took his first shot, giving the laptop time to fully digitalize the image. He then immediately began repositioning emitter and screen. Mahmood wanted eight good shots of each device, as they lay, then another three from underneath and one from above. At a bit over a ton, each, there wasn't going to be any rotating of the bombs along their long axes for better scans.

Ignoring Daoud, for the moment—*he knows his job*—Mahmood turned his attention back to the screen on the Detective-EX. It showed: "Classify Mode." Mahmood set that to running. It wasn't long before the screen added: "Found nuclear plutonium" followed shortly by "Count for >5 minutes for Weapons/Reactor grade."

By the time Daoud had finished his first half dozen scans, the screen showed, unmistakably: "Pu" followed by "Weapons grade Pu."

Now let's check for tritium.

The technique was called "computed tomography," and, it wasn't, in principle, all that different from the medical version. Indeed, used at a precision fixed site, it was quite similar. Daoud didn't have that fixed site, of course, nor anything like the usual degree of precision. Instead, he had to rely on the X-ray blocking tape to make common reference points, plus manual identification of known similars within the device.

That coiled wire on number three is *the same coiled wire in number five. Yes! We have a match. Now . . . let's match detonators . . .*

It took a fair amount of processing power, plus ScanView software, to turn those matches, from a dozen distinct X-ray scans of a complex device, into a reliable, digital, three-dimensional model of that device. Daoud's laptop didn't have it. Another computer in the baggage, however, did. That was currently humming away, building, connecting, discarding . . .

"So you're certain they're real?" Janail asked, when Mahmood came to report in his decadently plush stateroom aboard the *Resurrection*.

"As certain as I or anyone but the Russian can be," the scientist replied. "I know the core of each is weapons grade Plutonium 239. I know that they're of a proper size and mass, for both the primary and the sparkplug. I know the 'hohlraum' is present for each. I know that the test set says the detonators are functional. I know that the tritium reservoirs are full. I know that the thirty-two blocks of explosive, for each, to implode the plutonium are solid—no cracks or defects—and the detonators are properly positioned within them. I know that the sixty-four detonators and wires for each are the right number. I know that the wires *appear* to be of a uniform length, but I can't be certain because some are coiled. The test set says they're the same, but it could lie.

"Still, I think they're real."

★ CHAPTER NINE ★

All the news that fits.
—Jann Wenner

Captain's Quarters, MV *Richard Bland*, South Atlantic

Pearson looked half in shock, sitting his captain's chair, left elbow resting on the chair's arm and the underside of his nose on his index finger. In his right hand, hanging low across the chair's other arm, he held a piece of paper. This he passed to Warrington wordlessly as soon as the other entered the cabin.

"So they really did it," said Warrington, after he'd read. "Then again, it isn't like we weren't expecting it."

The captain shook his head, *No, it isn't as if we weren't expecting it*.

"Still," continued Warrington, "they could have told us something about casualties beyond, 'Heavy but not crippling.' They could have said something about civilian casualties."

"I asked," the skipper replied. "They told me, 'When

we know; you'll know.' I think maybe they're still digging in the rubble. And that's going to take a back seat to—"

Stocker's grim face appeared at the hatch. "You wanted me, Skipper?"

Warrington waved him in and passed him the decoded message.

"Crap," said the Canadian ex-pat. "Not many of my men are married with families on base, but they've all got family out in the country, out where the Venezuelans are occupying. They're not going to be happy over this, not a bit."

"Not happy over the attack," Warrington asked, "or not happy that we're sailing away from it."

"Both."

"Yeah . . . both. Question is, how do we tell them what we know and, worse, what we don't know?"

"I can make the announcement," Pearson offered Warrington, "But they're mostly your men."

"Actually," Warrington replied, chin pointing at Stocker, "they're mostly his. But I'm senior; I'll tell them."

"Do you want me to have the mess deck TV turned on?" Pearson asked.

"After I finish talking," Warrington agreed. "But can you show me what CNN's saying before I go face the men?"

"Easy," Pearson answered. "*My* television isn't on a kill switch."

Stocker shook his head with disbelief. "A peacekeeping operation? Those CNN assholes are billing it as a peacekeeping operation? The jets that bombed the shit out of Camp Fulton, the housing areas, the fucking post hospital were keeping the fucking peace?"

Pearson made a scissors motion with two fingers. "Oh, it's just a misspelling, I'm sure. See, from Venezuela's and Chavez's point of view they *are* just keeping a *piece*."

Mess Deck, MV *Richard Bland*, South Atlantic

"At ease," Warrington ordered, after the senior noncom for the expedition, Sergeant Major Pierantoni, had reported and walked off to one side. Though there was an elevated and railed balcony of sorts, sternward, he stood at the same level of the mess deck as the assembled men. Most of them were in formation, five blocks for the infantry company, a single block for the rump of the special operations company, and a couple of double ranks for the naval crew and aviation detachment. Only the cooks, standing forward, weren't in ranks and they, after all, had a pressing job to do.

"No," Warrington amended, making come hither motions with the fingers of both hands, "fuck 'at ease.' I hate raising my voice. Break ranks and cluster 'round. And you spoons in the back; set your burners to simmer and get your butts on over here, too."

Waiting a few moments for the men to gather, he made a patting gesture with one hand and ordered, "First five . . . ranks, take a knee. Or sit; I don't care.

"About twelve hours ago, the war started back on . . . in Guyana, I mean." Again Warrington waited a few moments, not only for the news to sink in but for the muttering to die down.

"As far as I know, it began with an aerial attack on our base. Regiment reports that casualties are 'heavy, but not crippling.' Exactly what that means I can't be sure of. I'd *guess*—and it's only a guess—that 'heavy but not crippling' means somewhere between fifty and a hundred military dead, and two or three times that in wounded. I have no idea what there might be in civilian dead. I do know that some of the housing areas were hit and that the hospital was mostly obliterated. If –"

"Jesus!" shouted someone from the line company portion of the mob, "Mah wif due to delivah de baby 'bou' now! We gotta go back!".

"Nobody's going back," Warrington said. "Just get the notion out of your heads. We couldn't if we wanted to. The Venezuelan navy's not much, but it's a lot more than this barge can take on. And they'll be all off the coast. Again, *nobody's* going back."

Whatever the mostly American and Euro crew of the aviation detachment and spec ops company thought of that, they kept to themselves. The, for the most part, Guyanans of the line company didn't. They were unhappy, pissed off, disgusted, and—based on some of the fallen faces—demoralized.

Based on some of the ugly glances directed at both Warrington and the Spec Ops company, some of them blamed the First Worlders.

And, thought Warrington, *since this sort of thing is normally our job, I suppose I can understand some of that*.

Headquarters, True Cinnamon Siblings (TCS), Manila, Republic of the Philippines

The building was an old, multistory batching plant, just north of the intersection of North Bay Boulevard and Lapu-Lapu Ave. TCS had acquired it for pretty much a song, having made the previous owners one of those traditional "offers you can't refuse." It wasn't actually within the boundaries of Tondo, but then, the gang had been growing for some time. Culturally, it was Tondo. It was TCS.

The building served the gang well enough, having storage space, offices, and room—once a few modifications were made—for fairly decent living quarters for some of the higher ups in the organization. Diwata Velasquez, for example, the senior member of TCS's management committee, lived there.

In some places, the news of the kidnapping of a very rich man would have gone stale by now. Lucio Ayala, however, was so very rich, and the Philippines so insular in so many ways, the kidnapping was still number one headline material, as often as not.

"Tsk," said Diwata, at seeing the news for the umpteenth time. She then repeated, "Tsk. Damned politicals. They'll ruin everything for everyone."

She had been, so it was reported, quite a beauty in her youth, before being deported from the United States—San Diego, specifically—and before running to fat. The years since had not been especially kind. The tattoos didn't help, though they were de rigueur in her little (rather, not so little, anymore) social group.

In her right hand Diwata held a small black box, about the size of a pack of cigarettes. In the other, she held an actual cigarette from which she occasionally flicked an ash onto the concrete floor of her gang's headquarters.

"Got to admire the balls of the thing, though," she admitted.

"That you do," agreed her—male—assistant, Lucas, recently back from collecting a not-insubstantial ransom from a family in Singapore. "And just imagine what *we* could do with that kind of money."

"That kind of money," she corrected, "also means bringing a ton of shit down on you. The Ayala family isn't especially noted for rules and law, any more than we are. Whoever grabbed Ayala is in for a shitstorm.

"No . . . we'll keep in business the way we always have—retail. On which subject,"—she held out the small black box—"I want this attached underneath Ben Arroyo's new business van. Anybody he's making deliveries to, I want us to know about."

Safe House Alpha, Hagonoy, Bulacan, Luzon, Republic of the Philippines

There were a number of choices when one had zero actionable intelligence to drive or support a critical mission. A popular choice, in some circles, was to throw one's hands up in despair, wail over life's difficult lot, curse fate, slam doors, and then crawl into a consoling bottle of the good stuff. Politicians had it easier. Though few of them even knew the difference between actionable intelligence and the wish for same, for just about all of that breed it was sufficient to puff and preen and make pompous pronouncements. The clever press either found a smart corporal and asked him or her for a spare clue or, and this had become an increasingly popular choice over the years, bewailed the sheer impossibility of the mission. The idiot press, conversely, wrote up something inane, ran that through their bureau's Department of Enhanced Inanity for editing, then published that.

Terry's team had none of those luxuries. In the absence of actionable intelligence, the standard was, "Develop some." That's where Aida's pilfered list came in. That, and a box of goodies brought by Graft as baggage aboard his aircraft.

As he inspected them, the sergeant clucked over his charges like a mother hen. Slightly smaller than a pack of cigarettes, the GPS trackers—two dozen of them—each came with a piece of covered tape attached, for when the integral magnet just wasn't enough. Once the covers were removed, the user had only to slap them somewhere unobtrusive—oh, and not too dirty—and they'd stay there till long after the batteries ran down. They were slightly rough surfaced, more or less pebbly, the better to allow dirt to build up for improved camouflage.

"I don't know where we're going to get more of these once this supply's gone," Graft mourned.

"Mail order?" Semmerlin suggested.

"Nah . . . the company that made them got sued into oblivion by a class of outraged adulterous and soon-to-be-ex wives and husbands who convinced a court that the things infringed their privacy."

"Surely there are other makers."

Graft shrugged as he deftly fingered a battery into its receiving well. "You would think so, but the others saw the writing on the wall and have eased out of the market. And I don't think the regiment can make them on its own."

"So we use them sparingly and recover them if we can," Semmerlin said.

Shaking his head dubiously, Graft answered, "That'll only extend the time until we run out."

"Dude, *that*'s all we *do* as an organization; extend time."

"Yeah . . . that, and hope the horse will learn to sing."

Ermita, Manila, Republic of the Philippines

It wasn't every country where it could be said that the American embassy and one of the major red light districts were in close proximity. Ermita, however, was at least one such. Some of the local inhabitants, perhaps, found a certain poetry in that, or at least a degree of symmetry.

Occasionally, some local political poobah or another would make an effort to move the hookers elsewhere. It never mattered for more than a short time. They always returned. En masse. A cynical observer would have said the embassy operated as a hooker magnet. A more observant cynic would have answered, "No . . . it's not the embassy. It's the sundry humanitarian organizations that have clustered close to the embassy." The wisest and most observant cynic would have said, "It's both."

★ ★ ★

If nothing else had improved since the Second Great Depression, at least gas was cheap. The air was full of fumes, from myriad taxis. Under that lay the aroma of garbage that was just a few days past the time it should have been disposed of. Through the stench, Mrs. Ayala's man, Pedro, wound the taxi through crawling traffic, a sea of lightly clad professional ladies, not all of whom were necessarily female, and the usual collection of half- or entirely drunk foreigners—some with round eyes, some with slanted—looking for a bargain. There was a continuous cacophony of beeping, interspersed with a great deal of mostly good-natured cursing from both drivers and girls. Pedro cursed, himself, from time to time.

If the locals found symmetry in embassy and street walkers operating so closely together, so did Welch, Lox, and the other two members of Welch's advance party, Graft and Semmerlin. Semmerlin spat in the direction of the embassy as Pedro drove past it. There was precisely no love lost between the Department of State of the United States and virtually any member or former member of America's armed forces.

Even as Semmerlin spat, Graft caught the eye of a short but still fairly leggy, and otherwise quite delicate looking, Filipina hooker dressed—to the extent she was dressed—mostly in red. The old soldier whistled a few bars of an old tune by Chris de Burgh, then vocally supplemented the tune with the letters "L-B-F-M . . . "

"Everything in its own time, Sergeant Graft," Welch said, thinking to avoid offending Pedro. Welch had seen the girl, too.

"Yessir." Graft, taking the hint, shut up.

"Don't bother me," said Pedro, with a shrug. "She little. She brown. She not much more than machine for fucking."

Welch sat up front, beside Pedro, with Lox sandwiched in the back between the other two. Lox had an open folder on his lap. Welch had a laptop with integral GPS on his.

Pedro had managed to fill about nine tenth's of the shopping list. For the rest: "Working on it. Few days."

Everybody had a hidden pistol, with suppressor, and a fairly legal *appearing* license to carry it. Everyone but Lox likewise carried a knife and a TASER pistol. Everybody had a local cell phone. (Actually, everybody had two of them, one provided by Mrs. Ayala's man, Pedro, which they didn't trust, and another obtained by Lox, which they didn't let Pedro see.) All of them wore light cotton suits. In the trunk were a couple of sets of night vision goggles. None of the heavier weapons Pedro had acquired were there. It wouldn't be too hard to pass off a pistol, with license, as legal, should a cop stop them. It might take a substantial bribe, of course, but still not too hard. Machine guns, submachine guns, and assault rifles, however, were an altogether different story.

In his right breast pocket Graft kept a sub-cigarette pack-sized GPS tracking device, suitable for attachment to a vehicle. The tracking device operated off of a long life battery, good for at least two weeks. It could be attached directly to a vehicle's battery, for more or less infinite operational life. Two weeks, though, was thought more than sufficient life expectancy for this particular job.

"Ahead, on the right," Lox said, pointing his chin in the direction of a *kei*, or bantam, car. Welch turned his eyes only to glimpse a blue Suzuki bearing the license plate, JBB 806. Between the numbers and letters was the image of a monument, an obelisk surrounded by statuary, appearing between the numbers and letters. A motto, "MATATAG NA REPUBLIKA," was inscribed below. The Suzuki was one identified in Aida's file as belonging to a journalist—if that was quite the word—apparently in deep sympathy with various Moro groups, likewise with the remnants of the Huks, and, it was believed, often enough in close contact. In addition to the name, the car model, and the license number, the file also gave the locale of the journalist's little piece on the side, along with a few other possible addresses.

Pedro's taxi slowed to a stop about fifteen yards shy of the Suzuki. "Gentlemen," Welch announced over his left shoulder, "your show. Pick you up four blocks down and right one."

Graft, Lox, and Semmerlin formed in just that order, left to right, and began a slow walk down the sidewalk, stopping occasionally to let Lox chat up the streetwalkers in Tagalog.

"Damned shame we don't have time to sample the merchandise," Semmerlin observed.

"Maybe later," Lox replied, turning briefly from the girl he'd been talking to. He returned his attention to the girl, then quoted a price calculated to be insulting. Infuriated, she said, "*Jackol*,"—go jerk off—then turned her nose up, spun on her heel, and stormed off.

It wasn't more than a few more steps after that that they'd reached the blue Suzuki. Semmerlin stumbled on the uneven pavement. Oddly, the pavement was no more uneven here than it had been for the last fifteen yards. Still, Semmerlin went down to hands and knees. Lox and Graft both bent to assist their comrade, though Lox angled right while Graft turned just slightly left.

Lox assisted Semmerlin back to his feet, providing a barrier to vision with their legs. After a few moments, Graft likewise stood.

Lox asked, "Any trouble getting it attached?"

"Nah," Graft replied. "It's tighter than a houri's hole."

"Good. Let's step it up, gentlemen, and get back to the taxi. We've got two more to peg tonight."

Safe House Bravo, South Green Heights Village, Muntinlupa City, Manila Metro Area, Republic of the Philippines

For certain kinds of deliveries, Ben Arroyo preferred the night. It wasn't that there were fewer police out, and certainly not that there were fewer criminals. But the beat cops could be more easily bribed with no one watching—if a bribe were even necessary; he was, after all, a reserve cop himself—while the criminals could be more easily shot and their bodies disposed of.

'Course, the criminals who are after my merchandise can also more easily ambush me. But that's just one of life's little chances. And, anyway, Peter did insist on a discreet delivery.

Initially, Ben headed homeward on the not entirely

indefensible theory that a criminal gang, looking to grab his merchandise, would figure he'd be much less likely to be carrying anything worthwhile from his business to his house. About half way there he was confident enough that he wasn't being followed to turn off that route and head in the direction of the address Lox had given him.

Tondo, Manila, Republic of the Philippines

"Eighty Suliven Alvendia Ave, Muntinlupa," Diwata read off from her computer screen. "Gotta love modern technology, while it lasts." Looking up from the screen, she asked Lucas, "Got it?"

He repeated it back to her, then asked, "Sure, but what about it? And what do you want us to do with the information?"

"Ben doesn't make night deliveries to just anybody. And that's a rich fart area. Whoever moved in and bought from Ben has money.

"Find a house nearby, not too cheap, not too expensive."

"Okay," he agreed. "A kidnapping job? We can do that. Rich Kano, maybe? The house is to recon the place? A secure place to assemble a kidnapping team?"

"Yes to all that, but"—she turned her attention back to the screen, typing in a job search—"Ha! They're looking for a cook and maid. Get one of our working girls, one of the better looking ones, without any tattoos, to go apply for the job. An English speaker who can cook. Use one with a kid and take the kid for insurance."

Lucas thought about that briefly, then said, "Maricel

or Lydia; we've kept both of them clean and tat free, for higher end work." After another few moments, he'd decided. "Maricel; Lydia's English is marginal and Maricel's is almost native."

★ CHAPTER TEN ★

For the lips of a strange woman drop *as* an
honeycomb, and her mouth *is* smoother than oil.
—Proverbs 5:3, King James Version

Safe House Bravo, Muntinlupa, Republic of the Philippines

The other half of Graft's ODA—Sergeants Baker and Malone, Staff Sergeants Perez, Washington, and Zimmerman, under Sergeant First Class Benson—had a mission list that, for the nonce, amounted to housekeeping. That word—housekeeping—tended to mean a somewhat different thing to the military. Oh, yes, they'd swept the place, in more senses than one, dusted a bit, set up their rather Spartan personal quarters. But day-to-day mopping and dusting? That was a bit beneath them. And cooking was right out, if it could be avoided. Sure, there was a security issue. But there was also a security issue, as in being way too glaringly different, to not having domestic help.

Malone had the job of finding a live-in housekeeper/cook, though Lox had put the ad up for them, since he spoke

Tagalog. They'd weighed the odds between going to an agency and putting up an ad. An agency might have produced a woman with a background check. Just as likely, in this degraded day, however, that background check would have been purely fraudulent. Moreover, it might have accompanied a police informer, or a gang member. You just didn't know anymore. All things considered, they'd decided there was a little more, a very slight bit more, security in randomness.

Malone thought the job interview was going exceptionally well, especially since this one, Maricel, swallowed.

He looked down at the woman, who in turn looked up hopefully, and said, "You're hired."

Safe House Alpha, Hagonoy, Bulacan, Luzon, Republic of the Philippines

The estate, though it came with a small boat, was not on the sea. Rather, it was several miles upriver, in a triangular valley of about a kilometer on a side. A stream from a spring ran through the valley, joining the river by a small boathouse. What the land had once been used for, Welch and his men couldn't be sure. There were both jungle-covered terraces running up the sides of the surrounding hills and some indicators that a portion of the valley, at least, had once been quarried. Most of the land was treed. It was every bit as isolated and quiet as Mrs. Ayala had said. To add to the isolation, the perimeter was surrounded by upright sheets of partially buried perforated steel planking that had once been intended to form an ad hoc airstrip. Because of the manganese in the steel of the PSP, it hadn't even rusted noticeably, though it appeared to have been up for a long time.

The main building, erected on stilts, was about forty feet on a side and built into the side of one of the surrounding hills. The stilts were there not as a precaution against flooding, but to reduce the access of crawling insects and snakes. In this it was only partially successful, possibly because the house wasn't completely on stilts. Towards the back, and below the main level, there were more rooms, more than half underground. The walls of some of those had some odd graffiti, apparently Japanese, that no one in the party could read.

Semmerlin had taken one look at the stilts and felt an immense wave of satisfaction. *Good. Keep the snakes out, too. I hate snakes.*

There were also a number of outbuildings, which Graft, Semmerlin, and the rest were busy turning into interrogation chambers.

Pedro brought the morning papers, daily, to the room the men had dubbed, "operations." Those papers Lox poured over, also daily, for anything of intelligence value. Two televisions, one tuned to CNN and the other to local news, supplemented the written word. From all of them Lox scrawled notes on a yellow legal pad. There hadn't been much to scrawl. The kidnapping had been announced, and a video statement from the victim released, but only that.

It's interesting though, Lox thought, *and just possibly significant, that the byline in the paper lists one of the reporters we put a marker on.* Of that he made a note.

The laptop noted and recorded the movements of the seven cars that the team had placed tracking devices on, over three days and nights. So far, though, there'd been nothing untoward. One of the cars, owned by a politician, went from home to the legislature to an apartment building presumed to hold the pol's mistress and then home again. The vehicles of the two "journalists" likewise had done nothing too terribly suspicious. One car, belonging to a high mucky-muck in an international humanitarian NGO acted a bit oddly, but a check of addresses and Aida's report suggested that that had more to do with the drug trade than terrorism. From the others? Nothing.

The laptop didn't need to be monitored; it kept track of the movements automatically.

At the sound of the old wooden floor, creaking under the walk of someone substantial, Lox looked up from his work with the morning papers.

"Anything?" Welch asked.

"Nothing."

"Crap."

Lox smiled. "We knew this way would be slow and difficult."

"Yeah," Welch agreed. "But I hate just sitting around on my ass. What are we going to do if these guys we marked are clean?"

Lox shook his head. "Kiss seventy million bucks goodbye? Watch while Mrs. Ayala pays twice that to her husband's kidnappers? Maybe watch a city go boom?"

Lox's voice grew contemplative. "I think," he said, "that given a choice between her husband safe in her arms and a city going boom, Mrs. Ayala wouldn't hesitate to let a city be destroyed. And that would be true even if it were a Philippine city, let alone a western one."

Terry looked around the room, then bent over, took Lox's pen in hand, and wrote on the legal pad, *If all else fails, we could do a rescue at the moment of transfer.*

Lox took back the pen and wrote, *Not a chance that old woman will let us anywhere near a transfer. Besides, whoever in her family set this up would tip off the Harrikat if we get close to them.*

Welch nodded, then muttered, "I suppose so." Turning away, he walked to the windows fronting the place. From there, one could see over the PSP fencing toward the front of the estate. Not that one could see much; the jungle that lined the river began not far from the fence.

I truly hate to fail, Terry thought, staring out the windows at the seemingly solid jungle past the fence. *If I'd known how unlikely it was going to be that we'd succeed here, I think I'd have bowed out. Thrown my weight, such as it is, behind Boxer's attempt to derail the project. And I'd be comfortably at home with my woman.*

And I really don't see how we're going to pull this off.

Caban Island, Pilas Group, Basilan Province, Republic of the Philippines

One of his guards, a surly looking Moro with a scar that ran from the right side of his forehead, across a clouded eye, and then down his brown cheek, tugged at Lucio Ayala's chain.

"Up old man," said the guard, giving the chain another painful tug. "The chief wants to talk with you. After that, you have an appointment with some news people."

Slowly, unsteadily, Ayala arose to his feet. Already, and it hadn't been so very long since his abduction, what fat he'd had was beginning to melt off, the result of bad food and not even enough of that. To add to his misery, the chain around his leg had created running sores, one which might already be infected. The old man felt weak, and tired, and pretty much hopeless.

The guard gave a vicious tug to the chain, causing Ayala to cry out with pain as he fell to the mucky floor of the hut. The guard stepped up, taking up the chain's slack as he did, and rolled the prisoner around with his booted foot.

"Nothing personal, old man," the guard said. "But we have a choice of beating you up to make the right impression to your family on television, or covering you with muck. The chief thought muck would be better, since you probably couldn't take a beating."

Old man Ayala stumbled along, as slowly as he thought he could get away with. His head was down even while his eyes searched frantically for some flower or leaf unusual enough to identify the island on which he was being held. *It doesn't matter whether I know what it is, or where I am. As long as somebody can identify it.* Sadly, there was nothing that struck him as particularly unusual.

Nothing. Shit. I'd try Morse Code from my army days if I knew where I was, and remembered it. "Basilan," they said. But this is too small—it feels too small—to be the main island. Still . . . it might cut down the search area.

What are those codes? What letters would I need? I can skip vowels. N and R, for near. B, S, L and N, again, for the area. N is . . . ummm . . . What was that mnemonic. Ah . . . N for November . . . AU- tumn. Stressed, unstressed; a dash and a dot. Yes, that's it. R is . . .

"In there, old man," the guard said, pointing at the entrance to a grass hut.

. . . ro-MER-o. Dot-dash-dot. I think. Hard to remember. B is Bravo. What the hell was Bravo? Something with clapping in it.

Mohagher Kulat, a television journalist, and his cameraman, a Mr. Iqbal, made some final adjustments to the second of two video recorders. "We're ready, boss," Iqbal announced.

Kulat was only notionally a Moslem. He did have the name and the ancestry, but as far as he cared, Islam could go to hell. Oh, sure, he mouthed the pieties when it seemed useful, as it had seemed useful for this. And he had the preference for family, though that was a cultural issue, by no means unique to the Philippines, and not a religious one.

Mostly, as with most journalists, he just wanted to make a name for himself, and took what risks were required for that.

Standing up from the log on which he'd sat while Iqbal did the final focusing, Kulat walked the three steps to another and sat down beside the leader of the group, Janail Hapilon. Janail had a pair of pruning shears at his feet.

"You are planning something dramatic?" Kulat asked, his fingers loosely waving in the direction of the shears.

Janail nodded, without a word.

This is good, thought Kulat. *Good for ratings, good for me, hence good.*

Caban Island, Pilas Group, Basilan Province, Republic of the Philippines

There were two TV cameras set up on tripods when Ayala entered the hut. Lights accompanying those ensured that his eyes didn't have to adjust to the gloom. His guard, still holding the chain with one hand, pushed him roughly in the direction of a horizontal log.

"Sit, Mr. Ayala," the kidnapper he knew only as Janail commanded. Janail wore a scarf, more or less a modified keffiyeh, over his head and across his face. Beside him, on the ground, was a pair of what looked like pruning shears.

"This man"—Janail's head nodded in the direction of a clean cut young Filipino, wearing bushtrousers and an open-necked shirt, seated between the cameras—"has come to interview you. Answer his questions."

Ayala nodded his understanding and agreement. Sighing, he reached both hands up to his temples, as if to massage away a headache.

The interview was long, much longer, really, than an old, sick and frail man's constitution could readily stand. Trying to send a message while chained and guarded, too, sapped some of Ayala's stamina.

Still, eventually the questions ended. When they did, the guard took Ayala's left arm in his own hands, grasping it tightly at the wrist. Then Janail picked up what were, in fact, pruning shears, and snipped off the old man's left little finger, between the knuckle and the joint. The finger fell to the hut's dirt floor, curling and uncurling a few times under its own direction. Ayala, likewise, clutched the tiny spurting stump and fell over, screaming. Over that screaming, Janail announced to the camera, "A piece a month until our righteous demands are met. We will be in contact."

Safe House, Hagonoy, Bulacan, Luzon, Republic of the Philippines

"Terry! Terry! Come quick; I've got something."

Welch burst into the operations room a few moments later, dripping and wrapped in a towel. "This had better be—"

Lox cut him off with a wave of his hand, then pointed at the television screen that carried the local news.

"So they made a propaganda tape?" Terry said. "So what? It's routine. And routine that the press helps them."

"Watch the fingers of his right hand," Lox replied.

Terry did watch for a few moments. "So what? So he's nervous?"

"Nope. He's sending Morse."

Welch looked carefully. "I don't see it."

"Look again; three fingers rubbing versus one tapping. He's sending 'NRBSLN.' 'Near Basilan,' would be my guess."

Again, Welch looked closely at the screen. At length,

he agreed, "Okay, I can see that. Still, so what? We figured he was somewhere in that area."

Whatever Lox was about to say was lost as a shrieking Madame Ayala burst into the house. At that same time, the camera homed in on Mr. Ayala's right hand, then followed his snipped off, twitching finger down to the dirt.

"I want those motherfuckers *crucified*!" It was at an amazing volume, given the tiny source.

"Bet she didn't learn *that* at Mount Holyoke," Lox muttered.

"An extra twenty-five million if you bring me that bastard *alive*!"

"And, interestingly, only one of the cars we've been tracking went to either the docks or an airport in the last few days."

"More if you can get me his *family*!"

Still speaking softly, Lox added, "So I think we have an initial target. Finally."

Mrs. Ayala stood then at the entrance to operations, her dainty, bejeweled hands clutching either side of the door. Her face was inhuman in its fury, which was all the more disconcerting because that face rode above a frame that could make five feet only in high heels.

"*Blllooooood*!"

★ CHAPTER ELEVEN ★

There are, as it turns out, only two different modes
of loyalty that arise spontaneously. The first, of course,
is the family. The second is the boys' gang.
—Lee Harris, *Civilization and Its Enemies*

MV *Richard Bland*, South Atlantic

There were other naval types for whom, of course, the
meeting was the be all and end all of existence. Having
suffered through more than a few of those, in his Navy time,
Captain Pearson liked to keep his meetings infrequent and
short. *At least where possible.*

The meeting, as were most, was held in the conference
room not far from the captain's quarters. The room was
spic and span, the walls decorated with nautical themes,
and the Formica conference table top, though old, was
gleaming. *I might have to tolerate leaving rust marks on
the hull, but I don't have to put up with sloppiness inside.*

Despite—or perhaps equally because of—having
given Sergeant Hallinan three days confinement on bread

and water, the ship seethed. *It was*, thought Captain Pearson, *something you can feel, even if you can't see it. The line grunts detest the special operators and the feeling is returned in full. This is out of my league to handle. And then there's the medical supply issue . . .*

"TIC Chick and I can draw blood from the crew we have aboard, to build up a store," Cagle said, "but we're still stuck for the drugs. None of the regimental shipping is conveniently placed to meet us, mid-ocean . . . or anywhere on any ocean."

"We sure as shit can't make landfall," said Warrington, "not with what we're carrying. So we're fucked?"

Cagle grinned. "Not necessarily. Interestingly enough, some pirates from the Horn of Africa area—they've taken to calling it Punt, of late—recently grabbed a humanitarian aid ship, a *medical* ship. They're from MSF, Doctors Without Borders, so that's probably going to have everything we need."

"Rescue the ship and crew?" asked Captain Pearson. "I think that's more attention than we can afford."

"Fuck 'em," said Stocker, heatedly. "Tranzi bastards are as responsible as anyone for the mess the world's in."

"Yeah, maybe," Cagle half-agreed.

"Capture at sea?" asked the skipper. "Take the boat, take what we need, move the crew over, then sink it?"

Warrington shook his head; the captain's power really stopped at the edge of his command and surely didn't cover ordering an operation not in his mission statement. "We're killers, not murderers. If we took the ship, we'd probably have to let the aid workers go. And we could never guarantee or take their word that they'd be quiet."

"Just a thought. But we wouldn't have to let them go."

"Doesn't matter," Cagle said, "it's already landed."

"Buy from the pirates?" suggested Stocker's XO, Simon Blackmore. Blond, blue-eyed, standing about five-nine and with broad shoulders and a powerful chest, the young Welchman was formerly of Her Majesty's Royal Gurkha Rifles. He, like a dozen of his brother officers, had been put on the beach when the Brigade of Gurkhas, in another ill-considered financial austerity measure, had collapsed from two battalions, that down from four, further down to one. The regiment had snapped up a couple of those officers and a larger number of the middling senior noncoms. It would have snapped up some of the Gurkha rank and file, too, but they were too bloody expensive for machine gun fodder.

Once quite broad, Blackmore's sense of humor had become somewhat impaired since being robbed of his regimental home. And the regiment, AKA M Day, was . . . trying, in both senses. He wasn't sure at all that he belonged here.

Simon continued, "I mean, really; how much do we need, weight and cube wise? Wouldn't it fit in one of the CH-750's? Two at the outside? And there's not a lot of news coming out of Punt to give us away; now is there?"

"We could probably buy the aid workers," suggested Pearson. "Then we could hold them until the mission was done."

"Out of our price range," said Warrington. "Easily run a million bucks a head, as hostages. And there's probably what, forty of 'em?"

"Fifty-two," said Cagle. "That would eat the profit for the mission almost entirely."

"Let's just defer a decision on the tranzis," Warrington said. "Maybe we'll save them; maybe we won't. Depends."

"Fuck 'em, anyway," Stocker repeated. "Not our mission. Not our problem. *Not* our people. In any sense."

"Do we have any connections in Punt?" Pearson queried.

Warrington sighed. "Since we killed a rather large number of them some years back, probably not good ones."

"They don't know who did that, or that we're affiliated with the group that did," said Stocker.

"If you were them, would you take any chances on heavily armed white foreigners who come from the sea?" asked Cagle.

"Put that way," Stocker conceded, "I suppose not."

"Don't worry about it, in any case," Cagle said. "The people who took the ship aren't the same group the regiment blitzed. Besides, *I* have a pretty good connection in the area."

"From what?" asked Stocker, gaping.

"I . . . ummm . . . used to do humanitarian aid work there."

"Dickhead."

Before Cagle could form a retort, the hatch to the conference room sprung open. Framed in the grommet-lined steel was Sergeant Major Pierantoni. He took a half step forward, folded his arms, and leaned against one side of the hatch.

"While all you high and mighty sorts are solving not

only our problems, but the world's, I thought you might like to know that A FUCKING RIOT HAS BROKEN OUT ON THE MESS DECK!"

Warrington's head sank on his chest. *The hard stuff we can find a solution to. It's the easy shit—or what* ought *to be the easy shit—that bites us in the ass.*

Looking up at Pierantoni, Warrington asked, "Who the fuck started it?"

"No clue, Boss. Doubt we'll ever find out, either. But I think we ought to get our asses down there before serious blood gets spilled."

"Right," Warrington answered. "And Skipper? I think you might better arm your crew."

Mess Deck, MV *Richard Bland,* South Atlantic

The only bright spot was that in one corner of the mess deck two of Stocker's four Gurkhas, kukris drawn menacingly, had cornered a dozen or so of Charlie Company's brawlers, holding them in place by sheer intimidation, while a third Gurkha guarded the backs of those two, holding off several of Warrington's men. The khukri of the latter, glinting under the artificial light, shifted like lightning, left to right and back, punctuated with barely perceivable flicks.

The fourth Gurkha was probably off meditating some-where.

Otherwise, though, things were pretty dark. In the center, four Charlies had one of Alpha's operators down, taking turns kicking him in the sides and belly. Off by the serving line, an Alpha, Feeney by name, appeared to be drowning a Charlie in a large vat of warming soup. As Warrington watched, Feeney pulled the Charlie trooper out, reddish soup—or perhaps soup and blood—streaming from face and hair. He pulled him out, but only long enough to set him upright, land several solid punches, grab him, and stuff his head back into the mess.

Most of the other three corners were just a wild melee, with no discernible winners. If Charlie had the numbers, Alpha had the experience.

"Wade in to break it up?" Stocker asked.

"Provided we are breaking it up," Warrington replied. "To which end, you and yours go after yours and get them in the corner with the Gurkhas. Me and mine . . . well . . . first we'd better save that poor bastard from drowning. But we'll push our own into the opposite corner. After that . . . Vug, I dunno.

"On which happy note, A Company, such as you are, follow meeeee!"

On the plus side, thought Cagle, standing just behind Warrington, *TIC Chick and I are going to get a serious work out.*

Stocker nodded once, briskly, and told his exec, "Simon, go reinforce the Gurkhas. Deck anyone who gets in your way. The rest of us will start breaking them up and pushing our troops to you."

"Aye, sir," the lieutenant replied. With a gulp, he stepped into the anarchic mess. After a few hesitant steps, he had to jump back for a moment as a Charlie company body sailed across his path, arms flailing and face spitting teeth and blood. He looked in the direction from which the soldier had come and pointed at an Alpha, just recovering from the punch he'd thrown.

"Freeze, Sergeant!"

For a moment the trooper, Sergeant Hallinan, in fact, seemed disinclined to obey. He took two lurching steps forward, then hesitated.

If I strike an officer, thought the sergeant, *Warrington will have the skipper put up a yardarm and hang me from it. That, or bread and water for a fucking year. Mmm . . . not how I wanted to die, actually, either hanging or boredom.*

"Ye . . . yessir," Hallinan answered.

Simon pointed again at the corner opposite the one where his Gurkhas were holding some of the company's men prisoner. "Go there. Now."

"Yessir."

Past Hallinan, Warrington and Pierantoni trotted for the soup vat, pushing scrappers out of the way or jumping over the semi-comatose, as needs must. There, they heard their operator, Sergeant Feeney, staring down into the soup and laughing maniacally. "Ha, ha, no more bubbles from you, motherfucker!"

The sergeant major kidney punched Feeney from behind, then grabbed his hair and pulled him over backwards. The soldier from C Company came up into the air with him. He didn't seem to be breathing.

"Mister Cagle!" Pierantoni called over his left shoulder, "This one's for you!" Then he let go of Feeney's hair, taking instead a grip on his collar and belt, and began to run him straight into the wall of the corner Warrington had designated. Feeney slammed off the wall and then fell into a heap.

Looking around for someone with a degree of his wits about him, Pierantoni settled on one. "You! Sergeant Hallinan! You're in charge of this mess until further notice. Sit on Feeney if you have to, and take charge of the rest as we send them to you."

"Yes, Sergeant Major," Hallinan replied.

Sometimes they came in of their own accord, more or less. Sometimes they were forcibly carried over by Stocker or his first sergeant. In one case, one of the captive Charlies, just awakening from a punch-induced unconsciousness, turned and began to go for the XO. A mild—for certain values of mild—tap from the hilt of a Gurkha kukri split the soldier's scalp and laid him out in a heap on the deck.

"Thanks, Sergeant Balbahadur," Simon said. The Gurkha sergeant shrugged: *Just my job, sir.*

At about that time, a file of shotgun-armed sailors appeared with their captain. Pearson gave the order, "Lock and load," loudly enough for everyone on the mess deck to hear. Whoever's attention that failed to garner, the sound of multiple shotgun slides being worked—Ka-ka-ka-*chunk*-*k*-*k*—got *everyone*'s notice.

Captain's Quarters, MV *Richard Bland,* South Atlantic

"Okay," Warrington asked, "besides us and the squids, who *isn't* under arrest?"

The A Company XO sported a huge and ugly shiner. He wasn't the only one with injuries among the command groups. And Cagle and TIC Chick were still busy down below sewing torn flesh and passing out Motrin and cold packs.

Stocker answered, "My three Gurkhas and seventeen others who weren't on the mess deck at the time. All the rest are on deck with shotgun bearing sailors watching them."

"Of us? Nobody," said Sergeant Major Pierantoni. "Somehow every one of them managed to get into it. The aviators stayed out, sensibly."

Pierantoni pointed at Warrington's eye and asked, "And, by the way, what are you going to do about that? Legally, I mean."

"Nothing. I never saw who landed it on me." Warrington looked around the room and added, "I think it would be better if none of us saw anything that could lead to charges."

"What about Feeney and the guy in the soup?" asked Pearson.

Stocker cleared his throat and said, "Private Cuthbridge will live. Besides, it was a clear cut case of self-defense."

Pearson sputtered, "Self def—"

"It was self defense," Warrington said. "For everybody. Self-defense, got it?"

Seeing that the captain was inclined to disagree, Warrington added, "We can't do anything about it, Skipper, not and have a hope of completing the mission."

"My ass," Pearson said. "We *already* don't have a hope

of completing the mission with two companies that are supposed to work in harmony and hate each others' guts."

"I know," Warrington said. "And I wish I knew something we could do about that."

One of Pearson's crew knocked on the hatchway. "Enter," said the captain.

"This just in, sir," the rating said, handing over a printed off sheet from CNN.

Pearson read it, then began to laugh. "Best news I've had lately," he finally forced out, passing the sheet to Warrington.

"What is it?" Stocker demanded.

Warrington, likewise laughing now, wiped a tear—wincing—from his blackened eye. "The regiment has mined the shit out of Venezuela."

★ CHAPTER TWELVE ★

The media's power is frail.
Without the people's support, it can be shut off
with the ease of turning a light switch.
—Corazon Aquino

**Safe House Alpha, Hagonoy, Bulacan, Luzon,
Republic of the Philippines**

Mrs. Ayala sat in a shadowy alcove of the small outbuilding, Pedro and her other most trusted guard to either side of her and slightly in front. On a strong wooden frame, set at an angle and bolted to wall and floor, lay a pale and terrified looking journalist, with a very bright light focused on his face. The journalist, one Mohagher Kulat, was buck naked, something that Lox was mildly surprised to see bothered Mrs. Ayala not a bit.

Given that, though, he thought, *I'm unsurprised to discover that she is completely unbothered by what we're about to do to this poor bastard. Then again, if I'd seen my wife's finger snipped off on national television, I might be disinclined to Christian charity, as well.*

Still, I'm glad it wasn't a woman we grabbed.

Kulat had been taken from the street in front of his house, at about the same time as a different half of Welch's team had grabbed his cameraman, a Mr. Iqbal. Iqbal's auto had been driven off by Welch, while Kulat had been bustled into the trunk of Pedro's taxi. They'd both arrived at the safe house in a state of chemically-induced unconsciousness. There, they'd been stripped, bound, and prepared for questioning.

Wires ran from the journalist's genitalia to a field telephone. It was World War Two surplus, but it would do. There were more sophisticated methods of electrical torture, but Lox's background was Army rather than police, hence field expedient oriented when it came to coercive methods of interrogation.

Lox reached out a meaty hand, slapping the journalist across the face hard enough to split his lip. It was also hard enough to get his complete and undivided attention, quite despite the lingering effects of the drugs used to subdue him.

"Hello, Mr. Kulat," Lox said. "Before you ask, my name is of no use to you. Suffice to think of me as the man you are going to tell everything I ask you to tell me."

"Fuck you," the journalist said, blood spraying from his split lip.

Lox smiled as he wiped the spray from his face. He turned to Semmerlin, manning the field telephone, and said, "Go."

Semmerlin began turning the crank ferociously. Hand-generated electricity coursed up the wires and through Kulat's genitalia. He screamed and writhed, his back arching half a yard from the platform to which he was bound.

"Intermittent," Lox ordered. Semmerlin slowed the spin of the crank, just enough to let Kulat's back slump to his platform, then cranked it ferociously again, pulling another agonized shriek from the man's throat and again causing his body to deform itself into a stiff arch. This he repeated, half a dozen times, until Lox held up a restraining hand.

"You owe me an apology," Lox said. When none was forthcoming, he signaled Semmerlin to begin the process again. After several more minutes in mindless, gibbering agony, the prisoner took advantage of a short lapse in the current to scream, "I'msorryI'msorryI'msorry . . . please *I'm SORRY!*"

"Good," Lox agreed. "And now that we've gotten over our little impoliteness, let me tell you what's going on."

Lox seemed to hesitate for a moment. "Hmmm, on further reflection, let's talk a little about morality, since the human mind is capable of all kinds of self-delusion if it thinks itself to be uniquely in the right. This is especially true of journalists, it seems.

"You have a wife and children, do you not, Mr. Kulat?"

Kulat tensed, not answering. If these madmen didn't know about his family they would be safer.

"It was a rhetorical question, Mr. Kulat," Lox said. "Through our contacts with the police"—that was *almost* a complete lie, but Lox thought it might be useful to have Kulat think it was so—"we know you do. And we're not, for the moment, at least, interested in them. This could, of course, change."

Lox let the threat hang in the air for a few moments, then said, "I would like you to imagine whichever one it is in the world you most love, in the hands of your enemies. Perhaps it's your wife, or your son. Maybe it's a father or mother. No matter, just imagine. Put your best loved face to that image in your mind.

"Now picture that best loved face, and the human being behind it, kidnapped, mistreated, tortured, dismembered. What would you not do to save them?

"What if the person who had the key to saving them were, like yourself, a member of the press? Would you care much about freedom of the press, in that case? Would you care enough to let that best beloved suffer a horrible life and then die a worse death?

"If you didn't know how to save them, would it be wrong for you to hire someone who did?"

Lox gave a grim smile. "I ask you these things, Mr. Kulat, so that you will understand that you are the key to saving someone else's best beloved, and there is no limit to what we will do to you, on behalf of our principal, to get that person back, whole and safe. What you would do, or would hire someone to do, we will do. In case you didn't understand that, what you would do, we *will* do. And freedom of the press means less than nothing to us. Indeed, we tend to blame you—all of you—for the state the world is in."

Lox reached into a pocket and pulled out a pair of rubber medical gloves. These he put on. From a different pocket he took a set of cheap steel vise grips. Those he adjusted, then carefully closed on one of Kulat's testicles. The vise grips were just tight enough to be noticed, not so tight as to really hurt.

"Electricity is good for this purpose," Lox advised, "but there's always the risk of cardiac arrest. And, besides, some people are more terrified of physical damage, especially to their reproductive systems, than of mere pain. Your persona suggests that kind of vanity."

Lox's voice changed from conversational to hard. "Your cameraman is being held in a different chamber of this compound. I am going to ask you questions. He will be asked the same questions. If your answers do not match, there will be pain and there *will* be damage."

With a grin, Lox asked, "Now, to begin, what is the airspeed of an unladen European swallow?"

Safe House Bravo, Muntinlupa, Manila, Republic of the Philippines

Maricel was considerably more American in her ancestry than she was Filipina. Her great-great-grandmother, who had been in the same line of work (well, at different times in *both* of Maricel's current lines of work), had gotten herself knocked up by the artillery major (white, of course, in those olden days) in whose house she'd taken domestic service, not so very long after the end of the Philippine Insurrection. The major had bought her off with what, at the time, she'd thought was a fair and generous settlement. It hadn't lasted, of course, which was why great-great-grandma, and later the half Kano great-grandma, had both ended up working various knocking shops. This was also how great-grandma had ended up giving birth to the child of either the 31st Infantry Regiment or the 200th

Coast Artillery Regiment. That was as much as she'd been able to narrow down grandma's paternity.

Three quarters American, and substantially white, grandma had been in great demand—practically a whiff of home—for Soldiers, Sailors, Airmen, and Marines on R&R from Vietnam. This was how Maricel's mother had ended up seven-sixteenths American white, seven-sixteenths American black, and a bare one-eighth Filipina. Mom had not the first clue to her paternity. Neither did grandma. When you're dealing that kind of a volume business . . .

Maricel's mother had broken that long line of honorable service to the U.S. Armed Forces, managing to get herself pregnant with a Swiss businessman, on vacation from a dowdy wife. This made Maricel half Swiss, seven thirty-seconds American white, seven thirty-seconds American black, and a bare one sixteenth Filipina. She was considerably taller than the local norm, and, despite the black heritage, considerably lighter. Thus, instead of being an LBFM, she was more in the lines of a Large, Off-white, Fucking Machine, an LOWFM.

And though there was not a trace of genetic predisposition to prostitution in Maricel's make up, memes propagate just as well as genes do, if not even better. The memes she'd grown up with included sex as being about as sacred as going to the bathroom and sex as about the only way to make a living as a bastard girl of only marginal local ancestry . . . those, and that the more you did it, and the better you did it, the more money you could make and the sooner you could retire before your looks and allure fled.

★ ★ ★

Maricel carefully did up Sergeant Malone's zipper and belt before rising to her feet. She rebuttoned her own blouse as she rose. She had much larger breasts (see ancestry, such as it was, given above) than the typical Filipina and had learned at mother's and grandma's knee that men liked to play with them while being blown.

"So it's no problem to take the day off, boss?"

Malone shook his head. "Nah. Everyone's entitled to a day off now and again. Go see your family and relax. We can send out for Chinese or something."

"No need, boss. I stayed up late making *champorado* for your breakfast and a nice pork *adobo* for your lunch. I'll be back in time for dinner."

"Nah," Malone replied. "We'll still send out for Chinese for dinner. You take the *whole* day off. Be back in time to make breakfast the day after tomorrow."

"Yes, boss. Thank you, boss. I promise something extra special then." Whether she meant extra special in terms of eating, or extra special in terms of being eaten, she left hanging.

Before she left, Malone slipped a ten down her shirt to nestle between her breasts. With a quick glance at the darkened window, Malone said, "You'd better hurry; it's getting late."

Leaving, she called over her shoulder, "Since you're going to send out, Fu Lin Gardens and Gloriamaris are both pretty good."

There had once, and in the not so distant past, been public transportation in this part of Muntinlupa City. Not that the residents had needed it; they'd all had cars. It had been mostly for the domestic help. Those days were past, buried under "austerity measures" that were closer to survival measures for the local government. Sure, the well-to-do types could have afforded the taxes. They simply would not, and would give more to any political group that would keep them from paying taxes than the taxes themselves cost.

Thus, Maricel had to walk more than three miles to Dr. Santos Avenue to pick up a bus to take her, not home to her mother and grandmother, but to Tondo, to TCS, to report in and to see the child that was—she was a hooker; she was *not* stupid—plainly a hostage for her good behavior.

Once past the well-to-do area, streetlights became a memory of a happier and more prosperous day. That is to say, the poles were there but nobody had replaced the burnt out lamps in, oh, a very long time, long enough that people had, at some level, begun to forget that the poles even had a purpose. They were just there, dysfunctional and useless as all the other trappings of civilization.

Only once was she accosted. After she hissed, "TCS," the man fled away. If anything, she was in greater danger from the broken sidewalks and potholed streets that, like the streetlamps, nobody was taking care of anymore.

On the bus, once she reached a still functioning line, Maricel had time to think. *This wouldn't be such a bad life, if I had my baby with me. Every one of them but Zimmerman uses me just about every day, which I could take or leave, but every one of them slips me at least ten bucks, forty-thousand pesos, whenever they do. Plus my maid's salary. And I get to keep it all, rather than the lousy hundred bucks I might make a week, servicing fifty guys, under TCS. And the quarters would more than do for the baby and me, both. Damn, why is it all the really nice arrangements never last?*

Tondo, Manila, Republic of the Philippines

However brave a show she'd put on while walking the streets, Maricel couldn't breathe easy and relax until she'd passed through the borders of Tondo, to the safety of her own people, her own tribe.

In that secure cocoon, now, Maricel and Lucas sat on opposite sides of an old metal table, off in a private corner of the gang's headquarters. Lucas was project officer, so to speak, for the enterprise, as he was for most high profile kidnappings.

"There are six of them," Maricel reported. "One of them's in charge, Mr. Benson. Supposedly some high up Kano executive. But even if he's dressing like one, he doesn't *act* like an executive. I don't know what he acts like. He sings a lot, weird Kano songs I never heard before: 'Rickity-Tickity-Tin, Goodbye, Mom, I'm off to drop the bomb.' Things like that."

And maybe I don't know *because the Americans pulled out their combat forces a long time before I turned thirteen and went into the life. Mother or grandma, though, might know. And once, just once, one of them called Benson, "Sarge."*

"I mean, if everybody but the big boss used me I'd put it down to him being married and faithful, but not minding what the peons do, and that would be that. But it's not like that."

"Doesn't matter," Lucas said. "What's their security like?"

"Typically four of them will be gone for a while on any given day, mostly in the day but sometimes at night. There are *always* at least two of them on guard, one inside and one walking between the house and the wall around it. And when they're on guard they are *scarily* alert. And very heavily armed.

"And . . . "—the girl struggled for the right words— ". . . they're strange, you know. They all make use of me, except for one, Zimmerman. But, tell me, how often does an executive adopt share and share alike with his minions? And they're not sharing because they're kinky, or anything. Pretty vanilla, as a matter of fact. Just *tsupa* and the occasional fuck. No gang bangs. No lez shows, not even a suggestion. No whips and chains."

She hesitated for a moment, then amended, "Well . . . one of them wanted my ass, once, but that's not really kinky."

"Takes all kinds," Lucas said, with a shrug. "You see anything we can't handle?"

"I dunno," Maricel answered. "They've got the guns. They've got body armor that they wear *religiously* when they're working. Some funny goggles that see in the dark; one of them showed me once."

Again, Lucas shrugged. "Okay, so they're an unusually good personal security team. Nothing we can't handle if we go about it the right way. Have you paced off the house?"

Maricel nodded.

Pushing a pad of paper and a pen across the table, Lucas commanded, "Sketch it out."

"What about my *baby*?"

Lucas held up a palm and waved it in negation. "*After* you make me a sketch of the place. And then, I think, I'll have to give you a little something to put the guards to sleep, because, realistically speaking, they sound a little tough to take on without some extra advantage."

Maricel shivered slightly, then said, "In case I wasn't clear enough, these are not some run-of-the-mill business types that you can drug and rob or drug and kidnap. You want me to drug them? Then *you* figure out how to give it to them at one time, then have it act on them all at the same time, or in a set sequence, when they're all different sizes and weights, while not only getting the armed guard on the inside but also the one outside? When I'm probably going to have to be fucking one of them."

Lucas rocked his head from side to side, then reached for his cell. "Okay, good point. I'll check with Loo Fung and see what he might come up with from China."

Safe House Bravo, Muntinlupa, Manila, Republic of the Philippines

"Hey, Sarge, are there any egg rolls left?" asked Malone.

Benson shook his head, answering, in a New England accent, "Nah; that asshole Bakah took the last one. And when did you say Maricel gets back? And if you call me 'Sahge' again, I'm gonna kick yah ass."

"Sorry, Mr. Benson. Tomorrow morning."

Benson puffed out his cheeks and blew air through his lips in a raspberry. "I am *really* not comf'table having a potential spy in the house with us. Even if she's both a Christian and a very good self propelled vacuum cleanah."

Malone gave a one-shouldered shrug. "It's like Lox and Graft said; we either accept that risk or we accept the greater risk of standing out more than we do and getting the attention of some people we really don't want to notice us."

"Yeah," Benson conceded, "but I still don't like it."

★ CHAPTER THIRTEEN ★

We are dropping down the ladder rung by rung
— Kipling, "Gentlemen Rankers"

**Interrogation Room #1, Safe House Alpha,
Hagonoy, Bulacan, Luzon, Republic of the Philippines**

It was easy to be brave and defiant, Kulat discovered, just so long as there was no possibility of your bravery and defiance being tested. When they were tested, when they were *seriously* tested, by, say, having a set of vise grips tightened on one's testicles, or having electricity sent coursing from one's anus to one's penis, or having a blow torch played over one's toes . . . then bravery and defiance tended to fall away.

Now, having endured all those things, defiance was a dim memory and bravery a concept totally devoid of meaning. Now it was, *Oh, God . . . please . . .* please, *ask me something I can answer.* Anything *I can answer. Please . . . just stop hurting me.*

In his agony, he wasn't quite sure if he'd merely thought that, or whispered it.

He sobbed quietly, half from the pain that had not yet gone away, and perhaps never would, and half from the humiliation of begging and pleading. They'd hosed him off after the session, but he could still smell the shit he'd deposited on the concrete floor.

There was the sound of a turning doorknob, followed by a thin sliver of light appearing at the door's edge. Kulat screamed.

In a nearby room, likewise dug into the hill behind the main house, Lox had an ear piece stuck in one ear. He was listening for any softer sounds coming from Kulat's cell.

"I don't get that first question you asked," Mrs. Ayala told Lox. She could hear the prisoner weeping—sobbing really—inside. This was understandable, since the vise grips had been adjusted shut enough to more than half crush one testicle. "For that matter, I don't understand *any* of the questions you asked."

Lox looked vaguely ill, though Madame seemed pleased enough with progress so far.

"To convince him that we're madmen who can, if he tries really hard, be placated. To make him want to satisfy our most absurd requests. To rob him of reason. To train him not to lie."

"You seem to know your business," Mrs. Ayala complimented.

"Not really," Lox disagreed. "Oh, I know the principles of the thing. But a really good interrogator could get as much information, faster, with less coercion. There's always *some* coercion, of course; there probably hasn't been a totally noncoercive involuntary custodial interrogation in history, and only liars and fools think there has. Sadly, the world has a shortage of really good interrogators and so we must make do with me."

"So long as you can find where my husband is being held."

"We probably can," Lox nodded agreement, "but it possibly may not be from these two. Even if they only lead us to someone who knows where your husband is, I'll be minimally satisfied."

"Why wouldn't they know?" she asked, bright eyes flashing. "They were there."

"I'd be very surprised if they weren't blindfolded for the trip," Lox replied. "At least once they were away from shore."

The woman's face sank to match her heart. "If they don't know . . ."

"Don't worry, Madame," Lox reassured her. "They either know or they know who does know or, and this is quite likely, they can describe enough of the area where your husband is being held for us to figure it out by map and terrain analysis."

"What are you going to do with them once you've got all the information we need?" she asked.

"Kill 'em, I suppose; it's become that kind of a world. And even if it weren't, we can't let them go after what's been done to them."

"I assume, then, that you would like the deaths to give a certain impression?"

"Talk to Welch," Lox answered. "It's his area of specialization, not mine."

"I'll talk to him," she said. "I need to talk to him. My

husband's kidnappers have sent me a demand, and a set of instructions. As for this one; I'll do the killing." Her tone brooked no quarrel. "Rather, Pedro and I will."

"That's fine," Lox agreed, "but there are certain parameters you must meet or the information we've gathered will soon be useless."

He heard a word, a bare whisper, in his earpiece. "And on that note, it's about time to get back to work."

As soon as Lox had the door opened by three quarters of an inch, his ears were assailed by a long, loud, and—for the pure terror in it—heartrending scream. He opened the door fully, walked into the interrogation cell, and slapped Kulat several times across the face to make him shut up. Then he bent slightly and began turning the knob to release the vise grips from his victim's testicles.

"Oh, thank you . . . thank you," Kulat whimpered.

"Mr. Kulat," Lox said, "it would be normal, at about this time in your interrogation, to introduce you to what we call 'the good cop.' This would be someone who would pretend to be your friend, to have your best interests at heart, to stop the pain if only, if *only*, you would cooperate. We don't have the time or the people for that."

"But you don't really need that crutch, do you, Mr. Kulat? You really do want to cooperate now, don't you?"

"Oh, yes . . . oh, yes . . . just ask me something I know, something I *can* answer."

"Very well," Lox agreed. "But you must remember that your cameraman is as eager to talk to us as you claim to be. And if your answers do not match, there will be more pain and more damage."

"Let me talk to him," Kulat begged. "I'll convince him to cooperate."

"No," said Lox, somewhat regretfully, "that doesn't really work. You will answer separately until your answers match."

"Describe the beach where you landed!" Lox demanded.

"There was a high cliff, to the left!" Kulat exclaimed frantically. "We pulled up to a short pier . . . "

"How many piers were there?"

"One!"

Lox signaled Semmerlin to start the electricity flowing.

"Two, there were TWO!" Kulat screamed, between spasms.

The juice cut out after a moment. Lox asked, "Which of the two was longer, north or south?"

"Nor . . . aiaiaiai! Southsouthsouth!"

"The first bunker, guarding the trail from the beach, what was in it?"

"A mach . . . aiaiaiai. Nonono . . . sorrysorry . . . please, no more pain . . . it was a cannon of some kind."

"Describe it."

"Big . . . three, maybe four inches across, the part I saw. It was something funny shaped on that end, like a cone."

"A recoilless rifle?"

The answer was a sort of long, drawn out, moan. "Yes . . . I think so . . . I hope so. But please, no more pain? *Please?*"

★ ★ ★

"Look at this diagram," Lox said, pointing to a large sheet of white paper with penciled in symbols. His finger traced a dotted line. "You and Mr. Iqbal came in along this trail"—the finger tapped—"past these two bunkers." The finger floated to the right and up. "What was here?"

"A tent," Kulat answered. "A big tent with smoke coming from the ground nearby. It was thin smoke, coming from a hundred holes. You could barely notice it until you smelled it."

"Did they feed you there?"

"No. No, but when they brought us food it came from there on big leaves."

"A mess tent, then." Lox's finger drifted. "And what was here . . . ?"

Both Kulat and Iqbal had been given their clothes back and released from their bindings. With Sergeants Trimble and Yamada as guards, Lox escorted them to a different cell, this one without any instruments of torture. Instead, there were some cots, a couple of bottles, and some packaged food.

"We can't let you go until our mission is complete," Lox informed them. "You'll be staying here while you're with us. The clear bottle is water; the darker one is a *tore* of Tanduay rum." Tanduay—or at least this mark of Tanduay—was perhaps not the highest-end rum distilled in the Philippines, but it would do. This particular bottle had been further laced with a modicum of opium. Mrs. Ayala's man, Pedro, was nothing if not resourceful.

"If your religious scruples forbid you from drinking it, that's on you. You might find that it helps the pain, though, and, if memory serves, alcohol is permissible as a medicine."

In a side room in the main house, Lox poured a San Miguel pilsner for Madame. He placed the amber-filled glass on the table next to her. Also on the table was a voice activated tape recorder, and a speaker that certainly had some desktop computer in its ancestry.

"And now?" Madame asked, picking up and sipping at the beer.

"And now we listen. It's just possible, not likely, but possible, that they'll talk about something they managed to hide from us. It's even more likely they'll confirm what they told us separately, once they start comparing notes."

"And if not?"

"We've learned all we can learn in the time we have before they have to make an appearance back in the real world. Maybe if there's something dramatic, we might put them through the ringer again. But, if not, tonight you can have them."

"Good," she agreed, her voice filled with anticipation.

"Killing them doesn't bother you?" Lox asked.

The old woman chuckled. "Mr. Lox, my husband and I were not always so very respectable. I've killed before. And you, does it bother you to torture?"

"I never have before," he answered. "And it makes me sick."

"Really?" She seemed surprised. "Where did you learn? You seemed quite competent."

"Oh," Lox admitted, "I got it out of a book by some hack science fiction writer."

Safe House Alpha, Hagonoy, Bulacan, Luzon, Republic of the Philippines

Whether Kulat and Iqbal were actually drunk by the time the clock had turned past midnight made little difference. A quick glance at the bottle indicated that they would be, in conjunction with the opium, drunk enough for pliability and drunk enough to have the booze show up in their bloodstreams, if anybody bothered to check. If the fire Mrs. Ayala planned left enough for a check of the blood.

"Load them," she told Pedro and her other most trusted guard. Taking one each over their shoulders, Madame's men dumped the two doomed journalists into vehicle trunks, one in the taxi's trunk, the other in Iqbal's, atop the camera, tripod, and sound equipment. Then she, her guard, and Welch loaded.

The two-vehicle convoy then drove north, before turning east at Cabanatuan. Ultimately, they stopped in the deserted section of road in Aurora Memorial National Park.

Once she'd picked her spot, Madame had the drugged and intoxicated journalists detrunked and laid on either side of Iqbal's auto. "Measure him, Pedro," she commanded.

"Yes, Madame."

Pedro took Iqbal and put him in the driver's seat. Then he rotated him forward and up, as if he'd been tossed that way by a collision. Pedro's eye carefully noted where Iqbal's head would strike the windshield, and his body the steering wheel. He then placed the body back on the ground and went to his taxi for a sledgehammer. With this he gave the cameraman a light rap on the skull, no more than enough to split the skin and perhaps cause some minor fracturing of the bone. The cameraman's ribs received heavier blows, heavy enough, perhaps, to have killed him on their own, eventually.

Kulat received similar treatment. Welch, standing with his arms crossed over his chest, nodded with satisfaction.

"Now wreck the car, Pedro."

"Yes, Madame."

For this, Pedro retrieved from his taxi a crash helmet, as well as some padding for his legs. He sat in the driver's seat of Iqbal's vehicle, put on the helmet, and placed the heavy padding in front of his legs. Then he put on the lap and shoulder belt and started the engine.

With a short, three-point turn, Pedro turned the car around and then drove about a hundred meters back in the direction from which they'd come. There he made another change of direction. After crossing himself, Pedro slammed down on the gas and sped up the road. At just past the place where his taxi rested, he ripped the wheel to his right, aiming for a stout tree. The car smashed into the tree foursquare and head on, crumpling the front and causing steam to jet out through the now bent hood. Pedro was thrown forward to the limits of his restraining belt.

As he emerged, shaken, the other guard was already carrying Kulat to the passenger side. Pedro shook his head to clear it, then lifted Iqbal and carted him across the road. Mrs. Ayala retrieved the padding, then demanded Pedro's helmet. Both of these she placed in the taxi.

"Shoot several holes in the car, Pedro," she said. When he hesitated, she asked, "You don't understand why?"

"No, Madame."

She sighed. Pedro was a good man, loyal and true. He was also bright enough, and very resourceful. What he wasn't was subtle.

"It doesn't matter if the police think these men were murdered," she explained. "Indeed, Mr. Welch"—she inclined her head in his direction—"has told me he wants them to. And I can buy our way out of any prosecution or investigation, even if they should equate the murder with us. What matters is that the people holding my husband not know these two spilled their guts. If they found out, they'd move and the information we've gained would become useless. For that, it is better that this look like a simple double murder, here on a lonely stretch of road, while they were in hot pursuit of another story or, better, being pursued. For that, we need bullet holes."

"Fair enough," Pedro agreed, drawing his pistol and emptying it into various random and chosen spots around the car. One of these—the only nonrandom spot—was the gasoline tank. With a flashlight, he began to search for the spent casings.

"Do you think they'll wake up enough to feel this?" Mrs. Ayala asked, as she bent down with a cigarette lighter in one hand. Pedro shook his head. Madame sighed, "I suppose not, but I hope they do."

Hell hath no fury, thought Welch, watching the gasoline take fire and the flames race to where more fuel poured from the ruptured tank.

"Now, tell me about the demands and instructions they sent you."

Welch, Lox, and Graft were seated at one end of a table holding a bucket of ice, three glasses, and a bottle, a tore, of Tanduay. Theirs was of a rather better mark than what they'd left for Kulat and Iqbal. The label said "1854," though, of course, it wasn't nearly that old. Fifteen years, though? That, it was.

Moreover, this tore wasn't laced with opium.

At the other end—though not far away; it wasn't a big table—was a computer, with the best map Lox had been able to find of the Pilas Group of islands. In the center of the image was one island labeled "Caban Island," blown up as far as it would go before it turned fuzzy.

"That's it," Lox said. "Everything matches. Nothing else in the area really does. Two piers, the cliff south of the beach, the layout of the huts. Can't see the bunkers but I imagine the Harrikat have learned a thing or two about camouflage by now. On the other hand,"—Lox reached out and tapped the screen with his finger—"if you look closely you can see the smoke coming up out of the ground in lines. That's the mess tent Kulat and Iqbal identified. He's there—on that island—if he's anywhere."

"That's going to be a pure bitch," Welch observed. "We've got no good ins. We can't lift enough people to matter with the two gunships. And, even if we could, there's no LZ big enough to get more than one bird in at a time. If we land on the beach, by boat or, if we had them, helicopters, he's dead before we've gotten to the first huts. Not sure that a whole bunch of ours wouldn't be dead, too."

"We've got to get someone in there," said Graft, "to find and secure him while the rest of the force lands, however they end up landing."

"Suggestions?" Welch asked.

Graft shook his head, but the gesture had more of despair to it than negation. His finger tapped the map at the southwestern edge of the island. "Two men," he said. "That's all we can get in with the two SeaBobs. They go in underwater to this cliff. Then they free climb up the cliff—yeah, it'll be a bitch. They take out the guards—there have gotta be guards there; it's the highest point on the island—to clear the way for follow-on forces to come in by Zodiac. If they can find Ayala and get him back to that point, with plenty of gunship support the company can hold the Harrikat off until we get the infantry company ashore.

"Shit."

"Why 'shit'?" Welch asked.

"Because I'm the best free climber in the company, that's why 'shit.' And I am *not* looking forward to this."

"It's something to study, anyway," Welch said, noncommittally.

★ CHAPTER FOURTEEN ★

Australia wanted the Gurkhas in 1990. Even today, Australia recruits Gurkhas who have served as much as 15 years with the British forces, which shows how highly they are regarded. It's possible they, or other nations, would be interested if Britain no longer wanted us.
—Chhatra Rai, Gurkha Veteran

MV *Richard Bland*, South of Mauritius

The ship functioned well enough, still, but only as a kind of a floating prison. The various military contingents lived separately and messed at separate times, with armed guards from the aviation detachment, the landing craft crew, headquarters and support, and the *Bland*, itself, ensuring peace. They got an hour a day, more or less, to exercise and breathe fresh air on the containers, topside.

There were a few exceptions, the Gurkhas who'd tried to keep peace during the riot, and the officers and senior noncoms, other than most of the senior non-coms from the spec ops company, almost all of whom had been in the thick of it.

Having nothing much else to do today, what with his troops locked down, Sergeant Balbahadur mostly stayed on deck, practicing with his pipes. After all, war pipes, in the close confines of the ship, tended to be kind of. . . . *loud*.

"Sergeant Hallinan, Sergeant Feeney, it's your time to go topside."

There were two armed guards, both naval. Warrington had been insistent. "One might tempt them."

Hallinan nodded and stood. "C'mon, Feeney, we've got our daily break from staring at the corrugated walls."

Hallinan felt miserable and had ever since the riot. Deep in his bones he was sure, absolutely *certain*, that it was all his fault. *I could have just put the goddamned rifle on safe, then taken it up with the chain of command later. But nooo, I had to be a wise ass. And now the whole fucking mission is up in the air. Jesus, fuck me to tears; I never expected anything like this.*

A baker's dozen of them—A and C companies, both—slowly assembled on the mess deck, just in time to see fourteen others marched down from topside and returned, still under guard, to their quarters. The men who'd escorted Feeney and Hallinan turned them over to four other guards, then went back for a couple more. It took fifteen minutes, at least, to round up the entire party. That hour's break tended to be less than that. Once they were all present one of the guards opened up a hatch at the high end of a ladder—actually a set of stairs but it would never do in naval circles to call something by its everyday name—and motioned them up. The men climbed four ladders before reaching the level of the top containers. There another hatch was opened. As it was, Hallinan heard the strains of what he thought he recognized as *The Black Bear* . . .

"On the pipes? Who's paying the pipes? Who for the love of God even *could* be playing the pipes, here?"

"One of the Gurkhas," replied a petty officer, Kirkpatrick, normally in charge of the LCM and now bearing a loaded shotgun. The petty officer rolled his eyes, adding, "He's been at it all fucking day, too."

By the time Hallinan reached the Gurkha, the tune had changed from "The Black Bear" to "Scots Wha Hae." That one, Hallinan knew. He stood there, perhaps a bit dumb *looking*, but definitely not dumb as he sang along:

"Scots wha hae wi' Wallace bled,
Scots wham Bruce has often led,
Welcome tae yer gory bed . . . "

Sergeant Balbahadur could hardly smile, what with the blowpipe stuck in his mouth. He did take his right hand off the chanter—screwing up a note in the process—to encourage Hallinan to sing along, but louder.

"Now's the day and now's the hour.
See the front of battle lour.
See approach proud Edward's power.
Chains and slavery . . .
. . . Let us do or dee!"

The Gurkha finished the piece with a couple of flourishes, then let it die away with a sound not entirely dissimilar to what one might hear from three cats caught in a blender.

"Where did you learn the song?" Balbahadur asked. His English was replete with received pronunciation, something unusual in a Gurkha.

"From my grandmother, who got it from her mother," Hallinan said. "Where did you learn the pipes? And to speak English like that. I heard the others speaking once and they have a pretty strong accent."

"I learned from Second Battalion, Gurkha Rifles," answered Balbahadur. "Both things, I mean. We—the Brigade of Gurkhas—picked up the pipes from Scots regiments, in India. Oh, a long time ago, it was. I picked up the English because, well, I was a line boy, born within the regiment. The others aren't. And they tell me *I* have a terrible Brit accent in Nepali.

"My father was Gurkha Rifles. So was his father and his grandfather. And I was born in the UK, at the Royal Victoria Hospital, in Folkestone."

Balbahadur held out his hand to shake, giving his name—"Or just Bal, for short"—and asking, "And you are?"

"Hallinan, Alex, Bal. Are you sure you want to shake *my* hand? I mean, this"—Hallinan indicated the guards and quasi prisoners with a wave of his hand—"is all my fault."

"Oh, bullshit," the Gurkha said. "You think that little thing with the safety—oh, yes, we *all* heard about it—caused all this? Nonsense; you're not that important, Al."

"No," Balbahadur insisted, "you didn't start this. It started over pay."

"What?"

"It started with the pay differential between Euros, Americans, and honorary westerners like me and the other Gurkhas, and the Guyanan locals. Yeah, they make two-three-four times what they could expect to make in Guyana, if they could even find a job. And, yeah, the pay index holds out the promise of making the same pay as we do, eventually. Though it doesn't hold out the hope, ever, of making the same cost of living allowance because there *is* no cost of living allowance for Guyanans. It's all based on having to support a family in America or Europe. Which is, frankly, bullshit, because almost everyone with a family has that family in corporate housing, right around Camp Fulton.

"That's okay when they're home, and it should be okay now, for the ones still back there, when they're home fighting for their home against Venezuela. But when they get shipped overseas, while their families are in danger, at home, it's just not enough money. No, not even with the combat pay, which they're going to get two or three months of for maybe an hour's fighting."

"But we *can't* pay them to U.S. or Euro scales," Hallinan objected. "If we did, we couldn't support the entire regiment with the Euros and Americans. And without the Euros and Americans, nobody would hire the regiment for anything. Then there'd be no regiment, no jobs, and *no* pay."

Balbahadur grinned. "You know that. I know that. Logically *they* should know that, too. And, logically, they *do*. But it's not about logic; it's about how they *feel*. And the pay differential makes them feel like second class citizens. Which is why they're so goddamned resentful."

Hallinan shrugged. "Yeah, I suppose. Above my pay grade. I don't suppose you have a solution?"

"Above my pay grade, too," Balbahadur admitted. "But that's where it all started. Add in that no Guyanan has yet been allowed to buy a share in the regiment . . ."

"Sucks, doesn't it?" Hallinan agreed.

"Oh, it's fine for me and mine," Balbahadur said. "Fine for you. But it sucks for them. And this is what wrecked the Brigade of Gurkhas, you know."

"Huh? How so?"

Balbahadur looked heavenward, as if asking the gods why his regiment had had to be mostly dismantled. "Well . . . used to be the Gurkhas got paid a pittance; it was set by treaty between India and the UK. But as the Empire closed down, and the Gurkhas had to be moved home, or to Hong Kong, or Singapore, or Brunei, the British Army found it *had* to start paying fairly. They hid it as cost of living allowances for quite a while, so as not to violate the treaty with India. Eventually, though, it was simpler to just make for pay parity and to hell with the treaty.

"This got pushed by the courts into parity for retirement pensions, right to live in the UK, a whole bunch of things. Very quickly it became obvious that Gurkhas weren't such a bargain after all. Oh, we were good, yes, but no better than a good British regiment. And we couldn't be used for some things; try, for example, putting a Gurkha whose English was, at best, pretty marginal out on the streets of Belfast or Londonderry to keep order. Not such a good idea? Ministry of Defense didn't think so, either.

"So, in a time of tightening budgets, they let the Gurkhas go, for the most part. One battalion is all that's left, plus a few demonstration troops at Sandhurst. And we're mostly line boys now. The British Army takes in less than eighty new Gurkhas a year, and Nepal's share is about twenty. And Gurkha pay sent back to Nepal used to be really important to a damned poor country.

"So a loud-mouthed actress, whose father was an officer in the Brigade, did some good for a few, for a while, and damaged an infinite number, forever."

Balbahadur laughed lightly. "You've heard that two wrongs don't make a right? Well, sometimes two rights make an infinite wrong."

"I'm wiring base," Pearson said to Warrington. The captain stood on the bridge, facing forward over the deck where Hallinan and Balbahadur were talking, the guards dutifully standing over them and the rest. "This mission is a failure from the word go. There's no way we can proceed."

"I wish you wouldn't do that," Warrington said. "I really do. We've still got three weeks or so to turn this around."

Pearson snorted. "I'm a Christian. I believe God made the Heavens and the Earth in seven days, whatever a 'day' may mean to God. But I'm not a fool. I *don't* believe you can make a combat effective force out of this mutually hostile rabble in the three weeks or so we've got left."

"So what have you lost by letting me try?" Warrington pleaded. "We can't go home anyway. The worst that happens is you burn up fuel. So?"

"No," Pearson said. "The worst that happens is that the next riot gets completely out of hand and somebody gets killed."

"Ah, but I have a cunning plan . . ."

"Oh, Jesus."

"By the way," Warrington asked with a grin, "what's illumination going to be like for the next few nights?"

"All right, you cunts; you want out of durance vile? This is your route."

The moon was up, but presented only a thin sliver of weak light, not enough to illuminate more than the grossest outlines of the ship, its structure, and the containers. In that nearly three-feet-up-a-well-digger's-ass-at-midnight darkness, four lines and four knots of troops, all mixed in as randomly as Warrington, Pierantoni, and Stocker could deliberately make them, waited for the word to start assembling the flight deck from the perforated steel planking. The lines were for the drudgery of moving the sections of Marsden Matting from the containers to where they were to be assembled. The knots, and each of those contained both line infantry and special operations types, were to do the actual assembly.

A bare minimum of the tiny, 4.5mm, chemlights marked the edges of the ad hoc airstrip and special danger areas. The greenish spark and faint glow they gave off was barely adequate to the purpose.

"The standard is one hour for a field of sixty feet by three hundred," Warrington reminded them. "Now GO!"

With a collective groan, the men of A and C companies began. Although they'd rehearsed the procedure in a small way first, in the light, down on the mess deck, dark multiplied the problems to infinity.

"Oooowww . . . you've got my fucking finger stuck . . .

Back off! Back off! . . . Goddamnit, ease it over! . . . Get off my foot, asshole!...Where's the half piece for the edge? . . . Shit! Get a medic; I think my leg's broken . . . End piece here! End piece here! . . . Mediiiccc! . . ."

"Sergeant Major P?" Warrington called out.

"Here, sir."

"Take charge of this shit. Don't let 'em kill each other. I'm going to go see how Blackmore, Cagle, and the landing party are coming along."

"Sir."

When Warrington reached the mess deck, Cagle, who—having a contact on the ground was effectively intel officer for the mission—was giving the situation brief. Behind him, on the big TV screen, was a Google satellite image of the objective area. Cagle pointed at it.

"That's the city of Bajuni," Cagle explained. "My contact tell me it doesn't look much like that anymore. Mostly it's ruined and burned. It would be more burned except that there was never much wood in its construction, being mostly mud brick.

"There is no civil order there; there is no law, not even Sharia. Rule is broken down between about nine different gangs, some pirates, some not. There used to be a ruling clan, the Marehan. That's over; they're just another one of the rival gangs. Rather, they're several of the rival gangs since even that clan broke up." Cagle pushed a button and the screen changed to superimpose the rough boundaries of the gangs that ruled the city and the surrounding countryside.

"The NGO's mostly gave up on the place a few years

ago. The press has long since pulled out. Now nobody cares about it."

With another push of the button a rough oval appeared, encompassing a set of docks, some warehouses, and a ship rather smaller than the *Bland*. "That's our objective area. It's entirely within the sliver ruled by the rump of the Marehan, so, as long as we don't wander, we shouldn't have to fight more than one gang. They've no armor; just some technicals. For indirect they've a fair number of mortars, heavy and light, but few of those have sights and ammunition is limited.

"Mind you, the other gangs could, in time, summon about five thousand fighters. So speed is going to be very goddamned important."

"And there's another thing." Cagle looked directly at Warrington, standing behind the mass of men seated on the floor and at the mess tables. "The price for the medicines we need is fair, but it includes evacuation of fifteen people, twelve men, a woman, and two children. One of those is the current chief of the Marehan, who wants out before it's too late. The rest are his family and close advisors and guards."

"We can do that," Warrington agreed. "Simon, what's that do to your load plan and egress plan?"

"As long as we can get them to the LCM, we can get them out. We're only going to load it with two Elands, one infantry platoon, plus a squad for portage, Sergeant Balbahadur on pipes, and the mortar section. Should be plenty of redundant carrying capacity."

The chief of the boat, no longer on guard duty, agreed but added, "There won't be a lot of room for baggage."

"I passed on that they'll have to travel light. They'll be bringing about half a ton of gold, and one bag per person, but that's it."

"Doable then," the chief said.

"Thing is," Cagle added, "we've had dealings, indirect dealings, with at least three of the adults before."

★ CHAPTER FIFTEEN ★

She signed and she swore
that she never would deceive me
But the devil take the women
for they never can be easy.
—"Whiskey in the Jar," Irish Traditional

Safe House Bravo, Muntinlupa, Manila, Republic of the Philippines

In the end, Loo Fung had come through, as Lucas had known he would. What he'd come through with was a drug—a sleep drug—and instructions on dosage for a given effect and given delay. Once known as almorexant, the drug had been abandoned by its U.S. developer, GlaxoSmithKlein, because of its unfortunate, if merely occasional, side effects and the potentially huge legal liabilities that would have flowed from them. China, conversely, had figured, *Eh? What's a little depression, hypotension, slowed heart rate, and blunted stress response if there's a buck—or a yuan—to be made? And besides, the doctors can always take any patients with bad side effects off the medication before it gets too serious. Moreover, in our current state of lawless industrial feudalism masquerading as communism, we can buy off any inquiries and settle with the families of any victims for mere* fen *on the* yuan.

What almorexant did, basically, was block the receptors for orexin, a chemical naturally produced by the brain, in the hypothalamus, specifically, which kept both people and lower animals awake. Block the orexin? *Flump*, sleep. And the great thing about it, Loo Fung had explained, was that there would none of the other symptoms of knockout drugs, no blurry or swimming vision, no nausea, no dizziness, nothing.

Of course, it couldn't be as simple as that for Maricel. Get everybody, including the guards, to start nodding off at the same time and it would likely, a) induce great suspicion and, hence, b) get her killed. Moreover, with the odd schedules the group she kept house for ran, she had to wait for a time when a) everybody was home, especially the big boss, Benson, and b) when everybody was involved in planning their own little things, rather than the entire group planning together.

It was a week and another day off before everything was just right and she could send Lucas the message: *Tonight*.

It was a strain on Maricel to keep her stress and fear—and her anticipation and excitement, as well—from showing. Then again, she'd been acting for her entire postpubescent life and, as importantly, fooling men for all that time. That this was a little more life and death didn't really change that.

She'd long since noticed a tendency for the rest of the crew to fuck off a bit without Mr. Benson riding herd on them. Thus, when for dinner on the big day she served everybody *tocino* and rice for a main course, then *halo-halo* for dessert, Benson's dessert had a little something extra in it, but only a little. Two hours after dinner he began yawning. A half hour after that, he finally gave up and took himself off to bed. Maricel heard, "I really have a yen, to go back once again . . ."

His last words before leaving the square-columned living room were, "It's my night, Maricel, but I'm just too tired. Tighten up one of the other boys."

Oh, I will. Everyone except the ones on duty. Whatever else they might do, the boys take that very seriously.

Next down was Perez. Bringing two clean rum and cokes for Baker and Malone, both balanced in one dainty hand, with the other she handed Perez a San Miguel Red Horse with just that little something extra. Before he was half through with the beer, Perez likewise excused himself to bed.

"Goddamn; I'm tired."

Since he was the only one at that moment who was sleepy, nobody gave it a second thought.

Two down, four to go.

Malone and Baker were even easier, since, post-Perez, they decided to double team her—one at each end—on the living room ottoman, the dining room table, and one of the stools of the wet bar. For her part, Maricel put in her usual Academy Award quality performance and soon enough, all screwed out, the two sergeants left for sleep.

In a way, that's bad, she thought, *since people who fall asleep naturally might just wake up naturally. Note to self and Lucas, take out Baker and Malone first, after the guards.*

Zimmerman, the interior guard at the moment, had wandered through the living room during the festivities. He'd seen it all before so paid them essentially no attention. Maricel thought him the nicest guy in a pretty pleasant bunch, really. *And he's never once used me, though I made the offer. Nice too that, to avoid insulting me, he just framed it as loyalty to his wife, back home . . . wherever home is.*

Next, after tugging her clothes back on and adjusting them, Maricel went to the kitchen and put on a pot of coffee. Taking two cups from a cabinet, and a two ounce vial from her purse, she put a quantity of almorexant, suspended in a liquid medium, in each of the cups, then swirled the liquid around before setting the cups down to dry. On a small tray she assembled some creamer, sugar, and a diet sweetener. Zimmerman stopped by once, on his rounds, to ask about the coffee.

"Few minutes, boss," she said, looking up from her cell phone and the text message she was preparing for Lucas. Earlier she'd sent him an alert that tonight everyone would be there.

"I can't wait," Zimmerman replied, stifling a yawn. Slinging his submachine gun, he took one of the cups from Maricel's tray and then, ignoring both creamer and sweetener, took the glass pot from under the still brewing coffee and poured it into the cup. A few drops fell from the coffeemaker's basket to sizzle on the hot metal circle below, before Zimmerman replaced the pot, allowing the fresh coffee to flow freely.

Serendipity works, thought Maricel, as soon as she heard the *flump* from Zimmerman's falling body. *Five down; one to go.*

She finished her message to Lucas—the last line being, *"remember they're all armed,"* then dropped her phone into a pocket. After waiting a few minutes for the coffee to finish, she poured the other tainted cup full, set it on the tray, and walked out to where the last of the lot, Washington, the only black in the group, stood his shift.

Pity about Washington, she thought. *He's the only one well hung enough for me to actually feel something besides weight.*

Tsk-tsking, she helped ease a swaying Washington to the ground. Her size, from her mainly European, Euro-American, and African-American genetic heritage, was a big help there. Then she reached into her pocket, pulled out her cell, brought up the draft message, and sent it on.

Come and get it.

"Wake up, *tarantados!*" said Lucas. The gang chieftain sat beside the driver's seat of a large van; one with surprisingly fresh paint. It was parked three blocks away from the Kanos' place. They'd been sitting there since about twenty minutes after receiving Maricel's first message.

There were seven in the van, including Lucas, though it had room to put in seats for fourteen. All seven were armed. Among the others were Rafael, driving, and

Crisanto, the kidnap team leader. Crisanto was one of the very few, and highly prized, members of TCS with a substantial military background, in his case in the Philippine Marine Corps. Under different circumstances, he'd have been a prized accession for M Day, as well.

The seven were crowded toward the front. The back had been left seatless, to allow a flat place to pile the presumptively unconscious prisoners.

The van moved gently and quietly from its parking spot. This far from the center of town there was no traffic to speak of. In mere minutes—obeying the posted speed limits the whole way—it was in front of the safe house, with Lucas, Crisanto, and four more piling out to where Maricel waited.

"Remember," she hissed, "two of them are *not* drugged. Be careful!"

"We know," Lucas replied as he pushed past her. "Get in the van."

"And don't . . ." Whatever she had been about to say was lost. Nobody was listening. Indeed, nobody was even talking, snapping and pointing fingers substituting for vocal commands.

Crisanto pointed down at Washington and snapped his fingers. Immediately, two of his men bent over the prostrate black, flipped him to his belly, then taped his hands together at the wrists and his feet at the ankles. One pulled a sap from his belt and gave the bound prisoner a none-too-gentle rap on the head. It wouldn't kill him . . . probably . . . but would ensure that he wouldn't be calling out to anyone if the drug wore off. Washington's submachine gun went by its sling over the kidnapper's shoulder. The night vision goggles were left draped around the Kano's neck. They could be recovered later.

Lucas, Crisanto, and two others pushed on into the house, padding gently on bare feet. Another snap and a point and those two were on Zimmerman. They both squatted to one side, grabbed the American's clothing, and hoisted him over to his front. Short strips of duct tape were pulled from pockets and quickly and expertly applied. By that time, the first pair, those who had bound Washington, were in the house. Crisanto pointed decisively up the stairs. With brisk nods the kidnappers began to ascend.

Baker, who wasn't precisely young anymore, grumbled as he stumbled across his darkened room to the doorway that led to the hallway bath. "Goddamned, bladder. If they'd told me I'd be pissing half a dozen times a night once I hit forty-five; I'd have arranged to die young."

It was an emergency thing; Baker didn't have time to put on his armor.

After flicking on the light to find the doorknob, a blinking Baker stepped out into the dusky tiled hall. Only to bump into a little tattooed, barefoot and brown guy, with a gun . . . who duly panicked, putting three rounds in rapid succession into Baker's abdomen. He didn't have to go to the bathroom after that though he did have to scream.

"What the F . . . !" Malone, the only member of Benson's half team who was both unshot and undrugged, was out of bed, alert, if confused—and not a little frightened, within a fraction of a second of the last shot being fired. His rifle was handy enough, but at the probable ranges inside a house a large bore pistol, with its superior knock-down power, was better. He eased his pistol out of the shoulder holster resting on the night table beside the bed.

Malone squatted down and duck walked to his door as fast as worn and arthritic knees would carry him. Pistol aimed up at forty-five degrees in his right hand, his left began to turn the knob, slowly, gently, and quietly. He hadn't quite finished the motion when the door thudded with a kick and flew open.

The muzzle of some kind of firearm—Malone guessed a pistol—flashed about eighteen inches above his head, generally horizontally. It was close enough to hurt, close enough to burn, but wasn't aimed at the low spot he'd taken. Malone fired two rounds. The next muzzle flash went up toward the ceiling. He shifted himself and his aim to a dimly sensed presence farther back in the hallway, firing twice more. He couldn't be sure, thereafter, whether the flop he'd heard was a body or a man trying desperately to find some cover.

Shouts and a scream told the American that there was more than one stranger in the house. *Oh, shit! Baker's down. Shit, fuck, suck . . . we're being raided. But* why? *And what about the guards? And where the fuck are Benson and Perez? And poor Maricel's probably scared shitless.*

It was that last, the thought of a helpless woman cowering under her bed, that sent Malone out—still squatting—into the darkened hallway.

★ ★ ★

Goddammit! Crisanto mentally cursed, as soon as he heard the first shot. *Stupid, fucking, hot-rodding, undisciplined rabble. And Lucas thinks I can make something out of this shit!*

Though his service with the Philippine Marines had been prematurely truncated by court-martial—a little matter of losing track of a truck carrying seventeen Singapore-built light machine guns and about half a million rounds of ammunition—Crisanto was still proud of his service, in both senses, and still measured all things by the standards—the tactical and disciplinary standards, if not the moral ones—of the Philippine Marines. It wouldn't have been so bad if the weapons hadn't been, most embarrassingly, the property of the Philippine Army, on loan to the Corps. But, as Crisanto had told his lawyer, "If they'd been Marine property, I'd never have sold them to the New People's Army. But *Army* guns? What's the big deal? It's not like they were fucking Moros, after all."

The lawyer hadn't been impressed with that argument, nor had the judge been impressed with the arguments the lawyer *had* come up with. In the end, only lack of certain evidence had kept Crisanto from a very hard period of penal servitude. At least, that was the official reason. Unofficially, Crisanto had had to pay over everything he'd made on the deal to the judge. He'd still been discharged. At loose ends, thereafter, and broke, to boot, he'd wandered home, to his old neighborhood of Tondo, only to discover it was under new management. Since he'd needed a job, and TCS had needed some military expertise it just didn't have, it had been a perfect match.

Or almost perfect; there was still the little problem of trying to instill some discipline into the human material.

Nerves or anger, or just too small a target, when Crisanto saw the very top of the Kano's head rising over the edge of the top step, he fired . . . and missed. On the plus side, when the Kano fired back his three rounds impacted the wall, about five feet over Crisanto's head sending plaster dust and shards to air and floor. It was a reasonable guess that neither of them ever got a good look at, let alone a sight picture on, the other.

Dumbass! Dumbass! DUMBASS! Malone thought. *Seven rounds and one in the chamber. And I've fired seven and left the other magazines back in the room. And the last three were a complete waste. Dumbass, dipshit, cocksucker. I almost deserve what's coming.*

But deserve it or not, I'd rather avoid it.

Keeping the pistol horizontal, he duckwalked back to his room door and slithered inside. Only then, only when he was behind cover, did he stand and race for the other three magazines. He rotated his body to bring the pistol over the bed, then pressed the round magazine release. The empty mag fell without a sound audible from more than a few inches away. The fresh mag went in with an audible click, but he didn't really care about that.

What the hell happened to the rest of them? Jesus! What about the guards. Risk it? Got to.

"Bennssonn! Perrezzz!" Nothing. No answer.

"Crap," Malone whispered. He tried again. Still nothing.

Maybe they got away. That . . . or they're dead . . . or they're down. Not here and fighting, that's for sure. So . . . a little Drizzle-drazzle; "time for this one to come home."

Dressing took one more hand free than Malone had. Instead, he stuffed his cell into his trousers, slid the magazines into the elastic band of his underwear, put the trousers over one shoulder and went to the window. His free hand punched through the screen, then bent and pulled back, taking the screen with it.

Course, I'm screwed if they're covering this side of the building. "Help me, Mister Wizard!"

Bare feet were fine, superior even, for smooth floors. For smooth, bloody floors, however, they really weren't worth a damn. For smooth, bloody floors, with two bodies to trip the feet without stopping the torso, they were completely worthless. Crisanto went flying over the body of one of his erstwhile underlings. As he did, he thought he saw the top of a head disappearing from the bottom of a window frame. His torso did stop, eventually, but only after his own head struck the wall at the opposite end of the hallway.

He came to, some minutes later, with Lucas standing over him, the lights on, and the only body in evidence one of the Kanos.

"Wha . . . ?"

"They were still alive," Lucas answered. "I had the boys put them in the van. They might make it."

Nodding hurt, Crisanto discovered. "The targets?"

"Four of them, stretched out unconscious in the back of the van. Time to go, though."

"I wanna punish the motherfucker who shot my boys?"

"Him, we'll probably never get. But we'll still punish him," Lucas agreed. "We'll punish him all the same."

★★★
PART II:
Coast of
East Africa
★★★

★ CHAPTER SIXTEEN ★

Dawn, and as the sun breaks through
the piercing chill of night on the
plain outside Korem it lights up a biblical famine,
now, in the Twentieth Century. This place, say
workers here, is the closest thing to hell on earth.
—Michael Buerk, BBC Correspondent,
24 October, 1984

MV *Richard Bland*, Coast of Africa, off the city of Bajuni

These were—or at least had been, when there'd been enough trade to justify the effort—pirate waters. Now the pirates had to range much farther afield to earn their daily kat. There were always armed guards on the deck of the *Bland*, even when they weren't involved in guarding their own. Now, though, a platoon of armed troopers manned heavy machine guns lining both sides of the ship, just in case some pirate hadn't gotten the word. As a class, pirates were not, after all, *cum laude*.

More stood at the bow and stern, likewise manning heavy weapons. All, bow, stern, and amidships, were

178   ★*Tom Kratman*★

dressed up in full torso armor, with ceramic inserts, helmeted, and with boom mikes swinging from somewhere just behind the ear to just in front of their mouths.

While another platoon, reinforced, and laden even more than the deck guards, prepared to load, the remainder of the company, also reinforced—by the aviation detachment and ship's crew, assembled the flight deck. Two of the three cranes squealed as they lowered the landing craft, already part loaded, and a section of the floating platform that eased the use of rubber boats.

The steel cables lowering the LCM stopped their tortured squealing as the boat reached and then settled into the water. Lieutenant Simon Blackmore, ground commander for the mission, pulled his night vision goggles down over his face and looked over the gunwale, down at the landing craft. The coxswain who had ridden down with one other crewman, waved an infrared chemlight. *All okay.*

Blackmore shifted his shoulders under the armor. The beastly stuff was damned uncomfortable.

"Right then," Blackmore said to the reinforced squad lined up at the gunwale to either side of him, "over the side with the net." He joined with the troopers, straining and grunting, to lift the heavy net up over the gunwales.

The moon was still down, and wouldn't be up for another two and a half hours. Until it arose, Bajuni would be lit only by fires, and only a few of those. Cagle stared across the water, musing back on the good he'd once hoped to do here. He did so with regret, and that mixed in with a sense of profound hopelessness and helplessness.

The world was not supposed to turn out this way.

"Once the world went into full-blown depression," Cagle said to Warrington, standing on the deck, waiting for the landing craft to be lowered to the water and secured, "the never-ending supply of bleeding heart humanitarian aid mostly dried up. The smart locals got out and linked up with their bank accounts in Switzerland or Lebanon or the Caribbean. But the ruler of this place wasn't smart. He spent his money, most of it, trying to help people weather the storm. Even brought in my contact from a hostile tribe to help; they having some history together."

"The kid we rescued a few years back?" asked Warrington.

"Yeah. His old man died, leaving him the chief. But without an endless supply of funds and food, he wasn't able even to hold his extended clan together. It broke up into septs, or even smaller groupings. Some are outright gangs. And all of those were at war with every other in no time.

"Might have been different," Cagle added, "if we hadn't so thoroughly financially raped and shot up the major opposing clan. But we did and that removed the threat that helped keep the Marehan together."

"We did what we were contracted to do," Warrington countered. "And it might not have been different, either."

Cagle sighed. "I know . . . and it was before my time with the regiment, anyway. But I wonder if the old chief, Khalid, would have been so enthusiastic about us smashing the Habar Afaan if he'd foreseen where that would lead."

"Don't worry about it," Warrington said. "That kind of prescience exists only in fiction."

"Are you sure we should be doing this?" Cagle asked. "The skipper expects the weather to pick up."

"Even if we didn't need the drugs," Warrington answered, "I'd order this anyway. And, yeah, the weather's going to get worse. But now's the time the light data suits; so now it has to be. Why? Because we *absolutely* need a common mission to bring this crew together."

"Is that why you put the kid in charge?" Cagle asked.

"That, and that Lieutenant Blackmore is both new and neutral, whereas Stocker and I are neither."

"Besides that," Cagle said, "the kid handled the riot pretty well. No more force than needed. No less, either. And impartially."

Bajuni, former Federation of Sharia Courts, Africa

"Would you have come to us if you had known how it would end?" asked Adam, erstwhile chief of the disintegrated Marehan, of Labaan, his former captor and friend. Both men had Kalashnikovs slung over their shoulders.

How it was ending was with Adam's family, the solitary Labaan, a dozen loyal guards with their wives and children, three pallets of medicine, and about a quarter of a ton of gold, waiting in the darkness not too far from the sea. There were no electric lights, not anywhere in the city. Oh, a few people still had generators, and some of those may have had gas, but incandescent light bulbs had become quite precious of late. There were a few fires, but very few, there being so little left to burn. The night was lit, where it was, by the flash of tracers, or the thunder-accompanied lightening of exploding mortar shells. The other fragments of the sundered clan were moving in for the kill, albeit slowly, each in dread fear that some other fragment might manage to scavenge a little more off the bones of the dead city than they could.

One of the very few generators remaining, and a gallon of so of rare for the area gasoline, powered the computer through which Labaan had been contacted by, and kept in contact with, their rescuers. That hummed next to the pile of luggage, with a single one of the older boys in attendance.

"I didn't have a lot of choice," Labaan answered. His voice held the trace of a chuckle, as if he found life, the universe, and everything some vast comedy routine. "Gutaale, upon him be peace, never quite forgave me for your rescue, even though I had nothing to do with it, and did everything I could to prevent it. If I hadn't come, I was for the chop. At least I was once the madness began to take him.

"So, not only would I have come, my young friend, I am eternally grateful that you found a place for me. As time went on, Gutaale developed some very advanced and sophisticated ideas on how to do away with those who had displeased him."

At that last a shuddering Adam stole a glance in the direction from which he had last heard the sound of his wife and children. *If we don't escape, what will happen to them? Chains and bondage, rape and all other forms of degradation, isn't advanced. It's the oldest thing in the world.*

"It might have gone better for you, you know,"

said Labaan, "if you hadn't tried to *really* outlaw slavery here."

"No choice," answered the younger man. "It was a condition of Makeda becoming my wife."

"The more fool her," Labaan said, "and the more fool *you*, especially since absolutely nothing can be done about it. And there'll be more people enslaved as a result of the breakdown than ever were in normal times."

The older man sighed and shook his head. "But . . . never mind. Everyone makes mistakes."

MV *Richard Bland,* Coast of Africa, off the city of Bajuni

Stocker was stuck with Warrington up on the bridge. No matter, Kiertzner was there to see young Lieutenant Blackmore over the side. It was the boy's first real mission with the regiment, and though he hadn't volunteered the information, the first sergeant knew it was also his first combat mission.

The boy was nervous, understandably. The first sergeant slapped him on the shoulder, saying, "Wish I were going with you, sir, for the sheer fun of it." Then, leaning close, he whispered, "The thing you're feeling inside right now, the nervousness, is only fear of being afraid. I've been there and done that. Now let me tell you a little secret. You're going to be too *busy* to be afraid. You won't have time for it. Period." Raising his voice again, Kiertzner finished, in a frightfully "posh" accent, "Now over the side with you, sir, like a good lad."

The wind had picked up and, with it, the waves.

To the *Bland* it made a little difference, but nothing the maneuvering thrusters and stabilization system couldn't handle. To the men of Second Battalion, trying to inflate the rubber boats, and the crew of the LCM, on the other hand, it was royal pain, with the boats barely controllable against the push of the breeze and the LCM rocking badly in the now choppy sea.

The landing party had practiced with the nets, of course, in the temporarily darkened spaces of the mess deck. It isn't quite the same though, when it's not only the ship moving, but the other vessel you're trying to board is bobbing like a cork and only half succeeding in keeping station against the mother ship.

Descending, as was proper, first of all the landing party, Simon Blackmore shivered on the swinging net. He'd grown up on stories—old soldiers' stories—of men losing their grip on the nets, falling, and, under the weight of their equipment, sinking like rocks, never to be seen again. In the abstract, he knew that the LCM was only ten meters or so below. The rhythmic pounding of metal on metal would have told him that, even if he hadn't known. But in the real, and *really* dark at the moment, world, it might as well have been a mile down.

And I wish that bloody landing craft would stop banging against the side of the Bland. *Reminds me of scissors . . . or a mechanized guillotine in a metal-working shop. Crap!* "Too busy," *the man said. Hah.*

The net was too long; that was one of the mistakes. For a tiny extra increment of safety, the coxswain, Kirkpatrick, had his crew haul up as much as they could of the thing,

draping the fold over the inside of the landing craft. The
edge still hung well down to the sea.

Looking through his NVG's, Kirkpatrick saw a dim
shape descending the net. *From the shape, I'd say it's that
new limey exec from Charlie, Fourth; the one who came
with the Gurkhas.* Two of the LCM crew were already
moving to guide the lieutenant's legs down safely into the
well of the boat.

"Thanks, gentlemen," Kirkpatrick heard, as the man's
feet touched the sloshing steel deck. Yep, the Brit.

He saw the lieutenant—*What was the boy's name?
Oh, yeah; Blackmore*—turn and put his attention to
helping the next boarder safely down off the net. The
boat's crew assisted. Satisfied, the coxswain put all of his
attention into keeping the LCM as flush as possible
against the hull of the *Bland*. It wasn't easy, what with the
waves coming from bow on.

Bajuni, former Federation of Sharia Courts, Africa

The firing was getting closer now, Adam could hear, a tide
of fire coming in. *Though it's coming from everywhere but
the sea. My troops are beginning to abandon me, I think. I
can't blame them; after all, I'm abandoning them. Not that
I have any choice, not if I'm going to save my own family.*

"There was a time in Europe, an event, long, long ago,
where somebody invited in every neighboring tribe to
exterminate a tribe he didn't have time or inclination to
obliterate himself. What was that, Labaan?"

"Caesar, with the Eburones," the older and better

educated man said. "But this isn't the same. These scavengers weren't invited by anybody."

"I suppose not," Adam conceded. "But they're coming in the same way, anyway."

"They won't come fast," Labaan said. "Half the gold in the clan treasury has been scattered out, in little birdseed trails that lead to one another, with trip flares to make sure they see it. If they're not already, they'll be fighting among themselves soon.

"But I do hope our rescuers get here in good time."

MV *Richard Bland*, Coast of Africa, off the city of Bajuni

About half the passengers for the LCM were loaded when the wave struck. The ramped bow had ricocheted off the steel hull, leaving an angled gap between them. It only moved about a foot and a half, Kirkpatrick later recalled, but that was enough.

In the funnel formed between the landing craft and the *Bland*, the wave raised itself higher than it would normally have been. This caused the LCM to roll slightly to starboard, even as it was pushed another foot or so away from the hull. The net, folded over the gunwale of the LCM, but with its bottom still in the water, was pulled by both the sea's drag and the top, which was still attached to the mother ship. At the same time, the half dozen troops climbing down swung inward, pulling on the net enough that, with the various other tugs, it came completely free of the landing craft, unfurling into the water and swinging toward the ship.

A soldier from C Company, a Guyanan, had one of his feet resting on the net, not far above the landing craft's gunwale. The other foot was searching for purchase on a lower section. As the net unfurled from where it had been gathered, it fell with a whizzing sound, then hit, flat and wet, against the *Bland*'s hull. It slammed that soldier into the hull, knocking him half silly. Even so, he managed to keep his hands and the one foot on the net.

Kirkpatrick reacted automatically to the surge, swinging the LCM back in. Unfortunately, in the way of waves, following the rise there was a dip. This made what would have been an economical shifting into just that little bit too much. The LCM, at full load displacing about sixty-four tons, slammed back against the *Bland*. The loose leg was caught and neatly severed.

Knocked silly or not, the soldier screamed his agony and let go the net. He fell backwards. Had anyone been expecting any of this, they might have caught him . . . if they'd seen him. But, no, it was too quick and far too dark. No one was ready; no one moved quickly enough to catch the flailing, shrieking trooper. With the LCM bouncing off the mother ship again, a space opened up. Into that space the trooper fell, beginning to pinwheel, striking his helmeted head on the hull, pinwheeling the other way, and then making a single splash before disappearing under the waves.

Simon didn't know exactly what had happened, or to whom. But he dropped his rucksack and armor, began shedding other equipment, and then started to weave his way through the obstacle course of heavy equipment and men, toward the net.

"What?" He shouted, over the roar of wind and engine and rising hubbub from the men. "Who?"

Sergeant Balbahadur cupped one of his hands to speak into his officer's ear. "One of the men, sir. Went down in between the ship and the boat. Lost. We don't know who."

"Fuck!" Simon didn't bother to strip off his shirt. He began climbing the gunwale, clearly intending to dive in for his lost trooper.

Balbahadur dropped his pipes and tackled his officer to the sodden deck. "I said, sir, 'lost.' He's gone, and there's nothing to be done about it. By now, loaded as we are—as he was, he's fifty or a hundred feet down. Lost, sir. *Gone*. Now carry *on*, sir."

Bajuni, former Federation of Sharia Courts, Africa

A sudden firefight erupted to the southeast, too far away to be any of the thin—and ever thinning—line of defenders. Labaan laughed, pointing in the general direction of sky-borne tracers.

"Heh; money well spent, that was," he chortled.

Adam said, "I wonder if we couldn't have bought them off with the gold?"

Labaan shook his head. "We'd only have whet their appetites for more, and more, and finally still more. They'd never had stayed—"

"Labaan!" called out one of the dozen remaining faithful security guards, this one sitting between a generator and a small satellite dish, his face lit by a laptop's glow. "Message. They're coming. Twenty minutes."

★ CHAPTER SEVENTEEN ★

There's no point in being Irish if you don't know
that the world is going to break your heart, eventually.
—Daniel Patrick Moynihan.

Off Bajuni, former Federation of Sharia Courts, Africa

Finally loaded and underway, the landing craft wasn't so
much plowing through the waves as wallowing in them,
rocking from side to side in a beat just arrhythmic enough
to set almost every nonsailor aboard to hurling chunks
over the side or to the deck. Of course, crowded as they
were, even if a suffering footsoldier intended to hurl onto
the deck, as often as not the space was covered with the
body of another troop. The boat reeked.

That was perhaps the only advantage to the men from
Second Battalion in the rubber boats trailing the LCM. In
smaller craft, being tossed about more violently, those
men were as sick as or sicker than the landing craft's
passengers. But they, at least, could be certain of being
able to vomit over the side.

★ ★ ★

Blackmore would have felt sick, even if the waves weren't inducing most of the men to vomit over the side or, if slow or unlucky, or standing next to someone unlucky, on the deck. More or less. Simon had other cause to feel ill.

Losing a man like that? Before we even pulled away from the ship? Jesus, what a waste. And I don't know what unit he was from, what with all or parts of five platoons and sections aboard. The platoon leader, Sergeant Moore, hasn't a clue yet, either. In any case, I'm not looking forward to explaining to either Warrington or Stocker what happened. Even if it wasn't anybody's fault.

The only man aboard who had actually seen and understood what had happened was Kirkpatrick, the coxswain. And, even though at an intellectual level he understood what had happened and knew it was just one of those things, at an emotional level he was eaten up with guilt from the crown of his head to his waterlogged feet. Unlike most of the grunts, he wasn't seasick; he was heartsick.

Zigged when you should have zagged, dumbass . . . all your fault . . . that poor bastard . . . food for the fish . . . my fault . . . oh, God, all my fault . . . why, why, WHY couldn't I have just held steady for a few seconds . . . fuckfuckfuck . . .

Still, as Doctor Johnson said, there's nothing like a sentence of death—even if only potential—to concentrate the mind. As the craft neared shore, both Simon and

Kirkpatrick realized that they had more pressing issues than waste or personal guilt.

Bajuni, former Federation of Sharia Courts, Africa

The tenth ounce gold coins scattered about could only do so much. Whoever had been fighting over them scant minutes before; someone had apparently won. There'd been a few lesser skirmishes, but those had apparently settled quickly.

Ashore, Labaan and one assistant strained to hear the approaching motors. So far, there was nothing.

Or maybe, thought Labaan, *we just can't hear it over the other sounds.*

They had no high tech, barring only the old laptop and its appurtenances, left a few hundred meters behind. Certainly they had none of the night vision gear M Day's troopers did. But they had a couple of things going for them. Neither Labaan nor his assistant were, strictly speaking, city boys, even if cities were not entirely strange to them. Having grown up outside of cities, and being, of late, in a city that was one in name only, both their hearing and their eyes were keen.

The assistant, being younger, had the keener of both. He tapped Labaan and pointed out to sea. "There. Maybe a kilo and a half. I wouldn't see it at all except that the waves are tossing them around so much."

Labaan nodded, not in agreement—he didn't see a thing yet—but in understanding and trust. "Light the beacons," he ordered.

★ ★ ★

There it is, thought Kirkpatrick, swinging his wheel slightly to the starboard. To two of his crew, standing to either side, he ordered, "Standby on the fifties." "Standby," in this case, meant lock and load. Locking and loading their Degtyarev-built KORD machine guns meant lifting the feed tray covers and inspecting by touch, laying down the belt of ammunition, then reseating the covers, and jerking the charging handles rearward. Once the handles were released, the bolts slammed home with an audible *clang*.

The troops in the well deck felt the craft change course slightly even over the rocking and pounding of the waves. A couple up by the ramp shouted back to the others that the beacons were in sight. The six men of the armored car crews bent to unbuckle their charges, pulling the releases to loosen the straps and then unhooking the ends from the shackles on the Elands. Then they climbed aboard, leaving the hatches open and their heads or heads and torsos sticking out above. The infantry all backed away as far as they could.

Simon's RTO, or radio telephone operator, tapped him with the handset. "It's the ship," he said.

"Blackmore." When there's nobody else it could be, and the radios hop frequencies more than six thousand times a minute, things like code words and call signs become unnecessary to the point of silly.

"Simon," said Warrington over the radio, "the choppers just took off. They should be passing you in about a minute, minute and a half. They'll contact you in the next forty-five seconds or so. The fixed wings are standing by.

You secure something that will do for an airstrip and they can be there in about two minutes.

"Have you figured out yet who you lost while boarding?"

"Roger, roger, and no."

"Damn . . . all right. Too late to worry about it now. Until you get back, just concentrate on the mission."

"Roger."

The two gunships passed overhead, one to either side. They churned through the air, moving about four hundred meters past the shoreline, then split to search out the perimeter. In his own headset he heard first one pilot, then the other, confirm to Blackmore, "Few armed men, no more than expected. But there's a serious knot of what look like women and kids. Low level fighting pretty much everywhere else." The crews of the gunships were Russians but, after this many years in the regiment, their English was pretty good.

"Roger," Blackmore answered. "Keep moving. Keep low. They're not supposed to have any MANPADS"— Man-portable Air Defense Systems, Stingers and Strelas—"but you never know."

"Roger."

The Old Port was defined by a thick, south-jutting peninsula, from the tip of which ran a west-southwest running breakwater. This peninsula, mostly bare with just some scrub and a couple of palm trees, passed the LCM to its left. Aiming for the eastern shoulder of the spit of land, Kirkpatrick throttled back as the craft neared shore, letting momentum and the waves carry it in for the most part. He felt the grinding of sand under the hull, slowing the craft. He waited until all forward motion was gone, then flipped the lever to drop the ramp. He gave a little more gas to the engines—well, diesel, technically—to keep his craft firmly hugging the shore.

Grunts began spilling out the front, splitting into three files and the little knot of headquarters and the portage squad. One or two stopped briefly, bent over and painted the shore in dull vomit. More infantry, or technically special operators, from the rubber boats joined them. The HQ types, under their lieutenant, collected off to the right of the ramp—right, rather than starboard, since they were on solid ground now. The mortar section staggered to the left under the weight of their guns and a frightful amount of ammunition.

As soon as the foot soldiers were out of the way, the Elands launched themselves forward, wheels initially spinning on the wet deck until friction had evaporated the seawater. Momentum, once gained, carried them bouncing over the lip of the well deck and onto the ramp. Momentum, gravity, and diesel saw them to the sand and rocks. At the shore they split up, one left, one right, inching forward while the turrets slowly traversed. Inside, the gunners' eyes stayed glued to their sights, peering into the greenish images, looking for armed strangers with hostile intent.

Two unarmed strangers with their hands up approached the headquarters cautiously.

"You're Labaan?" Blackmore asked.

"Yes," the African answered in accented but very clear English. "Cagle told me you would be Lieutenant Blackmore."

"I am. What's with the group of women and children? I understood we were to evacuate only a few, but our aviation people tell me there's a substantial number."

"The families of the few loyal men leaving with us," Labaan said. "Did Cagle misunderstand?" he asked ingenuously.

"I don't know . . . wait a minute." Blackmore made a gesture to his RTO, who passed over the handset.

"Captain Warrington, Blackmore. We've got a much larger number of civvies than I was led to believe. What do you want me to do about them?"

"Taking them is a condition of getting the medicine you need," Labaan interrupted. "The medicines don't go unless my chief goes. My chief won't go without his wife and children. And his wife, the saucy bitch, won't leave without the others."

"I think we have to take them," Simon added, into the radio. He asked Labaan, "How many?"

"About a hundred and twenty."

"Wait, over."

MV *Richard Bland*, Coast of Africa city of Bajuni, Africa

Cagle shrugged. "He didn't say a word about any others."

"Trying to pull a fast one?" Warrington asked.

Shaking his head, Cagle answered, "Probably not; he's not really the type, unless it's his job to be sneaky. On the other hand, maybe it was his job. Even so, probably miscommunication." *But I'm going to have a few choice words with the fucker, anyway.*

"We can fit them," said the captain. "And there's plenty of food."

"There'll be some dietary laws issues, I suppose," said Cagle. "But we can figure something out on that."

"I could care less about all that shit," Warrington said. "A lot more important and immediate is that we were supposed to get in, grab the meds and the few passengers we were expecting, and get out. One lift. This will take . . . what?" he asked Pearson.

"The LCMs can handle eighty combat equipped troops. So one lift for all the extra passengers. Range is theoretically a hundred and thirty miles. Realistically, about two-thirds of that. Still, it's only adding ten or twelve miles, so there's plenty of fuel."

Warrington grimaced. "How do we unload them in the dark? We lost one of our own and he was *trained* for this shit."

"We can rig up a cargo net around a pallet and use a crane as an elevator. That's too slow for equipped troops, at maybe a dozen men per lift, but we can probably stuff forty or fifty women and kids in one lift. Add maybe twenty to thirty minutes to the problem."

"Right." Warrington picked up the handset. He thought, "Order-counterorder-disorder." How do I reduce the disorder?

"Simon, go ahead and shunt the civvies into the LCM– all of them, at one time, and I don't care if they have to breathe by the numbers. Your operational cycle is put in abeyance for the duration of one boatload of civvies. Everything else goes as planned, except establish a defensive perimeter, just in case."

"Already doing that, sir."

Unseen in the far distance, Warrington smiled. *Stout lad.*

"I think we ought to launch the RPV," Pearson said. "This crap is starting to get out of hand."

"No, Skipper," Warrington said. "I've got two of everything else, and three of the Elands, one more than I need, so I don't mind risking the loss of one. But I've only got the one RPV, so I can't risk it."

"Your call," Pearson conceded.

Bajuni, former Federation of Sharia Courts, Africa

Simon's mind raced to formulate a plan to suit the change.

"We'll take your people," he told Labaan. "Get them down here, quickly."

Labaan spoke a few words in the local language. His assistant went running off farther inland.

"Just out of curiosity," Simon asked, "how did that relief ship that provided the medicine get here?"

Labaan smiled. "We captured it on the sea, to . . . ummm . . . keep it from the hands of our enemies."

"What about the crew?"

"They were to be sold as slaves, without my chief's knowledge. Right now they're locked up below decks."

"Slaves?" Simon sounded incredulous. Labaan, after all, seemed a civilized and even cultured man.

"Sure," the latter answered. "Why not? They're the people who've done more to ruin this continent than anyone up to and including the European imperialists. Seems only fair."

"Oh," Simon said, shaking his head, "you and Captain Stocker are just going to *love* each other. How many are there?"

"Fifty-two."

"Guards?"

"Just three, at any one time," Labaan said. "But they're ours. Well . . . probably ours"—Labaan out a hand out and wagged it—"loyalties have gotten pretty fuzzy of late.

"But you don't really *want* those people back, do you? I mean, I've met a lot of western do-gooders but these ones were so stupid they didn't or couldn't even realize just how bad things had gotten here. Or just who we might blame for that."

"Oh. Oh, shit." He took up the handset once again. "Warrington; Blackmore. We have a chance to rescue the aid workers, if you're interested."

MV *Richard Bland*, Coast of Africa city of Bajuni, Africa

"Fuck 'em," said Stocker, standing on the bridge next to the main radio. "Useless tranzi assholes, eh? Let 'em be sold; they brought us to this."

Cagle rolled his eyes. "No, they didn't. Oh, sure, they had a part in it. Weigh that part against the financial idiots who dropped the world into a depression.

"Besides, they're our people," he said. "Maybe misguided, maybe ignorant, maybe even stupid, but still ours."

"Not *my* people," Stocker insisted.

Warrington waved one hand for silence. "Suppose we do?" he asked Pearson.

The skipper shrugged. "Food, billeting and LCM fuel are the same; no real problem. And maybe we could stuff them on the same lift as we're going to use for the other civvies. But we couldn't let them go until well after our mission was complete. They really wouldn't like that. And any good will you're thinking the regiment might acquire from saving them—assuming the regiment survives the current contretemps with Venezuela, a highly questionable proposition—is likely to be lost when they aren't allowed to go when and where they want to. These people are, by definition, willfully *stupid*."

Stocker relented ever so slightly. "Well, we could have a couple of them walk the plank, then send video tapes and demand ransoms for the rest."

Warrington shot him a dirty look.

"I wasn't entirely serious. Not *entirely*."

"Hmmm . . . you weren't entirely joking, either. In any case, no, we won't do it for the ransoms. And not for any questionable goodwill. But, you know, soldiers—romantically self-pitying bastards that we are—*live* for the chance to do good, for the glory of the thing. We'll save them, but only because of the good it will do the morale of this detachment."

"They can do more good than that," Cagle said. "That's not just a freighter. I know the organization it came from. I'd be very surprised if it doesn't contain four to a half a dozen pretty damned well-qualified doctors and a dozen experienced nurses. And if they're political idiots, it doesn't mean they're medical idiots.

"Another thing is . . . well . . . I don't know how much you know about sub-Saharan Africa. It's a mess, always has been. And there's a tendency there to irrationally blame perfectly innocent people for their problems, particularly if they're frustrated and can't get at whoever is really to blame. I see bad things happening to those aid workers, precisely because we'll have frustrated the people coming for Adam and his crew."

"Hadn't really thought about those," Warrington admitted. "Be nice to have adequate medical staff if you and TIC Chick can't handle the load. And, yeah, I can see a pretty ugly massacre if we leave the humanitarians behind."

He keyed the mike. "Simon, you are authorized to attempt a rescue of the aid workers, but only if you can do so while maintaining the integrity of your defensive perimeter, and only if it isn't going to cost us anyone, or certainly not more than a man or two. Send back the meds, the gold, and the aid pukes with the second lift out. Extraction of your people will be third."

"Roger. Wilco."

Turning to Stocker, Warrington said, "I'm really taking some risk here. The solution to most risks is greater force. So I want you to start getting the rest of your company, and the last team of mine, ready to go in and relieve young Blackmore if things go to shit.

"And, Skipper," he added to Pearson, "if we do have to send in the rest of the force, your boys will have to man the machine guns along the gunwales on their own."

"We can do that. For that matter, I can put the cooks on them."

★ CHAPTER EIGHTEEN ★

"We're not something wriggling with too many legs
that you found in your sleeping bag. The proper tone
of voice is *Mercenaries*!—with a glad cry."
—Miles Vorkosigan, in *Borders of Infinity*,
by Lois McMaster Bujold

Bajuni, former Federation of Sharia Courts, Africa

*Hmmm . . . who actually knows how to do a hostage
rescue, which, sortakinda, this is. Aha . . .*

"Sergeant Major Pierantoni!" Simon shouted out, over
the pounding of the surf. His heart was pounding, too, but
more from excitement than fear.

"Here, sir." The return call came from farther inland.
Pierantoni and the rest of the Second Battalion men were
better equipped than the regular grunts, each man having
a personal radio and a boom mike that curved around his
face to just a couple of inches from his lips. But if the
lieutenant hadn't used it, why should Pierantoni make an
issue of it? Besides, you could follow a voice to a person a
lot easier than you could follow a radio signal.

"I need you and one team for another mission."

"Be right there, sir."

"Labaan, I'll want you to go with the Sergeant Major when he gets here."

The old man nodded, then unslung his Kalashnikov and partially unseated the bolt, then felt through the ejection port to ensure he had a round in the chamber.

Simon still couldn't see crap without his NVG's. No matter; voice worked even in the dark. "Sergeant Moore?"

"Sir!"

"Get one of the Elands ready to go with the Sergeant Major. And start leading the civilians to the LCM."

"Sir!"

"Porter squad?"

"Sir!"

Simon went quiet for a moment. *My God,* he thought, in a moment's confusion, *I just realized that this is the first time I've felt at home since joining M Day, Incorporated. Maybe because it's the first time I've really had a chance to do an officer's work—not just bloody be-damned paperwork—with good troops.*

"Sir?"

"What?" The lieutenant shook his head. "Oh, sorry, Sergeant. I just had a blinding flash of the obvious. Never mind. Report to Sergeant Moore and help him get a makeshift airstrip cleared for the fixed wings."

"Yes, sir."

Who would have thought it?

Under cover of a shack, under the red beam from

Pierantoni's flashlight, Labaan traced out a sand sketch of the area around the humanitarian ship.

Pointing, he said, "The guards are one on the gangway, one walking around on top of the superstructure, and one on the door to where we locked up the aid workers. They're probably not going to be a problem though. Just let me go first; they're used to taking orders from me, even if I'm from the wrong tribe. What's *going* to be a problem is if we don't get there quickly, before one of the other fragments of the old clan arrive."

Pierantoni puffed out his cheeks, blowing air through clenched lips. Every passing minute the firing came just that little bit closer. *This is* not *my idea of planning for a hostage rescue: "Hey, let's just go do it." But the old man is fundamentally right. What's easy now will become a lot harder—maybe impossible—if we don't move quick.*

"Is there a ladder from the pier down to the water?" he asked.

"There are," Labaan answered, pointing to a spot on the dirt sketch he'd made. "Here . . . and another one about *here*."

Pierantoni nodded. "Good, because I *really* don't like the idea of trying to herd a gaggle of empty headed NGO pukes through what passes for streets in this place."

"You want to take them out by water?" Labaan asked.

"We've got the four rubber boats most of my people came in on. Pull 'em up to the ladders, fill 'em with tranzis, then take them here and dump them off. After that, they're the lieutenant's problems."

"If you're going to get them out by boat," Labaan observed, "then you had best leave the armored car here.

Those things are all over Africa, and I've never yet seen one swim."

"Some of them can," Pierantoni said, "but we never bought the modification kits for ours. We should have. And you're right. Mostly."

At Labaan's quizzical look, Pierantoni said, "We'll need all four boats for that many passengers. I'll want to put six men in the boats, four to steer, one in charge, and one with no other purpose than manning a machine gun and watching out. That leaves eight of us, me, you, and the other half of the team, to get there, get the tranzis freed, and get them organized—cat herding—and loaded. I'll have the Eland—that's the name of the armored car— follow us, escort us, about halfway there. Then it can go back and take up a position to cover the withdrawal of the rubber boats."

Labaan pointed again to a narrow peninsula on the sketch. "Here. From here they can see all the way across the water to the ship, and also cover a fair piece of the dock, itself."

"Works," Pierantoni agreed. Obviously the old man had been around a bit.

Though the regiment had some odds and ends pieces of equipment in the inventory, the standard general purpose machine gun was the Russian Pecheneg. This was a mix of, mostly, the older PKM, upgraded with a finned barrel to increase cooling, and with a shroud derived from the American-designed, mostly British-built, Lewis Gun. The PKM was a good piece, in most respects, but had the worst barrel changing mechanism in machine gun history, a sliding bar with a half-moon indent that often had to be hammered out of position to release the barrel. This could be both difficult and painful if the barrel were hot, which was about the only reason to change barrels anyway.

That's where the shroud and the fins on the barrel came in. Muzzle blast drew air up it through oval slots cut out of the shroud's rear. This passed over the fins, keeping the gun cool enough that, in normal practice, barrel changes weren't required. It *had* been fired, for testing, in continuous bursts of up to six-hundred rounds without jamming, overheating or damaging the barrel. It was probably the only non-water cooled machine gun in the world, in general issue, firing a full powered cartridge, of which this could be said.

Sergeant Alex Hallinan, cradling a Pecheneg in his arms, with the sling wrapped around his left hand, sat roughly amidships in the second Zodiac in the four boat column. He, like the other five men in the boats, had a set of NVG's perched on his face.

Feeney, of soup-vat fame, guided the boat, his right hand gripping the "throttle" on its electric outboard. He had the power dialed down, keeping his place and his spacing from the lead boat. It would take a while for the other half of the team to reach the NGO ship; no sense in beating them there.

About halfway to the waiting ship, the lead boat stopped in the water. Feeney likewise cut power, as did the two boats behind him.

The Eland escorted Pierantoni and the other seven about half way to the ship. Through the winding streets of the city, this worked out to about a third of a mile of travel. Progress was swift; they met no hostiles on the way, even if the sounds of skirmishing ahead said they were not all that far away.

"As a matter of fact," muttered Pierantoni, "it is suspiciously swift." He called a halt in place, the men automatically fanning out to the buildings on either side while the Eland scanned ahead with its superior night vision equipment.

Suddenly, completely without warning, the Eland's 90mm gun barked, raising a cloud of dust from the bare street and knocking paint chips off the crumbling ruins to either side. Though the gun was fairly soft in its recoil, the armored car rocked back on its suspension, even so. The sergeant major, and every other dismounted man within fifty meters, winced.

"What was it?" Pierantoni demanded via the radio.

"Knot o' armed men," replied the Eland's Guyano-Hindu commander. "Dey have at least one RPG"—rocket propelled grenade launcher—"and meh saw no reason to take de chance."

Them's the rules in a place without civilization, Pierantoni silently agreed. *What is not positively identified as friendly must be presumed hostile. Especially if armed.*

"You hit 'em?"

"We use de beehive on de short fuse. Dey're colanders."

"Anything else out there?" the sergeant major asked.

"Not'ing dat shows up on de t'ermal, Sarn't Major."

"Roger. Eland stay here and cover. Do *not* use canister while we're in your line of fire. The rest of us are moving up on foot two blocks. At that point we'll take a left. Once we're out of sight, Eland, beat feet back to the overwatch position I showed you. Shouldn't be anyone to fuck with you all the way back."

"Roger."

The moon was still a thin sliver of a crescent, lying low over the sea. It didn't give off enough light that any of the men in the rubber boats felt they had to worry. It *did* give off enough to make out the white painted hull of a ship. They still didn't know its name or, really, much care.

Hallinan flipped up his NVG's and crouched forward, settling his right eye into the eyepiece of the thermal scope mounted to his Pecheneg.

"Hallinan here. I can make out the guy walking post up on the superstructure," he whispered into the small boom mike. "Just him, though. He definitely notices the gunships circling, but doesn't seem to want to make that one overtly hostile act."

Feeney added, "The Eland just pulled up on the shore a few hundred meters behind us."

"And meh sees you, too," said the Eland commander, on the same radio push.

Labaan stood at the pier, at the base of the gangway— or "brow," as the Navy would call it—looking up at the silhouette of a very nervous-seeming guard.

Inwardly, he sighed. *I suppose in this case honesty is not the best policy. Hmmm . . . lie through my teeth completely or just shade the truth a bit? I think . . . lie.*

"It's Labaan," he shouted up. "The American Marines

have landed. Adam, the chief, has been taken hostage, as has his family. They are willing to trade him for the people we're holding. You may not be able to see them, but there is a squad of them not far from me. If we do not surrender the hostages, they promise to kill everyone and everything."

"What should I do, Labaan?" the guard called back. "And what the fuck caused the Americans to take an interest in this place again?"

"To the last," Labaan replied, "I don't know. For the other, just place your rifle on the deck, put your hands over your head, and stand out of the way. They'll probably treat you a little roughly, but that's only for their security. They promise me you won't be harmed if you cooperate."

"Okay . . . okay, I'm putting my rifle down. Tell them not to shoot."

OKAY! thought Pierantoni, as two of his men forced the guard to the deck, flipped him over, and taped his hands behind his back. The other four, plus Labaan, were still scampering up the gangway. *That's one down. There's still someone on the superstructure. Rather not kill anybody we don't have to, but*—

Crack! The first bullet ricocheted, whining, off the deck an imperceptible fraction of a millisecond before the muzzle's report reached Pierantoni's ears. This was followed by a long, wildly unaimed, burst of fire that hit nobody but caused several of them to nearly shit themselves.

The sergeant major and the two with him scurried or rolled into whatever protection there was, flush against the bulkhead. The other five became involved in a temporary traffic jam—arms caught in legs caught in rifle slings caught around necks—as they tried just that little bit too hard to get out of the line of fire.

"Shit!" said Pierantoni.

Pierantoni heard in his earpiece Hallinan's voice. "I hear firing. I've got no, repeat *no*, line of sight."

"Ah, but meh do," announced the Guyanan in the Eland. There was a double report, first from the cannon across the water and then, louder, because closer, from the shell as it exploded just above the superstructure. A body—or enough pieces to make up a body; a 90mm was *not* a contemptible shell—flew off the superstructure, silent and dead. It passed, in loose formation, by the three men cowering on deck and the tangled five on the gangway before splashing to the dirty water below.

"Like meh say before; he a colander."

Pierantoni posted two men as guards on the deck. Then he, Labaan, and the four remaining passed through a hatchway. The passages inside were lit only by dim red emergency lights, apparently running off the batteries. Pierantoni asked about those. "The batteries should be dead by now. What's it been? A month?"

"We run the auxiliary generators every few days to keep the batteries up and the medicines cooled," Labaan answered. "The fuel's too valuable to waste much of it, though, even at current prices. When you've got nothing, fifty cents a gallon is quite a bit."

"Yeah, I suppose. Lead on."

Labaan unslung his rifle from his shoulder and took it in both hands. "The prisoners are down two flights and toward the stern," he said. "You won't want to be using a grenade down there. Even rifle fire would be pretty hard on the ears. So . . . give me a chance to talk the last guard out of his rifle."

"Sure," Pierantoni agreed, "you can try to save the guy. But if he so much as points the muzzle away from the deck, he's dead." *And if I had a forty-five with subsonic ammunition and a suppressor, I wouldn't bother. One of the little problems that pop up with ad hoc missions.*

"I understand," Labaan agreed. "And that's fair enough."

While a western-trained guard might have asked something like, "Who goes there, friend or foe?" the local just raised his rifle and shot. Fortunately, what with the light being all but nonexistent, coupled with the Inshallah School of Marksmanship, he missed Labaan. Labaan returned fire—wincing with pain at the drumming in his ears. He missed, too, but could at least blame it on the light. Pierantoni, on the other hand, didn't miss, despite having to fire around a corner, and with his off hand. Then again, he had a thermal sight on his rifle.

"Are you sure there were only the three?" the sergeant major asked Labaan.

"Very sure."

"All right. Let's get that hatch open."

Labaan was used to the hatch. He stood, walked to it, stepping gingerly over the leaking corpse on the deck, and spun the wheel. As soon as the bolts unseated with a loud *click,* he pulled the door open.

Pierantoni had reached him by that time so, with

Labaan, he was treated to the complete orchestra of screaming and the full aroma of unwashed bodies and human waste.

"You didn't let them go to the bathroom?" Pierantoni asked, a measure of disgust creeping into his voice.

"We gave them buckets," Labaan answered. "Good enough for us; good enough for them. It's just that the guards just didn't change them all that often."

"Jesus." Then, putting his head through the hatchway, Pierantoni announced, falsely, "U.S. Army. This is a rescue. Now shut the fuck up."

"You don't like these people any better than I do, do you?" Labaan asked.

The sergeant major thought about that for all of a quarter of a second. "No. If it came down to it, the dead guard had more value to me than they do. He still does, for that matter."

"But—"

"But the mission I was given wasn't to save the guard."

"Sarn't Major P?" Pierantoni heard in his earpiece, coming from one of the men left topside.

"Yeah, Rogers?"

"Have we still got priority on the gunships?" The voice sounded amazingly calm, even conversational.

"Yyeeaahh . . . why?"

Rogers suddenly sounded much less calm and conversational. "Because we've got about two or three hundred armed men starting to cross the parking lot between the ship and the town. I think just the two of us up here are at least a little outnumbered."

★ CHAPTER NINETEEN ★

Close air support covereth a multitude of sins.
—Howard Tayler, Maxim Four of *Schlock Mercenary*'s
The Seventy Maxims of Maximally
Effective Mercenaries

Bajuni, former Federation of Sharia Courts, Africa

Standing on the beach, Simon watched the LCM pull away with a full load of civilians, their few guards, the gold, and the required medicines. *Glad to get them out of my hair*, he thought, *even if they were generally pretty cooperative. Glad, too, we didn't need the airstrip. And it gives me an extra squad, now that I need one.*

Adam had, over his apparent wife's protests, elected to stay behind. "You might need some local insight," he'd told Simon. With a shrug, he added, "I might have it."

Blackmore had heard a couple, or maybe three, explosions off to his right, where he'd sent Pierantoni and one of the spec ops teams to collect up the tranzis. The gunships were still noisily beating the air overhead. And from off in the distance, if not so far off as they had been, came the sounds of anywhere from dozens to scores of minor firefights.

"That's mostly my cousins, fighting amongst themselves," Adam volunteered. "Can't be many of my own followers left."

"Fighting for *what*?" Simon asked.

"The gold. The ship. The aid workers. The medicines. The freaking food. To get rid of me and try to make a claim to right of succession. All those things . . . and because we really don't know much of anything else."

Ahead and to the right, out on the peninsula, an Eland's cannon boomed across water and sand. Another shot followed on that one within seconds.

Simon held up one hand for silence. Pierantoni— every word punctuated by firing—was shouting in his ear. The short version was, "I need the gunships. *Now!*"

Pierantoni and four men were up on deck now, trading shots with the locals. The incoming fire generally ricocheted off the steel of the ship and bounced upwards with an unnerving shriek.

The other two, plus Labaan, were helping guide the humanitarians up on deck. These emerged by staggering ones and twos from the hatchway behind the sergeant major.

"Get on your bellies and crawl to the other side!" Pierantoni shouted. At least one didn't get it, or didn't get it in time. A long machine gun burst from somewhere ashore pinned the former hostage to the bulkhead, dancing with the impacts. When it let off the dead man slid down the white painted wall, leaving a long, wide splotch of blood behind him. A woman, and at least two of the men, screamed.

"Labaan!"

"I'm here," answered the African, from the other side of the hatchway.

"No way we can get them down to the dock. Is there another way off the ship? An emergency ladder or something."

"Maybe. I'll go look."

One of the former hostages offered, "There are two on the other side. I can point them out."

"Do it. Zodiacs?"

"We're here," came the answer over the radio. "Don't think we can help you fight them off. No cover at all out here, of course."

"Don't want you to," Pierantoni said. "I want you to get in the lee of the ship from the fire and stand by."

"Wilco."

M Day had been given its MI-28's as a gift of sorts, or perhaps a payback, for rescuing the son-in-law of a fairly highly placed member of Russia's FSB, the successor to the "disbanded" KGB. Although there were newer helicopter gunships in the world, the MI-28 remained one of the better ones. It was not only all-weather and limited-visibility capable, and armed to the teeth, but, like its Hind predecessor, could carry either extra ammunition or a small number of passengers in a compartment.

Armaments varied. It could normally carry up to forty unguided rockets and another sixteen anti-tank guided missiles, along with two hundred and fifty rounds for its 30mm chin gun. In their current configuration, both gunships carried eight ATGMs, ten 122mm rockets with *Ugroza* guidance packages, and forty 80mm unguided rockets. They had the guidance packages available for those, but simply decided they wouldn't be needed. Besides, the guidance packages weren't cheap.

As they were upon receipt, the MI-28's remained crewed by Russians, with Russian ground crews still back aboard the *Bland*. Fortunately, over the space of five years, the Russians had learned to speak the regiment's language, English, rather well. They mostly kept their accents, however. Among themselves, naturally, they tended to converse still in Russian.

"*Starshina* Pierantoni; *Praporschik* Slepnyov. What you gots?"

"Starshina" wasn't actually equivalent to Pierantoni's rank, but was about as close as Russian military terminology could come.

The sergeant major could speak or at least get by in several languages: English, Spanish, Portuguese, Arabic, and Pashto. Of Russian, however—*I don't know enough Russian to negotiate a blowjob from a whore*. He stuck with English.

"I've got four rubber boats in the water and fifty-two . . . no, make that fifty-one, now, hostages. Plus eight of my own people on the ship. We can all fit the boats, which I'm bringing alongside on the friendly side. But those things are pretty slow. And loading's going to be slow. I need the bad guys held back for about twenty or thirty minutes, while we load, and then kept back another fifteen or so while we putt-putt across the water.

"They're mostly in the long parking lot, northwest of the ship, and the buildings north of the parking lot.

"There's going to be a space of time, when I pull my own people from the side of the ship to the boats, when nobody's returning fire. They'll sure as shit rush the ship then. And we can't get at the gangway to haul it in. Not even sure we should—as long as it's there it'll keep their attention and keep them from finding some other way to get at us."

"Okay," agreed Slepnyov. "Best way do this: Self and wing man go west, swing north, then east. Come along parallel to long parking lot. Fire off maybe six or eight smaller rockets, each. Cut in behind ship, turn around, and pop up over. Then fire chin gun, let know we still here. Drive away to west and north. Probably can't evict from buildings."

"Works for me. Do it."

"Roger." Slepnyov said that last without a trace of accent.

"This is it," said the hostage, breathing heavily with fear and stress. He pointed to a narrow hatch that seemed to lead into the superstructure. "There's another one farther forward."

He opened the hatch and began pulling out a flexible ladder. Almost immediately, two lights on the ladder began to blink. Labaan took hold of it and began to feed it over the side. "Go get the other one ready," he said.

★ ★ ★

Though there were still bullets cracking the air over-head, they were all *far* overhead. Even so, even though they were approximately as safe as in their mothers' arms, the people awaiting transport out—or, at least, some of them—wept or screamed whenever a particularly low-flying projectile passed over. When the two gunships began their run, several hundred meters away and closing, their fire lighting up the sky like God's own personal strobe light, they all screamed.

"Jesus, people," shouted the sergeant major, "will you all just shut the fuck up?" *Man, I can't stand whiners.*

Hallinan's boat, Feeney steering, followed the lead Zodiac to the nearer of the two ladders that had appeared, blinking in the gloom. The other two went forward to where another ladder, likewise blinking, had been lowered down the side. Feeney cut power and waited while the first boat filled. This took a while; people just released from durance vile usually lacked strength and coordination, both. Still, there were no mishaps as the first fifteen people made their way down, some of them crying, others still trembling with shock.

The chief of that boat put his hand up, catching one of the females on the ass. She huffed and began to curse.

"Shut up, honey," that sergeant said. "Now hold your place, like a good girl, until the next boat comes along."

Turning to the man on the motor, the sergeant said, "We're full up. Pull us back to the peninsula."

Without a word, the steersman applied power. The boat surged forward, then began a long, sweeping curve away from the ship. The sweep of the curb tightened considerably, once they were about thirty feet from the hull. Feeney, likewise applying a little juice, moved in to take the first boat's place. Once the blinking ladder was alongside, he reversed thrust to stop the forward motion, then cut power completely. Hallinan crawled to the ladder and grabbed hold with one hand. With the other he helped down the still muttering woman whose ass had been used as a stop signal.

"Go sit up by the bow," he told her. "*Don't* touch the machine gun."

"I wouldn't touch the obscenity if my life depended on it," she answered, with a verbal sneer.

"Good. See that you don't."

The next one was directed to the stern, where Feeney pushed him to the starboard side. "Sit. Shut up."

Overhead, one of the men kept up a long string of bitter complaints, ranging from the unnecessarily violent rescue to the failure to give the hostages' well being first priority, to the failure to secure the area so that they could leave like the heroic and noble ladies and gentlemen they were. When the MI-28's passed nearby, then rose to take a position over the Zodiac, he raised his voice to make sure everyone heard how badly abused he was, how worthy of sympathy, and how contemptuous of his rescuers.

"Stupid soldiers," said the aid worker, in a British, more specially a "received pronunciation" accent. "Bloody-handed murderers."

As if to punctuate, the MI-28 nearest to directly over-head let out a long burst with its chin gun. Spent casings rained down, mostly splashing in the water though one managed to land on the whiner's shoulder, eliciting an indignant, much aggrieved howl.

"Inconsiderate morons!"

Hallinan shook his head. *Is this guy incapable of drawing the logical inferences of his own claims? If he really believed we're as bad as all that, then insulting us is the* last *thing he ought to want to do.*

He directed the complainer to the portside space nearest to Feeney. *Which may be a mistake*, thought Hallinan. *Or maybe it isn't.*

"Slepnyov? Pierantoni."

"Here, *Starshina*."

"To my profoundly mixed feelings, we've got the last of the civvies out. I need you to cover our withdrawal. We'll need about eight minutes to load the last boat."

"Wilco," Slepnyov answered. "We do other swing by but from opposite direction, east to west. We expend last of on-board ammunition, so if you get in trouble after that, you on own until we rearm at ship."

"Works."

Hallinan winced at the words of the tranzi seated next to Feeney: "I *demand* that you take us to the British embassy."

"You 'demand' it, do you?" asked Feeney, conversationally.

"Yes, I—"

Uh, oh. Wrong choice of words.

Sergeant Feeney leaned over the tiller of his outboard, placing his right hand flat on the Brit's chest. One push and the man was over the side, struggling in the water. "Swim to the embassy, bitch," the sergeant said.

"Wait," the splashing ex-hostage sputtered. "Wait! Help me."

"Fuck you," muttered Feeney, who made no move to bring the boat around, nor even to face around. He didn't, therefore, see that the Brit was swimming after the boat. "I fucking hate limeys, anyway."

That latter comment wasn't precisely true. Feeney liked British soldiers very well indeed. What he hated were British civilians. But then, he hated *all* civilians.

"You'll all be up on charges," said the woman who'd earlier objecting to having her ass used as a brake. "Now I insist you go back and recover Dr. Saffron."

"Ummm . . . no," said Hallinan. "I don't know what the sergeant major told you people, but we're not going to be on anyone's charge sheet. You see, you are all the guests of M Day, Incorporated."

There was a collective gasp of horror from the civilians aboard.

"That's right," continued Hallinan, affably enough, even cheerily, "mercenaries. 'The frightful ones.' Lawless. Uncontrolled. Not answerable to the community of the very, very caring and sensitive. And we don't really give a shit about or for any of you. Now shut the fuck up before Sergeant Feeney decides that more of you need swimming lessons."

And let's hope that keeps them quiet before another one pisses Feeney off. I swear he's starting to worry me.

"Start loading," Pierantoni shouted to the men with him. "I'll be along."

While the MI-28's danced a tango overhead, lashing

out at the parking lot and the buildings beyond, crumpling and setting alight buildings and automobiles, Sergeant Major Pierantoni spent a few minutes ensuring that, even if there were a pursuit, it would run into a snag.

From a pouch on his load-bearing equipment he took a single fragmentation grenade. From another he lifted a small spool of wire. *Never know when wire's going to come in handy.* He flicked the safety clip off and laid the grenade on the deck, after which he unwound a short length of wire.

Be better if I still had the cardboard cylinder this came in, he mused, as he tied a loop of wire around the metal spoon of the grenade. *But, needs must . . .*

The running end of the wire he bent and twisted, spinning the twist until the wire broke. That end he tied off to a stanchion inside the gunwale. He then took the recently broken end and tied it to the thin neck of the grenade just under the spoon. Stretching the wire across the lip of the gangway, he tied it off to another small stanchion. Only then did he remove the ring and pin from the grenade.

The moon was up enough now to allow a cursory visual inspection of his little trap. Satisfied, he felt a moment's amusement at sundry treaties purporting to ban landmines, the framers of which treaties never seemed to realize that there were such things as field expedients.

"Ought to give 'em a moment's pause, anyway," he muttered as, still crouching, he began the short shuffle around to the other side, the ladder, and safety.

★ CHAPTER TWENTY ★

[Contrast] the behavior of the men on the *Titanic*
who . . . went down with the ship and those of the
École Polytechnique in Montreal decades later who,
ordered to leave the classroom by a lone gunman,
meekly did as they were told and stood passively in the
corridor as he shot all the women. Even if I'm wetting
my panties, it's better to have the social norm of the
Titanic and fail to live up to it than to have the social
norm of the Polytechnique and sink with it.
—Mark Steyn

Bajuni, former Federation of Sharia Courts, Africa

The first contact by anyone on Blackmore's thin perimeter
was over on the left, and just slightly north of the western
shoulder of the peninsula that defined the beginnings of
the Old Port. Sergeant Moore had posted a single
machine gun team there, three men with a Pecheneg,
covering the major avenue of approach, the street. They'd
taken up position under a car sitting above the crumbling

pavement, with several concrete blocks under each wheelless rim. When a dozen or so locals had come scampering up the street, quite possibly mindlessly fleeing the mayhem being inflicted on their brethren by the two gunships, the gunner had opened up with a fifteen-second burst, making the underside of the car flash like a strobe, expending that entire belt of ammunition, and leading five or six of the hostiles in a nice rendition of the Spandau Ballet. The others dove to the sides of the street, taking what cover they could, and returning a none-too-accurate fire.

Nice t'ing about de Pecheneg, thought the gunner, as his assistant helped feed in another belt. *You can fire off de whole belt wit'out overheatin' de bitch.*

The team's diminutive Anglo-Nepali squad leader was crouched behind the car in seconds. Odd bullets impacted on the frame and body, but many more of them hit the street or passed harmless overhead. "What'a' you got?"

The gunner reported, adding, "De fire's comin' fum de six o' eight I didn't get."

"Right," said the Gurkha, wincing from the passage of an altogether too close miss. It was a tracer and its passage left a dark line burned into the sergeant's retina. "Wriggle back out of there. I'll show you an alternate position."

"Wilco, Sergean'."

That was the first contact, outside of the aid ship. Within twenty minutes, almost every one of the men was engaged, this even after tossing in the extra squad that had done for porter and crowd control duty, and the special ops team that hadn't accompanied Pierantoni. The mortar section had chunked out enough rounds that they were already reporting, "Low on HE." The CH-750's quickly expended their very limited on-board ammunition and punched out, heading for the ship to be rearmed.

One Eland was in front of Blackmore, facing and firing west up the main coastal avenue. The other was maybe one hundred and fifty meters to the east, likewise engaging up the main drag to the east-northeast. The enemy wasn't showing himself enough, generally speaking, to justify using the cannon. Mostly the Elands supported with their machine guns, for which they carried, oh, a *lot* more ammunition than any ground-pounding machine gun team could hope to.

It was mostly exchange of fire, with few being hit on either side, and no one seeming particularly keen on getting to knife fighting range. The few friendly casualties were carried back, mostly in fireman's carries, to an ad hoc aid station set up right in front of the LCM landing point.

Simon knelt in the moon's shadow, beside a mud brick shack, maybe sixty or seventy meters from the spot of beach where the LCM had deposited him. His RTO crouched beside him. Adam sat with his back to the wall.

At the sound of booted feet, crunching on gravel, pounding hard toward him, Simon *almost* fired.

He hoped he got his muzzle down before Sergeant Major Pierantoni noticed.

"Glad you think before shooting," said the sergeant major. "Sir."

Damn; he noticed.

Without waiting to be asked, the sergeant major said,

"I've got the ex-hostages down by the landing point. Hallinan and Feeney are guarding. I needed to leave Hallinan because, frankly, sir, while Feeney needs some psychiatric help, Hallinan can usually talk sense to him. Most of the tranzis are snubbing us but a couple have kicked in to help with the wounded. The rest of mine are dragging the boats to the east side of the spit."

"Your other team is on line to the east," Simon said. "You can find them by the sound of the Eland. So far, they're doing fine. No casualties, last they reported."

"Who *are* these guys?" Pierantoni asked rhetorically.

Unexpectedly, Adam answered. "To the east is probably my cousin Nadif's band. Just rifles and machine guns, and a few RPG's. Northeast and north is my cousin Asad. He's got everything except tanks and aircraft. Well . . . he *has* tanks, two of them, but they don't run. Northwest is my uncle, Korfa. His faction's small, but relatively well trained. At least Labaan—"

"Here, Adam."

"—Labaan says they are. Me, I don't know enough to say. And west is either my cousin, Abdikarim, or my cousin, Taban. Or both."

"Both, I think," added Labaan. "I saw too many bodies and parts of bodies for it just to have been one faction."

"Think they're cooperating?" asked Adam.

"Anything's possible, for a rich enough prize or a bad enough threat," said the older man. "Possible for a *while* anyway."

At that moment, the Eland to the front fired its cannon. Dust flew out from the cracks of the adobe shack. A fraction of a second later there was a much smaller boom, farther west. Then there came the sound of a muted massacre, screaming, coughing—from blood-filling lungs—and sobbing, as flechettes apparently butchered some knot or other of some cousin or other's band.

"I used to think," said Labaan, softly and sadly, "that nations in Africa were a mistake, that we should have organized on blood, clan and tribe. Now that I see blood ties breaking down, I don't know what to think."

While I understand your feelings, old man, thought Pierantoni, *who gives a shit right now?*

He didn't say anything to that effect though. *What the hell; under similar circumstances I might be a little melancholy too.* Instead, the sergeant major asked, "Whatcha gonna do, PL?"

No way a Brit's going to get that joke. "When Murphy shows up and shit goes to hell, whatcha gonna do PL?"

MV *Richard Bland*, Coast of Africa, city of Bajuni, Africa

The crane was *still* hauling up loads of displaced locals. Oh, they were cooperating, as well as they could. It was just slow. And Warrington didn't want them trying to scamper up the nets.

On one wall of the red-lit bridge, a headset-wearing trooper had scrubbed away the previous operations matrix—which made damned little sense anymore—and plugged in new, additional tasks, numbers, and timelines. All of those were at least somewhat iffy.

Stocker snarled. He was none too happy about having his XO and some of his troops out on the bleeding edge and himself left behind, anyway. "The problem is the damned tranzis. We should just leave them behind, use the cover of the aircraft to help our people get out, and then *get out*."

"You ever take in a stray dog, Andrew?" asked Warrington.

"Well . . . yeah. So what, eh?"

"You can leave a stray dog out on the street, no guilt involved. But once you take it in, even for a single meal, that dog becomes *your* responsibility. If you're a decent human being, it does, anyway. You can't just kick it out again."

"These aren't dogs," said the Canadian. "Dogs are loyal. Dogs are Plato's good citizens. Dogs didn't bring the world to the state it's in."

"Neither did these people," Warrington answered. "And certainly not intentionally. Ignorance . . . well . . . ignorance is just part of the natural state of man.

"No matter. I'm in charge and I say we're not leaving anyone behind. Not them. Not ours.

"But the problem remains. We can't get them and us out on the same lift. We knew that when we started. What we didn't know, not for sure was—"

The loudspeaker's mounted on the walls crackled with Simon's distorted voice, superimposed over the rattling of rifles and machine guns. "Where the fuck are my gunships? I need them ten minutes ago."

"The first one just took off," Warrington answered into the mike. "The other's going to be a while."

"Roger."

"What we didn't count on," Warrington continued,

"was the landing party getting decisively engaged. So we're going to have to break contact to get them out. Hardest thing in the world, you know. Not just withdrawal while in contact, which is very damned hard. *Amphibious* withdrawal while in contact. For that, we need to attack to get some breathing space.

"Assemble your remaining two platoons, minus, by the nets. When the locals are done offloading, even before they're done, if you can, load your boys up. Head in to one flank or the other—best we confer with Simon as to which one—and attack. Sweep them from the flank and drive them back. Once that's done, get the Elands loaded and as many troops as will fit. If we need to, we'll land the CH-750's on the ad hoc strip. Likewise, the gunships will return, rearm, and make a single pass, expending their next load of ammunition, then land to pick up six or eight. If it takes longer we'll have them rearm twice."

"You're making the problem worse, though," Stocker said. He didn't push the idea too vigorously, since he *really* wanted to get ashore and get stuck in. "We can't lift out the original load and fifty-odd tranzis in one lift; how do we get out another eighty people over and above the initial load?"

The loudspeakers crackled again. "Direct the second gunship to the mortars!" Boom. "I'm taking serious fucking mortar fire!" Boom. Boom. Boom. BOOM! "Jesus Christ, get those fucking mortars!"

"I never knew he swore," said Stocker, wonderingly. "I'll get my boys by the gunwales. Somebody here can figure out how to make the horse sing."

"The sergeant major's down! I've got wounded!"

Cagle added, "I think I'll be coming along, too. Give me five minutes to grab an aid bag and a couple more of supplies."

Warrington considered that. *Sure, nothing he can do here that TIC Chick, can't. And, speaking of which,* "Skipper, you can handle air-sea-ground ops as well as I can, as long as we're not talking about fixed bayonet levels of operations. Maybe even better. I think I'd better be going, too."

Pearson nodded, then held up one hand. "Ummm . . . we've never used them, but we have a load of Russki PFM-1 mines. Four or five men can carry about two thousand of them and arm and drop them behind as you clear the perimeter. That would buy a little more time. Help?"

"Four or five tow poppers per meter?" mused Warrington. "Might."

Bajuni, former Federation of Sharia Courts, Africa

"Jesus Christ, get those fucking mortars!" Simon shouted into his mike from under a pile of mud brick, blown on top of him when a largish mortar shell—his guess was a 120mm—landed inside the roofless shack next to which he'd set up his little command post.

Someone—Adam, Simon thought—was screaming, "My back! Allah . . . my back." Through the insulating layer of the mud bricks on his own back, the sound was distant. More worrisome was that it was only the one man screaming.

Coughing in the fumes from the shell filler and the dust from pulverized mud brick, Simon forced his own back up through the shards and looked around. Labaan was tending to Adam, who had gone from screaming to moaning. The old man seemed fairly hale, as much as one could tell by limited moonlight, anyway. Pierantoni was breathing, but otherwise still. His RTO was . . .

Shit; his fucking head is gone.

He still had hold of the mike. Lifting it to his lips he sent, "The sergeant major's down! I've got wounded!"

Simon shouted, "Medddiccc!" Then, inanely apologizing to the headless corpse—"I'm sorry, Private, I'm so very sorry."—Simon rolled it over and eased the radio pack straps out from the dead boy's arms. With a couple of low grunts he tugged the radio on over his own shoulders. His bulky armor made it a tight fit.

"Sergeant Moore, report."

The platoon leader sent back, "I just left second squad and the porter squad, way over on the left, and they're holding fine. I'm with third, in the center. They took a couple of casualties to the mortars, one dead, one wounded—"

"We will *not* leave our dead behind," said Blackmore.

"No, sir, we won't," agreed Moore. "The KIA's the squad leader, so I'm sticking here. From where I am, I can hear first's firing and they sound like they're holding on handily. I can't tell about the SF team on the extreme right."

"Roger, break," *Hmmm . . . what was that sergeant's name? Damn if I can remember. No matter, everybody's got a number.* "SF Team Three, report."

"They're out there in front of us; but they're kind of leaving us alone, EllTee," sent the American back. "We had some contact a bit ago, but they broke and ran. I think maybe they were spooked by our night vision capability. They don't seem to have any."

"Seems likely," Blackmore agreed. "That, or they just ran out of batteries for whatever they did have. Keep me posted."

"Wilco, EllTee. I sent my medic back to find you."

Simon shook his head. *Of all the wretched horrors the Americans have inflicted on God's language, English, there is nothing more vile than "EllTee."*

Someone took a knee next to Simon. "Sergeant Rogers," the man said. "You need a medic, sir?"

"Yes, Sergeant, that and litter bearers. Your sergeant major needs help, too."

"On it, sir."

"Very good. Sergeant Balbahadur!"

"Sir!" answered the Gurkha, from thirty or so meters off.

"Give us 'The Black Bear,' and make it loud!"

"Sir! And maybe a little 'Scots Wha Hae' after that?"

"Excellent choice."

Again the radio crackled. "Simon, Warrington. We're all a'comin' to the party. We're going to attack around the perimeter to get a little breathing space. Which flank do we go in on?"

"Right flank, sir," Blackmore replied, without hesitation. "I'll have your third team guide you in."

Behind Simon, a fearsome MI-28 cut its way through the air, the downdraft pushing out the waters beneath in an expanding circle. It hesitated a moment there, at the shoreline, then began a slow upward spiral. When it had reached a height of perhaps seven hundred feet the mortars fired again from inside the city.

"I haf ze bastards," announced Slepnyov, over the general push. "Urrah!"

★ CHAPTER TWENTY-ONE ★

Invincibility lies in the defense;
the possibility of victory in the attack.
—Sun Tzu

East of Bajuni, former Federation of Sharia Courts, Africa

Well ahead of the coxswain, half sheltering behind the ramp, Warrington and Stocker took alternate turns trying to peer to the shore and ducking spray. Wet and miserable or not, the position had two distinct advantages. Secondly, from that position they could, if just barely, make out the sound of Balbahadur's pipes, cutting through the sounds of firing, blasting, engines, and surf. Firstly, and rather more importantly, it was upwind of the puke on the deck.

Though if this son of a bitch bounces up and down anymore, thought Warrington, *I'm going to be adding some, right here.*

Warrington lowered himself from his perch and told Stocker, "Your turn. Take a look."

The whole point of the exercise—besides that we needed the meds, of course—was to bring the two units together.

Warrington inwardly grimaced, *Not that I ever thought or intended that the exercise would become quite so serious. Perhaps Emperor Mong was whispering in my ear as I slept.*

"Amphib's not really my thing," Warrington shouted, once a dripping Stocker ducked down behind the ramp. The Canuck wiped salt spray from his face, then shook his head like a wet dog's.

"Do we land inside our perimeter and fight out, then start the sweep, or save a few seconds by landing outside the perimeter and going directly over the shore?"

"No question," Stocker answered. "Cazz says there's nothing harder or more dangerous than a landing on a defended shore. 'The historical lesson is: If you don't have to—DON'T! It might work great; but if there's even one machine gun there we'll be fucked in the ass, no grease, and not even kissed afterwards, eh?"

"So land inside the perimeter?"

"I think I said that."

"Yeah, maybe, kinda, sorta. Besides, Team Three is supposed to be marking it for us, and they're not likely to go outside the perimeter. Go back to the rear and direct the coxswain."

"You mean 'go back aft'? Roger."

Rising and falling with the waves, spray spurting over above the bow to fall and soak the men within, the landing craft neared shore. Kirkpatrick, at the wheel, was pretty sure he could make out the lines of battle from the muzzle flashes and the occasional ricocheting tracer rising above the low buildings of the burg.

But nothing much over to the right, the boat chief thought. He noticed a man climbing the ladder to the helm. At first he thought he recognized Warrington, from his height and build. After a few moments, he decided it was the line dog commander, Stocker.

"Which way, Skipper?" Kirkpatrick asked, lifting his NVG's, one-handed, as Stocker mounted the quarterdeck. The coxswain had to shout; this far back the engines were sheer murder on the ears.

There wasn't any line of firing to guide them. Stocker flipped his still dripping NVG's over his eyes. *There! There's Team Three's signal. Dipshits must be using IR chemlights. Nobody told them to but . . . ah, well, you've gotta expect a certain amount of confusion. And, better still, the company piper is standing by the lights.*

"Bear a little to port," the Canadian ordered. "Little more . . . little starboard. Hold this heading."

"Aye, Skipper. I see the marker now."

The landing craft lurched to a sudden stop. Almost all the men in the well deck were thrown from their feet. Stocker was slammed forward; only the steel rail between the quarterdeck and the well deck kept him from being tossed in and quite possibly breaking his neck.

"Sandbar!" Kirkpatrick shouted. "Doubt I can get past it."

"Never . . . mind . . . drop . . . the . . . ramp," Stocker gasped. Being slammed into the railing had knocked some of the wind from the man.

"Aye." The LCM bounced slightly upward in a sort of

recoil caused by the sudden dropping of the heavy steel ramp, forward.

"GetoffgetoffgetoffgetthefuckOFF!" Warrington shouted, walking aft, picking up and pushing men toward the bow. Instead of being thrown to the deck, he'd been mashed into the ramp. At least that left him still standing, if somewhat bruised. By the time he'd gotten maybe a third of the way back through the well deck, the others had risen to their feet. At that point his major task became not being run over by the human stampede. He avoided it by joining it.

Stocker, breath mostly recovered now, stepped off the ramp and found himself in calf-deep salt water. He'd expected it from the cries of "shit" and "damn" he'd heard coming from those who preceded him.

Not so bad. Another step and the water had risen to his chest. *Crap.*

He flipped his NVG's back down, then did a long one hundred and eighty degree sweep. All around and ahead, armed men were pushing their way through the water, weapons raised high over the heads. In the case of the four RPG-29 crews, holding the weapons and ammunition above head was no mean feat.

"Turn the fuck around, Private Khan; you are walking out to sea. Follow the sound of the pipes."

Came back across the water, "Yes, sir. Sorry, sir."

"A little more to your left, Khan."

"Yes, sir. Thank you, sir."

Funny how the Indian Guyanans speak better English than the whites or the blacks. Course, Khan's one of the

Afghan Guyanans. A good-hearted trooper, if a little weak on swimming and direction.

Trudging onward, Stocker bumped up against a body floating face down in the water. *Shit; there's been no shooting at us. Where'd he come from?*

Patting around the corpse's back, he felt no load-bearing equipment or anything to indicate an origin with the corporation. Though it was still too dark to see what the wet material looked like, the clothing didn't feel like M Day issue. *Must have been a local. Oh, well.*

He pushed the body off to one side and resumed his trudge. Then he saw Cagle, probably the shortest man in the group, outside of the Gurkhas, struggling with his nose barely above water. Stocker switched directions to go and give the medico a helping hand. Behind him, the heightened roar of the diesels and the whine of the ramp being lifted told him that the LCM was backing off the sand bar to take on another load, off to the west.

Warrington saw through his goggles that the sudden drop to deeper-than-expected water had pretty badly disorganized the company. He was about to turn around and go after Cagle when he saw that Stocker had the same idea and was considerably closer.

And it won't get any better if they come ashore that way. What to do; what to do? Ah, I know. Use the terrain.

He told the piper to, "Can it for a while," then cupped his hands to shout out, "Stop at the shoreline, A Company, and take a knee. Platoon leaders and squad leaders, get control of your own men there."

"Captain Warrington?" asked an American voice

from farther inland. "I'm here to guide you to your jump off point."

"Give us a few, Sergeant. We need to get settled and set before we move."

"Yes, sir."

Turning to Sergeant Balbahadur, Warrington asked, "Can you play 'Gary Owen?'"

"Yes, sir," said the Gurkha. "Or pretty much anything."

"'Gary Owen' will do nicely. But wait until I give the signal. No need to kill any more people here than we must and, if we can make them run way, we won't have to kill them."

Pulling back the concealing, Velcro-fastened, band over his watch, Warrington did a quick estimate of how long it would be before the gunships, currently rearming back at the *Bland*, were back in play.

Chewing his lip, he thought, *Probably not before we're set to attack, even with this delay. And probably not worth waiting for them. Besides, rather have them fully armed if we need them later on. No, we'll wade in with what we have. That, and the fixed wings, which ought to be up in a couple of minutes.*

Besides, the hurry isn't in clearing the perimeter. The hurry's in getting everything and everyone extraneous out of our hair so that the rest can move in a hurry when they must.

"We're ready to go," Stocker reported, "Bayonets fixed and everything. I can't be one hundred percent sure, but I *think* I saw some people taking to their heels when they heard the clicks after, 'fix . . . bayonets.'"

"Might well have," Warrington agreed. "Sergeant Balbahadur?"

"Sir."

"You accompany Captain Stocker. 'Gary Owen' for as long as you and he can stand it, then whatever you like."

"And you?" Stocker asked.

"Here to control third team and the aviation until you're through and wheeling left. After that, outside the perimeter it's your show. I'm going to parallel you, inside, and make sure they restrict or cease fire as you pass."

Stocker breathed a little easier. "Ah. Good thought. Thank you."

Besides amphibious, there were other operations that were less than desirable to carry out. Airborne was another one where the lesson of history was, "If you don't have to, *don't*." Helicopter landings into hot (which is to say, contested) landing zones, or LZ's, were almost as problematic.

But there were some toughies that one really couldn't avoid. Among these were what is called "Passage of Lines," offensive or defensive. Those you had to do, whether attacking, patrolling, defending, or delaying. The problems with passage of lines included inherent confusion, misidentification—hence friendly fire, coordination, and the touchy question of who's in charge, and when. The problems become more severe, of course, with the size of the units involved. But even for a short company, and a single special operations detachment, there are still some issues. In this case, Warrington ordered that Stocker would assume responsibility for the front as soon as the mortars kicked in, then Third Team would take it over again after Stocker's boys wheeled left.

One fingered, and ever so gently, the SF sergeant, Staff Sergeant Story, by name and rank, nudged Private Khan's rifle up and to the right; away from his head, in other words.

"Sorry, Sergeant," Khan said.

"It's okay, son." *No sense in upsetting the boy before his first action, after all.* "Just be more careful in the future. And more quiet."

"Quiet?" Khan asked. "You don't think they know we're here?"

"Here, sure," Story replied. "But not exactly how many, or what we're getting ready to do?"

"You sure they're out there, Sergeant?"

Khan, two of the men of Third Team, the rest of Khan's fire team, and Khan's squad leader, all occupied a bare room, mostly roofless, almost windowless, in an abandoned mud brick house, fronting the street. One of the few shreds of roof remaining held an infrared chemlights, to mark their position. The entire line was similarly marked.

On the other side, so Khan's squad leader had been told, were the enemy.

"They haven't made a sound since we dropped a dozen or so of them," whispered Story. "But we didn't get them all and they all didn't run away, either. They're still there."

"This place is weird," said Khan, as softly as Story could have wished. "Where are the trees. I tripped over a stump just after landing. But no trees."

"Locals cut them down for firewood would be my guess," Story replied. "Nothing else to cook with. That's probably where the beams for this place went, too."

"Oh."

"It's what happens when everything falls apart."

"Mortars up," Stocker heard in his earpiece. "Roger," he replied. "Time of flight?"

"We firing high charge and elevation for dis range, to get between de buildings. Twenty-two secon's."

"Roger. Twenty-four rounds, prox"—proximity; air burst—"then twenty-four delay. Traverse and search. At my command."

"At you' command, over."

I love it when a plan comes together, thought the Canadian. *Even when it's a plan you've pulled out of your ass.*

"Fixed wings ninety seconds out," announced Warrington. He was looking down at his watch. Stocker felt his heart begin to race as the countdown dropped: "Forty-five . . . thirty . . . "

From off to their right they heard the tell-tale buzz of the CH-750s' small engines.

"I mark your position," announced the lead pilot. "We're coming in with two, repeat two, pods of 7.62 and one, repeat one, rocket pod, each."

"Save the rockets for a rainy day," Warrington said. "Give me a single pass each with machine guns, then standby."

"Roger. Starting our pass now."

★ CHAPTER TWENTY-TWO ★

Those skilled in the attack flash forth
as from the topmost heights of Heaven.
—Sun Tzu

Bajuni, former Federation of Sharia Courts, Africa

God's farting hail, thought Stocker, as the two CH-750's made their pass. The twin, four-barreled, machine gun pods mounted underwing provided the cosmic flatulence—*brrrrrp . . . brrrrrp*—while the expended casings, hitting the ground at a combined rate of a couple of hundred per second, provided the hail. They couldn't really hear it on the ground, but the planes actually had to crank up the gas to counteract the recoil force of the gun pods.

Somewhere to the east someone—possibly several someones—screamed in agony.

"And that's my cue." Into his boom mike Stocker ordered, "Mortars, fire."

"Shot, over." From behind him, to the west, came a series of bright flashes as the rounds dropped by the gunners thumped out. In less than ten seconds, the chief of the mortar section reported back, "Splash," followed in another thirty seconds by, "Rounds complete."

The captain didn't hear that last part, as the high explosive—admittedly not a lot, 60mm being such a small shell—began detonating about a hundred and twenty meters to his front. The flashes of the shells lit up a scene of wrecked, roofless, crumbling buildings, in silhouette, and more than a few bodies. Almost immediately those shells were joined by small arms fire, and four rounds from the two platoons' Vampire rocket launchers.

"Platoon leaders, start your assault. Sergeant Balbahadur, some music please, maestro."

"Roger . . . roger."

Balbahadur didn't respond verbally. He simply stuck the mouthpiece between his lips and began belting out the strains of 'Gary Owen.'

"It's your show now, buddy," Story told Khan's squad leader, at the first *crump* of landing 60mm shells.

"Roger. Second Squad, to de windows. On my command . . . FIRE!"

A wave of tracers from almost eighty rifles and machine guns washed out across the street. Khan added his own measure to the din, though he stopped firing when three sides of one of the buildings almost opposite his perch crumpled into a worse ruin than it already had been from the impact of a Vampire's fourteen pound shell. The Vampire, also known as an RPG-29, could punch through more than a dozen feet of log and earth. The foot or so of mud brick didn't stand a chance; it flew away, mostly in the form of powder.

★ ★ ★

Though every army's doctrine calls for a certain amount of spacing between soldiers, any number of factors—tight terrain, darkness, snow or rain, sand storms, buildings, or unusually high concentrations of the enemy—can cause that spacing to be reduced almost to the shoulder-to-shoulder point. Part of that is about control; the small unit leader can't control what he can't see. An equal part is moral; soldiers get distinctly uncomfortable when they can't see, or at least sense, their comrades. "Uncomfortable" is, in this case, code for "frightened."

So they cluster. And leaders rarely or never countermand the clustering until it gets very close, at least in those circumstances, because at least they can see and control the clusters, or the leaders of the clusters.

Night vision equipment is often of only marginal help with the problem.

The mix of mud brick dust and powder smoke half blinded Khan and did set him to violent coughing. The rest of his team were in about the same boat. They'd backed out through the back door of their assault position, leaving Sergeant Story behind, then clustered at one corner of that roofless building. At a command from their team leader, all five had sprinted across the street, stopping only at the far wall of the building Khan had seen mostly demolished by a Vampire shell.

There had been a couple of bodies—maybe living, maybe dead—on the floor of that wrecked shack. Neither had attempted to surrender, even if they'd been capable of the attempt. In the darkness, neither had been certain to have been wounded. Khan's team leader—the only man in the team equipped with NVG's—had been trained in a very harsh school: Unless it is absolutely obvious, the burden of proof of intent to surrender or having been rendered *hors de combat* by wounds is on the party wishing to surrender or to be recognized as *hors de combat*. He saw the bodies; they gave no indication of intent, so he put his rifle's muzzle to their heads, in turn, and donated a bullet to each man. *Bang. Bang.*

This was called either "making sure," or, in the alternative, "not taking any chances." The dead, in any case, didn't complain.

Stocker was centered between the two platoons. With him were the company supply sergeant and his assistant, plus some reinforcement from the communications section and the cooks. Pointing at the corner where the street met the beach, he said, "Sergeant, go start tossing the mines there. Be sure to toss a fair few out onto the sand, too. Then follow my trail, laying them behind you."

"Yessir," said the supply sergeant, a short, stocky, black Guyanan. He and the assistant trotted off, laden with mine-filled rucksacks, for the spot Stocker had indicated.

"Okay, boys," Stocker said into his radio, "start your left wheel now. Simon?"

"Here, sir," answered Blackmore.

"I've got the company now. Put your major effort into getting everything we can out of here on the next LCM lift."

"Already on it, Captain." The lieutenant's voice held a tone of personal hurt.

Crap; he thinks I'm here because he did something wrong. Hmmm, how to fix that without letting him know that I'm trying to fix it. Ah, I know; "it's all in the tone of voice"—stern, demanding, fair.

"You've done very well indeed, so far, Simon. See to it that the evacuation runs as well, eh? Good lad."

It wasn't hard for Warrington to keep track of how far Stocker's assault had gone. Not only were there plenty of tracers, and a fair number of hand grenade blasts, but Balbahadur's pipes pinpointed the center of the effort fairly precisely.

In his earpiece Warrington heard, "Slepnyov, Captain. Back on station . . . two minutes."

"Keep a low profile, Slep. We don't need anything right now but when we do . . . "

"Roger, Captain. We take up hover by beach."

"Works." *And besides, the sound will carry a long way into the city. Ought help keep the other side scared and running.*

"I want you to run to the landing craft, you pieces of shit."

Jesus, Feeney, thought Hallinan, standing by the boat's ramp, *what's gotten into you lately?*

Sergeant Feeney stood exactly on line between the aid workers and the boat, though he was much closer to the aid workers. Nobody moved, probably because they were terrified of getting any closer to the sergeant than necessary. Feeney flipped down his NVG's and strode to the nearest one, a female. He grabbed her by her hair and pulled her to her feet. Shaking her a few times, to ensure he had her undivided attention, he twisted her hair to point her face at the boat. Then he said, "Those lights out there are the landing craft, sweetie. Get your ass there. Now."

He released the woman's hair, then slapped her on the ass, before letting her fall to all fours. He applied a very mild boot to her posterior, knocking her to the sand. Weeping loudly, the woman struggled to her feet and then, hair flying, she ran off. It was with very mixed feelings that Feeney saw she was, in fact, heading in the right direction. He went to grab another one, then stopped himself. *This is taking too long. Way too long. But I know how to speed it up.*

Wading through the mass of terrified tranzis, Feeney stopped at the far, which is to say the northern, edge of them. He pulled a hand grenade from his assault vest and flipped off the safety clip. Pulling the ring, he tossed the grenade shoreward about fifty feet. Then he shouted, "Incoming! Run for your lives."

The words didn't do much good. But the explosion that came a few seconds later got them on their feet and scrambling very quickly indeed.

Yeah, that's the ticket. Yeah. Feeney smiled very broadly at the grainy-green image of a mass of humanitarians, tearing at each other to be the first aboard the boat.

An exhausted Dr. Saffron emerged from the water, seallike, which is to say on his sodden belly. Exhausted, and too terrified for his self-righteous anger to have any place, he began crawling toward the civilized sound of a big diesel engine, cranking away somewhere to his right front.

He heard an explosion, which was almost enough to turn him around and back toward the water. Then he heard familiar voices shrieking in fear. Mindlessly, he followed the familiar. Lifting his head up he saw another sign of civilization, the red and green running lights of what had to be a rescue craft of some kind. He continued in that direction, operating off little more than autopilot and a new found will to live.

Cagle thumbed his radio's transmit switch. "Warrington? Cagle."

"Warrington."

"Boss, I've got six wounded by the beach ready to load on the landing craft. Only problem is that one of them's not going to make it unless he gets to the ship and TIC Chick's care within about five minutes. A couple of others are iffy."

"Recommendation?" Warrington didn't even bother asking if all the wounded belonged to M Day. The world had become the kind of place where nobody really cared about the enemy's wounded.

"More a question," Cagle said. "Can we divert one of the gunships to carrying him out?"

"Done. Break, break. Slepnyov, did you copy that?"

"Roger."

"You or your wingman, don't care which one. Land as close to the LCM as practical and evacuate three of our wounded."

"Wilco, sir."

"There's no time to mark a PZ," Cagle added. "Just land and we'll get them to you."

"Watch tail," Slepnyov reminded, needlessly. "I'll land west of the boat and put my tail to the southwest."

"Roger. Works."

Saffron heard the helicopter as it touched down. If he'd been either less tired or more humble, he'd probably have realized that it hadn't necessarily landed where it had on his behalf. Sadly, he was both utterly exhausted and arrogant at an automatic and unconscious level. Using the last reserves of his meager strength, he forced himself to his feet and began to run toward the swimming lights.

Right into the tail rotor. Think: Cuisinart.

"What was that?" Slepnyov's co-pilot asked at the sudden shudder.

"Dunno. Check instruments."

"Mmmm . . . they say we're fine."

"Then we're fine. And here are our passengers now."

★ CHAPTER TWENTY-THREE ★

My center is giving way, my right is in retreat;
situation excellent. I shall attack.
—Ferdinand Foch

MV *Richard Bland*, Coastof Africa city of Bajuni

TIC Chick was standing by—more precisely, *kneeling* by, lest the rotor take her head off—as the small hatch on the side of the gunship popped open to reveal one of the medics, pressing a thick gauze bandage with one hand while the other held an IV bag high overhead. Behind the doctor, likewise on one knee, were half a dozen other medical personnel and three two-wheeled gurneys. The medic had probably kicked the latch to open the hatch.

A closer inspection, had it been possible, would have shown that the medic wasn't trying to stop the bleeding so much as to hold the patient's intestines in place, where a thick fragment of 120mm had ripped open his belly, spilling them to the earth. Odds were the intestines were, them-selves, ripped up, a sure path to major internal infections if not cleaned and repaired posthaste. The IV was there only to keep the man's veins from collapsing, which would have made further injections highly problematic.

"GET THIS ONE!" Screamed the medic, quite unnecessarily; TIC Chick and company were already at the hatch, struggling to get the wounded man out while keeping his guts in. In this they were not entirely successful, a small portion of the large intestine being torn open on an exposed screw head. A vile stench immediately filled the compartment.

"Get the gurney over here!" TIC Chick ordered. The patient was not small and she and two assistants barely sufficed to hold him up while holding him together. She needn't have shouted; one of the gurneys was wheeled under the man before she'd even finished.

"That's the worst one, TIC Chick," the medic shouted over the roar of the engines. "Gary said he ought to be your number-one priority."

The doctor bridled for a moment. *Harrumph. Telling me my business. Just because he's my husband . . . Well . . . no, because he knows my business about as well as I do.*

She took the IV bag from the medic and pointed in the direction of the superstructure. "Thataway! Now!"

Bajuni, former Federation of Sharia Courts, Africa

Warrington was facing north, in between the remnants of three small buildings. He could still hear Balbahadur's croaking out some awful Scottish medley, the sound coming from his front and a little bit to his right. Suddenly to his left front, an amazing volume of fire picked up.

Thumbing the radio switch, he asked, "Andrew, are you letting your piper fall behind?"

"No, boss," the Canuck replied. "He's right behind me and I'm right behind the juncture of the two platoons."

"Then what's all that firing to your west?"

"Best guess, some of the ones we've been driving ahead of us we drove into some other group we haven't reached yet."

With a rush of static, Sergeant Moore piped in, "I think I can vouch for that. The ones facing us here suddenly turned away. And they're fighting *somebody*. We're not taking any deliberate fire at the moment."

"Right," Warrington agreed. "Fine. 'Keep up the skeer.'"

"Huh?"

Chuckling, Warrington said, "Sometimes I forget you're from the great frozen north. Go look up Nathan Bedford Forrest some time."

"Yeah, sure, in my 'copious free time.' Hey, boss, I've got some fighting to do. Bug me later, huh?"

"Keep up the skeer, Captain."

"Roger. You know, if these guys had any unity of command, they'd have pushed us into the sea—or dumped our corpses there—a while ago . . . Hey, Khan, pot that bastard!"

It pretty much went with the territory; for a night attack, in close terrain, fancy formations and maneuvers were just a little too dangerous. Instead, everyone was kept on a very tight leash and, if not exactly on line, the fire teams—little knots of men moving and shooting together, under *tight* control by their team leaders—did form something like a line, or a serrated knife's edge.

Khan heard his captain's shout, but couldn't really see who the old man intended for him to shoot. *Be nice when I make it to team leader and they give me a set of those goggles.*

Then he didn't so much see as sense a shape, about two dozen feet to his right front. That shape was a little too far out to be friendly. Khan automatically closed his left eye, then fired a short burst from the hip. In the muzzle flash he could see a man, lifting a rifle, and wearing local clothing. He fired again, and then again, though those was only in the same general direction, as the muzzle flash had temporarily done for his night vision in his firing eye.

Three bursts? Well, fire discipline was nice, but at close quarters, when you want someone down, you want him down *right away*.

Wonder what kept that guy here; most of the others have run. Probably in terror of Sergeant Balbahadur's pipes. God knows, they terrify me. Funny, I thought I'd be bothered by killing somebody, and these poor bastards never did me any harm. But they're not my family. My *family's on either side of me. So screw 'em.*

Khan didn't know it, and he couldn't have seen it even had he known, but the rightmost man in the platoon to the right practically brushed his sleeve on a soccer stadium where a late member of the regiment, Master Sergeant "Buckwheat" Fulton, had once done to death an improbably large number of the locals for stoning a young girl whose crime had consisted of being raped.

★ ★ ★

Stocker heard in his ear, "Rightmos' man be at de stadium, Skipper."

"Roger. Break, break. Both platoons, our heading is now two hundred and twenty-five, I say again, two hundred and twenty-five degrees. Keep pushing 'em."

"Wilco . . . wilco."

The men who followed Adam's uncle Korfa were, as advertised, relatively well trained. Why not? He, himself, was a man of some education, to include some fairly advanced military education from not only the United States, but also the United Kingdom and the former Soviet Union, depending on who was buttering his former country's bread at the time. What he'd learned, his men had learned.

And they'd, generally speaking, learned well. They'd pressed whoever the hell it was had landed on their turf pretty hard before the swarm of two other gangs tried to flee through them. They really hadn't known what it was that hit them. One minute, there was nothing but the occasional shot to the flanks, more for morale and warning than with any deadly intent. The next there was a mass of firing somewhere off to the east. Then, after perhaps another twenty minutes, a mob—there was really no other word—of terrified refugees had begun pouring through their lines, chased by some kind of shrieking demon.

Some of Korfa's men had stood and fought, if it could be said that one is fighting while gunning down men who had no thought of anything but escape. Still others had joined the stampede.

"And if I ever find out who," Korfa muttered, "they'll wish their mothers had strangled them in the cradle."

Korfa wasn't fooled by the sound. *No demon*, he knew. *Now I know exactly what it is. The fucking British have sent in the Highlanders. I can't face that. Take on an isolated company of Americans when I've got three or four thousand followers and the Americans tied their own hands behind their backs? That I can do. But we're a skirmisher people. This chin up, stand and be still to the Birkenhead drill bullshit is not my people's cup of tea. And if those are British regulars, in numbers—and the speed they've been moving says they've got the numbers—then my best bet is just to say to hell with the aid workers, to hell with their ship, and to hell with their medical equipment and supplies.*

There must have been British subjects among the hostages my nephew took and, for a change, the Brits decided to act like men.

Can't advance; the fire's too fierce. Can't stay here; I don't even think half my men are left. Time to leave, get out of their way, then reorganize and come back after they pass. That, *we know how to do.*

"Warrington? Stocker."

"Go ahead, Andrew."

"There's nothing to my front and that's got me worried. Maybe there's nothing there, but then again, maybe there are and this group has some discipline and is just waiting. Can we have the gunships do an overflight?"

"Roger. Break, break. Slep, you back from the dustoff?"

"I am back."

"How did my man do?"

"Was alive when he gots pulled from my helicopter."

"Okay, good. I want you to do a flyover, all around the perimeter. In particular, I want you to have a close look at the area southwest of the football field."

"Wilco. On it now."

"Andrew?"

"Stocker here."

"Much as I hate for you to lose your momentum, I'd hate it more if you got caught in the open by steady, approximately trained, troops. Hold up until Slepnyov has a look."

"Wilco."

The MI-28 was a *very* capable helicopter. The Russians built a good helicopter, in general—oh, sure, short on creature comforts and bitching tiring to fly—but the MI-28 was better than most. And, most importantly, it had something nobody else on the ground did, a truly powerful thermal imager. Even the ones in the Elands were small change in comparison.

With it, Slepnyov could see, "The area Captain Stocker clear out . . . they starting filter back. Ones and twos, mostly."

"Expected that," Warrington said. "It's a skirmisher military culture. Rarely stand and fight to the death. Rarely entirely give up, either."

And, eventually, unless you're willing to turn barbarian yourself and go all Einsatzgruppen *on them, the skirmishers will wear you out. It's as valid as our methods of war, by the only criterion that matters: Winning.*

"Yes," Slepnyov agreed. "Almost nobody . . . immediate front of Captain Stocker's men. Few I can see are . . . dead, I think. Or maybe wounded. Or maybe . . . what's that Americanism? Ah, yes, 'playing possum.' But of people who look ready to fight, I see none.

"There's a knot, maybe a hundred or two, still fighting down by the west shoulder of the peninsula. But it's clear until there."

"Can you run them off?" Warrington asked. "That's where I want Stocker to pass lines back to our side."

"Prob'ly. Sure can try."

"Do it. Don't expend more than half your on-board ammunition at the attempt, though."

"Roger. Urrah!"

Okay . . . now, once Stocker's boys are safe behind the lines, how are we going to thin the line to unass this AO?

MV *Richard Bland*, Coast of Africa city of Bajuni, Africa

"Fuck the tranzis," Pearson said. "The wounded have priority."

"Authority to use force to make it clear to them?" Feeney asked, over the radio. His voice held a definite tone of eager anticipation.

"Whatever it takes," the captain ordered.

"Roger."

Yep, definitely eager anticipation, thought the skipper. *Oh, well. Feeney, whatever his faults, should be able to explain their position in life to them.* He promptly put the aid workers out of his mind, rotating his chair and looking shoreward to where two intermittent streams of tracers leapt from the sky to the ground.

So far, so good, there. At least from the few snatches of radio traffic we've been able to pick up from the line dogs. Awful damned pricey though. Speaking of which . . .

Pearson punched the intercom button to sick bay and asked, "TIC Chick?"

"I'm kind of busy right now, Skipper." She was, indeed, quite busy, her arms more or less draped in intestine, and another eight feet she'd had to cut away sitting on a stainless steel table beside her.

"I know. Heads up; you're going to be busier still."

"How many?" she asked, peering intently at a bit of odiferous flesh as she wove her needle to and fro. "And how bad?"

"Nineteen, and mostly not so bad. All but two are conscious, Sergeant Feeney reports. Not happy, but conscious."

"Okay. Teams are standing by. Wish to fuck Gary were here to help."

"I can probably get you some help," Pearson said. *It won't be happy help, most likely, though.*

"From where?"

"The aid workers. There are doctors there."

"Oh, right. Yeah; forgot. Send 'em down."

"Roger. Wait." He went back to the radio. "Sergeant Feeney?"

"Here, Skipper."

"Next load, doctors and RN's."

"Already sorting them that way, Captain. Fact is, a

couple of the shitheads went up with the first load because our wounded needed them."

"Very good, Sergeant." *And just because you're a maniac doesn't mean you're stupid.*

★ CHAPTER TWENTY-FOUR ★

I have no right to rank with such great captains,
for I have never commanded a retreat.
—Moltke, the Elder

Bajuni, former Federation of Sharia Courts, Africa

Stocker's wounded and his two dead had been passed through the lines previously, whenever there'd been a convenient, or inconvenient, for that matter, slowdown in the pace of the assault. That made the final passage back into friendly lines that much easier. The commander stood by, Balbahadur's pipes—"Lilliburlero" was the tune now—still motivating the men but, more importantly for the moment, marking the point of passage. Stocker's first sergeant counted the boys through, confirming with the squad leaders and platoon sergeants that everyone was accounted for. Tail end charlies for the event were the supply sergeant and his assistant, pulling the pins to arm and then tossing PFM-1S toe poppers for all they were worth. All Hansel-and-Gretel-like, they'd left a broad swath of the nasty little things along their sweeping route around the perimeter, in every building along that route, and up and down the alleys. Safety pins pulled, the mines would generally arm themselves within as little as a minute, and certainly within ten minutes. They had an integral twenty-four hour self-destruct mechanism, though as with much former Soviet and modern Russian material, reliability was a matter of conjecture.

That the PFM-1S's rarely killed was not generally considered a good reason to blow one's toes off by stepping on one. There was some reason to believe—the sudden bang followed by the heartrending shriek—that a couple of the local skirmishers, closing back in behind them, had found this out the hard way.

More or less by luck of the draw, or at least by placement, Khan's fire team, a machine gun crew and a Vampire crew, plus one of the two Elands, had ended up covering the supply sergeant and his small party. Nobody was shooting at them, at the moment, what with the pasting they'd gotten from the gunships. They weren't taking any chances anyway, especially now that the moon, thin sliver that it was, was casting down just about enough light to allow something like target identification and deliberate aiming. The machine gun and Eland fired at anything remotely suspicious, though the rocket launcher was holding its fire for something more worthwhile.

Then came the word for those last ten, and the Eland, to pull back.

It was almost entirely quiet inside the perimeter. So far, at least, the mines were doing their job keeping the locals at bay. Slepnyov had said they were rallying, but only by ones and twos. And those ones and twos were advancing very cautiously.

"We can account for everyone except one man," Stocker reported to Warrington.

"That guy who went down between the ship and the LCM?" the latter asked.

"Must be. I've got the two platoons I brought in waiting for the LCM down by the beach. Moore's platoon is still on the line, along with your Third Team. How do you want us to handle disengagement?"

Warrington had been thinking about that quite a bit over the last hour. "One thing I *don't* want is the Elands sliding into a bunch of packed troopers in the LCM's well deck."

"Right; they have to pull out first. I figured that much."

"I can have Third Team sprint for the Zodiacs still on the shore. Can Moore extend his line to cover their sector?"

"He's already doing it," Stocker answered.

"Good . . . wait a sec." Warrington called his third team and told them, "As soon as the line dogs replace you, get the hell on the Zodiacs and head for the ship."

"Wilco."

Turning back to Stocker, Warrington continued, "All right. Once Simon has the Elands and the bulk of your company loaded, tell Moore to run like the wind for the LCM. I'll stay here, along with Balbahadur—"

"*We'll* stay here."

Chuckling, Warrington agreed, "Fair enough. You and I and the Gurkha will stay here, just watching and, if needed, firing until the LCM takes off. Then I'll call in one of Slepnyov's gunships to pick us up while the other one patrols the perimeter."

"Wish to hell," Stocker said, "that we'd thought to bring some claymores along for Moore's people to set on trip wires."

"Can't think of everything. But you're right. I wish we had, too."

Uncle Korfa hadn't known, hadn't even suspected, there were mines placed out until, entering a wreck of a building with some of his personal guard, one of the guards had knelt by a window and promptly had his knee blasted into ruin. It was fortunate, in a way, that it was so dark. Korfa wasn't sure how the rest would have taken the sight of mangled flesh, pulverized bone, and squirting blood. He'd had the man carried away to what passed for a doctor for his gang.

Well, to be fair, none of that would bother them ordinarily. But that, coupled with the knowledge that the ground itself has become untrustworthy? That would . . . do something to them, and not anything too very good.

Taking one knee himself, albeit very carefully, he took from a pocket and flicked into life his cigarette lighter. Sure enough there was a small, odd little butterflylike device a couple of feet away. Bending lower still, he examined it closely. *That small? Can't be too powerful. We can clear them safely, I think.*

"Go find some branches," he ordered, "some brooms, anything we use to sweep the ground ahead of us. And hurry! The medicines and the hostages are likely gone, but if we move quickly we may be able to grab some new hostages and trade for what we need."

He, more than the other gang leaders—there really wasn't a better word to describe them—also had a better idea of what had gone on the last few hours. It wasn't entirely accurate, of course, but it was close.

Some westerners—based on the bagpipes, I'd have to say "Brits"—objected to Adam's grabbing a ship full of aid workers. They landed a force—there's probably a cruiser or something as big, right off shore—and rescued them. Or—and this is possible, too—the hostages were the price of getting Adam, his family, and the few men still loyal to him, out of here.

But things went slower than they anticipated, so we had time to engage them closely. They had to land more force maybe than they'd planned on. That force is going to take time to get off the shore. And they'll be going out in dribs and drabs. That will be our chance, if any time will be.

"Elands to the landing craft; go!" Stocker ordered over the radio. The armored car chiefs acknowledged the order. Even if they hadn't, Stocker could still have heard the previously idling engines purr into high gear. In mere seconds, both of them appeared, bounding over the dunes, racing for the LCM.

Both stopped about fifty meters shy of the landing craft. For a half a minute or so they maneuvered to line themselves up, one behind the other, in a straight line to the bow. Both rotated their guns to the rear, one over the left rear fender, the other over the right. Then, gunning his engine, the first driver made a high speed dash. He hit the ramp, then bounced up, still going forward. The bounce ended about halfway down the well deck. Again, the thing bounced, though not as high or as far. By the time it touched down again, the wheels were spinning in reverse. This did no noticeable good; the front of the thing smashed into the forward bulkhead of the engine room, almost knocking Kirkpatrick from his feet. The second Eland followed, not quite as fast. No matter; it smashed into the first one.

"We on," the section leader for the armored cars reported. "We beat up and bruised, but we on. Tying de bitches down, now."

"Mortars, expend all remaining ammunition on targets three, four, and seven." Those were major avenues leading into the beach area.

"Shot, over."

"Simon, start loading second platoon on the LCM."

"Wilco," answered the exec.

"Rounds complete," announced the mortar chief.

"Mortars out of action; report to the exec for boarding."

"Wilco."

At the same time, Stocker saw the Third Team, from way over on the right, more or less duck walking across the sand in a ragged line. When they reached the first series of dunes they stood up, albeit still somewhat bent over, and began to sprint to where they'd staked down the Zodiacs.

"Slep? Warrington."

"Here, Captain."

In truth, neither of the helicopters was quite "here." Both were snaking back and forth about a quarter of a mile out to sea.

"This is going to be touchy, Slep. In about eight minutes, or maybe a cunt hair less, the line dogs are going to bug out for the LCM. That's going to leave me, Stocker, and Balbahadur on the beach. I want one gunship, your choice, to go all medieval on what used to be the perimeter. Expend all ammo. Kill anything that moves. Then. Come. Get. Us. We'll make ourselves very obvious. We'll be the guys running for the beach like the devil's on our tails. Two tall skinny white dudes and a little bit of a Gurkha with some pipes under his arm.

"After the one bird expends its ammo, I want the second one to cover our retreat. Once we're airborne, get the fuck out of Dodge and head for the ship."

"You gots it. My wing man will do first run. I cover after."

"I'll tell you when to start."

From the ship's bridge Pearson piped in. "Tracy, if you want I can have the CH-750's rearmed and airborne in that time."

"No, Skipper," Warrington sent back. "Strike them down or there'll never be room for the gunships. Or, if there will, we'll still be taking a risk we don't need to take."

"Your call."

"Warrington? Cagle."

"Go ahead, Gary."

"Is there any chance we can have the gunships sink the aid ship?"

"What?" Warrington asked, incredulously. If there was

anything he'd have expected from the medico, it wasn't destroying valuable medical supplies and equipment. "You've got to be shitting me."

Over the radio, damn procedures, Cagle sighed. "No . . . I'm not. Those supplies are going to kill more people fighting over them than they could possibly save. Sink the ship, if we can."

It took a long pause before Warrington answered. "No. I understand your position. But I'm not going to destroy medical supplies and equipment. If they want to fight over it, that's their problem."

"Okay. But I wish you would."

"They're all in, except for Moore's platoon, Captain," Simon reported. "They're hanging off the barrels of the Elands and breathing by the numbers but they're all aboard. With enough space for Moore."

"Very good, Simon," Stocker said. "Break, break. Sergeant Moore?"

"Moore, sir."

"Expend all ammunition and then hit the road, Sergeant. Now is not the time for good order and discipline. Do the move as quietly as possible; use the fire to cover the bulk of it, but fucking *move*!"

Suddenly the entire perimeter lit up as by a thousand strobe lights as Moore's platoon fired, bursts and full automatic, mostly. Within two or three minutes, every round from half the platoon was gone. Within an equal space of time, which time was used by the previously firing teams to bug out without being noticed, the rest had fired off everything they had, to include the rockets for the Vampires.

"Going now, sir."

"Simon?"

"Here, sir."

"As soon as Moore's boys get there and are all accounted for, you join them and get out of here. Don't wait for an order."

"What about you, the piper, and Warrington, sir?"

"Didn't I tell you? Hmmm . . . maybe not. We're leaving like gentlemen, on the last bird out."

"Yes, sir."

It had been fairly slow going, but eventually Uncle Korfa's boys had beaten a safe path through the mines. It would have been quicker, perhaps, except that about twenty meters into the presumed obstacle, the enemy—*Must be Brits*—opened fire at a fantastic rate, as if they were going to attack again. It took Korfa and his close underlings several minutes to get the frightened men back to their mine clearing duty, once the fire stopped.

But, after the delay, by the time they had a route through the mines, the LCM had raised ramp and was wallowing out, low in the water, leaving Warrington, Stocker, and Balbahadur alone.

"This is what we call a classic shitty feeling," Warrington said. Each of the three, he, Stocker, and Balbahadur, were on one knee. That latter was still playing his pipes, rifle slung across his back. The former two had their rifles aimed inland, sweeping left to right for some sign of a closing enemy.

Stocker was thinking almost exactly the same thing.

Instead of voicing that sentiment, though, he said, "At least we've still got the gunships with us."

"Yeah . . . speaking of which . . . " Warrington keyed his radio and said, "Slep, Warrington. Whichever one of you is going to pick us up, have the other go ahead and clear the perimeter."

"Roger."

Both gunships had been hovering out to sea, their rotors a distant *whopwhopwhop*. In mere seconds, that distant sound had gotten quite close. The helicopter passed about four hundred meters to the right rear of the small stay-behind party then, guiding on the small infrared chemlights that dotted the erstwhile perimeter, it began to pound.

"Amazing," Stocker said, in awe, "just how much firepower one of those things can bring to bear when it wants to."

"Yeah, no shit."

Korfa and his men, now through the mines, heard the chopper coming as plainly as had the three on the beach. Korfa physically pointed the point man at a building, ordering, "Quick! Take shelter in it."

The gunship's weapons man smiled at the distinct silhouettes of a dozen men, shining clearly in his thermal even through the mud brick wall. He muttered something in Russian that could have been approximately translated as, "Dumb fucks."

From his panel, the gunner initially selected his preferred weapon for something like this, an antitank guided missile, or ATGM. The AT-9 *Ataka*, with its more than fifteen pound warhead, was really overkill. "But there's no kill like an overkill." He'd have used the AT-9, but, since the target was so close, less than the missile's arming range, he changed his selection to one of the pods of unguided rockets.

Then he pressed the firing button.

From Korfa's perspective, the first rocket flew too high, impacting a building some distance to the west. The second, however, hit one corner of the mud brick building, blowing that corner both off and in, and sending two of his men flying. The next one hit inside the roofless house, blowing the wall outward, killing three men outright, and blowing in the eardrums of the remainder. The fourth hit the wall by which Korfa had stood for shelter. After that, he didn't know anything at all.

Heads down, and staying far, far from the tail rotor, the stay behind party sprinted for the invitingly opened hatch. Balbahadur tried to get his captain to go first, but Stocker and Warrington were having none of that. They picked up the Gurkha bodily and tossed him in.

Next, Warrington thumped Stocker hard and pointed. Shrugging, Stocker climbed through the hatch, stepping on Balbahadur's feet as he scrambled for the tiny chair. Warrington launched himself inward, though he stopped short as his load-bearing vest caught on the hatch's bottom edge. No matter, Balbahadur and Stocker leaned over, caught his arms, and physically pulled him through.

Warrington cursed the whole time; the edge of that hatch was *kinda sharp, you motherfuckers*.

Lastly, ignoring the pained scrapings on his lower abdomen, thighs, knees and shins, Warrington thumbed his radio one final time for the evening.

"Get us the fuck out of here."

★★★
PART III:
Republic of the Philippines, and at sea
★★★

★ CHAPTER TWENTY-FIVE ★

Our age is witnessing the ultimate climax,
the cashing-in on a long process of destruction,
at the end of the road laid out by Kant.
—Ayn Rand,
"The Cashing-In: The Student 'Rebellion'"

Safe House Bravo, South Green Heights Village,
Muntinlupa City, Manila Metro Area, Republic of the Philippines

It was rare for the local police to respond so quickly to a kidnapping. It wasn't a lot after midnight when the first squad car showed up. This was not because of indifference on the part of the police. Rather, a kidnapping tended to be a very quiet affair because of the local gangs' usual MO: a Mickey Finn or force majeure, followed by a quiet disappearance.

In this case the gunshots, in a neighborhood that never expected to hear any, had caused a call to the local police station.

There hadn't been all that much for the police to glean

at the site. There was a body, very dead, on the floor. There were no passports or wallets, nothing to ID the corpse, and no cell phones. There was no landline and, given that they had no idea about what the cell phone numbers, if any, had been, no leads there. There were additional bloodstains, but no bodies to go with those. No weapons, though there were a fair number of expended shell casings.

Supposedly, from what the neighbors said, there had been an SUV. Where it was now was anyone's guess; it certainly wasn't in the carport. The neighbors also reported that the place had been occupied by what they thought looked like Kanos, who spoke English—and a huge percentage of Filipinos could speak that, while the rest would at least recognize it when they heard it—with a single local girl as a domestic. They thought there had been at least three Kanos, and maybe as many as eight.

The local domestics thought it a little odd that the Kanos' girl avoided them like the plague. Also odd was that she looked less Filipina than she did an amalgam of pretty much everybody who'd ever passed through the islands, and was much larger than most.

Beyond that trivia, there just wasn't a lot to work with.

"Work with me here, Malone," said Lox, in exasperation, over the cell phone. He was hunched over a map displayed on his laptop, while Sergeant Ferd Franceschi drove.

The news of the hit—as far as Malone knew it had been a hit, rather than a kidnapping—had hit the other safe house like a ton of bricks. Terry's first thought was that it had been the work of the Harrikat. But . . .

"No way, Terry," Lox had said, back at Alpha. "They don't even know we exist. No . . . this is something else."

"I'm *trying*," Malone insisted, much more loudly than one would expect of someone in his predicament. This was because of some music, singing actually, coming from a nearby building. "But I don't know what street I'm on, and, if they're out looking for me, if I come out from these bushes I'm not going to be hard to notice with my white chest and bare feet."

"What's that music behind you?" Lox asked.

"I dunno. It's in Tagalog, though the tune seems familiar."

"Okay, shut up and hold your cell's microphone toward it."

Lox listened carefully for several minutes, then looked down at his map again. Despite the circumstances, he laughed. "I'm pretty sure I know where you are, Malone. We'll be there is about twenty minutes."

Lox and Franceschi both had their pistols out—and the latter had a Sterling submachine gun tucked in by his right leg—when their car came to a stop. Lox reached back—*Oh, my fucking back; I'm sooo getting too old for this shit*—and unlatched the rear door, pushing it open. For lack of a better method at hand, that would do as a near recognition signal.

"I just saw a door open," said Malone.

"That's us. *Sprint!*"

Half naked, barefoot, pistol in one hand and cell phone in the other, Malone burst out of the bushes in which he'd taken cover and ran for all he was worth across the neat grass of—as it turned out—the Muntinlupa Church of Christ. He didn't so much take a seat in the car as dove in, head first, before twisting to get his hand on the door's handle. He really didn't need to; as soon as Ferd felt the car shudder, he gunned the engine, the forward momentum swinging the open door back and shut.

"Back to base, Ferd," Lox ordered.

Safe House Alpha, Hagonoy, Bulacan, Luzon, Republic of the Philippines

"Who did it?" Welch demanded.

"No clue, sir," Malone answered. "I barely got a glimpse of some shadows. Little guys. Locals. That much I can say. I'd guess, from voices, there were half a dozen or so." The sergeant scrunched his eyes, thinking *hard*.

"I *think* the one I'm sure I shot was tattooed."

"Pattern?" Lox asked.

Malone shook his head. "No clue. It was too quick."

Welch's disgust was palpable. "How did they find you? Why did they target you? Don't bother answering; it was rhetorical."

Lox offered, "Could have been anything . . . the neighbors . . . following their SUV when they were out on recon . . . their maid."

Malone carefully avoided mentioning just why he'd chosen Maricel.

"Any chance it was our principal?" Welch asked.

"I can't rule it out," said Lox. "But I also can't see a motive."

"No . . . no, it makes no sense. Goddam . . . " Welch's cell phone rang before he could finish. He picked it up, looked at the tiny screen, and saw it was Benson.

Tondo, Manila, Republic of the Philippines

All four of the prisoners were tied to chairs in a back office of TCS's headquarters. There was a puddle of vomit on the floor next to the big black. Standing in front of them, Diwata scrolled through the numbers on Benson's cell until she came to the one labeled, "Boss."

"Who is this 'Boss'?" she asked Benson. She sounded as if she'd been brought up in California.

The sergeant simply glared at her. The drug had worn off by now and he'd spent the last fifteen minutes coming up with a story. Fortunately, the people who had them hadn't been clever enough to separate them before interrogation, so at least the others would have the basis for the same story.

Lucas raised his foot and smashed it down on Benson's bare and unprotected instep. The sergeant grimaced, but made no sound.

"The lady asked you a question, Kano. Answer it or next time will be your balls."

"He ansahs to Terry," Benson said. He didn't think these people would be particularly expert at torture. He also didn't see the point in finding out, personally, just how inexpert they might be.

"I don't know his last name" Benson lied. "I was nevah told. He runs guns, drugs sometimes. People sometimes.

I was hired to do reconnaissance and security. I don't know anything else about his business."

Diwata looked intently at Benson's ashen face, seeking the lie. She didn't see it. *Though that doesn't mean it isn't there. Hard to read Kanos, sometimes.*

"Your people sometimes call you 'Sarge,' I understand."

"A couple of us served togethah before," Benson said, thinking, *That fucking idiot, Malone.* That brought another thought . . . distant at first, hard to grab hold of. Then, *Oh, crap. That maid Malone hired; she's the only one who ever heard it. She was working for these people.*

"I'm going to call your boss," Diwata said, "and tell him what we want for your safe return. You shut up until I tell you otherwise. Don't try to pass him any information; the price you'll pay for it is really high."

"I don't have any information," Benson lied.

Safe House Alpha, Hagonoy, Bulacan, Luzon, Republic of the Philippines

The phone was still ringing, unanswered.

"It'll be them, probably," Lox said, "whoever has our people. Assuming they're still alive. Act—talk—sleepy, as if you didn't know anything about this. Listen carefully. Get their demands, if any. Ask to speak to one of one of our men."

Welch nodded, then said, "Everybody shut up. Lox, you get a pen and paper in case someone has a bright idea to pass me." Then he pushed the answer button, followed by the speaker key, and said, in as sleepy-sounding a voice as he could muster, "Hello?"

"Terry?" asked the female voice on the other end.

"Yes."

"My name doesn't matter," the female said. "Though if you need something to call me, call me 'Princess.' I have some of your people here with me. Benson, whom they call 'Sarge,' Zimmerman, Perez, and Washington. We're sorry, truly sorry, about the one we shot. We won't charge you for him. For the other four, though, if you want them back, it will be four million dollars. In a week we'll kill one of them. But the price for the other three will still be four million dollars. In another week, we'll kill a second one. The price after that will still be four million dollars. If you don't talk to me now, we'll hang one right away, video record it, and put the video online. Then I'll call you again, and tell you again, that in a week we'll kill another one, but the price will still be four million dollars."

"I see," Terry agreed. He made his voice sound more naturally awake now. "How do I know you have my people?"

"How do you think I got this cell phone?" Diwata countered. "No matter; you can talk to one of them briefly."

Tondo, Manila, Republic of the Philippines

Diwata held the phone up to Benson's ear. "Again, no games," she warned.

"This is Sahgeant Benson, Terry. We're all heah, just

like the lady said. I'm worried about the maid, though. I don't know about her. I'm awful concerned about her, Terry."

"Forget her," Diwata said. "She's none of your business."

Safe House Alpha, Hagonoy, Bulacan, Luzon, Republic of the Philippines

Welch almost said, "Screw the maid." Then he wondered, *Why would Benson think I'd care?* He shot Malone a questioning look. *And why did Benson admit to his rank?*

Malone looked away and chewed his lip.

The voice on the phone changed back to the woman. "Happy now?"

"Happier," Terry replied. "Don't do anything drastic, Princess. I'll pay to get my people back. But it's going to take some time to raise the cash."

"You have a week. Call this number when you have it, and we can arrange the exchange. If it takes longer, the exchange will be easier, because there'll be fewer people involved. Goodbye."

"Goodbye," Welch whispered to the silent phone. He shut it off, then turned to Malone. "Is there a little something you haven't been telling us, Sergeant?"

Malone sat in front of a laptop, scrolling through the pictures of the literally thousands of escorts available in the Manila area.

Meanwhile, Welch, Graft, and Lox considered the options.

"Will the regiment pay?" the latter asked. "I mean, we've never set a policy, officially, because we've never had to. But the whole ethos of the organization would be *'don't* pay.'"

"That's easy to say," Graft said, "when it's strangers. When it's your own people, though, it becomes a little different." He shrugged. "Four million sounds like a lot of money. Hell, it *is* a lot of money. But there's no value you can place, in dollars and cents, on your friends."

Welch's mouth formed a moue. "*My* instinct is don't pay. My feelings, though, say, 'whatever it takes.' Well . . . half my feelings. The rest of them say, 'Get even, with interest.'

"Here's what we're going to do: If the girl was, in fact, a hooker or escort used for bait for kidnappings, we're going to try to find her, take her, and wring her dry. Don't care what it costs her; don't care in the slightest. The bitch, if we find her, is already dead, anyway.

"Meanwhile, I'm going to message the regiment, explaining what happened—shit, I'm going to hate explaining *this*; you fuckhead, Malone—and asking for a bank draft. I'm also going to need some advice from Boxer. If regiment won't provide, I'm going to ask our principal for an advance against expenses.

"If the girl, if we can find her, provides enough information for a rescue we'll do that. If not, we pay to get out people back. Then we do the original mission. Then we punish whoever took them in ways that will give their great-grandchildren nightmares."

Lox nodded. "If you've got the time, I've got a book on my reader, from some hack sci fi writer, that has a lot to say about punishing people."

★ CHAPTER TWENTY-SIX ★

Misery, mutilation, destruction, terror,
starvation and death characterize the process of war
and form a principal part of the product.
—Lewis Mumford

**Caban Island, Pilas Group, Basilan Province,
Republic of the Philippines**

There were two slaves kneeling on the dirt floor of Janail's
command hut, their hands bound behind them and their
faces pressed to the dirt. A pair of guards flanked each of
them, though one was a boy of perhaps fifteen and the
other a girl not much past twelve. The boy's body shouted
defiance, despite the dirty foot pressing his neck down.
The girl, on the other hand, shuddered with sobbing, her
tears wetting the dirt to either side of her nose.

One of Janail's many jobs, as leader of the Harrikat,
was to serve as a judge. Sometimes this was both tedious
and dangerous, as when two of his followers had an issue
with each other. Wherever justice might lay, there was
always the risk of the loser of the case going *juramentado*,

which was to say, in this sort of case, arming himself, possibly drugging himself, and going berserk against the judge who had ruled against him and anyone else unwise or unlucky enough to get in his way.

As a general rule, Janail had found it wise to recompense the loser from his own purse and possessions, thus maintaining the loser's honor and giving him no good excuse for going on a killing spree.

Most cases, however, were much, much easier. Of those, the ones involving the many Christian slaves on the island were easiest of all. Really, there were only four punishments. Women and girls were usually beaten, but sometimes beheaded. Men and boys were sometimes whipped, but about as commonly crucified. Three permanent crosses were kept north of the camp for just this purpose, while the whipping posts and chopping block were located down by the mosque. Conversely, the females could be beaten pretty much anywhere, with no real ceremony required.

Barring only a few that he'd given to the personal use of his *Datus*, the rest of the slaves were more or less public property. That meant that for any serious punishment the slaves always had to be brought to Janail for judgment, since public property, in this case, meant his property.

The nice thing about passing judgment on the Christian slaves was that Janail detested Filipino Christians and rather enjoyed punishing them.

"What did these two do?" asked Janail, as he walked between the slaves before turning to sit on his throne. His right palm came to rest on the copy of the Koran resting there, albeit mostly for show.

"We caught them making for the small boats," answered Molok, one of Janail's senior datus. "They had a parcel of food and two canteens stolen from stores."

"Related?" Janail asked.

"Brother and sister," answered Molok. "We grabbed them from a coastal village not far from Ipil."

"Been here long?"

"No," Molok replied. "Maybe three or four weeks."

"The rules were explained to them?"

"Yes," the datu said. "As soon as they arrived."

"Tsk, And they still didn't listen." Janail put his elbows on the arms of this throne and rested his chin on his clasped hands. "Are we short slaves?"

"No, not really," Molok said, curling his lip and shaking his head.

Janail made a show of consulting the Koran before giving his judgment.

"Crucify the boy." The girl screamed and the boy tried to rise to run before his guards kicked him over then dragged him to his feet.

"What about the girl?" Molok asked.

Janail shook his head. "No . . . I take a certain limited pride in tempering justice with mercy. The girl's not entirely responsible. We'll leave her her life but beat her—not too severely—and then—since she's old enough—she can entertain the guard shack for the next three nights."

"As you command," Molok said, bowing his head slightly and beginning to withdraw.

"On second thought," Janail amended, "have the girl watch what's done to her brother. It may save us having to kill her, later on, too."

★ ★ ★

No one actually knows where crucifixion began, or how whoever it was figured out that hanging someone with their arms above forty-five degrees would eventually cause death. It is possible, at least, that a few civil servants, in the middle of administering a judicial whipping somewhere, somewhen in Achaemenid Persia, decided to take a break for a cup of wine at the nearest public house. Perhaps they joked with their hanging victim, "Don't go away, Rustam; we'll be back."

Also, perhaps, as such things go, with one cup turning to two, to three, to an hour or so, they returned to find their charge, still hanging by his wrists with his feet just above ground, but now rather dead: "Doubt the whipping did it, we'd hardly given him a dozen strokes. Let's bring out another and see if we can't duplicate it."

Perhaps thus was born the scientific method.

As it has turned out, nails aren't necessary; tieing will do nicely. Nor is the crosspiece necessary, since the victim may be nailed or tied to the upright to the same effect. Indeed, as those long ago enforcers of Persian justice may have found, as did more modern researchers in Dachau, the upright piece isn't necessary either. A victim may be hauled up by a single rope tied to the wrists, with death following in, typically, about an hour.

There are, of course, those who feel that an hour's worth of slow suffocation isn't quite enlightening enough as regards the witnesses. For these purposes, the upright piece, the "stirpes," in Latin, is most useful since the feet can be affixed as well, with the knees bent. Done this way, death by crucifixion can take days. And the cross piece, the *patibulum*, also has its uses, for better efficiency, since the victims tied arms can simply be draped over it, or separately pulled by rope up to it, without all the bother of having to take down and erect the cross.

The girl—her given name was Maria—wept not for herself, though she knew what lay in store for her, but for her brother, Roberto. There were already two bodies hanging there, rotting and half eaten by birds. The idea that that would be her beloved brother . . . Maria began to shriek. On her knees she begged and pleaded, promising anything and everything she could, and some things she could not, for their captors to spare Roberto's life. The Moros were having none of it. And besides, "Don't be silly, girl; we'll take what we want from you with or without your permission."

For convenience's sake, one of the Moros punched Roberto in the solar plexus, just before untying his wrists. That reduced his struggles to a bare minimum as those wrists were rebound to long ropes draped over the *patibulum*. A few long pulls and the boy hung with his feet a yard or so above the ground.

There were already a couple of stout spikes driven into the stirpes. Loops of rope were run around these and around the boy's ankles, then tightened.

None of that was actually very painful. The downside of that was that without pain, the victim might show defiance. This was not to be tolerated, nor even risked. Pain there must be and pain there was as the Moros placed two circles of wood over the boy's heels, then took two long spikes and drove them through the wood, through the flesh, through the bone, into the stout stirpes below. The boy shrieked like a little girl, which shrieks were echoed by his young sister, with each hammer blow.

Then they peeled Maria away from the base of her brother's cross and dragged her by her hair to the guard shack.

Alone in his hut, the hut covered by the light-blocking jungle of the island, at night, with only a candle lit, sitting on a thin cushion, staring into the flickering light, Janail's innards were in turmoil. One might have thought that the earlier crucifixion, or the boy's screaming still filtering through the jungle from the north were the source, but no. Neither was it the sobbing girl whose multi-hour gang rape proceeded apace from a bit to the south. No, Janail was worried about his money and his nukes.

The Russian is threatening to sell to someone else. Chopping off one of the old bastard's fingers didn't get me immediate delivery. And now he's sick and the doctor says he might not make it if I chop off another one. 'Weak heart,' he says. 'Got to expect that in an old man.'

I could chop another one and publish the video, then demand a partial payment up front. Ah, but no, what's the use of that. One nuke gets me nothing. They either won't believe I have it or, if I use it, that will be it.

He stood up, the abrupt motion unsettling the air and causing the candle to flicker. Shadows danced around the hut's woven grass walls.

Pacing, Janail continued to ponder. *But . . . no, not necessarily. If I have one I can claim to have another.*

Would they take the risk that I might not? Would they risk millions of people?

Then again, Prokopchenko insisted they were a package deal, so what good does partial payment, that won't cover the both, do me? None.

Does he actually have another buyer? Who are you kidding, Janail? Be a realist. He has as many buyers as he wants. The only limit is on how many he's willing to let know what merchandise he has on offer.

Could I take them from him? Janail laughed at the notion. *Hah. He's got dozens of well armed, highly trained guards. I saw dozens. But it felt like hundreds. And that—hundreds—wouldn't surprise me a bit. Nor is his yacht a lobby, nor the sea a crowded city, where it's easy to sneak up on someone or set an ambush. Nor do I have anyone aboard to help. Even if I did, there's no telling what Prokopchenko would do if he were attacked and was losing.*

I have no desire to be at the center of . . . what's that Americanism? Oh, yes, an "Earth-shattering kaboom."

So what, in the name of the god in which I no longer believe, do I do?

Yacht *Resurrection*, between the coast of Kudat and the island of Pulau Banggi, South China Sea

There were really only three places Prokopchenko felt truly safe. One was in his palace—no other word would really do—outside Moscow. Another was his dacha and its compound, on the sea, west of Rostov on the Don. The third—sometimes—was on the *Resurrection*.

The *Resurrection* was problematic; there were just so many places he couldn't go, or, if he went, couldn't safely stay. Pirates? Bah; he could handle any pirates and no worries about some silly international tribunal bringing charges for it. There would be—rather, had been—no survivors, after all. No, if he had to, his yacht could take on every pirate in the world, simultaneously.

It was the regular forces that were a problem. The Vietnamese and Chinese were always out in the Spratlys, these days, looking to intimidate the other and, on occasion, actually engaging. Sometimes the Filipinos took a hand, too. The yacht was no match for a frigate.

And the regular ports? The bribes to keep the local "authorities" off his ship were endless and, if not precisely insupportable, insulting beyond Prokopchenko's willingness to bear.

So I'm stuck here, the Russian fumed, lying on his back, hands behind his head, dick recently wet, with Daria occasionally raising a snore beside him.

I'm stuck here with a mere one girl to entertain me, moving from one section of empty sea to another, with the nearest thing of interest the occasional at sea resupply. Well, that and watching my puts on the market.

Maybe sail to someplace approximately civilized and take the helicopter to land to find a few more women? Risky. Needlessly risky. I'm not precisely a wanted man, not by the authorities, but any number of local criminal gangs—local to wherever—would like to get their hands on me. And the fucking "civilized" ports, of course, won't let me take adequate security along. Idiots.

I wish that goddamned wog would hurry up and get

me my money, so I can give him the devices, so he can detonate one, so I can use that detonation as a kind of Reichstag fire to take power back home. Of course, it's risky, being in the same area and being a suspect for the delivery. But this is something I can't trust anyone else with. God, I despise humanity.

In that kind of foul mood Prokopchenko slapped the Ukrainian girl, saying, "Wake up and use your stupid mouth for something besides breathing through. It's what you're paid for."

Caban Island, Pilas Group, Basilan Province, Republic of the Philippines

What was, to Janail, mere distant screaming from the raped girl was, to his main prisoner, much closer and more personal. Her ordeal took place a bare thirty feet from where Ayala lay. It sounded like it was in the same hut.

Poor little shit, though Ayala.

His finger stump had stopped aching some time ago. From what Ayala could glean from the "doctor's" expression, this was not necessarily a good thing.

At the doctor's insistence they'd made Ayala something like a bed, and given him a thin blanket and, probably too late, a mosquito net. Neither of these, despite the tropic heat, kept him from shivering. He was still chained to his rock, in any case, though in his condition that was probably superfluous.

The infection in my hand or a touch of malaria? the old

man wondered. *No matter; either will be the death of me. And fairly soon, I think.*

I always thought that I'd die before my Paloma. No fear there. But I thought I'd die with a priest at one hand, my confession said, and Paloma holding the other. Now? No priest, no confession, no salvation. And the burden of my sins is heavy . . . heavy. And no Paloma.

I wish I could get her a message. I'd tell her to forget about me, forget about the ransom, and use the money for revenge. "Vengeance is mine,' sayeth the Lord." That's what the priests say, isn't it? Well, if I'm going to Hell anyway, what's a little more reason?

And if, somehow, by the grace of God, I ever get out of this alive, my entire fortune is going to revenge, and the fucking Moros' great-great-great grandchildren are going to shudder and scream at the mention of my name.

If . . . by the grace of God . . .

The shivering ceased as Ayala felt a wave of warmth come over him. *Oh, shit. Now comes the fever and the shakes.*

Just across the trail, a young girl shrieked anew as her masters tore her sphincter for about the fourth time this evening.

Allah not making an answer, Janail was left on his own. Slinging his rifle over one shoulder, he left his hut and walked to the shore to the north, where some low cliffs kept back the sea. On the way he passed by the crucifixion site, a couple of bodies, dead and stinking with decomposition, and one fifteen year old Filipino, struggling and, in effect, torturing himself to death.

Janail spent a moment looking up at the writhing body, just barely discernable in the jungle gloom. With an indifferent shrug, he continued on.

The old man's a wasting asset. I use him, or I lose him, anyway. So next week we're going to make another video, taking another finger. If he dies in the course of making it, so be it. We can cut that out of the recording. His family won't know, and the one in his family who has been helping us would rejoice if he did.

Reaching the low cliffs to the north, Janail sat, cross legged, looking to sea and thinking hard upon his unenviable plight.

After all, I'm only taking one chance among many. If he doesn't die this time he surely will next. And I never intended to give him back. At some point in time, we're going to be left with a corpse anyway. If we have the money, well and good; he becomes a corpse after that. If he dies before we have the money . . . well, we'd have had to bluff anyway.

Hmmm. That leads to an interesting thought. What if we take not one finger, then change his clothes a bit, then take another finger, maybe with a slightly different camera angle. Then we wash him up, bandage him, dirty the bandage, and change his clothes. Another slightly different camera angle . . . then a toe . . .

Yes, that's the trick. We'll take six months worth of videos in a single day. He'll probably die but that doesn't matter if we have the means to keep terrorizing his family.

Ah, Janail, you are brilliant..

Hmmm . . . should I get that cooperative journalist back? No, I think we can handle this better on our own, without any distractions. And better have the doctor get him as strong as possible so that he lasts long enough. I'll give the doctor that week.

I wonder, should we take as many parts as we possibly can before he dies? Mmm . . . no. Six—or five, even, if he doesn't last that long—should be more than enough. Anything beyond that—on the off chance he does last that long—would be gratuitous and I am, after all, a civilized man.

"Old man, get up," announced the guard, pulling on the chain that ran from Ayala's leg to the rock. The guard was one of two. In another time, a stronger Mr. Ayala might have been flattered that they felt he needed two guards. Now? Now he couldn't possibly care if they'd sent a regiment.

"Get up." *Tug. Tug.* "The boss wants to speak with you."

Ayala wasn't sure he even *could* rise. A quick inventory suggested it was possible. Another hard tug from the guard indicated it was necessary. Weakly, he forced himself to a sitting position, then to his feet. He started to fall over before the guard, younger, taller, fitter, and much, much healthier, caught him, one handed.

Ayala took one look at the camera, set up on its tripod, and turned to flee. The senior of the two guards caught him by his filthy, ragged collar, pulled back, spun him, and then cuffed him hard enough to split his lip.

By the collar, Ayala was dragged to his chief kidnapper's chair and thrown, roughly, to the ground.

Two men, both armed and wiry-looking, stood behind and to either side of the chair, which seemed to Ayala to be a sort of rude jungle throne. The men had their faces covered with thick gauze, wrapped around them, starting at the neck, then spiraling up to form something like turbans. Janail was similarly masked.

Behind them a green banner was hung, proclaiming something—Ayala had not clue one as to what—in Arabic script.

Janail nodded to the cameraman, who started recording.

In English, the language he and the Ayala clan shared best, he said, "I warned you what would happen if our demands were not met. I sent you instructions. You have not contacted me. You have not met my demands. This is the price of your intransigence."

"Take him."

The two veiled guards behind Janail came out from behind his pseudo-throne. One pushed Ayala over into the dirt. The other grabbed his leg and yanked, presenting the bare foot to Janail.

Janail picked up the same set of shears he'd used before. They were rustier now. He held them before him a bit for the cameraman to focus on.

"Please? Oh, plleassse! Nooo," begged the old man.

"Whine to your vile and decadent clan of oppressors," Janail responded, loudly enough for the microphone on the camera to pick up. "Only they can help you."

Twisting around in his seat, Janail locked one of Ayala's skinny ankles in a vise grip, forcing down the lesser toes as he did. Then he carefully placed the shears around the big toe. Squeezing once drew both blood and a shriek that would have made a kinder man blanch. Janail didn't care in the slightest.

The shears met bone, which resisted for a bit. The old bone was no match, though, for the strength behind the shears, especially once Janail began twisting them with his wrist. If anything, the old man's screaming redoubled.

The bone split with a audible crunch. Clamping down on the shears' handle, Janail severed the last shreds of flesh. Ayala's big toe popped off, flying several feet to the dirt. The camera followed its path, then held steady on the pitiful, bloodied bit of flesh for several long moments, Then, finally, it returned to the victim, lying on his back in the dirt and sobbing like a young child.

"Next month, it will be another piece," Janail finished, making an imperious gesture to stop the cameraman's recording.

"Ooo*kay*," the terrorist chieftain said, with enthusiasm, still in English. Reverting to his own language, and rubbing his hands together, he said. "That went pretty well. Now take him, bandage his foot up, but make the bandage look old and dirty. Clean him up a little. Change his shirt. Comb his hair. Then bring him back and we'll do number two. A finger this time, I think."

Quivering with shame, humiliation, disease, infection, and pain, the old man was dragged off to prepare him for his second ordeal.

★ CHAPTER TWENTY-SEVEN ★

And that is called asking for Dane-geld,
And the people who ask it explain
That you've only to pay 'em the Dane-geld
And then you'll get rid of the Dane!
—Rudyard Kipling, "Dane-geld"

Malate, Manila, Republic of the Philippines.

Aida wore a light sweater, pink, when she arrived. She'd been her before, and always found the air conditioning set too low.

Pedro's head was down, shaking back and forth slightly in a way that suggested he didn't even realize he was doing it. "She's in the TV room, Aida," he said. "She's in a bad way."

Aida nodded. She knew the gist of it but not the details. "How did the recording get here?" she asked.

"Junior found the disk on the front lawn. I suppose somebody frisbeed it in."

Aida grimaced. "Yeah, I suppose. Where is Junior? And why aren't you with the Kanos?"

"Junior's gone to the office. Says he can't stand to see his mother like this. They called me back to see if I could help with Madame."

Pedro sighed. "Aida, I'm not going to try to take your gun. But I'd appreciate it if you didn't let Madame see it. That's how bad a way she's in."

"Point taken," Aida agreed. "Though she's not nearly that weak. You don't have to escort me; I'll find her myself."

"Won't be hard, even if she's moved. And I've sent for the head of the Kanos. And a doctor who won't ask too many questions."

Long before even reaching the corridor that led to the "TV Room"—it was much more of a high end commercial theater in miniature—Aida heard the keening. It was high pitched, repetitive, and really not quite human-sounding.

Oh, dear.

The first thing Aida saw on the one hundred and eighty-four inch screen, mounted to one wall—yes, the peasantry could no longer have cheap, incandescent bulbs; this meant little to the very rich—was a very sharp image of something she could not, at first, identify. The screen was locked on that image. She stared for some moments, then drew her breath in sharply once she realized she was looking at a bloodied human toe, fuzzily displayed about twenty times life-size on the screen.

Aida couldn't see the tiny woman, being rather short herself and Paloma Ayala being dwarfed by the seat back. She didn't need to see, though, to know where Mrs. Ayala was; the keening sufficed for that. She walked forward about twenty feet and turned left, toward Madame. Mrs. Ayala had her arms crossed in front of her. She was rocking back and forth, rhythmically, tears pouring down her face, ruining her makeup. Paloma's hair was a torn-up mess. She had nothing around her neck, at the moment, though there were a number of mixed pearls and diamonds scattered across the floor. Even her customary crucifix was nowhere to be seen.

Taking a seat next to the stricken old woman, Aida reached out one arm, patting her back in a sort of *there, there* gesture.

Paloma turned toward Aida, then, still keening, rocking, and weeping, and buried her face in the other woman's shoulder. Automatically Aida wrapped her in a one-armed hug, then began stroking the tangled mess of Mrs. Ayala's hair with the other hand. *There, there.*

Aida rested her own cheek on the top of Paloma's head. "I'm so sorry, cousin. I'm so very, very sorry."

Shuddering, Paloma finally got a few words out, the words broken by sobs, sniffles, and shudders bordering on the epileptic. "I've . . . got . . . to . . . pay them, Aida. He's . . . old . . . older than me. He can't . . . take that." She wailed, "Aiaiaiaiai . . . he'll . . . aiaiaiai . . . he'll die!"

"If you pay them," Aida said, softly, "he'll surely die."

At those words, Paloma went into an even worse bout of pseudo-epileptic contractions.

Welch looked around the expansive and ornate— ornate almost to the point of tackiness—estate. *"Let me tell you of the very rich. They are different from you and me."*

"What happened?" Welch asked of Pedro, by the entrance into the mansion from the porte cochere.

Welch had a sudden, odd thought. *I like this guy because, not only doesn't he hesitate to do what's needed, I'm twice as big as he is and he's not remotely intimidated by that.*

"We got a video disk," the sometime taxi driver, sometime arms provider, and full-time bodyguard and doer-of-needful-things replied. "The Harrikat took off the old man's toe. I've seen the recording. He looked . . . bad. Really bad. I think Madame wants to pay the ransom."

"That would be . . . unwise," Welch said.

Pedro agreed. "You know that. I know that. So does Aida, who's in with her now. But Madame, she don't know anything except that the one person she loves most in the world is being slowly chopped to bits, that she can't stand that, and that she'll do anything to make it stop."

"You can kind of understand."

Welch nodded ponderously. "I *do* understand. It's still unwise."

"Yeah. C'mon, Mr. Welch, I'll bring you to her."

God, thought Welch, *I hate to see a woman cry. It just flips all kinds of genetic switches.*

Aida had wiped Paloma's runny nose and more or less reorganized her hair. The makeup was mostly rubbed off and resting among the fibers of Aida's sweater. It wasn't quite so uniformly pink anymore. About the stream of tears, she hadn't been able to do much.

Aida and Welch exchanged glances. Reluctantly, the woman said, "She wants to pay the Harrikat."

"I cannot even begin to explain what a bad idea that is, Madame."

Paloma couldn't speak; sobbing, she pointed a trembling hand more or less at the screen with its big bloody toe.

"Yes, I understand that. But if you pay there is no chance you will see your husband again. You'll see another ransom demand, for even more money, perhaps. But him? No, no; he's the goose with the golden eggs."

"When can you do a rescue then?" Aida asked. "He's not going to survive through much more of this."

That last set Paloma Ayala to howling: *Aiaiaiaiai . . . aiaiaiaia . . . aiaiaiaiai*

"We're pretty sure we know where he is. Madame was there for that. The rest of my force arrives in three days. We go in three or four days after that. Call it a week from now."

"Can you guarantee to save him?"

Welch shook his head. "I told Madame up front, there are no guarantees in this kind of thing, only odds. We have a preliminary plan, and I think we have a good chance . . . a *very* good chance. But no more."

Later, after Madame had been sedated and put to bed, Aida and Welch reviewed the video.

"Disgusting . . . disgusting . . . disgusting." Aida said it about every four seconds of the few minutes' duration.

"I need a copy of it," Welch said, when it was finished.

"Why? There's nothing there to see."

"You never know," Welch said, "And Lox is remarkably good at ferreting out things you wouldn't normally see."

Aida was a policewoman, and a good one. She knew that, on the global scale, Filipino police were about as good—if also about as corrupt—as could be expected in a poor country. She also knew there were capabilities that her force couldn't even dream of having. The Kanos just might.

"I'll have a copy made and give it to Pedro for you," she agreed.

Welch hesitated a moment, then said, "Ralph told me I could trust you. He told me before we left and he wrote it again, just recently. Can I trust you, Aida?"

She shrugged. "Depends on with or about what?"

Welch looked around, then stood up, walked to the theater door, and closed it. Returning to his seat next to Aida, he asked, "Any chance this place is bugged?"

Aida scoffed. "You seriously think the old man, or his wife, would ever set up something that might allow their conversations to be recorded or tapped?"

"Good point," he agreed. "I need some help. Some of my people have been grabbed . . . kidnapped."

"Muntinlupa?" she asked. At his confirming nod, she said, "Yes, I saw a report on that." She paraphrased, "One obvious Kano dead. Bloodstains. Some shooting besides. Maid was probably working for the kidnappers. Probably TCS."

"How'd you know about the maid?" Welch asked.

"It's their style."

"Yes . . . well, I brought in extra people, a half dozen of them, that Madame didn't know about."

"Why?"

Welch snorted. "Because I don't trust her."

"That's sensible," Aida agreed.

"Yeah, but I was too clever by half. They have four of my people. And I need them."

"Can't mount a rescue for them," she cautioned. "The papers would be all over it. And then the Harrikat would know you're here."

"Can the police do anything?"

Aida scoffed. again. "Sorry, but TCS's area has long since become a no go zone. We need to send the army in, but the pols don't want to admit it's gotten that bad.

"There is one good thing," she said.

"What's that?"

"Well, unlike the politicians, TCS, when bought, stays bought. They're a business; some ways just like any other. If you give them the ransom, they'll give you your people. They always have. Bad advertising if they didn't, ya know?"

"Will they actually kill my people?" Welch asked.

"Only if you don't pay." Aida answered. "Then? No question about it.

"The only real problem might be if one of them got killed. Then they've got another advertising issue going on: 'Don't resist us.'"

"Shit."

"No," Aida said, "you can't just grab some of theirs to trade. It wouldn't work unless you got the very highest leaders, and they're all in Tondo, surrounded by hundreds of armed men. Well trained? Maybe not. But there are a lot of them. That's *how* their area became no go to the police."

"Could we grab some of their wives? Kids? Husbands?"

Aida shook her head. "Same problem; they're all in Tondo."

Terry stood and paced for a bit, then asked, "What about the gangs around them?"

"Hate each other. Shoot on sight levels of hate, if one is found in the wrong area. The other . . . mmm . . . five or so . . . they hate TCS, too. Maybe even more, because TCS has been so successful. But they'd turn on your people, too, if you tried to go through them, which you would have to. There's a rough balance of power now. They wouldn't upset that lightly. And there are a couple of safe areas, exits in and out, where nobody shoots at anybody, by mutual agreement."

"Okay," Welch said. "Let me think on that problem for a bit. What's their method for trading the prisoners for their ransoms?"

"It's a multi step process," Aida explained. "You have a way to contact them? Maybe the victims' cell phones?"

If he wasn't convinced before, that detail convinced Welch the woman knew what she was talking about. "Yes, I have a way."

"When you tell them you have the ransom, they'll give you a time to be at some particular place. That place may or may not be covered by their people. No matter, they'll send you three, four, maybe five more places and one of those *will* be covered, to make sure you're not being tailed, and don't have a force with you."

"Day or night?" he asked.

"No set pattern. Odds are . . . day, though. They're not stupid and know what they don't have. Day means their eyes are as good as yours. Night means you might have an advantage they can't match.

"They'll be at the place where the exchange is to take place well in advance, one or two hours, anyway, well before they tell you where to finally go. You won't have a chance to set up an ambush or a rescue there."

"Do they prefer rural exchanges or urban?" Welch asked.

"Generally, urban. They know the police have qualms about a major firefight in a crowded area."

"We're not police."

"Yes," Aida agreed, "and they know you aren't. That doesn't mean they'd discount the possibility you might have police backup. And you've got another advantage and a disadvantage TCS doesn't know about, or at least probably doesn't know about. If they knew who and what you were, they'd probably have left your people alone in the first place. Since they didn't leave them alone, they don't know what you might, just might, be able to do."

"Yeah," Welch agreed, "ignorance can be a dangerous thing. And, you know, if they have an advertising and public relations issue with one of their being killed, so do we.

"I don't suppose you have a way to communicate with the leaders of the other gangs?"

"Could be," Aida admitted.

"Do you have a list of places where they've done exchanges before, and with whom?"

"I can get it."

"What will we owe you?" Welch asked.

"Nothing. I really don't like the idea of some self-declared foreigners claiming sovereignty inside *my* country. I'll get you the file on TCS, too."

★CHAPTER TWENTY-EIGHT★

No man will be a sailor who has contrivance
enough to get himself into jail; for being in a ship is
being in a jail, with the chance of being drowned.
—Dr. Samuel Johnson

MV *Richard Bland*, Laccadive Sea, southeast of the Maldives

Even from the top of the superstructure, no land was in
sight. Neither were there any ships of any size. There
were a couple of fishing boats, small things, probably
family owned and operated. But those were far away and
hard to see.

There might have been satellites overhead, thus the
aviation mechanics worked their birds—all of which had
seen some pretty hard use at Bajuni—under double tarps,
stretched out between the containers that formed walls on
a lower, open area. Even without the chance of a satellite
overhead, the tarps would still have been doubled. If they
hadn't, the maintenance area would have been an
absolute oven. As was, with the breeze from the forward

motion of the ship, it really wasn't bad. The tarps wouldn't necessarily protect the gunships and CH-750's from observation, but it would probably take a human being to dial up the requisite filters to spot them, not a mere computer program.

Bland was a much happier ship—*much*—than it had been not so very long ago. Despite their losses, success had proven a sovereign remedy for most of their ills. Better still, with the women of Adam's followers aboard, a new line of cooking had been added to the galley's repertoire. They were grateful to have been saved, even if their current accommodations were a little suboptimal, and had kicked in to help where and when they could.

Besides, though the men were under tight enough discipline that there had been no incidents between Adam's people's women and them, it was just *pleasant*, very pleasant, to have the tall, generally attractive, and gracefully swaying women aboard.

"Okay," said Captain Pearson, "so you were fucking right. No need to gloat."

"*Not* gloating," insisted Warrington, with a wag of a finger. "Just happy."

"Bullshit," the skipper said. "I know a gloat when I see one."

Warrington shrugged, then held up thumb and forefinger, spaced closely. "Okay, maybe a *leettle* bit of gloating. But really, mostly I'm just pleased."

"We've still got problems, you know," Pearson said, with bad grace.

"Oh, many, many," Warrington agreed, cheerfully.

"My sergeant major is still concussed, puking his guts out at random intervals. We've got a hold full of some very unhappy humanitarians. Eventually some dipshit is going to try to get at the Marehan girls. Balbahadur's pipes still assault the air, with frightful regularity. And I have it from Welch that there are a couple of problems—and not small ones—on the other end. And then there's the question of Labaan, Adam, and the other men from Bajuni. They're all guilty of piracy and slave taking.

"Lots of problems, as you said."

"Yeah, and what are you going to do about them?"

"Easy. In the case of the Marehan I'm going to take the Foreign Legion approach: Who fucking cares what they did before? Kiertzner's being relieved of duty as first sergeant of C company and taking over as detachment sergeant major. I've got a double armed guard on the Marehans' section of the ship, on our side, and a quadruple guard on their side, of their own men. Welch's problems are not ours until we get there . . . three days?"

"About that," Pearson agreed.

"I confess, I don't have a solution to the problem of bagpipes in the middle of the night. And I'm not quite sure what to do about the tranzis, though I am leaning toward Stocker's suggestion of having them walk the plank. Well, except for some of the genuine medicos. Those, we can use."

"What the hell do they want, anyway?" the captain asked.

"Nothing unreasonable, really. They want to be let off at the nearest port."

Shaking his head violently, Pearson said, "We can't do that."

"Nope. Any idea what the law of the sea says?"

Laughing, Pearson said, "It says 'fuck 'em.' I'm not a lawyer, mind you, but as far as I can tell, none of these people fall precisely under any of the pertinent conventions and neither, exactly, do we."

"Wonderful thing," Warrington said, "the law. I wonder—"

The interrupting knock on the hatch stopped whatever Warrington had been about to say. Pearson demanded, "What is it?"

"Sir," said the rating at the hatch, "it's the civilians, down below. They're all up in arms."

"Oh," said Pearson, "the tranzis are revolting, are they?"

Warrington and Pearson trudged down the ladders to the mess level, then entered the mess deck. Lunch was due, in about an hour, its aroma permeating the air. The smell was unfamiliar, so it was probably the women from Bajuni taking their willing turn at mess duty.

Kiertzner sat by the port side of the mess deck, watching some instruction going on. Warrington didn't know what the subject was, and didn't think he had the time to find out. He did a double take, though, at the instructor. It was Sergeant Feeney, who seemed, at second look, to be very kindly and gently leading a platoon from C Company through assembly and disassembly of some of the off the wall weapons 2nd Battalion used.

"Wait a sec, Skipper," Warrington requested of

Pearson, before walking over to take a seat beside Kiertzner. "Ummm . . . Top . . . what's with Feeney?"

"You mean his suddenly taking a professional interest in the development of the Guyanans, sir?" Kiertzner asked.

"Well . . . umm . . . that, and that he's not trying to kill one of them. Or more than one."

"It's really very simple, sir," Kiertzner began to explain, in a received pronunciation accent that just about all the Americans found highly amusing. "Feeney is a borderline sociopath, a 'useful sociopath,' we sometimes say. But a useful sociopath isn't a sociopath at all. He's perfectly capable of relating to other human beings as morally important creatures in their own right. He simply defines 'human being' differently than do most. Indeed, at some level, the 'useful sociopath' is perhaps the sanest among us. He doesn't feel he should hate someone for looking a little different, and therefore, quite logically, sir, feels no need to love someone for looking a little bit the same.

"In any case, once the humanitarians showed up, they provided a sufficient 'other' for Feeney to elevate—and I'm sure he hasn't a clue that that's what's going on in his head—well . . . to elevate the Guyanans to provisional human beings, in his particular universe. Thus, as full human beings, albeit provisional, they're entitled to all the consideration, kindness, and care that he would normally give to any other full human beings, few as those may be.

"Do you see, sir?"

Warrington shook his head. "I'm honestly not sure, Top."

"Well . . . then just trust me, sir."

"Oh, I do. Still, it's odd. Tell you what, though, I think I'm going to need Feeney in about half an hour to impress some people with their position in life."

"The tranzis, sir?"

"Precisely."

Kiertzner smiled broadly and wickedly. "I'll make sure he's available, sir."

Oh, goody, thought Warrington, *at least they're not chanting, "Give Peace a Chance."*

What the humanitarians *were* doing, however, was throwing things—rations, furniture, garbage, the buckets they'd been given until the crane crew could dig down to the extra porta-potties—at the guards. And, though they'd been assigned six containers to sleep in, all had crowded into just one.

And then, of course, they sat down in that one, started rocking side to side, clapping, and singing, "All we are sayyyiiinnnggg . . ."

Warrington and Pearson stopped, the rating behind them and centered. Pearson crossed his arms while Warrington put hands on hips. Both smiled, evilly.

Evil smiles or not, the singing went on, ". . . is give peace a chance . . ."

Turning to the Captain, Warrington observed, "They seem ungrateful for their rescue."

"Dreadfully so," the *Bland*'s master agreed. "However, they're *your* charges. You rescued them. You figure out what to do about them."

Turning his head over one shoulder, Warrington told

the rating, "Please get me the acting sergeant major and Sergeant Feeney."

The rating shot a quizzical glance at his captain, who gave a couple of curt nods. *Do as the man says.*

The aid workers shut up when Warrington and the skipper walked right up to the opening, with the former banging on the corrugated metal sides of the thing for attention.

"What do you want?" *As if I didn't know already. I really hope they don't force me to make an object lesson of somebody. Yeah, morally I think they're crawling shits, but that doesn't mean they aren't technically useful. And they're more useful if I can trust at least some of them with the run of at least some of the ship.*

"We want to be released," said several of them, in unison. The other joined in, in a cacophony. "Wewewewawanttooobebererelealeasedeasedeased."

"You don't care for our hospitality?" Warrington asked.

"We want to go home! We don't want to have anything to do with your fucking evil corporation. You can't keep us here while you go make war on somebody, probably innocent Third World victims of corporate America."

"I see." He held up one finger and said, "Hold on a second."

At that time Acting Sergeant Major Kiertzner and Sergeant Feeney showed up. The aid workers all knew about Sergeant Feeney, the man who had pushed poor Doctor Saffron off the rubber boat, probably to drown. But seeing him in the dark, seated low, and seeing him in the light, standing, were two remarkably different things.

At about five foot ten, Feeney wasn't really that tall. Indeed, many of the aid workers had height on him. Where no two of them could match him, however, was in the shoulders, which seemed to be nearly as broad as he was tall. The sergeant had his sleeves rolled up. His arms would have done nicely for an illustration on the cover of a Conan the Barbarian novel. All of this was made worse, more intimidating anyway, by the sergeant's having about a twenty-nine inch waist. But the really horrifying thing was the face, and that wasn't even scarred. What it was, however, was the very platonic essence of *mean looking*.

The complaints dropped to a low rumble, and that with an undertone of terror, as soon as the tranzis got a good look, in the light, at Feeney.

"You wanted us, sir?" Kiertzner asked, conversationally, if artificially loudly.

Warrington matched volume. "Uh, yes, Sergeant Major." Officially, of course, Kiertzner was not, or not yet. But he had the job; he could have the title, too.

"What I would like is for you to supervise Sergeant Feeney in taking these people who don't appreciate our hospitality topside and having them walk the plank."

"Well, sir," Kiertzner said, "I'm not a sailor, really. Neither is Sergeant Feeney. We barely know our way from one end of a ship to the other. It would be a big help if the naval crew could set up the plank for us."

"Good point," Warrington agreed. "Uh, Skipper?"

Pearson had a hard time of it keeping a straight face. Raising his own voice helped a bit. "Yes, Major?"

"We do have a plank somewhere aboard ship, don't we?"

"We may have to look a bit," Pearson replied. "Why . . . it's been six months,"—he thought about that for a moment, as if puzzled—"yes, at least six, since we had anyone walk the plank. You wouldn't mind if I assemble the crew on deck to witness punishment, would you? You know how the men like a good show. They'll be happy to set it up for you."

"Your ship, sir. Your rules. And thank you, sir."

Warrington turned his attention back to his unwilling passengers and asked, "Are there any Olympic class swimmers here? Someone who could help the rest swim the roughly seventy-five miles to shore?" Seeing there were not, and seeing the suddenly blanched faces, he added, "Pity. Some of you might have made it that way. Oh, well, you insist on being released right away. It's a free world . . . sort of. So we'll make this one little accommodation.

"Oh," Warrington finished, before turning to leave, "if any of you believe in God, I suggest this would be a good time to make your peace with Him."

"They can't be serious," announced the woman whose rear end had once been used for a stop signal. Her name, not that anyone in M Day really cared, had turned out to be Jennifer Duke. "People don't do this sort of thing."

"*Our* kind of people don't," said a man seated next to her, one Sean Zink, rather more softly. "Who knows what their kind of people would do? Maybe we should have just shut up and been happy we weren't going to be sold as slaves in the Bajuni market."

"I still can't believe—"

Kiertzner harrumphed. "Sergeant Feeney, make a believer of that woman."

"Women and children first?"

"Something like that."

When Feeney walked into the container, his broad bulk seeming to fill the thing, all the others backed away as far as the close confines and the press of their own bodies would permit. The woman, too, attempted to scoot back. But there really wasn't any room. Feeney grabbed her by the hair and hoisted her to her feet.

That *hurt*. At about that time she decided that, yes, maybe these animals were serious and, yes, maybe she and the rest should have just shut up. *Did I assume that because some of them were white they were more civilized than the Africans who held us before? Oh, dear.*

"C'mon, sweetie," Feeney said, "this won't take long."

He stopped for a half second, then asked, "Sergeant Major, can I fuck her first?"

Kiertzner shook his head with disappointment (to say nothing of distaste, the woman was *most* unattractive). "Definitely *not*, Sergeant Feeney. Our mission is to toss them over the side, not to dally with them. And there's no *time*, Sergeant. You should *know* that. Where's your sense of *mission*, son?"

Feeney looked down at the deck, shamefaced. "Yes, Sergeant Major. Sorry, Sergeant Major. It just seemed like a waste. Oh, well. C'mon bitch."

The problem there, thought Kiertzner, *is that* I'm *acting, but Feeney is not.*

He's serious, thought the woman. *Ohmygodhe'sSERIOUS!*

She turned begging eyes to Kiertzner. "Please, I'll be good from now on. Don't hurt me."

Kiertzner shook his head, regretfully. "I'm sorry, Madam," he said, "but you made a request to be released immediately, which request both my commander and the captain of this vessel have approved. You will have to take this up with them.

"Off with her, Sergeant Feeney."

If anything, the refined accent in which those words were spoken added, and perhaps immeasurably, to the woman's horror.

★CHAPTER TWENTY-NINE★

Barbarism is needed every four or
five hundred years to bring the world back to life.
Otherwise it would die of civilization.
—Edmond de Goncourt

8767 Paseo de Roxas, Makati City, Manila, Republic of the Philippines

Welch looked ashen, that and confused, as he emerged from the tower fronting the triangular green parkway on the other side of the dual lane road. Lox, waiting at the entrance to the building, had to raise his voice to be heard over the sounds of traffic coming from the intersection to the east and the matching road—amusingly enough named for their principal client—to the west.

"What's wrong, Terry?"

Welch shook his head. Almost too softly to be heard, he answered, "The bank manager didn't understand why, either, but the Philippine government has ordered a stop on all transactions involving the corporation or Guyana. They wouldn't honor the draft."

"My guess," Lox said, "would be that the international community of the very caring and sensitive put a little pressure on them, all 'in the interests of peace,' of course, and probably all across the globe. That, or it's just the Philippine government trying to control the usual menu of problems. Shit. What are we going to do, boss?"

"I don't know. I'd considered asking our principal for an advance from escrow, but she's almost ready to throw in the towel, anyway. That might just push her over the edge, and without getting us the advance."

"Better think of something quick. We've got two days before they hang one of Benson's men."

Terry snapped then, something he rarely did. "God-damn-it, Lox, fucking tell me something I don't already know."

Lox blinked several times in shock. "Geez, sorry, Terry."

Ashamed, Welch shook his head. "No, *I'm* sorry. I shouldn't have snapped at you. But I don't know what to do. And it's making me sick. Jesus, I wish I'd never taken on this gig. *Nothing* is working out right."

Lox nodded. *I understand; fuggedaboutit*. Then he added, "Hey, I got a call while you were in the bank. If it helps any, Malone thinks he's identified the girl."

Safe House Alpha, Hagonoy, Bulacan, Luzon, Republic of the Philippines

The rest of the advance party was clustered around Malone, where he sat in front of a monitor. The sergeant's eyes were bloodshot and his face slack and weary. He hadn't slept since his half of the team had been taken.

Instead, he'd spent every moment pouring over the on line ads of Manila's *very* many escorts, prostitutes, and courtesans. There were over one hundred thousand women, and not a few transvestites, in the Manila area. Only the fact that most of them couldn't afford to take out an ad, that, and the search function, had let Malone whittle them down to a still huge number.

"I'm sorry, sir," Malone said. "Maybe they shouldn't all look alike to me, but they do. At least enough alike that it was too hard to tell. But I'm over ninety percent certain this is her. And none of the others fit the bill at all."

Malone's finger pointed at a—*Well*, thought Welch, *frankly good looking*—Filipina in a not very flattering or tasteful pose. *Besides, not his fault foreigners are hard to distinguish. To our brains, they* do *look more like each other than they look different to us. Damned shame reality is misogynist, racist, and mean.*

"*Not* a hundred percent. After fucking her in every God-damned hole, you still can't identify her?"

Malone hung his head. "No, sir. Not a hundred percent."

"Useless fuckwad," Terry said. Malone's chin dropped just that much more.

"Well, we're not going to kidnap and 'interrogate' some poor innocent hooker because Malone could only concentrate on his own dick. We need to make sure before we touch her."

"Graft?"

"Yessir."

"You take Malone and another man, maybe two—your call who, and how many—and get a hotel room or rooms. Make an arrangement for this girl"—he indicated the image on the screen with a gesture—"to do a house call. If it's her in person, take her and bring her here. If not, enjoy your blowjob and get Malone back on the computer to find the right girl. And bring me *that* girl."

"Yessir."

"Better get an expensive hotel. If she's in the business of marking clients for kidnapping, she'd never come to a cheap place. Wouldn't be good hunting territory."

"Lox?"

Lox felt a sudden wave of something like nausea—or, at least, anxiety—pass over him. He was pretty sure he knew what was coming. "Sir."

"You're not going to like this," Welch said, "but—on the off chance that Malone is slightly less of a fuckhead than all the recent evidence seems to suggest—you're going to have to interrogate a woman. And you're not going to be able to take much time over it."

Lox transformed his face into a stone mask. What he did to any personal feelings he might have had—concerning that or anything else—were entombed with the face. Without a word he left the room, the building, and then went to his interrogation room.

"Aida's report on TCS is on my desk, Lox," Welch called to the warrant officer's back.

Hotel Dusit Thani, Makati City, Manila, Republic of the Philippines

Welch had said, "A hotel room or rooms." Graft didn't feel like being doctrinaire about it; he got two suites.

"The girl's more likely to make an effort to show up someplace nice," was Graft's stated reasoning. "Besides, they'll be better insulated for sound."

The suites, well furnished and about eight hundred square feet, each, were nice, and also well insulated. Light gold carpets matched darker gold drapes. The couches were striped, white, and a light green. There were even a few live plants.

Graft had taken three other men, including Malone. One of those, Ferd Franceschi, waited with him in the hotel room. Both had used false passports to register. Another man, Semmerlin, with a very tiny pen camera in his pocket, waited outside. Malone was in a nearby room, watching a laptop linked to both Semmerlin's camera and another in Graft's room, poised on the laptop and facing the hotel room door. A couple of unpacked bags had been left on display. It wouldn't do to make the girl bolt early by looking like anything but a western businessman, lonely and horny. That said, the bags contained nothing but chunks of wood, packed in crumpled newspaper. Everybody was linked by cells with Bluetooths. The laptop linked to Semmerlin and his pen-cam was the only thing that wasn't there just for display.

Ferd watched the thin parade of girls leaving taxis and chauffeured autos, displayed on the laptop's screen. Occasionally he whistled and occasionally he sighed. "What did you say these girls cost?"

"About sixty bucks," Graft answered. "For whatever you want to do to them."

"Jesus," the Aussie exclaimed. "That's shit. Those are some nice looking sheilas."

Graft laughed, cynically. "You think that's cheap? Out of that sixty, the girl will be lucky to see two. Shitty world, isn't it?"

"Yeah . . . right shitty."

A voice came from each man's Bluetooth. It was Malone.

"Semmerlin, that girl in the white dress with flowers printed on it. That's her, to about ninety-nine percent."

"Are you sure that's the girl who set you up?" Graft asked.

"No, ninety-nine percent, like I said. Not *much* doubt about it. I wasn't that sure from the pic on line. I'm that sure now."

"Well . . . Semmerlin, did you make the car she came in?"

"It was a taxi, Graft, no guard or chauffeur. It's gone. I got the phone number if you think it's necessary."

"Nah, we can probably forget about the taxi."

"What would you have done if it had been a dedicated driver?" Ferd asked.

All three, Graft, Semmerlin, and Malone, answered simultaneously, "Killed him." Semmerlin added, "Assuming the girl's one hundred percent, and then I'd have made it look like a robbery."

TCS had given Maricel several days off for a job well done. It wasn't an excessively generous organization, though. After her brief leave, she was instructed to get back to work. Her work, of course, was primarily prostitution, but with the related and significant side line of finding targets. Since TCS allowed her very little of the money she brought in via selling herself, finding an attractive mark to take for ransom, and the resulting bonus, were an important part of her livelihood, however infrequently the opportunity arose.

Fortunately, her mother, long since retired, ordinarily took care of Maricel's baby when she had to work. Her mother lived in Valenzuela City, well north of Tondo.

She'd worked the Dusit Thani many times before, so many, in fact, that she'd long since lost count. She actually liked it more than most places, because, for a working girl, the Dusit Thani was safe. That's why she'd been able to take a taxi, rather than have to wait for a guard and driver to take her. And, of course, without having to wait for a guard and driver, she hadn't had to tell TCS's "entertainment division" that she was on the job.

Some hotels made a girl registered there take the employee's entrance. The Dusit, however, didn't mind if you came in through the lobby provided you didn't *look* like a hooker. Maricel had taken some pains in that respect. It hadn't hurt that she'd had quite a bit of practice lately, in Muntinlupa, looking, dressing, and acting like a normal woman. Moreover, some of her unusually large earnings had gone into a couple of tasteful new dresses, a new purse, and a new pair of Italian heels to match.

Gliding past potted palms, she stopped off at the desk, to have the desk clerk call and announce her to the client. This he did in a very businesslike way. He knew, of course, what Maricel did for a living, but any show of knowing that might have detracted from the hotel's image and reputation.

"Mr. Springfield?" Well, that's what the guest's passport

had said. "There's a young lady who says you're expecting her . . . ah, yes, sir. I'll send her right up."

Waiting for the elevator, Maricel thought, *The American on the other end of the phone sounded pretty lonely. With any luck, this could turn into a long engagement and a nice tip, even if he turns out not to be a good candidate for kidnapping. They've never yet beaten me for only making a week's worth of money. They wouldn't this time, either. And, fair's fair, at least they leave me my tips.*

About ten seconds after opening the door for the girl and saying hello, which is to say, just enough time to close the door, walk to the chair, and start to undo his belt, Graft heard in his Bluetooth, "One hundred percent; that's her!"

Before the girl could even sink to her knees, Graft spun around, punched her just above her face—*Ugh, I hate doing that to a woman*—knocked her down, jumped over her, spun her belly down, and gave her a second punch in the kidneys. The girl didn't even have time to scream before the excruciating pain in her kidneys had her gasping like a dying fish.

"Ferd," ordered Graft, "needle!"

Franceschi came out of the bathroom, bearing a syringe in one hand. He tapped the syringe with one finger of the other, then bent and gave Maricel the injection full in the buttocks.

"Semmerlin, car, exit B, three minutes."

"Roger."

"Malone, evacuate."

"Roger."

"Leave the bags but *don't* forget to take the laptops. Ferd, give me a hand with this girl."

Safe House Alpha, Hagonoy, Bulacan, Luzon, Republic of the Philippines

Lox's face was still a stone mask when Ferd and Graft carried the girl in, each with her under an arm. She was still groggy, but not completely unconscious. She also had a large welt growing on her forehead that bid fair to turn into a major bruise.

"Take her clothes off and tie her to the table," he said tonelessly. "Then hook her up. Ferd, get on the field telephone; it's about time for you to find out just how shitty our job can be."

"Let's hope she's not a subbie," Graft joked.

"Wouldn't matter if she were," Lox said. If anything, his voice had grown even duller. "I don't know her safe word."

If he'd ever heard anything more heartbreaking in his life, Lox didn't know what it had been. Ferd, in a corner where the girl couldn't see, was wiping his eyes. The girl, herself, moaned and wept, repeating endlessly, "Please . . . please . . . don't hurt me anymore . . . I'm just a poor girl . . . I'm just a poor girl . . . please . . . "

Rather than having another witness to check stories against, Lox had had only the file. He began the . . . for lack of a better word, the training, of the girl with questions he could check against information in Aida's file in which he thought he could place high confidence. He'd also lied to her, telling her that they'd also grabbed another member of TCS to check her story against.

She'd broken very quickly. The problem, however, had been that the file lacked a great deal of the information desired . . . and the girl had lacked it, too. There'd been little choice, then, but to hurt her until it was really obvious, *painfully* obvious, that she just didn't know.

"C'mon, Ferd," Lox said, "time for a cigarette break."

Franceschi looked, quizzically. He knew Lox didn't smoke. Even so, when Lox went to the door, Ferd followed.

Ferd left Lox alone, sitting on the side steps, with his head in his hands, shaking. That's where and how Welch found him, though a puddle of pungent puke had been added since Ferd had left him there.

"Did you find out what we needed to know?"

"As much as she knew. It wasn't enough."

"Damn."

Lox raised his head. "Don't you *ever* ask me to do something like that again. Not. EVER. And we're *not* going to kill the girl."

Welch nodded. He understood. "I wasn't planning on it. And I won't; you did what had to be done, but there are limits to what you can ask of someone, even of the things that have to be done. As for offing her . . . we're going to have to think and talk about that one."

★CHAPTER THIRTY★

Depend upon it, sir,
when a man knows he is to be hanged in a fortnight,
it concentrates his mind wonderfully.
—Dr. Samuel Johnson

MV *Richard Bland*, Laccadive Sea, southeast of the Maldives

Jennifer Duke pleaded all the way to the galley area. She begged her way past the cooks and kitchen, and through the tables. She wept up the several ladders in the super-structure, on the way to the top level of containers. At the hatchway to the open deck behind the superstructure, with the sight, sound, and smell of the churning sea she was sure would be her grave, before her, she simply collapsed in quivering mass of human jelly.

Then, too, it might have been the funeral march Balbahadur was playing on his pipes that was the final straw.

Sergeant Feeney didn't care. Though his taste in women was of the "one hole's as good as another" variety, as far as he was concerned she was a lot closer in moral importance to jelly than to human. He applied a boot, perhaps a little harder than was strictly necessary, propelling her out onto the deck, face first.

Pearson had a modicum of his crew, all that weren't needed for other duties, standing by, in ranks. The few soldiers and airmen present just sort of milled about, until Warrington called, "Fall in."

"Get up, cunt," Feeney said, his voice cutting into her like a serrated knife, "or I'll kick you all the way to the gangway."

Sobbing loudly, with snot running down her face and across her mouth, then dripping from her chin, Jennifer rose to all fours, then to her knees. She recognized no one aboard, except for the two, Pearson and Warrington, who had sentenced her to death. Pearson was the closer of the two.

Whence the strength came, Jennifer was not quite sure. But wherever it came from, she found it. She propelled herself forward, from knees to feet, then pushed her feet into a near blur, racing for Pearson. Her run, and the jiggling of her jowls, caused runny snot to fly from her chin in all directions.

At the vessel's master, she fell to her knees again, wrapped both arms tightly around his thighs, and begged, "Please don't throw me overboard. I'll do anything. I'll sign anything. I'll be your ship's slave. But don't kill me."

"Major Warrington?" Pearson called out, though the other was a bare twenty feet away.

"Captain?" *Silly custom.*

"I believe this person has requested the hospitality of

my ship. She promises to be a good girl—isn't that right, madam?—if we just refrain from granting her request of only a few minutes ago. I have my doubts that she can be trusted. Will *you* take responsibility for her?"

"Jeez, Captain, I dunno . . . "

That last burst of strength had been all Duke had. She crawled the 20 feet to Warrington, clasping him around the ankles, still begging.

Warrington sighed, loudly and impatiently. That was for her benefit.

"Puh . . . puh . . . puh . . . puhleeze?"

He sighed again. "Oh, very well. But this is your very last chance to behave.

"Sergeant Hallinan?"

"Sir!"

"Take this woman to . . . oh, the clerk's office will do, I suppose. Have her write out, in her own hand, a request to be permitted to stay aboard ship and her appreciation for our making room for her, even though we can't bring her to port yet." Warrington mused for a moment, then added, "Oh, and an *earnest* desire to help us in our good work, in any capacity for which we find her suitable."

Hmmm . . . harpoon practice, maybe.

"Sir!" Hallinan broke ranks and walked over, then helped Duke to her feet. "Come on, ma'am, I'll help you to the clerk's place."

"Th . . . th . . . th . . . tha..a . . . a..ank you."

"Sergeant Feeney?"

"Sir." The sergeant sounded vaguely disappointed.

"Go get another one."

"Sir!"

★ ★ ★

"Are we going to have to pull this fucking charade with all fifty?" Pearson asked. "It'll take hours, maybe even days, if we start having to drag them all the way. I'm a busy man."

"Nah," Warrington replied. "Relax. Another half dozen or so and I'll have the acting sergeant major ask generally if there is anyone who doesn't want to walk the plank. They'll all take the offer; *depend* on it."

"And what if one of them refuses to back down?"

Warrington looked over the stern, contemplatively. "Then the sharks get a free meal. But it's not very likely. You very rarely have to carry through on a threat when it's really obvious that you can and *will*."

MV *Richard Bland*, Sunda Strait

Though it was a bit out of the way, and more than a bit more treacherous to navigate, Pearson had chosen the Sunda Strait, rather than the Straits of Malacca, to make *Bland*'s passage into the waters around Malaysia. It had been a close call. There were still some very hungry pirates infesting both passages, but the Indonesian Navy did a rather better job controlling them in the Sunda Strait, which was much closer to the capital of Jakarta. In some ways, the world's current economic circumstances helped there; Indonesia no longer had the money to pay for running and maintaining big, flashy, and essentially useless major warships. They had kept their corvettes and patrol boats, as well as a couple of the newer and more economical Dutch-built Sigma Class frigates. These were, in every way, more suitable to Indonesia's real security problems.

Of course, there were pirates and then there were pirates. The Indonesian government didn't object to merchant vessels being armed, not anymore. Even the blue hulled megayacht following the *Bland* had obvious armed guards fore and aft, as well as along the sides.

Still, Indonesia might have objected to a de facto assault carrier traveling its waters without declaring itself as such. Fortunately, to object the government had to know. To know, their own inspecting officials would have to tell them. To tell them, the inspecting officials would have had to feel that the bribes offered to keep their noses out of the hold were insulting.

Captain Pearson never gratuitously insulted anybody, and, hence, made sure that those officials' unofficial gratuities were adequate, plus a little . . . all in the interests of international chumship, freedom of the seas, and recognition of the very fine job done by Indonesia's gallant navy—where fine job was partially defined by several score crosses on Sumatra's coast, to the north, almost all of which bore the cold body of a pirate who had died, oh, a very hard death.

It had become a rather hard world. That was, in fact, why many people had turned to piracy. That was also why many others had turned to more traditional methods to combat piracy.

Sweeping the southern tip of Sumatra with a pair of very powerful binoculars, Pearson muttered, "Damn, that's a hard way to go. Two of those poor bastards are still writhing. Oh, well, so far as I know, Sura Five of the Koran doesn't require breaking the legs after three days."

Hmmm . . . there's a lesson there, I think.

Feeney stood almost unblinking and very nearly motionless in front of the container the humanitarians had been placed in for the passage. It just wouldn't do to have one of them find his or her way to the superstructure and drive up the bribe required by the Indonesians. Not even the doctors and RN's, who had been given almost the run of the ship after their enthusiastic—where "enthusiastic" meant scared shitless—conversion to the cause. They were scared shitless now, too, with that *ogre* standing watch over them.

Feeney wasn't precisely annoyed that he hadn't been really allowed to make any of them walk the plank, but it wouldn't be quite right to say he was happy with the officers' charade either.

Nothing showed on his face either way. In its way, that was more terrifying to the humanitarians than an expression of sheer hate would have been. Feeney simply didn't see them as human beings and they *knew* it.

Hallinan knew better than to startle Feeney when he was in the zone. From just to one side of a hatchway, behind a metal bulkhead—in other words, safe from a spraying shotgun—he coughed loudly enough to get Feeney's attention.

"What is it, Hallinan?" Feeney asked impatiently.

Hallinan showed himself in the hatchway. It was safe enough now that Feeney knew who he was. Even so, he unconsciously kept himself a little to one side of the opening, just in case.

"Skipper asked me to bring three of the aid workers up to the bridge. The Indonesians cast off a little while ago and there's something he wants them to see. Also, he said that the others can be released to their assigned duties."

"Who does this skipper want?"

"Duke, Zink, and Bourke."

"Right." Feeney pointed a thumb at the hatch. "You three. Go with Hallinan. Now!"

Jennifer Duke turned a ghastly white at what she saw through Pearson's binoculars. Bourke and Zink looked, if anything, worse. And Zink, in particular, looked a likely enough candidate for vomiting that Pearson had had one of his bridge crew guide him to stand over a trash can.

Duke couldn't stand to look very long. She pulled the glasses from her eyes and asked, meekly, "Why did you want me to see that, Captain?"

"Oh," Pearson replied, "I just thought it might help you understand the world as it has become, Ms. Duke. Being kidnapped and almost sold as slaves didn't seem to help but, then . . . humanitarians wouldn't feel their own pain and fear as well as someone else's, would they?"

"I'm sorry for those men . . . " she began, before the captain cut her off.

"Why? You should feel sorry for their victims, for the raided villages and the girls from those villages kidnapped, raped, and sold at public auction. You should feel sorry for the boatloads of people trying to get away from starvation in their homelands, caught on the high seas, robbed, and killed. Except, of course, for the young girls, who join their village sisters on the auction block."

"But that . . . that *atrocity*. No crime should . . . "

Again the captain cut her off. "Should and ought are mere meaningless fantasies, Ms. Duke. 'Is' and 'real' and 'works' are what matter. I suppose you can't quite see that.

"No matter, Ms. Duke, what you see or don't. It's become that kind of world. Best ask yourself why?"

Warrington entered the bridge, saying, "No more time for fun and games with the tranzis, Skipper. Terry just sent us the final op order. There aren't a lot of changes from the preliminary, but we've still got some work to do."

"What kind of changes are there?" Pearson asked.

"For the navy and air, nothing, really. For the ground . . . well, apparently Terry lost half of the team he had with him. And that's a whole other story, one we don't know the ending to. I'll fill you in later."

MV *Richard Bland*, Celebes Sea

A full dress rehearsal just wasn't possible aboard ship. This handicap was mitigated, at least partially, by the effective—if general—full dress rehearsal they'd done for Bajuni. Thus, while they couldn't go through every planned step on actual ground, they did have the kinks worked out of close air support, using the gunships, loading the landing craft, slinging it and the armored cars over the side, dusting off the wounded, etc.

And that's a lot better than nothing, Warrington

thought, looking over the leaders as they moved counters on a sand table constructed on the mess deck. *It was probably worth even what Bajuni cost us, not even counting the medicines we grabbed.*

Two toy gunships circled on wires attached to platforms over a very accurate scale model of the island where Lucio Ayala was being held. Below them, several green toy soldiers stood, plastic faces toward the north.

Though a lower rating, Kirkpatrick, the coxswain of the landing craft, had a big part in the sand table rehearsal, as he was going to have a big part in the operation. It might fairly be said that, without him, nothing was going to happen.

Reaching down, he moved the toy LCM representing his craft, to the shore of the target island.

"I am ashore," he announced. With a flick of a finger, the toy's ramp dropped.

Immediately the chief of the armored car section reached down to the toy LCM and moved from it to the shore the two models of Elands. "De armored car section has debarked." He then moved the toys to the right, as he faced the scale model island. "We's turning to de right, to cover de unloading of de troops."

Stocker's turn came. Setting a black painted toy soldier ashore, he said, "Company headquarters has debarked and established itself fifty meters inland from the landing beach."

The new First Platoon leader, Moore having moved up to take over the company first shirt slot, vice Kiertzner, placed a toy soldier, red colored, to the right of Stocker's, hard against the model island's "shore." "First platoon is ashore and moving north . . . "

Yep, better than nothing, Warrington thought.

"Second Platoon is falling in to the left of first . . . I am bringing the landing craft back to the *Bland* . . . We have reloaded . . . We are at the beach . . . De mortars . . . guns up . . . T'ird Platoon, droppin' off six shells per man wid de mortars, then swinging right . . ."

★ CHAPTER THIRTY-ONE ★

For when the gallows is high,
your journey is shorter to Heaven . . .
—William Maher,
"The Night Before Larry was Stretched,"

Safe House Alpha, Hagonoy, Bulacan, Luzon, Republic of the Philippines

Aida had been asked to stand by; she had a lot more experience in this kind of thing than did anyone in Welch's command. She sat, silent and listening, nearby, with a pad of paper and a pen to hand. She had no idea whatsoever about the girl imprisoned below.

"I need more time," Terry said into the cell phone. The phone's address panel said, "Benson." "The banks are being difficult. Don't hurt my people, just give me a few days."

Diwata's voice was hard and pitiless. If there was any soft and yielding femininity in it, it was hidden under a layer of iron . . . cold iron. "I gave you enough time," she said. "I warned you what would happen if our demands weren't met. Your time is up. So is the time for one of your people.

"In about an hour, if you're curious, you can go to uglystuff dot com and see for yourself.

"Now call me again when you have the money. In another week, you can check that site again to see why there are only two of your people left, and why the price for those two remains four million dollars."

"Jesus! Wait . . . wait . . . " The phone was dead.

TCS Headquarters, Tondo, Manila, Republic of the Philippines

There were half a dozen small cages, just big enough for a short man to lie down in, not big enough to sit or stand, in the basement. They were suitable for animals, not for men. Two were empty. The other four held Benson, Perez, Zimmerman, and Washington.

Diwata looked over the supine and cramped figures in the cages, judging, weighing. *Let's see . . . Terry sounded like a whiteass. He might not care about losing the hispanic or the black. And the "sarge" is probably the most important. He might not pay at all for the others. So . . . it's . . .*

"Take that one," she said, pointing at Zimmerman.

Zimmerman fought back, kicking at the hands reaching inside the cage for him. He was by no means a weakling, either. Eventually, though, Crisanto had had enough. Pushing a cattle prod through the mesh of the cage, he shocked Zimmerman senseless, while another man got a rope around one ankle. Then, their victim trembling from the electric shock, they dragged him by his ankle out onto the bare concrete floor.

Benson called out, "No, take me." Perez and Washington swore in every language they knew between them. The kidnappers ignored them all.

"I'm tired of the trouble these fucking Kanos cost me," Crisanto announced. "Tie the motherfucker's hands behind him. Then beat the shit out of him. Just don't kill him or knock him unconscious. He needs to be awake to do his little dance for the camera."

Though her face remained hard and stiff, Diwata smiled inside. *The worse he looks the better the threat. So long as he can still dance.*

After fifteen minutes or so she decided, "Enough. Get on with it. Oh, and take his clothes. There are a few details to this his friends ought to see."

"Yes, ma'am," her ex-Philippine Marine said, drawing his knife to cut away the shirt from the bound hands.

Beaten half to a pulp or not, Zimmerman began to struggle again as soon as he saw the rope and its menacing noose, dangling from a pipe overhead. It didn't matter; Crisanto, with a fair degree of training, himself, twisted one of Zimmerman's hands, bending his wrist, in a "come-along," then marched him to the rope. This was slipped over the victim's head, despite every effort on his part to twist out of the way.

Crisanto released the hand then, reaching up to tighten the noose. This wasn't easy; he'd tied the noose himself and he'd tied it *tight*. Once the noose was not quite snug about the neck, with the knot just under the left side of the jaw, in front of Zimmerman's ear, Crisanto backed off. He directed his followers, "Get on the rope."

Zimmerman thought of a line he'd read once, *When you're going to die, anyway, style counts.* Spitting a bloody gob onto the concrete floor, he said, "cocksuckers." Then he began to sing an old, old song. He'd never hated Filipinos, or any brown folk, until this minute. But, this minute, he sang, "Damn, damn, damn . . ."

Diwata, who had followed the execution party at a safe distance snapped her fingers at a man standing with a home video camera. The light on the camera said it was recording.

She snapped them again at Crisanto. He and his crew began to haul on the rope. Zimmerman had just gotten to, " . . . with a Krag," when he felt the hempen cord bite into his neck and the ground fall away from his toes.

One of the oddities of various reforms to capital punishment, exacted around the western world in the twentieth and twenty-first centuries, was that the reforms—outside of outright prohibition—were always presented as a more merciful, less painful form of killing, but always had as their real objective the sparing of the witnesses from sights more unpleasant than strictly necessary. Thus, for example, hanging—which, properly done, killed instantly—gave way to gas, which could take quite a while, to electricity, which basically cooked the victim, and ultimately to lethal injection. Some of the cocktails used in lethal injection caused the victim to suffocate slowly, over a period of ten or twelve minutes. But, since it *appeared* less painful, since the slowly suffocating victim couldn't call out for help, and since that appearance spared the witnesses psychic pain, it was simply assumed to *be* less painful.

Even with hanging, it was often assumed that the neck-breaking drop was more merciful than simply suspending the victim without any such drop. This, too, was false, or at least not necessarily true. A thin cord, as in the Austro-Hungarian pole-hanging method, for example, caused essentially instantaneous unconsciousness, by cutting off the blood supply to the brain. True death might take a while after that, but the hanged weren't feeling anything. Oh, yes, the legs might kick and the body shudder and writhe, but that was all automatic and meant, basically, nothing. Still, it *looked* cruel, and that was what mattered.

On the other hand, it was certainly possible for a suspension hanging to be very cruel indeed. Just tie the noose very tight, use a thick rope, make sure the knot is placed to give as much freedom to blood flow through the neck as possible, and hoist gently.

Safe House Alpha, Hagonoy, Bulacan, Luzon, Republic of the Philippines

Nobody cried, they just weren't that kind of men. But every man who watched the horrific drama play out on the monitor screen felt sick, and hopeless, and worthless, and helpless . . . and very, very hate-filled and angry.

They didn't swear or curse, none of them. Nobody vowed revenge; that was a given. M Day would repay this, with usury, if it took a hundred years. But they watched their comrade of years, Zimmerman, dance and kick and slowly turn blue as the noose tightened. They saw him lose bladder control, his penis jetting a stream of piss onto the concrete. Though he was turned toward the camera for most of his ordeal, they could tell when he lost sphincter control by the dark, runny lumps that ran down his legs and plopped to the floor.

In the end, his swollen, blackened tongue jutting out from a gasping mouth, Zimmerman's kicking and trembling ceased and all that was left was a lifeless body, twisting slowly in the air.

The men couldn't cry. Though few of them had ever given a thought to Andrew Jackson's mother, all would have understood completely her words to a very young future Old Hickory: "Girls are for crying; boys are for fighting."

Aida could cry and, though she didn't know the victim, she did, whimpering through her tears, "What a shitty world . . . poor, poor man . . . what a shitty, shitty world . . . " She finished with, "Those are *not* my countrymen. They are *not*!"

"The odd thing," Graft finally said, "is that Zim was one of the nicer ones among us."

Terry Welch felt he ought to say something, anything, but no consoling words came. In the end, he gulped, took a few breaths, and settled for, "Excuse me, I need to go study a map."

Caban Island, Pilas Group, Basilan Province, Republic of the Philippines

The doctor—that was all anyone on the island ever

called him—wasn't really a doctor. Oh, he'd begun medical school, right enough, at Manila Central. He'd even gotten through three of the required four years, with fair grades, too. Then—the doctor shook his head at his own foolishness—he'd gotten involved in a little local politics, of the Moro Liberation variety. One thing led to another and the other thing led to a bank robbery, in which he'd agreed to serve as a medic. The robbery had led to a police chase, a gun battle, and—

Why did I ever *get involved with that crap?*

He'd barely made if off of Luzon with his life. From there it had been several years with the Moro Liberation Front, then a spot of trouble (where trouble is defined as pissing off the head of movement and again having to flee for one's life), then finally with the Harrikat. They'd been desperate for a medico, even one without a license. And, since he'd had to flee anyway, and they were willing to help . . .

I should have stayed there. All the MLF would have done is killed me. They wouldn't have put my soul at risk.

The leader might be an atheist—the doctor suspected he was—but the doctor was emphatically not. That's what had led him into trouble in the first place.

Sitting on the dirt floor of the prisoner's little shelter, the doctor glanced from the medical text he'd been searching through to his quivering patient.

Poor old man's life is hanging by a thread. Maybe I did the wrong thing by persuading Janail to leave off after the toe and two fingers. The reason I gave, that he'd never make five cuts if they did four, was probably true.

Ayala moaned, delirious.

"And, old man, that might have been better for you."

The doctor had the infections in Ayala's foot and hand under control. That was a result of lots and lots of experience with dealing with jungle infections. The lungs were iffy, though. The doctor didn't have access to even fairly low medical technology; he was about at the level of Hippocrates, diagnosing by inference. He'd tried two types of the highly limited store of antibiotics he had on hand. They hadn't cured the almost cardboard like crackling the doctor could hear in Ayala's lungs, but at least it hadn't gotten any worse.

It might even have gotten a little better. He is, after all, a tough old bird, however sick, or he'd have been dead by now.

The lungs might be coming around or they might not. But that eighty-five year old heart? He'd had to administer CPR twice already, and he was still sure the old man had suffered some pretty severe ischemia.

Lucky, or maybe unlucky, that I saved that bottle of nitro pills I never thought to see a use for.

Alaya began a spasm of coughing. The doctor dropped his text, much less carefully than he should have, considering how nearly irreplaceable it was, and raced to his patient's side, taking one knee beside what passed for a bed.

The old man was breathing fast and shallowly. The doctor felt Ayala's skin. *Cool, but that might be the down-swing from the pneumonia I'm pretty sure he has. Maybe another aspirin . . . but what if he starts bleeding again?*

That might kill him, the doctor thought. *But if he's having a heart attack it* will *kill him.*

PART IV:
H Minus

★★★

★ CHAPTER THIRTY-TWO ★

I hate mankind, for I think myself one
of the best of them, and I know how bad I am.
—Joseph Baretti

Safe House Alpha, Hagonoy, Bulacan, Luzon, Republic of the Philippines

Not far from the main house, Maricel, trussed up like a chicken and certain she was for the chop, lay on one side next to a small, linear open area she distantly understood to be a dirt airstrip. Welch stood above and beside her, saying nothing.

She'd been left like that, on her side with no neck support, for the last half hour while a bunch of big strangers—nine or ten of them, she thought—busied themselves on all sides of the airstrip. None of them had said a word to her either, not even the one she recognized, Malone. There also seemed to be a couple of women, little ones, smaller than her, standing by.

For the most part, she couldn't see what the men were

doing. She could see that lights had begun to appear along what she guessed were the edges of the strip. In the distant glow of those lights, barely, she made out one man—*maybe the one who hurt me*—hunched over something or other.

Oh, God, please, please don't let them kill me. Please.

Maricel was pretty sure they were going to take her up in a plane and then throw her out, maybe over land, maybe over water.

Water, she decided. *Why tie my feet, too, unless they want me to drown*? She began to cry, until the big Kano ordered her, "Shut up."

The men had discussed what to do with her and the notion of paying the girl in kind for the death of their friend, and in precisely the same coin, had come up. Welch had squelched that, for the nonce, at least, not because he didn't think that, in a just world, it was appropriate. No, what saved her was the knowledge of what her interrogation had done to Lox, on the inside. He didn't think the men's condition would be improved by watching her choke, either; rather the opposite.

What we are *going to do with her, I'm just not sure*, he thought, standing there in the dark, waiting for his flight. *What I am sure about, though, is that we can't leave her here, unguarded, I need every man for the mission, and we can stow her away on the* Bland *until we figure it out. Besides, if we decide to kill her, I need a few more officers to constitute a court-martial. The men still won't like it, no matter what a couple of them might have said, but they'll be a little more accepting if the whole thing has at least the trappings of law.*

Fact is, though, that I don't want to kill the poor little shit anyway. Yeah, she was part—a big part—of a criminal conspiracy. Yeah, that conspiracy murdered two of my men. But . . . well . . . what the hell choice did she have? What the hell choice did she ever have, in her whole life?

The man who was hunched over, the one Maricel thought had tortured her, straightened. She heard the voice—*Yes, it's the same one*—call out, "The first plane's two minutes out, Terry."

Maricel heard the engine, a sort of anemic buzz, approaching. With each second, and each little increment of increase in the buzz, she prayed a little more fervently. Then, almost before she understood what had happened, the plane—tiny little thing—was on the ground, right before her eyes. A team of four, she thought, was actually picking up the tail to turn the thing around.

Two men—neither of them Malone—picked her up and carried her to the plane, her head hanging like a dog's. Neither of them was particularly gentle. Then again, neither of them had any reason to bear her good will.

What Maricel found particularly frightening was that neither of them took the chance to cop a feel or squeeze her ass.

I'm not even a woman to them. They're gonna kiiilllll me.

At the plane, the pilot had already tossed the door open. One of the men carrying Maricel, the one by her feet, said something she didn't quite catch. Then he let go of his end, letting her feet fall to the ground, while he fiddled with the chair inside the cabin. When he had that out of the way, the other began feeding her head first into the luggage space behind the passenger seat. Then both men forced her lower half in, apparently not much caring that the space was designed for light freight, not people . . . not even slender and not really so very tall people. Just being stuffed into position cost Maricel a few bruises and scrapes. Then they put the chair back into position. That cost her a little pain, too.

She wasn't thinking particularly clearly—and who could blame her for that? Had she been, she might have realized that there was no good way to get her out of the cargo compartment to dump her over water. The big Kano entered the plane, ass end first, sat back, and buckled himself in. From the dash he pulled a set of headphones with a boom mike, placing them over his head and adjusting his mike to sit about three fourths of an inch in front of his mouth. Somebody tossed him a bag from outside, then closed the door.

The plane shuddered and hummed as the pilot gave it some gas. Maricel felt it move, bouncing as it covered the rough strip.

The CH-750's were normally flown without a copilot. Not only wasn't there enough room for three—not comfortably, as Maricel could have testified if she hadn't been on the verge of pissing herself with fright—but the light planes normally carried a fairly heavy load of ordnance. Another pilot could have cut into that, considerably.

"You *sure* we've got enough lift for this thing, Jake?" Terry asked of the pilot.

"Close, sir, but yes. Two hundred and five for you.

Forty for your bag. Maybe one hundred and ten for the girl. Hundred and forty-five for me. Leaves us about sixty-five pounds. That's good because the air is hot and wet, so a little thin."

"Okay, just checking."

The pilot jerked a thumb to the rear, asking, "That the bitch that set up half of the team you had with you?"

"Yeah . . . that's her."

Using a falsetto stolen from an actress in one of the many films about Robin Hood, Jake said, "I likes me a good 'angin', I do."

"Might come to that, Jake. It just might come to that."

Jake chuckled, then adjusted the throttle. The engine began to hum, shaking the plane as it moved it. The lights the men had set up to either side passed slowly at first. Still, Terry counted only two on his side before Jake pulled the stick and the thing was airborne.

"Now let's hope we can get over the trees," Welch observed.

"Piece o' cake," the pilot replied.

The CH-750 was almost as capable of flying nap of the earth—that was when you were flying and could look *up* and still see trees—as a good, modern helicopter. There had been arguments at the club—sometimes rather *severe* ones—between helo pilots and the CH-750 pilots who insisted that they could do it better.

From Terry's point of view it didn't much matter; both sets of pilots were certifiable maniacs. This opinion wasn't reduced in the slightest when the CH-750's tricycle landing gear did, in fact, scrape the trees at one end of the strip.

He didn't attribute that to pilot error so much as that night vision goggles tended to rob depth perception.

"Sorry about that, sir."

The pilot couldn't see Welch's nod. He did hear him say, "Any one you can walk away from. As long as you can get us all to the ship . . . however many lifts it takes."

The pilot pushed on the stick, causing the plane to lose height as it followed the trees. At that point, Maricel *did* lose bladder control.

You could hardly blame her for that, either. After all, she'd never in her life flown before.

One of the tough parts of flying this area was that, as a former bastion—in every possible and historic sense—of the U.S. Armed Forces, the place was inundated with radar. While the U.S. was long gone, the Philippines' forces—who were certainly doing the best that could be expected given the economy—Air Force and Navy, in particular, kept up as much as possible. For example, while the former Naval Base at Subic Bay had been given up to civilian enterprise, San Miguel, to the northwest, was still a fully active naval station. That—not just San Miguel but all the active radars in the area—was why Jake had to keep so close to the trees that he'd be picking bark and leaves out of the landing gear for a week.

Fortunately, Jake had been stationed here before, with the Navy, and pretty much knew the radar patterns by heart. That's why he turned his tiny command to fly between the mountains of Bataan Natural Park and Mount Mariveles before slipping down to wave-top level for the trip out to the ship.

Thank God, thought Jake, *for what remains of the Global Positioning System*.

MV *Richard Bland*, South China Sea

The ship was heading due north, but going very slowly, just fast enough not to appear suspicious.

Pearson had better radar available than the one he was using. The problem was that that radar was military grade. A military grade radar, suddenly lighting up the world, close to an area hotly contested between the Philippines, China, and Vietnam, would have been like a nun, dressing up as a tart, wandering Times Square. It was bound to attract the unwanted and unwelcome attentions of all the wrong sorts of people.

Instead, his radar people worked with what they could, a not so very splendid civilian outfit, that wouldn't be noticed by the local authorities even if it could be picked up, but which also hadn't a prayer of picking up an itty bitty sport plane flying almost between the waves.

"Pity," said Warrington, standing on the bridge, looking forward over the deck of containers.

"What's that?" the skipper asked.

"Huh? Oh, I was thinking out loud . . . that it was a pity we couldn't modify these things so that there was a flight deck that ran all the way through, down below. Then we wouldn't have to bust people's asses setting up the PSP flight deck. We'd just open some doors, fore and aft, and there it would be."

"Harder than it sounds," Pearson replied. "You don't

notice it so much because you've gotten used to it, but this vessel jumps around quite a bit. That might pitch an incoming plane up in the air but, what the hell, the sky is big. Pitch a plane up with something that has a roof over it? No, thanks."

"Good point," agreed Warrington, cheerfully.

Pearson noticed the cheer. "What's got you so happy."

"Oh, I don't care for command, particularly. I like being in charge of a given mission, mind you, but the bullshit of legal and *technical* command is not my cup of tea. Welch is welcome to it."

The speaker on the bridge squawked with Jake's voice, saying he thought they were about three minutes out. One of the bridge crew, on a huge night vision scope, announced, without taking his eye from the rubber eyepiece, "I see them, bearing Green-Zero-nine-seven."

The captain automatically looked over his right shoulder but, of course, couldn't see damned thing.

Picking up a mike, Pearson ordered, "Give me a signal, Jake."

"He's wagging his wings," the observer announced.

"I see your wagging wings," said Pearson.

"That's me."

"C'mon home, honey, dinner's waitin'. But circle for a couple of minutes."

"Wilco."

Using the ship's intercom, Pearson further ordered, "B Bird, get ready to launch."

"She's up," replied the chief of the flight deck.

"Launch."

"Why the close timing?" Warrington asked.

"Stealth, really," the captain replied. Seeing that Warrington didn't quite understand, he added, "Just imagine if someone, somehow, is tracking Jake. And Jake suddenly disappears off their screen. Imagine the horror. Imagine the frantic calls for rescue. Imagine the stupid looks on our faces when somebody investigates and discovers that the innocent-seeming merchie is actually an assault carrier. With *captives* aboard, no less. Imagine looking out from between prison bars for a very, very long time.

"This way, if someone *is* tracking Jake, they see a plane. They lose a plane for a couple of seconds but, 'no problem, there it is. Dumb-assed pilot must have been playing footsie with the merchie.'"

"Ohhh."

"Oh."

Ayala Country Estate (Formerly Safe House Alpha), Hagonoy, Bulacan, Luzon, Republic of the Philippines

Lox watched the small plane take off into the night. He didn't know that particular pilot but, no sweat, Jake would be back for him. That penultimate flight carried Pedro and Mrs. Ayala. Aida and Pedro's partner had gone before. Pedro had also advised Lox, "Tell them, if you can, not to try to take our guns. It could be ugly. Oh, and not Aida's, either. She's a bitch."

"Welch knows," Lox had replied.

Both of those prior flights had flown out with the smaller Filipinos seated in tandem in the one passenger seat. It was tight, to be sure, but way better than the cargo space. Besides, none of them were big or anything like fat.

"It's going to be at least a half hour before Jake returns for me. Still, might as well get it over with now."

With that, Lox walked back to the house and grabbed two cans of gasoline. He poured most of one into each of the two interrogation rooms. The rest went into the one holding cell.

The police might someday investigate the events of the next two days. *Good luck to them*, Lox thought, as he flicked a lighter to life, *finding anything bigger than a useless scorched chromosome if they do.*

Fortunately, the estate was isolated, and the local fire department, with a bare thirteen men and women, plus old and obsolete equipment, was grossly overtasked already.

★ CHAPTER THIRTY-THREE ★

I suppose every man is shocked when he hears
how frequently soldiers are wishing for war.
The wish is not always sincere; the greater part
are content with sleep and lace, and counterfeit an
ardour which they do not feel; but those who desire it
most are neither prompted by malevolence nor
patriotism; they neither pant for laurels, nor delight
in blood; but long to be delivered from the tyranny of
idleness, and restored to the dignity of active beings.
—Dr. Samuel Johnson

**MV *Richard Bland*, Sulu Sea, Basilan Province,
Republic of the Philippines**

The *Bland*'s sole remote piloted vehicle, or RPV, didn't
need a deck to launch from. The entire thing, aircraft,
launch rail, and control station, fitted neatly inside a single
twenty foot container for storage and transport, with the
rail going above the container for launch.

Of course, a deck certainly made it easier to recover

the thing. Still, not much was deck was needed. Pearson's naval crew had laid enough Marsden Matting across already, as a first step in laying the entire deck for the CH-750's. What they had down already was more than sufficient for the Searchers. Indeed, it was almost sufficient to launch the CH-750's, if not quite enough when they were under full load. It was not enough to recover them.

Israel, from whom the regiment had bought their RPVs, had quite a selection available, from little hand-held jobs to large, long endurance, high payload aircraft that were a match or near match for—and in some ways the superior to—those made in the United States. M Day had none of the largest class, and some of the smallest, but had settled in the main on Israel's Searcher IIIN, in a clever little under the table deal with India coupled with a really *big* favor done on behalf of Israel. As both inside joke and memorial of the favor, the RPV had "Saint Rachel of IHOP" stenciled in small letters down both sides.

A fair amount of the space in the container, when in transit, was taken up by the aircraft itself. The control station took up slightly more. The various recon packages—from signal gathering to air sniffing to thermal imaging—took up still more. Even with that, the bulk of the space was taken up with dunnage—packages, frames, wooden and plastic beams and braces—to hold everything in place while in transit. Fortunately, Guyana—home base—was a place to have some pretty solid custom cabinetry made. Fancy? Maybe not. Solid? Absolutely.

The Searcher IIIN, N for "Navalized," was smaller than its predecessors, even quieter—and they'd been very quiet—had slightly improved range, and a better AI to bring the thing home in the event of communication failure. That said, reports from the front in Guyana had suggested there were some problems, as several had simply disappeared without any obvious cause.

Welch had asked for three or four RPV's for the mission, back at regimental headquarters. The regiment had let him have one.

Which was stupid as shit, Welch thought. *If there's any rule that ought to be tattooed on the foreheads of everyone in the military, everywhere, it's that if you absolutely must have one of anything, at the objective, you must start with more than one. The one we have, therefore, had better fucking work.*

Both Welch and Lox stood over the RPV's pilot, in the space vacated by the launch rail. But for the corrugated metal of the container walls, the baskets and the cabinets, and the fact that the whole assembly rocked with the ship, as far as either could tell they were in the cockpit of a rather sophisticated aircraft. The pilot had screens for everything, plus computers, controls that mimicked those found on manned planes, plus a truly bizarre looking virtual reality helmet, sitting on his dash, for when the TV screen might prove not quite enough.

"And we're . . . airborne," the pilot announced over his shoulder.

"Peter," said Welch, "stay here. Match what *Rachel* finds against what we think we know. I'm going the bridge and then to bid Graft and Semmerlin good bye and good luck."

★ ★ ★

Emerging onto the darkened deck, right up against the port gunwale where the control station had been set, Welch guessed from the sound that the full flight deck was maybe half laid. Consulting his watch and thinking back to the navy's operations order he'd listened to, he decided, *Pretty good time, so far.*

The way to the superstructure led along the gunwale, and past the launch rail and its bipedal supports. In the darkness he almost missed it—indeed, he almost tripped over it—because that bipod was already down and the flight crew struggling with pins to disassemble the entire apparatus. It just wouldn't do to have even fairly heavy metal objects lying around, once the flight deck became active.

Just shy of the superstructure, at the edge of the ad hoc runway, two containers were opened. There was just enough non-suspicious light coming from the superstructure's portholes for Terry to make them out, as well as the one CH-750 that sat fully out in front of one of them, with a part of the deck crew unfolding and locking down its wings under the supervision of Jake, Terry's pilot for the evacuation from the safe house in Hagonoy. Welch couldn't really see them very well, but there was also a line of rocket and machine guns pods sitting on the deck, waiting to be mounted.

One of the things Terry found surprising was how quiet it all was. *They must have rehearsed the shit out of all the crews. Kudos to Warrington and Pearson. Good damned thing, too. Even if I can't see them for beans, there have got to be some small craft out there. If one of them happened to be working for the bad guys, and reported suspicious sounds, our job could become a lot tougher.*

Everything had seemed fine on the bridge, with Pearson in total control of his part of the operation. By the time the ship was twenty miles west of Zamboanga City, the crew had lowered a floating platform over the starboard side and run a net from the gunwales down to the platform. Once the platform was down and confidently secured, three men crawled down the net, Welch, Semmerlin, and Graft. There, swaying with the wake-induced turbulence, they took control of the two SeaBobs as they were lowered, easing them down gently and accurately, then laid them out on the platform. The formerly bright yellow SeaBobs had been painted and then covered in dark tape, just to make sure. Two packages, containing arms, uniforms, ammunition, night vision, and radios came down next.

"Good luck," Welch said, just before the scuba-equipped Graft and Semmerlin eased themselves off the platform and into the water. He used a foot to push in the bundles of gear after them. Once the pair were well away, Terry climbed the cargo net back to the gunwale. There, the landing craft was uncovered, and hooked up to a crane.

Quietly, the SeaBobs carried the pair to a spot several hundred meters to the ship's starboard, where they waited until it was safe to head for their objective. After ten minutes' wait, Graft, the senior, said, "Let's go."

The ship veered north again, which course it would maintain until Graft reported he was at the objective. It would not launch the main force until he reported that the target was secured.

Caban Island, Pilas Group, Basilan Province, Republic of the Philippines

There was a cliff to the west and southwest quadrants of the island, perhaps eighty feet in height. It would not really suit to get an old and frail, quite likely also sick and weak, man down it to the sea. It could be done, but was a last option. Nor, for that matter, was it terribly suitable, which is to say it was completely *un*suitable, for an assault. Thus, there was good reason to believe it was only lightly guarded. Graft and Semmerlin, staying underwater except twice when they surfaced to get their bearings, rounded the island and headed for the base of that cliff.

MV *Richard Bland,* Sulu Sea, Basilan Province, Republic of the Philippines

The numbers of people on the island counted by the Searcher's thermal, about four hundred, wasn't a surprise. In that particular the Philippine Army report provided by Aida had been accurate. Bunkers and other fortifications, identified by the late Mr. Kulat and Mr. Iqbal were pretty much as Lox had squeezed out of them.

No real surprises, in any case, he thought.

That information was passed to the bridge, where one of Pearson's men duly annotated the map, changing the color codes for those items from "Suspected" to "Confirmed."

The heat signatures from the hut tentatively identified

as the hostage's, though, were problematic. There were two men outside, which was expected. But there were also two inside. One of them supine and the other one moving from one side of the hut to the other, with occasional stops at the supine one between the two.

No idea what that one is, but I'd better pass it to the bridge and to Terry.

The *Rachel* continued its overhead patrol, with the pilot being very careful to keep it out of any path that would place it directly between the island and the moon. The nav computer was absolutely crucial to that security measure.

Little by little, Lox was gratified to see, and one by one, the dots that indicated standing or seated men narrowed and stretched out, even as the few fires died away. The Harrikat, barring only the guards around the shore, two of them near the west side cliff, and a few more, were going to sleep.

Lox used the ship's intercom, which had been hooked into the control station. "Bridge, Lox. When he pops up to check in, advise Graft that there *are* two guards walking the length of his cliff, which is about what we expected. If he needs, I can advise him when they're at one extreme or the other."

"We'll patch you through to him directly," said the bridge.

"Roger, that would be better."

Caban Island, Pilas Group, Basilan Province, Republic of the Philippines

Graft and Semmerlin cut their motors when they were

still about a hundred meters from shore. That was far enough that the sounds of the waves beating on the cliff's base and the gravel and rocks in front of it should have covered any sound made by the sleds. Any closer? An unnecessary risk, they thought.

The SeaBobs and the packages they carted arose to the surface, dragging the men along with them. Commercial SeaBobs were naturally buoyant; these had been modified to be flooded and sunk if desired. From there, it was flipper work, men pushing devices rather than devices dragging men.

There was a different feel to the water, which feeling grew as the men neared shore. Eventually, Graft felt he could reach down and touch the gravel. He did; it was there. A wave picked him up, moved him, then set him down. Graft held in a curse as a barnacled rock scraped his knee, drawing blood.

Graft, followed by Semmerlin, stopped paddling and assumed more of a crouch. They still kept as much of their bodies in the water as possible. The cliff's base was perhaps fifty feet away, more heard than seen. At the base, they tied off their SeaBobs to a couple of rocks and sank them in place. It mattered little to the mission if the SeaBobs were lost, as they didn't have enough power remaining to get anywhere useful. It did matter that they not drift out where they might be seen or, worse, might wash ashore.

They'd recover them later, if they could.

Already Semmerlin was stripping down and fitting up. On went his uniform, boots, and combat harness. On went the Kevlar kneepads. He slung a suppressed .510 caliber subsonic rifle across his back. It had a loaded magazine but no round in the chamber. The pistol that went into a shoulder rig, on the other hand, was loaded, previously loaded, in fact; the sound of a slide being worked being altogether too loud and distinctive. On his head went a set of headphones with mike, those being hooked in to the radio at his belt. Over that he put on a climber's helmet modified to take a set of night vision goggles, with the goggles already mounted. He had a pair of thick leather gloves, but only put on one of them, hooking the other to a carabiner. For the other hand, he was likely to need fine sensing and control, groping his way up the cliff.

Heart pounding, with excitement more than fear or exertion, huddled at the cliff's base, with waves sometimes still washing around his ankles, Graft reported, "Pelican," over the radio, in a tense, subdued whisper. It meant: *We are safely ashore.*

The ship sent back, "Roger, be advised there are two guards along the cliff, but not directly above you. We're patching Lox through from now on. He'll keep you up to date."

"Roger," Graft acknowledged.

In the dank glow from the sliver of the moon, and even that mostly blocked by the cliff's height, Graft and Semmerlin were barely shadows to each other's eyes. The latter helped Graft on with his minimum required arms and equipment, that mostly being a helmet with NVG's, knee pads, a small personal radio with earpiece and boom mike, the silenced pistol in a shoulder rig, a long rope, a smaller piece of rope, and a sling clustered with spring-loaded camming devices, or SLCD's, and carabiners.

Much of the rest would come up on Semmerlin's back, after Graft had established a rope to the top of the cliff. The final load would be hauled up behind them, once the rope was set at the top.

Even with that, and lightly laden, Graft looked up at the near vertical face of the cliff at the base of which they'd landed and whispered, "Shit. This is *so* going to suck."

"Hey, cheer up," Semmerlin whispered back. "At least it's not sheer. There are hand– and footholds, and you'll find them."

"I'm over forty," Graft muttered. "Closer to fifty, in fact. And you think a few handholds are going to cheer me. Besides, I'm lead climber, remember?"

"Yeah, I remember. You're a better free climber than I am. So, okay, fine. Now just imagine trying to get up that son of a bitch—*silently*—if there weren't any handholds."

"Point," Graft agreed, putting on and buckling down a safety helmet. "Well . . . watch me, then."

Semmerlin nodded and slipped his night vision goggles over his face, waiting to turn the device on until it was well seated and none of the greenish glow from the amplification tubes could escape.

Free climbing was not quite the same thing as free soloing, the latter being a deliberately risk-taking venture, done without a partner and, broadly speaking, without safety equipment. Instead, free climbing involved the use of a safety rope, the kinds of devices on the sling across Graft's shoulder, and, most importantly, a belay man at the ground level to stop a fall, if required.

Under the circumstances, taking an unnecessary risk would have been, in the first place, potentially disastrous to their mission; and there were seventy million dollars riding on the successful retrieval of Louis Ayala, after all, and quite a bit more for the elimination of the group that had taken him. Moreover, Ayala's wife, Paloma, had offered that substantial bonus for inflicting some sheer frightfulness on his kidnappers.

Those bonuses were secondary, of course, payable only if Welch's crew could also return her husband to her. On the other hand, if it did turn out that Mr. Ayala was dead, or if he were killed in the rescue, Welch fully intended to make Mrs. Ayala an offer for revenge at the original price, anyway,

But, in the second place, needless risk was just box-o-rocks stupid, mission or no.

★ CHAPTER THIRTY-FOUR ★

The moral here is to never trust equipment, but oneself.
—Fiona Always

Caban Island, Pilas Group, Basilan Province, Republic of the Philippines

I'm not a big fan of stupid risks, either, thought Graft, standing directly at the base of the cliff. He rotated his night vision goggles down over his eyes, then adjust the focus for very close. He could, perhaps, have tried the thing by feel alone. *The problem is, though, that feel won't help you plan very far ahead.* Even so, he began by putting both hands flat against the surface, just getting a feel for the rock. *Not that I think this little ritual matters half a shit, but the guy who taught me always did it, and who am I to fuck with tradition?*

Removing his hands from flat against the rock, Graft began to squat down, tapping the cliff face lightly with his finger while he searched for an initial foothold. He found it, about three and a half feet above where sand and gravel met rock. *It isn't much, but it'll do.*

Satisfied with that, he stood again, reaching upward. There was only one good handhold within reach, a small ledge about eighteen inches overhead. Unfortunately, it was to the right of the foothold, so he'd have to use his ungloved right hand. At some point in time, if the pattern repeated, that would begin to wear and, worse, tire out his shooting hand.

Placing the toe of his left boot in the foothold and the stiffened fingers of his right hand on the tiny ledge, Graft hoisted himself up. After pausing briefly, he next sent his left hand questing for the next little ledge.

Graft's heart was beating fast, not so much with fear—though that may have been part of it—as with the exertion of forcing his nearly fifty-year-old body straight up a cliff.

I am so getting too old for this shit. And, speaking of shit . . .

Vainly, Graft's free hand sought another handhold. There was nothing within reach, either to left, or right, or straight up.

. . . I knew this would happen.

There was a crevice, of sorts, at about waist level. He examined it through the goggles, though they couldn't tell him all that much. Taking a camming device from the sling around his body, Graft unlocked the device with his thumb and two fingers, then tucked it into the crevice, as high as he could fit it in. Releasing his thumb, the device lodged itself in the crack. He gave it a long tug, to ensure it was set.

"Gimme a little slack," he radioed in a whisper to

Semmerlin, on belay, below. Feeling the rope about his waist and running through the carabiners he'd already set loosen, he snapped another carabiner around it, then lifted carabiner and rope, then connected the carabiner to the last cam he'd set.

"Take up all the slack. I'm going to need to use the rope to bear me while I inch up for a better hold."

"Roger," Semmerlin answered. After a few seconds, he added, "I've got you."

"Roger." Graft felt along the sling until he came to a mechanical prusiking device, an ascender, with a loop of rope already attached to it. This he clipped onto the camming device, setting the bottom of the loop about two and half feet above his right foot. After tugging the ascender to ensure it would hold, he set his foot in the loop and pushed his leg down, lifting himself that extra two and a half feet upward. From there . . .

Okay . . . if the crevice runs upward some, and opens and bit . . . and . . . yes! Sadly, it does me no good unless I can find a handhold or footrest to take the weight off the rope. Well . . . find one or make one. And I don't know that I'll find one, so . . .

Letting himself down that same two and a half feet, Graft's foot hunted for the previously used rest. Finding it, he let his weight all go to that foot. Then he pulled another camming device from the sling. To this he attached an independent loop of cord—not even quite rope, though strong enough—from his pocket. Once the loop was joined to the cam, he set that in the crevice, just below where he'd set the earlier cam. His free foot went into the loop.

"Slack the rope," he told Semmerlin over the short-range radio.

"You've got it."

Lifting himself, as he had before, by his precarious finger hold and the new loop, Graft took yet another cam in his free hand. When he'd raised himself as far as the loop would take him, he sought the upper extension of the crevice. Again, he thrust a cam into the crack and locked it down. Then, weight entirely supported by the loop and the fingers of one hand, he reached down, grasped the rope, and pulled it upward to hook it through the last used cam's attached carabiner.

"Take up the slack."

"Roger."

Graft lifted his NVG's for a moment, then looked down and saw nothing but blackness. He was high enough that the sound of surf had become a bit distant, as if heard through a wall. His best guess was that, of the eighty-odd feet he'd had to climb, sixty, perhaps sixty-five, of them were behind him.

Well . . . below me, anyway.

Worse than the height he'd reached, that more distant sound of the surf would no longer cover the sounds of his climbing quite so well.

On the plus side, though, I've got a marginally better chance of hearing it if they've actually got a roving patrol up above, and it comes close to my objective at some time when the RPV is elsewhere. Course, they've got an even better chance of hearing me than I do them.

I am so getting too old for this.

Flipping the goggles back down, he confirmed that he had a pretty fair position at the moment, with both feet, heel to heel, solidly set on a rather narrow ledge and one fist formed into a ball to lock it into a crevice. He'd already found several likely footholds over the next half dozen or so feet.

The rope around his waist, in multiple loops, was slack for the nonce. Once again he drew a camming device from the rope sling with his free hand. That went into the crevice, was locked down, and then the main rope was fed through the attached carabiner.

Raising one foot and planting it on a tiny toehold, Graft pulled with his fist-formed hand, lifting himself upward.

It was at that point that the rock around his fist gave way on one side. One second, his clenched first seemed firmly held. The next, and it had sprung free in a spray of decayed rock. Graft automatically threw his head back to protect his face and the goggles from the rough cliff side, zipping in a greenish blur past his eyes. As he fell, the rope around his waist whirred as it whipped the safety line through the carabiner on the camming device. As the slack ran out, he felt a sharp pull on his midsection. That pull was altogether too brief, however, as the now taut rope ripped the camming device right from the rock face.

MV *Richard Bland*, Sulu Sea

A radio operator, seated on the bridge, clutched one hand

to his right earphone. Still looking down, he announced, "Graft reports, 'Pelican'."

"Bring her around," Pearson ordered, then gave a heading.

"Aye, aye, Captain," the helmsman responded, repeating back the heading. Ponderously, the ship began to respond to the wheel, veering though about one hundred and eighty degrees until pointing south again.

"Ahead slow," the captain ordered. He rechecked the operations matrix, did a few quick calculations in his head, and let that order stand.

Amphibious operations *always* have command and control issues. Normally and routinely, these were solved, to the extent they could be, by the simple expedient of leaving the naval side in charge of everything until half the landing force was ashore, at which point the ground component commander took over everything, including, broadly, the dispositions and tasks of the navy.

It was both simpler and more complex, in this case. It was simpler because there was only the one ship, though it would be sending out a number of lesser craft and boats. It was more complex because regiment had placed Terry in overall charge.

That was where mechanical, formulaic solutions had to give way to human ones. Yes, Terry was in overall charge. That didn't mean he knew jack about the ship-side aspects of it. So he left Pearson in charge, maintaining for himself only the option of taking control—or, more tactfully, giving advice—if he thought it was needed. Pearson, meanwhile, understood fully that his ship didn't matter to the mission nearly as much as actions on the ground, so he conformed his actions to the needs of the ground commander—who was also Welch.

It worked reasonably well, really, though it might not have for a larger and more complex organization, one where the sheer size meant it was impossible for any large percentage of people to know, hence be able to trust one another.

The whole ship tingled. Both helicopters sat, covered but fully armed and waiting for the word to go. Both CH-750's, also armed, though much more lightly, idled at low just ahead of the superstructure. The nets were already rolled over the side, with the landing craft, bearing both armored cars, sitting just inward from the gunwales and long cables leading from their shackled to the crane, overhead. Forward of the landing craft, three rubber boats sufficient for the special operations portion of the landing force sat on deck. They'd be hoisted over at a signal. The special floating platform from which Graft and Semmerlin had departed swung overhead.

Even below, the people from Bajuni felt the excitement in the air. They were free to come and go but, since they weren't actually part of the regiment and there hadn't been time or space to train them to be, they'd been politely requested to keep out of the way. Being a polite folk, themselves, they did.

The humanitarians, on the other hand, were locked up in two groups. One of these was composed of the highly trained medical types, the doctors and the nurses, whose services just might, and probably would, be needed. The others—including Duke, Zink, and Bourke—were the human dunnage, the administrators; those, and the propagandists who may have been necessary to the making of the advertisements and briefings that would bring their organization money, but were completely unnecessary for an organization that got its funding from sources besides private contributions and government grants.

Stocker had observed, as they were marched off, "Eh? If the ship sinks, fuck 'em."

Terry was out on deck, doing a bit of LBWO—leadership by walking around. This involved letting the troops see you, talking to them in a confident tone of voice, asking questions—as much to let them know you were on top of things as to see if they were on top of things and ready.

Pearson still stood the bridge, monitoring the occasional traffic from Graft. That last was worrisome, because it had been a few minutes longer than expected since the last message.

A printer began to hum down in the commo shack. The rating on duty waited until it had finished, then read it. With an excited "Wow!" the sailor ran out of the shack, and up two sets of ladders, to the bridge. There he handed the message over to the captain.

Pearson, too, read the short message. Then he started to laugh, more or less like the man on a gurney who gets notice of a governor's reprieve, just as they're getting ready to stick a needle in his arm.

"Jesus!" Pearson shouted, between bouts of hilarity. "Jesus, they fucking did it." His fist pounded the padded arm of his chair for a few minutes. Then he read the rest of the message and said, softly, "Damn."

Hmmm . . . announcements? They deserve to know. But . . .

"Radar? Anybody significant very close?"

"No skipper. I can't vouch for a small boat, of course; this equipment's just not that good. But nothing as big as a patrol boat, no."

"Hmmm . . . we're too far away for there to be any little warning craft from the target. We're also too far away, for the next hour or so, for them to make any connection between us and the island. So, yeah. Okay." Pearson's finger hit the intercom button.

"Now hear this," he announced, in his best captain's voice. "All hands, now hear this. This is the captain speaking. Hold your cheering to a minimum. But the war in Guyana is over. Regiment won. Hugo Chavez is dead. And the Venezuelans have sued for peace. There are many, *many* prisoners. Your families are safe."

Orders or not, the ship, all decks, except for the humanitarians' cells and the Marehan, who mostly didn't understand English, just *erupted* in cheers. The aid workers, many of them, sat silent and stunned. Hugo Chavez had been something of a hero in certain circles.

"And now for the bad news. You grunts from Charlie Company . . . your battalion made history. But casualties are heavy. Likewise, you guys from the spec ops company; your battalion took out Chavez to force the peace. But casualties were also heavy. Aviation; your squadron didn't lose many people, but it's interesting that a majority of the regiment's serviceable, uninterned aircraft are currently sitting on the deck of the *Bland*. Navy got off lightly, but we also have about thirty-three percent of the landing craft the regiment now owns, also sitting on deck.

"A last thing for the people who knew him; Colonel Riley of First Battalion was killed in action.

"Regiment sends to us, 'Good luck and God speed.' That is all."

★★★

PART V:
H HOUR
★★★

★ CHAPTER THIRTY-FIVE ★

Dear Lord, please don't let me fuck up.
—Alan Shepherd (attributed)

Caban Island, Pilas Group, Basilan Province, Republic of the Philippines

Whether by God's grace, Murphy's finger, or the Emperor Mong's celestial command, the second camming device held. Graft wasn't sure that had happened until the taut rope and his own momentum slammed him—*hard*—into the rock face.

He hung there, limp and gasping, for long minutes while he tried to convince himself that a) he was still alive and b) this was a good thing. The second proposition, given the sundry pains and the near impossibility of drawing a breath, was the harder of the two.

"You all right, Graft?" asked Semmerlin. He'd seen the fall through his goggles and *just* managed to belay the rope before Graft had built up enough momentum to rip another cam from the wall.

Finally, convinced of the former and willing to accept the latter, even if only *arguendo*, Graft got one hand on the rope, righted himself, and began to reconquer the ground lost.

"Yeah . . . and thanks. I owe ya a beer."

"Cheap bastard."

Only once did he pause on the way up, and that was when a couple of passing pebbles suggested that his little misfortune might have attracted some unwanted attention. Even if he hadn't sensed the pebbles' passage, the softly spoken words, in Lox's voice, in his ear—"They're *right* above you, Graft"—would have stopped his ascent.

The Moros were really—like Zulus, Sikhs, and Gurkhas—among the world's naturally good soldiers. They needed intelligent leadership, of course, and perhaps a bit more than most, since some of their personal and cultural values were highly inconsistent with either mission accomplishment or personal survival. Among other things to their credit was responsibility for the U.S. Army dumping its inadequate .38 caliber pistols in favor of the much more reliably man-stopping .45. Having to use, as a matter of sheer survival, such a large bore pistol to deal with such tiny people said a great deal about Moro morale, guts, and enthusiasm, even if all three were often enhanced with drugs. Moreover, as often happens with a respectable enemy, many in U.S. forces during the Philippine Insurrection and the later Moro Rebellion thought a lot more highly of enemy Moros—and, frankly, liked them better—than they did Christian Filipinos, even when the latter had signed up on the Imperial side. Much the same thing was to happen again, six decades later and rather far to the northwest, in Vietnam. It was a fluke of, at least, American military psychology and didn't really say anything too very bad about either Christian Filipinos or Vietnamese of the former Army of the Republic of Vietnam.

In any case, one constant meme running through the U.S. Army for over a century, which meme transferred nicely to M Day, Incorporated, was, "Respect the abilities of the mean little bastards."

Graft froze in place. This wasn't easy as he had the fingers of one hand tentatively clutching a tiny ledge above him. Pain started small in those fingers, but spread across his hand, down his arm, to his shoulder, and to the muscles of his chest.

Damn the Insurrectos, he thought, as the agony spread. From above there came a faint sound of conversation. Slowly, and as carefully and quietly as possible, he removed his .45 from the shoulder rig in which it rested. That didn't help his overstrained other arm a bit, of course.

Cousins Mukdum and Baguinda were just two of Janail's three hundred and change followers on the island, exclusive of the mostly enslaved women who cooked, did laundry, and warmed some of the Datus' beds at night. Datu was, in this case, a title conferred on his officers by Janail, and had little relationship to the idea of noble birth that the word normally conveyed. Their only badges of office were the kris—the local term for the swords was "kalis"—Janail had bought for them at a market.

Neither foremost nor least among Janail's followers, it was just luck of the draw that had them standing watch over the long stretch of cliff that night. Mostly, they'd looked out over the sea, seeing little but the occasional brightly lit superstructure of a passing freighter, usually off at a considerable distance. The freighters had once been fair game, easy and profitable. Now there were few and those all armed.

Occasionally, they walked the length of the cliff, more for form's sake than in any expectation anyone would try to climb it. Mostly, they interspersed their patrol with long sits at one end or another, just chatting.

And then they heard, oh, *faintly*, mostly covered by the surf, an odd sound—a sort of whirring—followed by a nearly as faint a thump. That got them up off their butts, walking cautiously along the cliff's edge toward the sound.

"They're *right* above you, Graft," whispered the ear piece. "I mean *right* above you. Don't answer; that's how close they are. Two of them. One's staying a little shy of the cliff, if you're wondering. The other one would probably see you, if he had some night vision capability."

Graft didn't need that, except for the knowledge of the one that was hidden from view. It was the knowledge of that hidden one that kept him from firing at the one he could see, and probably screwing up everything in the process.

Instead he waited, one arm slowly turning to a kind of stone with outraged nerves running through it, the other pointed upward, aiming the silenced pistol at the stranger standing above him.

★ ★ ★

Baguinda laughed, calling back to Mukdum, "There's nothing there. Must have been a bird, or maybe a high wave. Maybe even a snake. Loose rock? I dunno."

"Well, come on then," the other replied. "I still need you to explain to me why we're not supposed to bury unwanted baby girls alive. Yes, yes, I understand that we're not. I just want you to explain Allah's reasoning, if you can."

"Sure, sure," replied Baguinda. "Be right there. Just give me a minute." With that, he undid his organization issued trousers, pulled out his penis, and took a long leak over the cliff.

This is just . . . wrong . . . on so many levels, thought Graft, as his goggles, neck, and shoulders were liberally sprinkled with foul, nasty, human urine. *I'm so going to make you pay for that, motherfucker.*

He still kept the same position, as steadily as humanly, or even inhumanly, possible. The goggles weren't worth a lot, at the moment, since tiny droplets were scattered on the lenses. Then the ship sent, "They've moved off, Graft, maybe a hundred and fifty meters to your right. You can go ahead now."

This close, Graft had to be absolutely positive that his camming device was secure and that he had a quick and solid way over the lip of the cliff. Yes, the RPV showed that the two guards were still off to the right, and just possibly asleep, though, with the Moros, that was not something to count on. But this had the potential to be disastrously noisy. As bad, he was about to go into the area that the moon *did* illuminate.

No second chances . . . no chance for mistakes. Do it by the fucking numbers, Graft.

Step one, he thought, *seat the camming device.* He did this, in a small crevice about six feet below the lip, then applied as much strength as he could to pulling it out. It held. *So far, so good.*

Step two, make a loop of rope. This wasn't a big deal. He did it, using teeth and one hand.

Step three, double the loop . . . step four, attach a carabiner . . . five...get the carabiner in the camming device . . . six . . . foot in the loop . . . goddamit quit wriggling, rope. Okay, got that.

Steps seven through one hundred and eight: get the pistol ready and breathe. *Crap, twenty years ago I wouldn't have needed the breather . . . .and my arms wouldn't have noticed the strain. Now? Shit, I've gotten too old. Step one hundred and nine, clean the lenses . . .*

With the loop set at a height that would lift Graft's waist to the cliff's lip, he pushed down with his leg. His pistol was in, close to his chest, as first head, then neck and shoulders, then his upper torso arose above that rocky edge. His goggled eyes snapped left, ahead, right, even as the pistol snapped out to follow his line of sight. *Yeah, so Lox said the RPV shows them not here? So? Who really trusts technology, anyway?*

"Congratulations," whispered Lox. "How's it feel to go 'where no man has gone before'? Now I suggest to you that you kill those two."

Graft didn't answer. He just thought, *Well, duh.*

Leaning forward, Graft laid his upper torso on the ground and began to wriggle forward towards a likely tree. At the tree he stopped, reluctantly laid his pistol on the ground, looped the rope around one leg, and began undoing the rope coil about his waist. Once it was free, he ran it around the tree and tied it off, just enough to keep it from coming loose. Then he retrieved his pistol. He felt a *lot* better with that in hand.

To Semmerlin he whispered, "Don't come up yet. The rope's not fully set and I have to get the guards."

"Roger. Waiting. Let me know."

"You can hook up the bundle."

"Doing it."

Unseen, Graft nodded. Rising to a crouch, he began to follow the cliff to his right, as a distance from it of perhaps a dozen feet. "How far are they from the cliff's edge?" he asked Lox.

"Right up on it."

Good.

Graft walked forward slowly and carefully, setting his feet down, outer edge first, then rolling them inward to smother any sound they might make. After traveling about a hundred meters that way, he heard the voices of the two Moros. As far as he could tell, they sounded like the ones he'd heard before. Graft moved forward until he was on line with a line drawn roughly perpendicular to the cliff, and running between the Moros. He'd gradually changed the orientation of his body as he moved, to keep the pistol pointed in their direction.

The .45 had been left, from the beginning, cocked and

locked, with only the grip safety to ensure against a premature discharge. That, too, was deactivated by Graft's grip. He changed his grip from one-handed to two. With the pistol thrust out ahead of him, he slowly crept closer to the unsuspecting Moros.

At a distance of about twenty feet, Graft stopped and lifted the goggles from his face. They were good for many things, but aiming at a close target wasn't among them. His pistol didn't have a laser aiming device; like a lot of special operations types, Graft didn't really trust anything that required batteries, and used those that did require them very sparingly, radios and night vision scopes and goggles being about the limit of his tolerance.

No matter, even through the trees overhead, the moon gave enough light to silhouette his targets.

Which one first? One had his rifle across his lap. The other's on the ground at his feet. Lap loses.

Graft fired twice, *pffft . . .* recover *. . . pffft.* The slide made more sound than the firing did. His target pitched forward onto his face.

The other Moro began to bend and turn. Again, Graft fired: *pffft . . . pffft.* That Moro, too, went down.

Now was not the time for subtlety. Bounding forward, Graft placed the muzzle of his .45 almost against the head of his first target and fired again. Brains splattered, some of the mass onto Graft's boots. Turning, he repeated the action with his second target. Again this was called, "overkill," or "making sure."

There were any number of human rights and international law lawyers and judges who would have claimed that Graft had just committed a war crime, since his targets were clearly *hors de combat* at the time of his fifth and sixth shots. Graft, however, was of a more practical and far less intellectual school. *Just making sure.*

"They're down," he said into the mike. He slowly pulled back the slide, ejecting one shell and loading the last one from that magazine, then took a spare magazine from a pouch and clicked it home. *Seven and one*, he thought, automatically. He then started rolling the bodies to the cliff. One after the other, down they went, with not a sound to be heard by anyone not actually on the beach. Certainly Graft didn't hear the bodies as the rocks below ruined them even further.

"Wait a few minutes, Semmerlin, while I go back and secure the rope properly. You can go ahead and mark the landing point for the next wave with a couple of IRs."

"Roger, doing it."

"*Bland?*"

"We copied."

MV *Richard Bland,* Sulu Sea

"Ahead slow," commanded Pearson. The ship shuddered as it began to lose way.

"Lower the loading platform." The crane whined slightly as it first picked up, then swung over the side, the floating platform used to load the Zodiac boats. The boats were already loaded and lashed down to the platform, while the men of A Company clustered by the nets nearest where the platform would be set down.

One of the naval crew guided the crane by intercom,

right until the platform softly splashed into the water. Then, at a signal, the operatives of A Company, under Warrington—Welch being stuck on the ship—began to scramble over. The first men at the bottom of the nets automatically began unlashing them and pushing them to the edge of the platform. Once all were down, they formed up to either side of the Zodiacs, picked up the boats, and walked forward into the salt. When the boats were fully in, the troops scrambled up from the water, over the gunwales, in an orgy of knees and elbows. The first men successfully aboard reached out to grab and pull in those who were still struggling.

Finally, where finally meant a mere couple of minutes, the boats were loaded and the men in their preassigned position. At command, the electric motors—large and fairly powerful, but very quiet—were started. Warrington, in the lead boat, gave the command, "Move out." Three boats, forming into a line, began to undulate through the choppy sea to the western—and now unguarded—side of the island.

★ CHAPTER THIRTY-SIX ★

Only those who lack it use the adjective
'excess' in front of testosterone.
—Dan Goodman

Caban Island, Pilas Group, Basilan Province, Republic of the Philippines

Graft and Semmerlin strained at the rope, hauling up the last of the equipment they'd brought with them. Naturally, the package stuck at the very edge of the cliff.

"Go get it," Graft ordered. "I can hold the rope here."

"Sure." Semmerlin sniffed "Hey, why do you smell like piss?"

"Just go do it."

Semmerlin slithered out and got his hands on the bundle. By main strength he and Graft pulled it up and over. They quickly untied the main rope. Then Semmerlin took a piece of dark duct tape and an infrared chemlight from his combat harness. He attached the plastic tube to a point a about twenty feet above the rope's free end, then tossed the rope back over the cliff.

From the bundle emerged all manner of wondrous things. First came two rope ladders. Each man took one of them to different trees flanking the main rope. To these the ladders were attached, then viciously pulled on to make sure they were secure. The ladders were pushed over the cliff as well, unrolling as they fell.

"You know," whispered Semmerlin, "for the very first time I begin to suspect this shit might actually *work*."

"Shhh," said Graft. "You want to jinx us, ya dumb ass?"

"Sorry."

Next came a brace of weapons, a suppressed .510 caliber rifle matching the one across Semmerlin's back, and a regimental standard Pecheneg machine gun. Graft laid the rifle beside himself. It would be his primary weapon for the festivities if and only if things got out of hand.

A dozen claymore mines came out, filling the local air with the pungent, plastic aroma of C-4. Though still in their bandoleers, eight of the mines had already been rigged with det cord to form two daisy chains of four each. Each man slung one set of daisy chained mines across his shoulder. The clackers were in the bandoleers. The other four mines had been left as singletons, though each was equipped with a trip wire device that merely needed arming and setting to become a rather effective booby trap.

Thermal scopes came out. Graft took the first and, after telling Semmerlin to turn around, affixed it to the latter's rifle. Then he did the same for his own, returning the rifle to its spot on the ground.

Semmerlin began pulling boxes of belted machine gun ammunition out, hanging these from his body as he did. Graft grabbed an entrenching tool and stuck it on his own gear.

This, plus draping themselves with still more goodies, didn't take very long. They'd rehearsed it, over and over, back on the ship, unpacking and repacking their equipment bundle over and over as they did.

Finally, fully accoutered, the two men patted themselves to make sure everything was in its proper place. They each did a couple of short leaps upward to ensure they weren't rattling, banging, or making any other distinctive sound. They then began the trek down to where they believed Mr. Ayala was being kept.

Their job was not actually to retrieve Ayala from the island. It was possible they could have, of course. But it was also risky, and would become especially risky once the presumptive means of early evacuation, the helicopters, were heard by the enemy. Instead, what Graft and Semmerlin were tasked to do was find him and secure him, then move him to as safe a spot as they could find, on the island, while the island was being cleared. Indeed, even the rest of A Company was not intended to clear the island, nor even help much. Once landed, they, too, had the job of securing Mr. Ayala, once the company, plus Graft and Semmerlin, linked up. Part of securing Ayala was keeping him alive, once secured. For that, Cagle had accompanied A Company.

Clearing the island, on the other hand, so that evacuation could proceed safely, once all the Moros were dead, was the job of C Company and the aviation detachment.

That's where the *serious* firepower was. At most, A Company could ease C Company's way, as Graft and Semmerlin had eased the way for the rest of A Company.

Part of Graft's and Semmerlin's shipboard rehearsal had been to ensure that they didn't clank when they walked. They didn't; everything was either wrapped in something soft or, if not, kept away from anything hard or metallic. Still, they were carrying enough sheer mass that walking was a little awkward, especially since they really had to stay off the trail that led from the cliff to the main Moro cantonment. Fortunately, the island being mostly jungle covered, the ground was actually fairly clear of vegetation other than large tree trunks. The NVG's, touch, and long experience helped guide them around those, though the goggles had a nasty tendency of making hanging vines look like draped snakes. *That* could be very creepy. No one ever quite got used to having what appeared to be a large fat snake suddenly and unexpectedly appear in their vision.

I fucking hate *snakes*, thought Semmerlin, jumping back from a swaying green apparition.

Navigation—or guidance, anyway—was helped a bit by the RPV. Its thermal imager was powerful enough to see them, at least most of the time, and would have provided warning if there'd been any unfriendly strangers, close by and ahead. This further allowed somewhat less careful walking, upright and hence faster, than if they'd been unescorted.

In a fairly short time they were at the edge of the cantonment. This was where things got dicey. Graft reported, just in case the RPV couldn't see them for the nonce, "Crater." *We are at the edge of the cantonment.*

MV *Richard Bland,* Sulu Sea

The operations chart suggested it, or perhaps demanded it, but Welch had to do his own calculations in his head. *The Zodiacs are forty-five minutes out from the cliff. Graft's almost at the target. The* Bland's *about twelve miles from the island. With slinging it over the side, and loading the troops, that's two and a quarter hours for the LCM. An hour and fifteen minutes for the Zodiacs to land, my people to scale the cliff, and to set up a perimeter to secure Mr. Ayala. I think . . .*

"Skipper, land the landing force."

"Aye, Major. All stop."

"All stop. Aye, aye, Skipper."

As usual, Kirkpatrick and his crew went over the side with their LCM. Someone had to be there to control the thing and cast off from the crane's cables. No sooner was the boat settled in the fairly comfortably calm water then the crew sprang to undo the shackles. Immediately, and enthusiastically, the men of C Company began surging over the gunwales and down the net. Only two platoons plus Stocker's headquarters were going in this load; the rest, under the exec, Simon Blackmore, would load and move to shore when the *Bland* had closed substantially on the island.

One reason, and not a small one, for the men's

enthusiasm was the news of their home regiment's success, back in South America. It had seemed so impossible—an impossibility weighing on their souls like a tombstone—that the news had propelled their morale to the very heights. They felt they could take on the world.

Balbahadur went with that first group. His pipes were silent and would remain so until contact was made. He thought, *No sense, after all, in warning them we're coming. Lots of sense in frightening the piss out of them once they know we're there.*

Caban Island, Pilas Group, Basilan Province, Republic of the Philippines

From behind, Semmerlin overwatched, looking through the thermal scope of his suppressed .510 caliber rifle. Flat on his belly, Graft aimed the claymore out to graze across the main trail junction leading, on the one hand, to the main pier and, on the other, to the cliffs. Sixth inch thick detonating cord led from one side of the claymore to the next in the series. The other side of that claymore had a standard blasting cap and wire. The wire already ran back to where Semmerlin overwatched. The clacker was, sensibly, in Graft's pocket.

Finished with sighting that mine, Graft dragged himself, his rifle, and the bag of claymores to the left, then began setting up the next in his series. Once finished with all four, he crawled back to the trunk of the grand old tree behind which Semmerlin covered and whispered, "Your turn."

Crawling off with his rifle cradled in his arms, Semmerlin left his Pecheneg resting on its bipod, aimed up the trail. He, too, took his clacker in his pocket. His area for his daisy chain was a little farther forward, almost at the one true building—an almost pagoda-looking mosque—the camp boasted. Once he was done, he crawled back. Then he and Graft connected four clackers to the four wires running from the ends of their daisy chains.

And now, thought Graft, finally standing to make his way into the camp, . . . *now it really gets dicey.*

The cantonment was surprisingly quiet, as Graft, sans most of his equipment, slipped from hut to hut, staying always in the shadows and trying to stay downwind. Fortunately, the camp remained quiet. If there were any dogs around—and there might well not have been since the Koran is not precisely a doggie fan book—they neither heard Graft nor caught his scent.

Somewhere in the village Graft heard in his earpiece Lox's voice, "I've lost you among all the other images. You're on your own."

Gee, thanks.

Well, it wasn't like I wasn't expecting it at some point. Now let's see . . . there's the mess area, I can smell the residual smoke and food. Hmmm . . . okay, past that and online, up the trail, is a bigger hut. That's the Harrikats' headquarters. So . . . Ayala is . . . there.

Graft had two choices, neither particularly good. He could try to slice his way into the hut, through the wall. If he had the wrong place, and it was just possible he might have, and more possible that Ayala had been moved, and if anyone was awake or awakened by the sound, he was screwed. On the other hand, while the normal entrance had two guards as of the last report, a disadvantage not to be underestimated but also a pretty good indicator that Ayala was there, he could make a pretty good effort at killing them before they got the alarm out. He opted for the normal entrance.

"Graft," came the whisper in his ear, "if that's you I see about fifty meters southeast of Ayala's hut, the number of guards remains two. There are maybe a dozen more, lying down, unless a couple of them are fucking a couple of others, in the long hut across the trail. I'd suggest you jump around or something, so I can know, but that's probably not such a great idea. For what it's worth, Terry says the rest of A Company will be climbing the cliff in ten minutes, and half of C Company is almost at the point where the Harrikat will be able to hear the LCM's motor anyway. He's putting the aircraft into the air. You're authorized to start the party."

Good timing. thanks. No, it's a really bad idea. And I can hear them, chatting.

Okay, now how do I do this? There's just not a lot of room for subtlety and cleverness. If I edge around the hut's wall, I'll see one first. But if I shoot him I won't have a shot at the other. If I expose myself to where I have decent shots at both, good chance they see me and raise an alarm. If I get in position to take one, and wait for the other to expose himself, good chance I get seen . . . like when the sun comes up, because I just might have to wait that long. And there's no time for that anyway.

If I were about five-four and skinny, I'd just walk right up to them. But I'm not . . . and there's not all that much time.

Brute force and ignorance it is, then. Oh, this is so gonna suck.

In fact, that—brute force and ignorance—wasn't precisely what Graft did. First, he got down on his belly and crawled to where he could see one of the guards. From its bandoleer, he gently took one of his two remaining claymores. This he set up on its legs, but without pushing them into the soil, and aimed at the guard. He then offset the aim almost entirely to the right, to make sure that none of the seven hundred-odd steel ball bearings in the thing went into the hut. Then he sunk the legs. Backing off, taking the clacker with him, he set the other claymore up at a safe distance from the first, and aimed at the guard shack across the trail . . . aimed *low*.

This is not *my first choice. But if I have to, then I have to . . .* With that, Graft settled down in the muck among the shadows, pistol in hand and the clackers at his feet, waiting and hoping for both guards to appear at one time.

That happened, but not in a way Graft would have chosen.

The further guard announced to the other, "Man, I have got to piss."

"Just wait for the relief," the other said. "You know what'll happen to us if you go to the latrines and you get caught."

"Fuck that," said the first. "I'll just go piss over behind

the hut. Won't take a minute and if the datu comes by you can tell him I heard a suspicious noise."

"Oh, man . . . you can't do that. Janail is *death* on pissing or shitting in the camp except in the designated latrines."

"Fuck him; he's not Allah."

With that, the first guard left his post and began walking in the direction of Graft, undoing the buttons of his trousers as he did. That had him automatically looking down when his right foot caught on something that he really didn't expect to be there. He stopped and bent over, feeling down.

Oh, no, thought Graft, seeing the Moro undoing his fly. *No, no, no; not again, not tonight. I'm all pissed out, frankly pissed off, and not going to get pissed on, again.*

When the Moro bent, he thought, *Uh, oh, I'm in trouble. Well fuck it, I see them both now.*

The better target was the farther one. Still wearing his goggles—no time to lift them off—Graft fired three shots, hitting the Moro twice in the chest and missing once entirely. His left hand was raising his goggles even as his right was bringing the .45 down again. The clanking of his pistol's slide brought the other Moro's head up, just before he got his eyes close enough to see what had snagged his foot. At a range of under fifteen feet, Graft fired again, putting his bullet just off center from the bridge of the Moro's nose. Brains, blood and bone flew out the back of his head, dropping him like a sack of potatoes.

Instantly Graft was on his feet, racing for the now uncovered entrance. He didn't bother finishing off the

Moro who would now never get to take his piss. He did donate a bullet to the head of the other one. And then he was in the entrance, almost face to face with another stranger.

While there is life there is hope, the doctor thought, in the near total darkness of the prisoner's hut. The one candle added but little light, and that more concealing than illuminating. *But as life flows away, so does hope. My patient will not last until morning. I have failed.*

It hurt, deep inside. Nearly weeping, the doctor thought, *I don't even have a decent needle for intravenous.* Shaking his head with frustration and despair, the doctor wondered, *Allah, why did You give me any skill at all in the practice of medicine only to deny me the means of using what skill I have? I confess, I will have questions of You in the hereafter.*

The doctor heard a couple of odd thumps and metallic sounds, then footfalls. He sensed a presence at the hut's entrance. He turned to vent his anger at whichever one of the guards had interrupted—

Oh, shit, the doctor thought, at seeing the very large, very plainly not Filipino man, in camouflage clothes and wearing some bizarre kind of mask over his face. *Not . . .*

And that was the last thought the doctor ever had in this world.

★ CHAPTER THIRTY-SEVEN ★

And when the thousand years are expired,
Satan shall be loosed out of his prison.
—Revelation 20:7, King James Version

**Caban Island, Pilas Group, Basilan Province,
Republic of the Philippines**

The first thing Graft did, after downing the Moro standing over the small, reclined body of a man, was grab the candle and hold it up by the man's face. The candle flickered, albeit not much, from the man's shallow breath. So wan was the man that it took Graft a few moments to confirm in his own mind the message he sent the *Bland:* "I have the target. Alive. Not well. *Really* not well."

Next, Graft went outside and grabbed the two dead guards by their collars, dragging them inside the hut before anyone stumbled over them. One of the corpses caught on something. When Graft went to inspect he saw it was a chain. Looking left he saw a rock. In the other direction the chain led to Ayala. *Shit!*

He followed the chain right to where he expected it, a

locked shackle around the old man's foot. The foot didn't, itself, look gangrenous, which eliminated Graft's first solution to the problem, severing the foot. *Double shit.*

The chain? *I've got nothing that can get through that big old iron bastard, not without a week to saw at it. How then . . . aha!*

Hmmm . . . that's going to draw a lot of attention, though. Well . . . I sorta planned for drawing a lot of attention at some point in time.

Crouching low, Graft left the hut again and bent to retrieve the claymore that one dead Moro had upset, its clacker, and the clacker for the other, the other being left pointing at the guard shack across the trail. Keeping his pistol in one hand—*Note to self:* Change the motherfucking *magazine, ya dumb ass*—made the retrieval awkward. Graft dropped the claymore once on the way.

Once back inside, after changing the magazine, he put down his pistol and pulled a knife, using the point to pry the claymore apart. After scooping out the C-4 from inside, being careful to retain as much of its flat form as possible, he placed the redundant body, plastic and ball bearings, aside. Reflattening the explosive as best he could by hand, he molded it into a V and placed the open end of the V down on the chain. There were formulae for that, but Graft went with Factor P, for plenty.

A pound and a quarter of C-4 ought to be plenty.

The C-4 was about equidistant between the rock and the prisoner. That was based on a crude, rather a purely unconscious, calculation, to keep as much of the blast away from both himself and the prisoner, while having to take no more of the chain than he possibly could avoid.

Frantically, Graft unscrewed the plug that held the cap in place and placed it at the V's very points.

Hmmm . . . need something to absorb the shock; the old man can't take much more. For that matter, I'm no fan of keeping close company with large booms. Oh well, nothing to hand besides some fresh meat. They'll do.

The doctor's body—though Graft thought of it only as the body of the one he shot inside the hut—came first. Graft dragged it to the chain and bent it into a C, on one side of the explosive V. Next came one of the Moros, he wasn't sure which one and didn't much care, either. That one, with the doctor, formed an oval around the C-4. The last one went atop those two.

"Gentlemen," Graft whispered into his mike, "I am starting the party in a few seconds. SITREP, please."

"We're coming up the ladders now," said Warrington. "*Rachel* reconfirmed the guards weren't replaced."

"Idling off the landing point," said Stocker. "We hit the beach three minutes after the order."

"Aviation's ready to go," said the commo man on the bridge of the *Bland.*

Okay, thought Graft, as he bent his own body over Ayala's to provide what protection he could. *And, Lord? For what we are about to receive.*

With that, Graft cupped a hand over his one open ear, tucked the other against his shoulder, and squeezed the clacker.

Shaped charges, which was what Graft had formed from the C-4, are much misunderstood. They don't, in the first place, really concentrate the explosion. In fact, the bulk of the blast goes outward. Conversely, a rather small percent of the total power is directed inward, at the focus of the cone. On the other hand, that relatively small percentage of the blast that is focused is *very* focused, enough so that the jet of hot gas and sometimes metal that it forms can get through a great deal of very tough stuff.

That's what the V of C-4 did, albeit less efficiently than the shaped charge norm; it sent a jet of gasses, effectively a hot knife, against the metal of the chain, which might as well have been butter. The chain was cut.

However, there's a price for everything. When the rest of the explosion hit the bodies Graft had placed around it . . .

Jesus, Graft thought, pulling a length of smoking intestine from his shoulder. *Fuck that was ugly*.

He wasn't too badly stunned, and his hearing was still fairly good. He could thank the Moros for that. *But I won't*.

Graft pulled on the chain attached to Ayala's leg. It moved lightly; the C-4 had done its job. Gathering the still fairly long segment of chain up, he placed it on the old man, then picked up and tossed the man over his shoulder. This was suboptimal but optimal required more time than he had.

Jesus, he doesn't weigh anything, hardly.

Already there was shouting coming from the guard shack opposite. Looking around, Graft saw that the C-4 had tossed one of the Moros more or less bodily through the walls of the hut, at least, there was now a big hole there. Crouching with Ayala still on his shoulder he fought his way through the hole, breaking bamboo and branch, shredding leaves and grass.

Once outside, Graft cut left, to the other claymore's clacker. He stooped down—*Oh, shit, my back*!—and grabbed it. One squeeze and there was another explosion, this one aimed and propelling its seven hundred-odd steel ball bearings fairly precisely at the guard shack. What happened there, Graft couldn't see. He could hear, however, a *most* satisfying chorus of screams and shrieks well blended with a lovely bass section of frothy coughing from bloody, violated lungs.

Roughly thirty fragments and ball bearings per vertical square meter was enough to pretty much do a dam-dam on anything living, down range.

Well, that gives me a little time.

The hut nearest the claymore caught fire almost instantly, the flames leaping up the walls to the roof.

Graft tossed his head back, flicking the night vision goggles up and away from his face. Firelight would do better for the nonce.

"Ssseeemmmeeerrrlllliiinnn!"

Maria, the small, young, and much abused slave girl, lay in a fetal position, eyes tightly clenched and sucking her thumb for a change, on the floor of the guard shack when the claymore went off. She didn't know what had caused it, but she could see the results once the blast shocked her eyes open and set the grass above alight.

There is a God, the girl thought, watching her rapists bleed out by the light of the burning roof. *There is a God, but I'd better get out of here.*

She didn't know how to use a rifle, but knives were pretty much universally understood, She took one from one of the bodies, then fled into the night in the direction she'd last seen her brother.

Once he heard the first boom, Semmerlin knew it was "weapons free." He immediately jacked the bolt on his rifle, sighted on a likely man-shaped glow in the scope, and squeezed off a round. The stock jammed hard against his shoulder as the rifle coughed, lightly. There wasn't a lot more sound than would have come from a .22 short.

From off in the distance came another loud explosion, followed quickly by flames rising to the sky.

Again he worked the bolt—*click-clack; click-clack*—launching a stubby brass casing up and to the right. Semmerlin sighted on a silhouette that seemed to be trying to pull on some trousers and squeezed. In both cases the big—forty-nine gram!—bullets moved slowly, at just over a thousand feet per second. But they passed through the light walls as easily as the thermal images had passed going in the opposite direction. And when they hit, they hit with about twenty-four *hundred* joules.

Both targets went down, dead maybe, but for sure at least dying. Not only did the heavy projectiles hit with massive force; being so wide they dumped virtually all their energy into the flesh in an instant.

Click-clack; click-clack.

Semmerlin swung the heavy rifle left, then right, searching for targets. Someone was standing in the open, facing away and waving a rifle. He seemed to be shouting. Some others ran toward that one. *Oh. A leader. Goody.*

Cough. The presumed leader, struck from behind, bent forward at the middle as he threw both arms out. His rifle was sent flying. The others gathered and stood around for just a moment, staring down at the body. If their leader had been shot why hadn't there been a sound of a shot? This was *not* fair.

Click-clack; click-clack. Cough.

He heard, "Ssseeemmmeeerrrlllliiinnn!"

No need to whisper now, really, Semmerlin answered, "Bugs, Mr. Rico. Zillions of 'em. I'm a burnin' 'em down."

Semmerlin swung right again. He saw Graft rounding a bend in the trail, feet a near blur. Looking more carefully, he thought, *Uh, oh.*

Dipshit, Graft thought, as his legs churned through the meters between himself and Semmerlin. Fast as he was running, he couldn't simply run. His head swung left to right—fortunately, the old man on his shoulder was so thin he didn't really interfere with the left view—looking for any threat to himself and his burden. Five times his pistol gave off its anemic cough, missing three times and hitting twice.

Since he ran into three armed Harrikat along his route, this was not quite enough.

In a mutual race to the death, Graft pulled his pistol down even as the Moro raised his rifle. Everything seemed to be in slow motion. The mercenary's vision narrowed at the edges to nothing more than his—*too slow, God-dammit*—pistol and the little man who was determined to kill him.

Then the Moro's chest just *exploded* in a shower of blood and meat. Arms twitched as his body twisted obscenely to the ground. Graft heard in his earpiece, "You owe me big time, sucker."

". . . sucker."

Semmerlin laughed inside. It wasn't every day you got one up on Graft. It was a fine feeling when you could.

He'd been counting his rounds carefully as he engaged. The magazine held seven rounds, of which he'd already fired six.

Bullets were flying now from both sides though. Graft probably needed suppression a little more than he needed a .510 caliber guardian angel. Semmerlin set the rifle aside and pulled the Pecheneg toward himself, settling his shoulder into the stock.

Yee haw! The Pecheneg spoke with considerable authority—about a hundred times—as he sent a long burst first to Graft's left, then to his right, to both cause the Harrikat to duck and discourage pursuit. *Brrrrrrrrppp. Brrrrrppp.*

"That was a little fucking close, shitbird."

"Bitch, bitch, bitch." *Brrrrrppp.* "Never happy." *Brrrrrppp.* "You'd complain"—*Brrrrppp.*—"if they were gonna hang you"—*Brrrrppp.*—"with a golden rope." *Brrrrrppp.*

Graft streaked by Semmerlin's firing position, unfriendly shots following closely.

"Keep going!" Semmerlin shouted. "I'll hold 'em here long enough."

Graft didn't need the advice. Still holding the frail little man over his left shoulder he sped past his partner, straight up the trail on his way to the cliff and safety.

★ CHAPTER THIRTY-EIGHT ★

All men dream, although not in the same way.
The ones who dream by night in the dusty shelters of
their minds, wake up the next day and discover that
it was just vanity; but the ones who dream by day are
dangerous men, because they can represent their
dreams with the eyes open to make them possible.
—T.E. Lawrence

**Caban Island, Pilas Group, Basilan Province,
Republic of the Philippines**

There's a time and place for stealth and then there's a
time and place for, "Get your fucking asses up the ladders!"

Warrington uttered those words roughly a millisecond
after hearing the first explosion coming from the enemy
camp, to his northeast. It wasn't as if the men on the
beach or scrambling up the rope ladders were slacking
off, but they had been trying to be careful and quiet.
There'd be no more of that; legs pumped and arms
grappled as they pushed up, one man's head often enough

close enough to smell another's ass, if he hadn't wiped properly.

The two and a half teams under Warrington represented about a platoon in manpower, or a little less. In power, though, there was little comparison. They had fully five Pechenegs and two recoilless rifles, with almost all the ammunition for the latter being antipersonnel. Every man had his own radio, and everyone had some kind of night vision capability, scope or goggles. Moreover, all the scopes were thermals. Every man carried at least one claymore. Perhaps best of all, they were sufficiently strong and fit that they ported about twice a normal infantryman's load in ammunition.

Feeney appeared at the edge of the cliff, recognizable by the outline of his ogre's shape. At the top he stopped and bent a knee, reaching down to haul his normal partner, Hallinan, up and over. At the other ladder Cagle, bowed under a positively *huge* aid bag, stopped about waist high at the lip, then swung a leg over. The next leg followed right enough, leaving Cagle fully prone almost at the cliff's edge. Then the medico pushed himself and his load up from prone to hands and knees, then stood up fully.

"Cagle, find a low spot."

"Roger." The medic trundled off. About fifteen meters from the cliff's edge he found something, terrain-wise, that would do, a shallow depression sheltered by a rock outcropping and with trees to either side. Dumping his bag to the ground, he took a couple of red chemlights from his load-bearing vest, bent them, shook them, and pinned them low, near the roots of the neighboring trees.

Shadows formed into small groups, then the groups

ran past Cagle's aid station toward the camp. They didn't go very far toward it, just enough to provide some standoff distance between the enemy they expected and the cliff. There was a minimum of shouting, though clearly they were being pushed, prodded, and folded into something resembling a cohesive perimeter. As soon as they were set, some of the men took over security, other broke out their "wretched little shovels" and began scraping out rough fighting positions, while still others began to set their claymores out, generally fifty feet to the front.

MV *Richard Bland*, Sulu Sea

The MI-28 gunships had already gone; a night vision scope pointed toward the island would have seen them, almost skimming the waves, about halfway between it and the ship. Following along with a pair of roaring *whooshes*, one after the other, the CH-750s sped down the Marsden Matting, lifting off long before they came even near the end of the strip. They sank under their loads, pulling up just before touching the sea. Both gained altitude, just enough, then veered toward the island.

Welch's eyes followed the light planes down the runway. Once they lifted, and got out from the mild glow of the chemlights placed along the runway, he lost them.

Terry became aware of a tiny shape standing next to him, likewise staring forward, though not necessarily comprehending what she saw. He didn't look. He didn't need to. Only one person aboard ship had that size, or that peculiarly aristocratic presence.

"Yes, Madame?" Terry asked Paloma Ayala, without looking away from the view presented through the bridge's forward windows.

"This will work, Major Welch?"

Madame was dressed as she always dressed, tastefully, richly . . . well. She wore pearls, remarkably large, perfect and—so Welch suspected—not at all cultured, as befitted her age and station. Her hand stroked a gold crucifix at her neck, as if seeking comfort from her God. She sounded quite calm, and so Welch would have taken her, had she not asked the same question roughly once every waking half hour since boarding the *Bland*.

Terry consulted his watch. *Yep, right on time.*

"I know," the woman said. "I *know*." Terrified for the fate of her husband, she allowed fear to creep into her voice. "But . . . but . . . my husband is my *soul mate*. I couldn't find another even if I were still young and beautiful. I *must* have him back."

Thinking of his own wife, Ayanna, back in Guyana and, so it had been reported to him, safe and home again following the war with Venezuela, Welch said, "Madame, I assure you, you are still beautiful." *And I understand about soul mates.*

"There are no guarantees in this sort of thing, Madame," Welch said, as he had said to her so many times before. "Anyone who says otherwise is a fool. Or a liar. Or both. But if I didn't think we had a good, even an excellent, chance of success, I wouldn't have come this far.

"For what it's worth, though there's a lot still to do, and the risks are still large, we have your husband away from the Harrikat."

Though at an intellectual level Paloma knew that that meant a lot less than she'd like it to, at a purely emotional level it was the next thing to Heaven. Tension drained from her shoulders at the news. She slumped and began, softly, to cry. "Thank you. No matter what . . . thank you."

Glad you're appreciative, Welch thought, *because I'm going to be asking for a very large favor here, very soon.*

Caban Island, Pilas Group, Basilan Province, Republic of the Philippines

The very first explosion had awakened Janail with a start. His first thought had been, *Oh, crap, one of the idiots dropped a match in the ammo dump. I'll have his balls—*

That thought cut off as he heard the next explosion, bare seconds later. *No . . . no, those were about the same power. That wouldn't happen at the ammo dump. Oh, shit.*

The slave girl at his side whimpered. He paid her no mind.

He raced half naked and shoeless, stopping only to grab a rifle, before emerging into the dirt road in front of his hut. Already flames were arching to the sky from a burning hut to the south. He guided himself like a homing pigeon toward those flames.

He heard the moans of the dying in what remained of the guard shack. *They don't matter,* he thought, turning away from that and toward Ayala's hut. The left side of his face nearly burned from the heat from the burning hut nearby. Already, the material of Ayala's hut was beginning to smoke.

The explosive blast inside had extinguished the candle. No matter, there was enough light leaking from outside through the entrance and the newer hole for him to see that not only was Ayala gone, but the entire area was littered with pieces of bodies.

"My prisoner," he murmured, "my money." Then he shouted, "My weapons!" With shoulders slumping he thought, *My sultanate.*

Whatever his others flaws and deficits, Janail didn't lack for either decisiveness or determination. Stepping back outside, he called for his datus, his officers. A tracer from somewhere to the south zipped by. Janail paid it no mind.

Small knots of the slave girls and their brats streamed by, heading to presumed safety in the north. As four of Janail's six datus gathered around him—*Who knows where the other two are?*—he set his mind and heart on winning. *They can't be off the island yet. If they were, there'd not be any firing. No, I have to assume Ayala is still here, somewhere. Where? Probably in the direction that firing is coming from. Sure, why not? They got ashore unseen. That means the cliff.*

"Camana, Ampuan," he addressed two of the datus. "Assemble your companies and drive to the cliff. Camana, you're in charge."

"Salic," Janail addressed the datu of his weapons company, "support them."

"Yes, Janail," answered the scar faced, older datu, in the turban.

"Be sure to spread them out. I haven't seen or heard any, but they may have aircraft in support. Now, all of you; go!"

With acknowledging head nods, those three sped off to gather their men, followed by their own radio telephone operators, or RTO's.

Janail didn't really care overmuch about the datu who served, in effect, as his number two. The missing company commander, though; he was important. Janail shouted out, "Molok?"

"Here, Janail," came the answer from the shadows. Datu Molok had been more sensible than most, taking up a covered position before a bullet found him.

"Get your men into their positions along the western beach. I don't know if there'll be more coming by sea, but I don't want it to surprise me, either."

"Ampatuan, your company is with me. Bring them here, but do not cluster them. Get me a radio and someone to carry it."

Something to the east and moderately high in the air fired, rockets and machine guns both. Further flames began rising from the direction of the piers.

Fuck, thought Janail, *they're going after the boats, too.*

Semmerlin fired a short burst at a head that poked around the mosque. The head was a little too quick for him; he missed. Where the Moro had gone, he couldn't be sure, though a fair bet was that he'd taken to ground and was crawling forward.

That wasn't the first miss he'd had, either. Not long after Graft had passed on his way to the cliff, the first Moros had begun showing up in something like an organized fashion. He'd dropped two, he thought, and those only because of surprise. Since then? No luck. If they showed themselves it wasn't for more than an instant.

Problem is, these little fucks are actually pretty good. If they'd just rush me I could drop a shit pot with the daisy chains. As is, there aren't enough to justify it.

I think maybe it's time for Mrs. Semmerlin's little boy to unass the AO.

And, since I'm not going to get a lot of use out of the daisy chains, I may as well expend them to drive the little shits' heads down. It'll give me some smoke to cover my withdrawal, too, which, given the light from the fires, I'm probably going to need.

As if to punctuate that last thought, a burst of fire from somewhere off to his left chipped bark just a few inches over Semmerlin's head.

Thinking, *Oh, Mommy, I'm a comin' home*, he reached for the clackers.

Datu Salic had three platoons in his company, one of mortars, one of heavy machine guns, and the other of recoilless rifles. The mortars could pretty much see to themselves. At least, they could once they got the ammunition from the dump and established radio contact with Camana. The heavy machine guns were way too heavy to move easily, and impossible with a useful load of ammunition. They were mounted on high tripods for antiaircraft work, with at least a fighting load of linked .50 caliber or 14.5mm, depending on the type of gun, piled behind them. They were Salic's least favored platoon, not because there was anything wrong with the men but because he was fairly sure that if the Philippine Armed

Forces decided to evict them from their little island the eviction notice would come in the form of some bomb-carrying aircraft he couldn't hope to touch with mere machine guns.

The recoilless rifles didn't need a lot of ammunition, being direct fire weapons. What they did need the crews were able to retrieve from the dump in passing.

Salic only had four of them, and those four were all U.S. designed, Chinese-built, M18, 57mm jobs. They were all pretty old, having seen service with the People's Liberation Army and the Moro Liberation Front, before finally being stolen from the latter by the Harrikat. Ammunition was fairly plentiful, if rather old and therefore a little iffy. It had a nice little high explosive warhead and a useful white phosphorus rounds, though the anti-tank warhead had never been worth much. Salic had only kept a couple of dozen of the latter, expending the rest for training purposes. He'd been just paranoid enough to have each crew load up with two of the AT rounds.

The crews, six or seven men per gun, were in a widely spaced column, trotting behind Salic, far enough from the steadily firing machine gun that he felt comfortable having them trot upright rather than crawl.

Two sets of explosions, so close together as to be almost indistinguishable, off to Salic's left front, had him and all his men diving for cover in a flash. Mere fractions of a second after that, explosions seemed to erupt all around, though none were precisely on target.

"What the fuck was that, Datu?" asked the recoilless platoon leader.

"I don't know," Salic answered. "But whatever it was I

didn't hear so much as a pebble reach us from the first blasts. Check that your men are all healthy and then get them back on their feet and into the trees."

Because I think we've got company up above and I wish I hadn't left all the heavy machine guns behind.

With one hand gripping his rifle around the stock and the other curled around the carrying handle of his Pecheneg, bent over at the waist so low that the firearms sometimes slapped the ground, Semmerlin sprinted back toward the cliff, staying just off the trail. He'd been on the right side, previously, so he looked for a place on the left side from which he could delay the Harrikats' advance. As the wise old sergeant had said, *Randomization is your friend.* He was definitely in doggie mode—which is to say, "any tree will do" mode.

He settled on something he found about two hundred meters back from his previous position. This was a large tree with the advantage of having a solid looking boulder between it and the trail. It was actually the boulder that had first attracted his attention. Between the two was a nice little gap, maybe eighteen inches across. The machine gun he reloaded and set aside, though he left it close enough to grab at need. The suppressed .510 caliber he also reloaded, with a seven-round magazine, and then settled himself and the rifle into a firing position from which he could cover the trail junction.

★ CHAPTER THIRTY-NINE ★

Surprises are foolish things. The pleasure is not enhanced and the inconvenience is often considerable.
—Jane Austen

Caban Island, Pilas Group, Basilan Province, Republic of the Philippines

"They were *there*," fumed Slepnyov to his gunner. The man's actual title was "Weapons and Navigation Officer," but "gunner" would do.

"I mean right *there*! Maybe thirty men carrying four or five, maybe even six heavy weapons. In the fucking open. Meat. Just meat. And then some fucking *asshole* on the ground had to set off some explosions and they all ducked. Why? Why, why, *why* did he have to do it while my finger was pressing the firing button? Why? A whole *pod* of rockets! Wasted. Why? Is there no *God*?"

"Slepnyov," answered the gunner wearily. "You—oh, deny it if you like, but I know better—are still, at heart, a communist. You *already* didn't believe in God."

"And there's my fucking proof!" the pilot snarled.

"Where'd they go by the way?" the gunner asked.

"Scattered and somewhere in the trees. We don't have any really superb weapons for people inside forests, you know. And there's *more* proof, as if I needed any."

Providing proof of friendly intent and disposition was always a tad problematic for those who just had to run towards groups of nervous, essentially trigger-happy, friends. For this there was something called the "running password." No, no, it didn't pass from mouth to mouth. Nor did it resemble a running joke. It was something the soldier shouted for all he was worth when running for his life from the enemy.

The running password had a couple of criteria associated with it. It had to be easy to remember, even when scared out of one's wits. It was good for it to be more or less unpronounceable by one's enemy-du-jour, words with "W," for example, if fighting Germans or Slavs; "L's" and "R's" were good for most Asians, "V" wasn't bad for Latins.

It was also supposed to be followed by a number, for the number of people attempting to pass lines. This could, in some circumstances, be a problem.

"Schickelgruber Twwwooo! Schickelgruber Twwwooo!" Graft screamed, as he passed between Feeney and Hallinan. He'd been shouting the same thing for about three hundred meters.

That one would have worked, even with a German, since the German would have pronounced it *too* correctly. The problem was in the "two."

"Hallinan," Feeney said dramatically, "I only saw one man pass by; Graft, I think it was. That means somebody's still out there . . . gotta be Semmerlin. One of our own is out there, Hallinan. I gotta go get him."

Hallinan himself wasn't sure. Unlike Feeney, he'd noticed the burden on Graft's back. Maybe that was the "two." But, on the other hand, there had been a two man team, so maybe "two" was Semmerlin, maybe shot and bleeding in their flight. Graft would have wanted to go back for him, if so, but Graft, Hallinan knew, was a real pro. He wouldn't have risked the mission for a single man, except when, as now, a single man *was* the mission. *Sooo . . . I dunno.*

"I gotta go get him, Hallinan. He's one of *ours*." As fiercely as Feeney despised those who were not "ours," his devotion to those who were was just as strong or stronger.

"I'll go with you." Keying his mike, Hallinan reported to his team leader, "Semmerlin's out there on his own. Feeney and I are going for him."

The team leader, not having any better information, passed that on to Warrington who said, "Roger."

The suppressed big bore rifle, Semmerlin discovered, was not entirely suitable for occasions when the enemy wasn't just standing there. Oh, sure, the forty-nine gram bullet was vicious if it hit, but, being subsonic, it took a whole second, more or less, for the bullet to travel to the target at three hundred meters. Since displacing back, he'd only gotten two of the Harrikat who'd gotten a little bold, themselves.

Now? Now they were crawling below his ability to see,

or making short rushes that made it almost impossible to lead them properly. And a few were spraying the trees around him, or bouncing bullets off his rock—*pretty sure that's just random; doubt they know exactly where I am*—none of which was doing a thing for his marksmanship.

And they *were* getting closer.

No, they don't know exactly where I am. But they've got at least a general idea. Time to go? I think maybe so.

A long burst, maybe twelve rounds, from a machine gun somewhere to his front, hammering a tree just behind him, convinced Semmerlin that getting up and running was not the best of all possible ideas.

But, crap, those little bastards are *getting close. Maybe not grenade range . . . yet. But close. Maybe a hundred twenty-five, hundred and fifty meters. Hmmm . . . dumbass, you should have set up a claymore on a trip wire when you first got here.*

Oh, well. No use crying about it.

Semmerlin began wriggling back, snakelike, away from the little gap between tree and rock. Once back he rolled to one side and slung the rifle across his back. Then taking the machine gun to cradle in his arms, still like a snake, he began crawling up the slope that led to the cliff.

The shore by the piers was only about two minutes away, as the LCM's bow arose and fell in the heightening waves close by the island. In his goggles Kirkpatrick saw one of the gunships lashing a tree line with its 30mm chin gun. The other rode shotgun on the landing craft, maybe two hundred meters behind the boat and a like distance to its right. By the piers, themselves, two small and one larger boat burned merrily. Whether that was from rockets, tracers, or some combination of the two, coupled with leaking fuel from gas tanks, the coxswain didn't know.

By the bow, Kirkpatrick saw the grunt commander, Stocker, peering out at the shore over the left corner of the ramp. There were no grunts directly behind him; they were leaving a little space for safety for the Elands, both of which were already almost completely unlashed and almost ready to be unleashed onto the shore.

Suddenly, the night was lit from behind as the MI-28 lashed out with half a pod of rockets. Kirkpatrick's goggles flared, went dark, then gradually came back from the effect of the explosive flashes erupting ashore. The gunship's chin gun kicked in. Smaller explosions, not quite enough to overload the light amplification tube in the goggles, lit up the shore.

Kirkpatrick hoped the supporting fire would be enough to kill or drive off anyone on the other side who might be waiting. He knew, however, that hope wasn't a plan, and that, historically, that never happened even if you were using sixteen-inch naval guns in support. Some of them *always* lived.

If they're there. Hmmm . . . the helicopter wouldn't have fired if they weren't, I suppose. After all, he can see. I hope the grunt commander can figure that out.

Still keeping his hands on the controls, Kirkpatrick lowered himself into the lightly armored wheelhouse. At a quarter of an inch of steel, the armor wasn't much. It was still better than nothing.

★ ★ ★

"Where's the aid station?" Graft called. "Where's the fucking aid station?"

"Over here, Graft," Cagle shouted back. "Follow the red chemlights."

Still with his small burden over his shoulder, Graft hurried over, dodging trees along the way. Cagle helped the sergeant ease Ayala from his shoulder, then lay him out on the ground. By the dull red of the lightsticks, Graft saw that Cagle had already scraped out a shallow trench for Ayala. He'd also hung several IV's from the nearby tree and rolled out his instruments. Cagle started an immediate search, mostly by touch, for any wounds.

"You done good," the medic said. "He hasn't been shot."

"I didn't check his vitals," Graft said, as Cagle began doing just that. The sergeant sounded apologetic, adding, "There just wasn't time."

"Not a problem," the medico answered. "Shit, his blood pressure's down to about the level of a corpse. Gonna be a bitch getting a needle in his veins in that condition . . ." Cagle grabbed another light and began searching Ayala's arm for some place he'd have a half decent chance of getting a needle stuck in. Tsk-tsking at the poor prospects, Cagle muttered, "Well . . . it's shit, but it'll have to do . . . goddamit, I missed."

"Train to standard, not to time," Graft said. "Stick the son of a bitch again."

"You've been listening to Riley's and Coffee's stories," Cagle accused.

"It's not a crime."

Paying no further mind to Graft, Cagle made another

attempt. The needle went into the skin easily, then the medico began to search with it, going by highly experienced feel for the vein. "Annnddd . . . there it is."

"You're good," Graft said admiringly.

"The best," the medico responded cheerily. "Well, except maybe for TIC Chick. And she's not so hot out with the snakes, bugs, and dark."

"Hey," Cagle said, "the radio's right there, patched in straight to TIC Chick. Get on it. As I give you symptoms and injuries relay them to my wife so she can get everything ready."

"Yeah, sure, fine," Graft replied. "But hurry it up, will ya, Doc. One of my men's still out there and I'd really like to get him back."

They'd been caught moving to the bunkers that covered the beach, but not quite at those bunkers, when the enemy struck. The delay, and getting caught, wasn't really anyone's fault, except maybe their enemies', but between the night, the surprise, the fear . . . it all took up time.

Molok felt his company—in Harrikat terms, that meant maybe sixty men—almost disintegrate around him. One moment they were moving forward with a purpose; the next they were just a bunch of frightened individuals, with no purpose higher than not getting perforated. First came the rockets—fifteen or twenty of them; he wasn't quite sure—some spilling out cargoes of flechettes, others impacting the ground and trees. The explosions were to be expected, but the sound of the flechettes was absolutely chilling, almost like a swarm of intelligent killer bees. He'd never faced flechettes before, hadn't even known they existed. But the killer bee sound, coupled with the two men in front of him who, by the light of the burning boats down at the shore, began spouting blood like a matched pair of obscene fountains, were enough to let him know that whatever they were, they were something particularly evil.

Those two died quietly, surprised, shocked, and bled out before pain could really register. Others didn't. After the passage of the killer bees, even after his ears had been assaulted by the rockets that struck the ground, Molok could hear screams coming from as many as half a dozen throats.

"Run for the bunkers!" he screamed to his men, getting up and sprinting himself. "It's your only chance!"

After the rockets, something a good distance out to sea began firing what had to be the mother of all machine guns. Molok couldn't really make out any details, by the thin moon and the flashing strobe light underneath, but as he ran he thought he saw a helicopter gunship. That was bad news. That meant he wasn't facing some rival Moro group, but probably Philippine regular forces. Maybe even Kanos.

With that dreary prospect in the back of his mind, he reached the command bunker overlooking the shore and dove in. The bunker was dark as an infidel's soul; Molok had to find the field telephone by touch. Once he did, he pulled it from its case and, holding it to one ear, stood to look out through the central of the bunker's three broad and narrow vision ports.

He felt another man crawling into the bunker behind him. "Who is it?" Molok asked, drawing his knife. The bunker was too close quarters for the rifle.

"Just me, Datu," said his RTO. The man sounded infinitely weary. "Sorry it took so long to get here. Something hit me in the thigh. Twice: A little pinhole on one side . . . on the other, a slice. It was gushing like a woman in season. I don't know what it was, but if I hadn't stopped to bandage it I'm not sure I'd have made it here at all.

"I brought the radio."

"I will call a medic," Molok said.

"No point, Datu. He was turned into a colander. I will live or not as Allah sees fit."

The radios carried by the individuals of A Company were very short range, no more than a quarter of a mile, ordinarily. Leaders had longer ranged sets, of course. Despite this, Feeney kept repeating into his set, "Don't worry, Semmerlin, we're coming for you." That Semmerlin didn't answer, especially since both Feeney and Hallinan presumed he'd been right on Graft's tail, was *most* worrying.

"We oughta go back," Hallinan said. "We're never going to find him this way."

"No," Feeney insisted. "You never leave your brother."

Again into the mike, Feeney whispered, "Semmerlin, don't worry; we're coming for you."

Both were almost surprised when Semmerlin's voice came back, fainter than a baby's breath, "Hold your position; I'll come to you. But you gotta be a little patient."

★ CHAPTER FORTY ★

Success is not final, failure is not fatal:
it is the courage to continue that counts.
—Winston Churchill

Caban Island, Pilas Group, Basilan Province, Republic of the Philippines

How the hell did I get in this position?

"This position" was, for Semmerlin, basically in a small depression, with a tree on each side, his rifle unloaded, and about a dozen Harrikat on all sides. How he'd gotten into such a unenviable position he wasn't quite sure, but thought it might have something to do with, *Give the little fuckers credit; they can* move *when they want to.*

What had actually happened was that he'd set off the two daisy chains, hitting nothing, screwing up Slepnyov's targeting, which had driven the Harrikats' recoilless rifle platoon to first duck, then run like hell for the tree line and past it, humping their guns with them. One minute he'd been crawling to the southwest, basically alone; the next they'd been *everywhere*.

I can see at least a dozen of them, and that's just in front of me. I'd guess from the sound that there are at least that many behind me, maybe more. That one fucker haranguing them sounds like he's addressing a good sized audience. And I've got no loaded rifle, my machine gun is kinda on the noisy side, and my pistol has only seven rounds in the mag and one in the chamber.

I am so fucked.

He remembered a couple of other items still draped to his body then, and, reconsidering, thought, *Or maybe not.*

Then *very* slowly, *very* quietly, and ever so carefully, Semmerlin's fingers began pulling out first one, then the other, of the two claymores remaining to him.

Each was already primed for tripwire operation. *Ah, but that won't do. No way I can quietly get them fixed to something, solidly enough to use the tripwires to detonate them. Nope, it's gotta be electric.*

And this is really *going to sting.*

After taking out the claymores, he pulled out the clackers and the caps, with their already attached wire. These he set down and concentrated on one claymore at a time. It took a little extra time but, not wanting to risk inadvertently setting off the trip wires—*Murphy rules!*—he unscrewed that adapter and set it carefully to one side. The plastic shipping plug came out next. He slid the wire through the slit in the plug and pulled it through to seat the cap right up against it. The cap then went into the claymore. A few twists to the plug and it and the cap were well enough seated. Then his fingers followed the wire to the spool, feeling for the connector. This he attached to the clacker. It wasn't exactly proper procedure, but proper procedure really didn't cover these particular circumstances.

The whole assembly, minus the clacker which stayed close to him, went to the other side of the tree in front of him.

Fortunately there's no range safety officer nearby to bitch about it.

Okay, now let's get the other one.

One of the boats by the pier suddenly blew up with a major burst of flame. The little one near it promptly sank, extinguishing its own fire. The remaining boat, the largest, continued to burn, lighting up both the beach and a low ridge lined with rather well-camouflaged bunkers.

Heavy machine gun fire from the LCM's two .50 calibers thumped overhead, thrashing at what was beginning to appear as a line of winking bunkers, facing the beach. They didn't seem to be doing all that much good, since the fire coming in—causing the sand to jump and the water to spout—wasn't lessening any. The detachment had known that defense line was there, courtesy of the late Kulat and Iqbal, but really hadn't expected the Harrikat to be able to man it quite so quickly.

One bunker in particular, off to the right edge of the beach, was being a serious pain in the ass.

"On the right! On the right!" Stocker shouted into his radio, speaking to the Eland section chief. "Get the fucking bunker on the right!"

Machine gun fire from that bunker rattled off the Eland's just-barely-adequate armor. It also swept the area in front of the landing craft, with occasional rounds pinging off the steel ramp and whining off into the air menacingly. Only Stocker and a single squad had managed to get off the boat—and that only because they took a not inconsiderable risk in following the Elands ashore— before the machine gun had made it impossible for any- one else to debark. At that, one body from that squad, perforated and ruined, bobbed in the waves to the left of the ramp.

Someday I'll probably convince myself that I was just excited, thought the Canadian. *But the truth is, right now I'm so scared I can't spit.*

Balbahadur was doing his bit from inside the well deck, the pipes encouraging the men to risk the fire and storm over the ramp. But they were only human. Nobody would move.

Can't say as I blame them, the Canuck captain thought. *Wouldn't do it myself if I hadn't had the armored car to follow for cover.*

"Meh sees him," answered the Eland section chief. "But only if I stands up in de turret. Wish is bad fo' meh health. I ain't got no good shot. Number two?"

"Meh on it," replied the other car commander. His turret traversed slowly under the power of a hand operated crank. The gun depressed a few inches, then raised almost too little to notice. When it spoke, a great flash of almost solid-seeming flame leapt forward from the muzzle. The entire car rocked back with the recoil. Downrange, a tiny fraction of a second later, a bunker was first lit up like Christmas, then wrapped in a dark cloud, before more flames burst out from the firing port.

"Meh loves me some HEAT, meh does," exulted the commander of Number Two.

Number One answered, "Yeah, but de HEAT no seem to work on all of dem. I hits meh one? It shoot right back, like twas nothin'."

Turning back to the open bow, maybe fifty feet behind him, Stocker did a rush, followed by a fall, a roll, and another rush, to get behind the left side gunwale of the boat.

Sticking his head around the corner—risking that head, in fact—he shouted into the well deck, "Get the fuck off this boat!" Nobody moved; all Stocker could see, and that not well, were the whites of eyes, as if saying, "Are you out of your fucking mind?"

"Balbahadur?"

"Sir?" answered the Gurkha piper, temporarily abandoning his pipes.

"'Blue Bonnets Over the Border' and use your boots if you have to, to move these people out!"

"Sir!"

"You heard the captain, you cunts!" the Gurkha shouted over the roar of battle. "Get off this boat."

Then, in fine Gurkha style, to show the way, Balbahadur resumed his playing, and marched—almost as if on parade—to the ramp. There he stopped, as calmly as might be imagined, marching back and forth across the ramp, port to starboard.

Bullets were still coming in—precisely from whence nobody could say—kicking up spouts of water and pinging off the steel of the hull. Balbahadur, true to his ancestors, paid them no mind whatsoever.

Khan, like the rest, sheltering in the questionable cover of the gunwale, stood up and shouted, "Come on, you pussies! If the sergeant can just stand there in the open, we can at least *move*." With that, the Afghan began running forward, slapping people's backs as he went, to spur them on. The two platoons, minus, of C Company, after an understandable moment's hesitation, began to flow across the ramp, around the piper, and onto the shore.

Behind them, Kirkpatrick raised the ramp and reversed engines, turning his wheel left and right to wiggle his boat off the shore. His machine gunners still kept up a steady fire—*For all the good it seems to be doing*, thought the coxswain—as he backed.

Commendations, Stocker thought, as his platoons spread out around him. *The writing of, eloquently, earliest convenience.*

Then he breathed a sigh of relief that what had been starting to look like a disaster was unfolding as something rather better than that. His RTO, who had been left behind on the LCM, now flopped to the prone next to the captain.

"Get me the gunships," Stocker ordered.

"Yessir, right away, sir. Sorry for being late, sir."

With impatience tempered by the knowledge that, after all, his men were only human, Stocker said, "Just do it."

"Yessir."

Stocker put his head up before it was driven down again by a low flying burst. Looking behind he saw that his men, the two platoons of them that were with him, were out of the boat and on the beach. That was the most he could say, though. Even the destruction of that bunker off to the right hadn't appreciably reduced the amount of incoming fire.

Crap. Not getting anywhere.

The RTO handed him the microphone, announcing, "The gunships, sir."

Stocker took two deep breaths to force some calm into his voice. This wasn't, he found, the easiest thing to do with bullets cracking overhead and hitting the sand to his front. He took a couple more, just to be sure.

Slepnyov and his wingman had pretty specific rules of engagement. It was at least *suspected* that the cantonment area on the island housed some substantial numbers of women, and quite possibly children, and that a fair number of those were probably slaves, Christian Filipinos and Filipinas, that the local government wouldn't be overjoyed to see slaughtered. Yes, of course the Ayala family had the pull to kill any official investigations. But, once her objective was met, Welch had had serious doubts that Mrs. Ayala's power, attitude, and interest would go all that far.

"We're just minions to her," Welch had briefed his subordinates, in a briefing from which Paloma had been tactfully excluded. "And, even if we were more, we've still got to live with ourselves. We do what's necessary, but gratuitous carnage is not in our SOP."

As far as it went, Slepnyov was happy with that restriction. After all, he hadn't taken any fire from the camp. Neither had his wingman. And the RPV hadn't noticed any antiaircraft weapons.

Though, of course, thought the Russian, *it might not. They're not necessarily all that big.*

The radio gave off a couple of the odd beeps that indicated a secure transmission. "Slep? Stocker."

"Slepnyov, Captain."

"I'm held up here, Slep, and falling behind schedule. Let me tell you what I've got."

"Go, Captain."

"My company," he said, "two platoons of it, plus the armored car section, are pinned down on the beach south of the piers. There's a line of bunkers to our west. The bunkers are pretty intelligently placed. We can see a few; others we can't, though, even with the Elands' thermals. They've got to be strongly built; I've *seen* the Elands' main guns hit a couple that just shrugged the hits off. I need something bigger. And I need it to hit them from either the north or south; the bunkers don't seem as strong except to the side facing us."

"I gots something for that, Captain. Can you say 'thermobaric'? Wait a minute."

Slepnyov, switched languages, sending a message in Russian to his wing man. Stocker picked up the message, without understanding a word of it. He didn't really need to, in detail. Both helicopters pulled pitch, noses rising as they changed direction. Then they headed out to sea, formed in echelon, and returned to take up a position somewhat shy of the camp area. A flash started at one of them, then streaked across the sky. To Slepnyov's south, to Stocker's west and front, where the flaming streak met the ground there was suddenly a massive blast.

Slepnyov grunted with satisfaction. The satisfaction

even grew a bit, as two tiny men staggered out of the bunker he'd targeted, one clutching his throat, the other tearing at his own eyes. The chin gun up front whined, then chattered. Both men, one after the other, began to do the Spandau Ballet as the ground erupted around them. They fell in ruined heaps of mangled flesh.

The second gunship likewise fired, its guided missile also touching the ground with cosmic thunder and a massive cloud.

"See?" said Slepnyov's gunner. "I *told* you there was a God."

"Yeah? Fuck off," answered the pilot, as he used his helmet's heads-up display to set another target for the gunner.

"Good choice," said the gunner, once the target was clear. He armed another F Model Ataka missile to deal with that bunker. "And hold her steady for a few seconds."

"Sure, but after this shot we have to move."

"Roger. Missile away."

Just off to the northwest edge of the camp, the Harrikats' heavy machine gun platoon leader, which is to say also the antiaircraft platoon leader, had no illusions about the capabilities and limitations of his guns. He'd been tempted to take a swing at the little buzzing aircraft that had made a couple of passes to the southwest, then really concentrated on lashing the mortars into the next world, but, *No . . . they're at extreme range, in the first place, and I can only see them when they fire, in the second place. Waste of ammunition, and sure to get us smashed flat to no good purpose. Like those helicopters up there. I can hear them. But see them well enough to engage? Not a chance.*

Something flashed above the platoon leader, and about four hundred meters to his east. Another flash and streak formed right after. From the platoon leader's perspective that second shot—if he had doubted it was a shot the amazingly robust explosion at the end of it would have removed those doubts—came from a bit farther away and somewhat to the north. There was a third shot. Then the sound of the helicopters changed slightly. They were moving.

Oh, please, merciful Lord, let them come closer. Let them come close enough that the flames from the huts let me and my men see them. Please? I'll free a couple of slaves if You do.

Like other fighting men, the Russians had many, many admirable qualities. Also like others, by no means excepting Americans, they had their flaws. Among these was a tendency to follow orders very literally. This had its place, of course. It also had places where it didn't belong.

The second of the two gunships also had a place it didn't belong. Rather, it had an area. This area was anywhere above the now mostly burning encampment where the light from the flames would illuminate the bottom of the helicopter. Unfortunately, Slepnyov had given that pilot his orders—"Echelon left, about three hundred meters"—and the pilot had followed those orders to the letter. This placed the gunship squarely over the brightest of the brightly burning huts, where the Harrikats could *see* it.

Three streams of bright green tracers arose from positions around the camp, followed, a second or so later, by a fourth. All four streams converged on the second gunship. The guns were a mix of ex-PLA and American, thus the streams came in two colors, two red, two green. The pilot's first warning was when some of the tracers passed by his helicopter's nose. The second warning came in the form of a 14.5mm bullet that went right through the thick almost-but-not-quite-bulletproof-enough canopy, splattering a goodly percentage of his gunner across the inside of the cockpit. The third warning—admittedly far too late—was a flashing red light on his instrument panel that informed him that he'd lost control of his tail rotor. The light didn't say why, but in fact a .50 caliber bullet had severed the rod. Without its counterbalancing tail rotor, the MI-28, under the torque from the main rotor, began to spin uncontrollably. Within three spins it was spinning vertically, and then vertically, but down.

Once he'd realized what happened, the pilot had just enough time to say, "God—" before slamming into the ground. *That*, given both the fuel on board and the mix of ordnance, led to a massive blast, big enough to catch two of the ground-based machine gun crews in its radius, and send the other two—minus the platoon leader who was so much strawberry jam at the time—running for the north, hoping to join with the women and children sheltering there. It also very nearly flattened the encampment, and put out most of the fires, partly by blast, and then by the thermobaric warheads using up all the free oxygen.

★ CHAPTER FORTY-ONE ★

It is a shameful thing for the soul to faint
while the body still perseveres.
—Marcus Aurelius

Caban Island, Pilas Group, Basilan Province, Republic of the Philippines

While the one hundred foot wire is there intended to be used, or at least a minimum of half of it is, it's actually fairly safe to detonate a claymore much closer to oneself than that, safety regulations, doctrine, and the manual notwithstanding. A couple of sandbags—perhaps three for the very safety conscious or paranoid—are enough to absorb all the plastic fragments the thing will kick back, allowing the soldier to set it off, safe from those fragments, at a distance of a meter or two. Sometimes, in certain kinds of units, a soldier attempting to break contact, and knowing in advance that he just might have to, will place an armed claymore right in the back pocket of his rucksack, then use the frame of the ruck as an ad hoc, hand-held, aiming device. *Uhuh, right about there . . . Boom*! Still . . . fairly safe, though the rucksack's contents are likely to become scrambled.

Fragments, however, are only one of the dangers to using a claymore, with its pound and a half of C-4, in close proximity. Trees or sandbags may partially deflect the blast, but it will still flow around them. This can . . . kind of hurt . . . at about a meter and a half's distance . . . with two of them—three pounds of C-4 . . . and no good way to cover one's ears.

Lord, for what I am about to receive, thought Semmerlin, as he flicked off the wire bails, the safeties, that otherwise prevented the clackers from being squeezed. He had his head down, of course, and one ear tucked as much into his shoulder as he could get it and the other at least generally towards the ground.

Semmerlin squeezed the clackers. For all practical purposes, the resulting explosions—almost but not quite simultaneous—picked him up and bounced him. He couldn't hear it, shoulder over ear or not, but the blasts, partially, and the fourteen hundred pellets, mostly, scythed down a good nineteen of the thirty-odd men around him. Almost none of them were killed outright. The rest, such as retained consciousness, shrieked.

Some, of course, were not hit; claymores rarely if ever scattered their pellets quite evenly. Moreover, some were off to the sides, simply out of the pattern of thrown fragments. Of those not hit, though, some stood their ground while others threw themselves to the ground—on the not-indefensible theory that they were under air or mortar attack. Some ran off. A couple of those running off did so screaming in fear or pain or both.

Thinking, to the very limited extent conscious thought was involved, *To Hell with the rifle; to Hell with the machine gun,* Semmerlin launched himself past the up slope tree and through the smoke from the claymore. Three more staggering steps and he tripped over the legless body of a Moro, already dead or dying; he couldn't tell and didn't much care. There were plenty of screamers around; what was another one, more or less?

Staggering or not, he was moving fast enough to fall, which fall he turned into a complete roll that left him back on his feet, though with his left hand still touching the ground for balance. He came up without his goggles— broken off and lost somewhere behind—leaving him about as blind as some of the Moros caught in the fragmentation pattern of the claymores; the ones who'd taken pellets in the eyes.

Gotta get out of here.

He really wasn't sure where he was going; he'd aimed at the tree because he'd known it was upslope. After the fall and the roll? *Jesus, get out of here, yeah. But for where?*

Automatically, his right hand reached for the suppressed pistol under his left armpit. He shook his head to try to clear his fuzzy mind. *Mistake! Big damn mistake!* Semmerlin felt a sudden, almost irresistible urge to throw up. Forcing it down, literally, he assumed a low crouch and began slowly creeping back upslope.

Stocker barely noticed the little explosions off to the

left. He was still mesmerized by the really big one in the cantonment area, and the way the surviving helicopter was doing its level best to imitate a giant, crushing ants, its stomping feet the unguided eight centimeter rockets, the chin gun the giant's thumb.

Watching the gunship dance over the remains of the camp, relighting the huts and finishing off any wounded that so much as twitched, Stocker thought, *Note to self: whoever is piloting that? Don't piss him off.*

At some point, once the pilot was satisfied that he'd killed everything below, the helicopter started to move north, following the refugees it hadn't been able to extinguish.

"No, no," Stocker muttered, "that's a bit much and you have a mission." Taking the radio's mike from the RTO he called for gunship. The Russian didn't—apparently wouldn't—answer, until Stocker reminded him with the question, "Are you a soldier or a petulant spoiled brat?"

"They killed my people," Slepnyov's voice came back, hate-filled and hurt-filled, both. "They must *pay.*"

"Yes," Stocker agreed, genially. He more or less understood where the Russian was coming from. "And we can kill them all . . . once we take the island. IN THE FUCKING INTERIM, THOUGH, I NEED SOME MORE FUCKING FIRE ON THOSE FUCKING BUNKERS! Is that clear enough?"

Chastened, the Russian's voice came back, "Yes, Captain. Sorry, Captain."

"I understand how you feel, Slep," Stocker consoled. "But let's do the job first and have fun later."

"Roger."

MV *Richard Bland,* just east of Caban Island

The *Bland* was about a hundred percent faster than the LCM, if it wanted to be. With the irregular waters and sea beds in and around the Pilas Group, its captain did *not* want to be. Still, he managed to pull within two and a half miles of the landing point by the time the LCM had unloaded, turned around, and come back for its second load. Even that was a little iffy; Pearson would never have risked it if there had been any chance that Harrikat mortars could have reached, or Harrikat observers could have spotted, his command.

The RPV had been looking for just those items, in fact, and among other things, and Pearson had been fully prepared to run like hell when it found them. Fortunately, it had found them early, and the two CH-750's had put all their effort, and two loads of ordnance, onto the Harrikat mortars before Pearson would venture in.

Now one of the CH-750's was rearming on deck, a very brief process, actually, given how little it could carry, while the rump of Stocker's company surged over the side and down the cargo nets to the LCM. The nearest crane, not being otherwise occupied, lowered a pallet of mortars, mortar ammunition, and sundry other expendables, mostly more ammunition.

All in all, mused Pearson, *things haven't gone too badly. What did the wise man say? "If you can get seventy percent out of a plan you're doing pretty good." We're probably doing a little better than that, with only one exception. We've got a multiplier to our plan, Mr. Ayala. If he doesn't live, then our seventy or eighty percent success gets multiplied by zero. And Cagle, ashore, has his doubts.*

Wish I hadn't had to have Ayala's wife escorted from the bridge, so Cagle could speak freely. But listening to her alternating wails and demands for immediate evacuation was just getting on my nerves. And once Cagle mentioned doubts? Jesus, what a bitch.

Caban Island, Pilas Group, Basilan Province, Republic of the Philippines

Both Feeney and Hallinan jumped in their skins when a firefight, a pretty *heavy* firefight, erupted behind them in the direction from which they'd come. Hallinan was fairly new, but Feeney had enough experience to make an informed judgment. "Four platoons, maybe five, of theirs," he whispered.

"How can you tell?" Hallinan asked, equally softly. There weren't any Harrikat around, so far as could be told, but since the twin explosions to the east maybe ten or twelve minutes prior, followed by a cacophony of shrieks and wails, some of which had come rather close, they still weren't taking any chances.

Feeney shrugged—useless gesture in the dark—and answered, "Just the volume of fire."

"I can only tell there's a bunch of them."

"Less than you might think. The Moros have always been tough and brave."

"You? A good word for our enemies."

"Playmates," Feeney corrected, "and I've got a lot higher opinion of them than I do of the humanitarians in the hold. Moro men are *men*."

"You're a very strange dude, Feeney."

"You don't know the half of it. Now where the fuck is Semmerlin?"

It was eerily quiet in Semmerlin's one-man-world at the moment. His hearing was damaged, he knew, and maybe irreparably. *But I'm not totally deaf. I can hear shooting, explosions. It just all sounds a mile away and like I'm down a well. Damn, I hope it recovers. I don't know anything but this shit. What would I do if I couldn't do it anymore? Don't even want to think about that.*

Shit, I've got to think about it. I can see where I'm supposed to go. Hard to miss with about ten thousand tracers crossing back and forth every minute. But I wouldn't hear a Moro if he were walking on my helmet . . . provided he was walking softly, anyway. Ah, crap, I need help.

He reached down to the belt around his waist and turned the volume or his radio all the way up. *I might not even hear that.* Then he called, "Feeney, Hallinan, I can't make it to you. You're gonna have to find me. My hearing's almost gone and I've lost my goggles. I can't see you either."

There was a moment's delay. When the answer came, it still sounded like it was coming into or from a deep, deep well. "Got an IR chemlight, brother?" Feeney asked. "Just pop one or two. We'll come to you."

★ ★ ★

Everything was harder in the dark. And chemlights helped only so much. The tracers flying back and forth overhead didn't help at all.

Cagle had Ayala's blood pressure up to something a little better than a corpse's. His hands took turns squeezing the bulb of a BVM, a Bag Valve Mask, a kind of hand operated artificial ventilator. And the old man seemed to be starting to breathe better, on his own, a little at least, That was probably the result of the quinolone cocktail Cagle had shot him up with, once he had the veins above collapse level.

He wouldn't have made it this far if he weren't a pretty tough old bird. And there's no proof that he's only got one strain of pneumonia going, if it is pneumonia. Quinolone might beat one, and leave the other.

Quinolones, while very powerful, had their downsides. Some variants, and the drug had many, as well as many generations, were extremely toxic. Some were carcinogenic.

But cancer is the least of your concerns, old man.

"Is he okay?" Graft asked. The sergeant had started slowly going into a frenzy, which state got worse as every minute passed with his man, Semmerlin, out alone.

"For now. You're worried about your soldier." It wasn't a question. Cagle jerked a thumb upward, with his free hand, and said, "Relax. If you haven't noticed it, *this* place isn't precisely safe anymore."

It had taken a while, a lot longer than Stocker was happy with. It had also taken a lot of fire, fire from the gunships—now gunship, singular—fire from the Elands, then, as those two had beaten down the enemy, fire from the company's own Vampires. Then the machine guns had started kicking in their rattle to some good effect.

Now the men of C Company, Third Battalion, were up and moving, by individuals, by fire teams, and over on the right, where the gunships had had their greatest effect, by squad, as one broke into the Harrikat defenses and began clearing them, right to left, with hand grenades.

Stocker was on his feet, though still covered by an Eland's bulky form, watching his men work their way through the defenses and, most importantly, making sure the fires shifted to the left as they did.

"Sir?"

Stocker turned around. It was the exec, Simon Blackmore.

"Sir, I've got the mortars and the last platoon. The mortars are setting up where we planned and rehearsed it. The LCM is waiting at the beach for a load of wounded. Where do you want the grunts thrown in?"

Stocker jabbed, repeatedly, with a knife hand. "Simon, that's Second platoon clearing from the right, and First providing fire support from the left. I want the Third to pass behind Second, along the beach, then cut inland. A Company's decisively engaged, but they're not losing. If they don't lose, the enemy must. When the enemy breaks, I want a platoon in place to keep them from getting somewhere where we'll have to dig them out.

"You understand?"

"Yessir."

"Good, go with them."

"Yessir."

"And Simon?"

"Yes, sir?"

Stocker sighed. "These are a lot tougher and better trained than the last ones. Be careful."

"Won't argue with those orders, sir."

★ CHAPTER FORTY-TWO ★

Falstaff:
To die is to be a counterfeit, for he is but the
counterfeit of a man who hath not the life of a man;
but to counterfeit dying when a man thereby liveth,
is to be no counterfeit, but the true and perfect image
of life indeed. The better part of valor is discretion,
in the which better part I have sav'd my life.
—William Shakespeare, *Henry the Fourth*

**Caban Island, Pilas Group, Basilan Province,
Republic of the Philippines**

Janail did a mental inventory of his assets and liabilities.
*My company on the beach doesn't seem to much exist
anymore. My mortars are gone. My antiaircraft platoon is
gone. I haven't heard from the antitank platoon in a while.
Camana is dead and Ampuan says that to show yourself
up by the cliffs is to die. My prisoner is gone, and I'm not
going to get him back. So my nuclear weapons and my
sultanate are gone, too.*

I wish I knew who it was who attacked me. Ampuan thinks it's the Kanos. That certainly matches the firepower they've used. And the vindictiveness with which they've used it, when they got hurt. Americans; they'll cross an icy river, in winter, in the middle of the night, to kill you in your sleep. On their Christmas. I'm so fucked.

"What can I save?" he asked himself. "Ampuan says it's not too late to pull out, that he and the two companies can run faster than the enemy can follow. And I've got this company with me, untouched.

"Suppose we pull north? I have defenses there. Also that's where the Christian slave women ran with their brats. Kanos or Filipinos, makes no difference where their, or anyone's, women and children are concerned. Yeah . . . yeah . . . that's the ticket. We can use the women and children as shields and trade them for safe passage out of here to somewhere else. Mindanao, I think. And maybe, if I can save enough, I can challenge the Liberation Front for leadership.

"Maybe all isn't lost quite yet."

Freshly rearmed and refueled, aloft and searching over the northern end of the island, Jake saw a large knot of *some* group or other clustered by the shore. He pulled his stick to the right, veering in that direction, to fly almost directly at them.

Those aren't Harrikat, he thought, looking left through his NVGs. *They're little guys, but they're not that little. And those aren't guys. And I don't see anything that resembles a rifle among them.*

And they're waving? Yeah. Not Harrikat. No way.

He called the bridge of the *Bland*, saying, "I've got something over a hundred people, all sort of hiding on the northern end of the island. Women. Kids, too, if I mark them right. They're looking for rescue, near as I can tell."

Sent the *Bland* back, "Roger, wait, out."

MV *Richard Bland*, just east of Caban Island

Welch and Pearson exchanged glances. The latter, shrugging, said, "Well, food's not even as much of an issue as it was with the Marehan and the humanitarians. We can dump them right back on Luzon. Like tomorrow."

"I don't have anyone to send for security," Welch objected.

"Don't have to," Pearson insisted. "We've got the one LCM, with two .50 calibers on it. Kirkpatrick's got two more men besides. I can shit another four, maybe. They can get them loaded and secure themselves while they're doing it."

Kiertzner piped in with his very posh accent, "All the same with you gentlemen, I'd like to go on that."

"See?" said Pearson. "Even the acting sergeant major thinks it's a good idea."

Kiertzner didn't add anything to that. He did think, *That's not precisely what I said. What I said was I'd like to go along. It might be a very bad idea indeed. On the other hand, I* really *don't like being stuck aboard ship when there's action going on.*

"And after the load of wounded they're putting on Kirkpatrick's boat, now, we'll have nothing we have to take out," Pearson continued. "Not until the island's cleared, anyway. And Stocker's going to have a sufficient area of the beach cleared for any more wounded we might take to get dusted off in just a bit."

Welch puffed his cheeks, doubtfully, and asked, "You're saying, 'Do it'?"

"Why not? And besides, we might need the good offices of the Philippine government here shortly, like when you go for Benson and his crew. This won't hurt that a bit.

"I can have the LCM bring the wounded they've got now back here. We unload them. Load up a few more men, under Kiertzner. Kirkpatrick goes in and pulls the civilians out. What could go wrong?"

While Welch was contemplating all the things that could go wrong, Lox, down in the RPV control station, piped in over the intercom. "Bridge, Lox. Quick picture: It looks like the Harrikat around A Company are pulling back. Might be for another push, or maybe a rush. Might be they're leaving. I think it's the latter, because that couple of platoons—or maybe it's a really small company—in the center are also starting to move back to the north.

"There are still stragglers all over the place, of course."

"Roger," Welch sent back. Then he had a thought. "Peter, if this group had a bunch of captured women, what language would those women speak?"

"Mostly Tagalog," the latter replied. "Some might speak Cebuano, too, but they'll still probably understand Tagalog. A lot of them—probably most—will speak at least some English, for that matter."

"Right," sent Welch. "Turn the intel gathering over

to the pilot. Come up on deck; I have another mission for you."

"Roger. Be right there. Out."

"So you're going to let us do it?" Pearson asked.

Welch gave him a dirty look. "You knew I would two minutes after you first broached the subject."

"Okay, so why are you agreeing?" the captain asked.

"Because of what you said about the Philippine government and because right now those women and kids can be evacuated before the Harrikat can hide behind them or use them for bargaining chips. I really don't want to get into an argument with our employer about killing the Harrikat if it means killing a bunch of women and kids. See, she won't care."

"They might not be the only group, you know," Pearson said.

"True," Welch agreed. "But it's better to get twenty or thirty killed exterminating the Harrikat than five times that many."

Caban Island, Pilas Group, Basilan Province, Republic of the Philippines

Feeney and Hallinan couldn't find Semmerlin. They guessed that he'd drifted down into a patch of low ground where it was very difficult to see the infrared chemlights. That both men had rifle mounted night vision devices, rather than goggles, made it harder still.

Feeney sent over the radio, "Semmerlin, where the fuck are you?"

"I haven't a fucking clue," came the answer. "And speak up."

"I swear," said Hallinan, with frustration, "or at least I could have sworn, that he was right around here."

"Yeah, I saw the lights, too," Feeney agreed, lifting his rifle to his shoulder, placing his eye against the rubber eyepiece of his scope, and sweeping left to right. "Damned scopes are good for a lot of things. This isn't one of them."

"Hey, Feeney; listen."

"Listen to what?"

"The firefight back by the cliffs."

Feeney lowered his rifle and listened for only a moment before asking, "What firefight?"

"Right. It's stopped. What's that mean?"

"Most likely that either the Harrikat won, or we did and they're pulling . . . oh, shit."

Both men instantly dropped to the ground, side by side, rifles to shoulders, and eyes to scopes, sweeping the ground in the direction from which they'd come. Hallinan was the first one to spot the retreating Moros. He elbowed Feeney lightly, to warn him, then whispered, "They're coming this way."

"Hold your fire," Feeney counseled. "There's too many of them."

"No shit?"

They heard someone call out a command. They didn't understand the language but the tone was unmistakable. The Moros began to congregate closer to where the Americans lay.

★ ★ ★

The two companies had started with about one hundred and thirty men and two datus. They had left maybe eighty and a single datu, Ampuan. The rest were dead or dying back up the slope. For that matter, not all the eighty were entirely hale. A good dozen, as far as Ampuan could tell, were being carried by the others. Like good Moros, those wounded didn't cry out, except for one trying to hold his guts in where something—maybe a bullet, maybe a mine—had basically disemboweled him. And even he had blood running down his face where he'd chewed his own lips to pulp trying to stifle the cries of pain.

We should put him out of his misery, Ampuan thought. *I saw what was left of the hut where the doctor had been. He'll get no medical care from us and that means it's just a lingering miserable death for him.*

I suppose we could leave him for the Kanos or the Filipinos, but they'll probably just burn him alive for their amusement. The times have sure changed from the old days.

Finally deciding, Ampuan called out softly, "Bring the wounded to me." The word passed and the bearers began carrying their charges toward Ampuan.

The first to arrive was a young boy, no more than fifteen years old, If Ampuan remembered correctly. The boy's eyes and face were mostly gone; the datu could tell that much by touch.

He gripped the boy's shoulder and asked, "Do you believe in Allah?"

"Yes, Datu," the boy said softy.

The datu drew his kalis, the local term for a kris. It was wavy and sharp as a nagging woman's tongue. "Go to Him, then, and know that the blessings of Paradise will be yours for your courage and faithfulness."

Ampuan drew the kalis across the boy's throat, opening it so that blood gushed out in a fountain. The spray stopped after a few moments. The boy went limp and unconscious instantly.

The next was walking, but held up by a man holding his left arm across the shoulders. "No need, Datu," said that one. "I will die, but not yet. And I can still fight. Leave me here to cover your withdrawal."

Ampuan agreed. "Find him a position from which he may still fight," he ordered the bearer.

The bearer began half-carrying that wounded man to a tree he could just make out among the shadows.

Feeney was possibly a lunatic but he was not a fool. He waited until the last possible moment to fire, just on the off chance that the Moros might move on or even stop short of his position. Still, with the one Moro bearing another almost stepping upon him, he had no choice. It was fire now or die damned soon.

He raised his rifle and shot twice, at a range of no more than a dozen feet. The first bullet passed through the wounded Moro, approximately center of mass, stopping the man's heart in mid-beat. The second blew the brains out of the back of the head of the one carrying him. They fell in a tangle of limbs.

Hallinan was expecting it, ever since he saw the one Moro bearing the other in his and Feeney's direction. He opened fire immediately after Feeney, knocking down one, then another, who had a radio on his back. He missed the third, cursing. After that there were no more targets visible as the Harrikat went to ground. Two seconds after that, both Feeney and Hallinan were quite thoroughly pinned, as dozens of Moro rifles and machine guns beat the air and ground around them, aiming for the muzzle flashes.

His RTO wouldn't answer. He couldn't call for help, even if Janail had had any to send. His men were shooting but he doubted they were hitting anything of importance except, given the darkness, maybe each other.

Ampuan really didn't know why the enemy had missed him. He suspected divine intervention. Allah's finger upon him or not, though, his heart beat a frantic tattoo. He still had his kalis in hand, which was perhaps something, but not much. Where his rifle was he had not a clue.

I'll find it later, if I can . . . that, or there should be someone else's lying around. His hand squeezed the ornate—cheap and tacky, but ornate—hilt of his kalis. *No use to that,* Ampuan thought. *But what do I have that might work?*

Transferring the blade to his left hand, his right searched along his ammunition belt for the grenades he kept there. These were homemade things, with friction pull igniters. Really, they weren't a lot more sophisticated than the grenades of the early part of the Great War, being merely a bamboo tube, the inside lined with nails, then filled with explosive and the friction igniter, the latter being fitted to a nonelectric blasting cap.

Ampuan's hand found one such and pulled it from his belt. He let go the kalis, then took in his fingers the little drilled out stone to which the pull cord for the igniter was attached.

Quality control for hand grenade manufacture, even in the high tech west, was a little questionable. In the local arms factory? *Forget that shit*. As soon as he pulled the cord, Ampuan threw his grenade in the direction of the muzzle flashes. Immediately, that questing right hand sought another grenade.

Feeney saw the first grenade, landing close by, by the sparking of the fuse. His firing hand left the pistol grip of his rifle, grabbed the thing automatically, and tossed it a few meters away. The blast was bad enough, at that distance, but most of the shrapnel went up and away. Two pieces found his right calf and thigh, however, tearing into the flesh below the skin and the cloth of his battle dress.

Son of a bitch!

He saw another rolling spark and, lifting his torso up, reached for it. Yes, he possibly could have ducked away but Hallinan probably did *not* see it. Whatever Feeney's flaws, and they were many, saving himself at the cost of a brother was not among them.

The grenade went off in his hand, peeling his arm back to the elbow and driving dozens of metal fragments deep into his neck. His body armor, itself studded with nails, could not help him there.

Hallinan, lying next to Feeney, felt blinding agony as something tore into his neck and, at the same time, flash and blast burned off most of the flesh on the right side of his face, totally ruining that eye. Dropping his rifle, both hands went to clutch at his own throat, where blood from a severed artery poured into his mouth and down his lungs.

He was on his back, twitching and gurgling, as Ampuan's kalis came down upon him, slicing him from the juncture of neck and shoulder all the way to his sternum.

★ CHAPTER FORTY-THREE ★

"My dear Pooh," said Owl in his superior way,
"don't you know what an Ambush is?"
—A. A. Milne, *Winnie the Pooh*

**Caban Island, Pilas Group, Basilan Province,
Republic of the Philippines**

After a long night of fighting and fear, the first hint of sun was beginning to peak over the horizon. Everything under the jungle roof was still dim and indistinct, the distant light being further scattered by the canopy overhead.

Warrington flipped open his compass, checked direction, then made a knife hand in the direction of the beach. The point man of one team nodded acknowledgement, then turned and began walking in that direction, his eyes darting left and right as he advanced. His team leader was behind him, with the other ten members of the team stretched out in a deep V, to the rear. The other whole team—though it wasn't very whole, being minus a couple of wounded, and four litter bearers—formed another, shallower V to the rear.

Warrington, a part of company headquarters, the rump of Graft's team, and Cagle, took center, Cagle holding an IV bag above the small frail form on the stretcher borne by two of Graft's men.

I don't know, thought Warrington, *but that maybe we should have rigged up to lower the old man down the cliff on a litter and taken him out by Zodiac. I don't know and I probably never will. Once the shooting started they might have had someone watching out for just that. Or they might not have. It was a gamble, like everything else in life.*

The point man passed a thin line of scattered Harrikat bodies, not far from where the front line had been. Pointing at one, he snapped his fingers. Transferring his rifle to his left hand and drawing a knife, one of the men in the team trotted out, took one knee, bent the Moro's head to expose his throat, and slashed it.

That was a war crime. Everyone knew it. No one cared. Nobody paid attention to the law of war anymore, at least when fighting those who themselves didn't. The idea that one should not finish off terrorist prisoners—at least after interrogating them, if that seemed worth doing—had become as laughable as the notion that a twelve-year-old should never pick up a rifle to defend his mother and sisters from rape and enslavement, or that a group of them couldn't join under an elder who knew what he was doing to provide a common defense to each boy's mother and sisters. It had become as laughable as the idea that a man, or a village, couldn't put out mines to provide early warning and defense.

So the notion that one should spare the lives of

those who feigned, or even might be feigning, death or incapacitating wounds—itself a war crime—had died. It had been laughed to death.

There was just enough light filtering through for Warrington to see the killing. He mentally shrugged. *Go ahead, indulge your intellectual fantasies without paying the slightest attention to the final result. Stretch the law of war past the breaking point and that's what you get; no respect for it, no respect for a law that only runs one way.*

It was a better world we had then than we have now. Pity those that killed that world couldn't have seen what they were doing.

Ampuan could *see* now; no more fear that with every step someone was tracking him in a rifle scope he couldn't match. No, instead each step was dogged with fear that someone was tracking him with iron sights.

He'd reformed the two companies into a single one, a very small single one. They were moving north, in a column of platoons, even as Warrington's little group was moving to the east-northeast. Ampuan's command had grown a bit as stragglers, a half dozen of them or so, from the various knots of fighting, had gravitated toward him. No doubt there were still others out there, alone or in twos and threes, lost, dazed, confused and waiting for death to find them.

Fortunately, they hadn't met any American or Filipino troops on the way north. *Maybe they got what they came for and left*, Ampuan thought. *But . . . no, I can still hear their aircraft. They're out there.*

Somewhere back by the cliffs, Camana's company had

lost its radio. That left Ampuan's. But the shot that had killed his RTO had also passed through the radio, itself. It was deader than chivalry. The datu could talk to no one who wasn't right near him.

But the silence, it talks to me. It tells me we have lost, totally. I hear no gunfire, none. Where is Janail? He should still be fighting, if anyone is. Is he destroyed, along with the last of the men with him? Has he surrendered? Ampuan mentally scoffed. Hardly anybody surrendered anymore. *No, not Janail. He is not among those who would give up.*

Janail and Ampatuan's company were a quarter of a mile from the northern tip of the island when one of the little infidel aircraft spotted them. The plane had fired only two rockets—*maybe all he has left,* Janail suspected— but lashed the company with machine gun fire, even so. He wasn't hitting much, *But, then, we aren't moving much either.*

Where is Ampuan and why doesn't he answer the radio? I need his men there to make the threat to kill all the slave women and their spawn credible.

With the very tip of the sun rising to port, Kirkpatrick eased his landing craft in to shore. There was no beach here, no place to drop the ramp. If the area wasn't quite the imposing cliffs found to the southwest, it was also no place to land vehicles, which was the major reason why the landing point selected for Stocker's company had been to the southeast.

As soon as the top edge of the ramp nosed into the

steep but low slope, Lox, Kiertzner, and four sailors armed with rifles swarmed up. Two other sailors stayed in the well deck, to help people down. A further two manned the heavy machine guns port and starboard of Kirkpatrick's wheelhouse.

The climb wasn't too hard. Even if the inside of the ramp was wet, it was also cleated to provide footrests and handholds, while the lip of the not-quite-cliff sat only a couple of feet above the top of the ramp.

Overhead and somewhat to the south, one of the CH-750's—*Jake's*, thought Lox—lashed at something uncomfortably close. Lox began calling out in Tagalog for the people there to come to him.

First to appear was a little knot of seven, four women, one of them little more than a girl, and three ragged children.

"I never thought . . . " one of the women began to say, in English, before breaking down in tears. Lox pointed in Kiertzner's direction, since the latter was waiting only a half dozen meters or so from the boat's ramp.

"It's okay, miss," Kiertzner said, very gently, taking the woman's arm and pointing her directly at the ramp. "We're here to take you home. Just walk that way; someone at the boat there will help you, help you all, down."

More people came, some seeming to rise from the ground, others to appear as if by magic out of the thin morning mist. Most of the adults spoke at least some English, but there were some children, unaccompanied by any adults, who spoke either Tagalog, or Cebuano. For the latter, Lox had to make do with sign language aided by the fact that *people* are herd animals, too. Some of the women helped, having picked up enough Cebuano during their captivity to make do.

There were only two men there. Neither was armed, not with so much as a penknife; the sailors searched them thoroughly for anything like that. They gave their names, in really excellent English, as Mahmood and Daoud.

Kiertzner wasn't sure what it was, though it might have been a vague recollection from his time on the fringes of Her Majesty's intelligence community. It might just have been the oddity of two obviously Muslim, and just as obviously not Moro, men among a bunch of mostly Christian slaves. Whatever it was, as soon as Mahmood and Daoud were down in the well deck, he ordered, "Tie those two up."

Janail didn't hear the boat at first, partly because of the lay of the land, partly because of the flailing aircraft overhead, and partly because he was preoccupied with his predicament. When he did hear it he acted decisively enough.

"On your feet," he shouted, rising himself. "The enemy are trying to steal our slaves! We must stop them. Follow the sound of the boat engines."

Whatever their fear of the aircraft might have been—and, again, the Moros were a people brave to a fault—the prospect of having their property stolen was much, much worse. As a single man, Ampatuan's company arose to their feet and began a mad dash for the sound of the LCM's diesels.

Lox's first warning was an infuriated mass shout,

coming from slightly to the south. One of the sailors fired first, but if he hit anything it was impossible for Lox to see.

Crap, he thought, *and we almost had them all loaded.*

"Run for the boat," he cried out, then repeated the command in Tagalog. "It's your only chance!"

The women, dragging and carrying children, swarmed past him in a rush, heading for the boat, for freedom, and safety.

Jake saw the wave of Moros rise up. He swooped again, delivering two long bursts from his gun pods. *No fucking good that was,* he mentally cursed.

"Where's the gunship?" he asked over the radio.

"Rearming," came the answer. "And Stocker still has priority."

"What about the other CH-750?"

"Sitting on flat part of the beach, waiting for the package to be delivered for a dustoff. And, before you ask, the RPV is being refueled."

"Crap! Well, fuck you all, then."

Pulling the odd, V-forked stick all the way back, practically into his shoulder, Jake climbed to the vertical, then continued on into a loop. Looking through the upper part of the windshield, as the loop continued on into an upside-down dive, he aimed by sight, feel, and experience alone, lashing the ground around the Harrikat with everything he had left.

"Ballsy bastards," he muttered, as the Moros continued their rush, despite his having apparently hit several of them.

★ ★ ★

Lox pulled his cheek away from his own rifle just long enough to see Kiertzner easing the last woman down the slope. Then he took the very last child and tossed it to someone waiting below.

"Lox, you and the bloody sailors, MOVE!" Kiertzner shouted.

Putting his eyes back to the front, Lox fired three more times before shouting, "You squids; get the hell out of Dodge."

The sailors didn't need any more encouragement. Brave enough, surely, this was still not their jobs, they weren't that good at it, and they knew it. All four of them emptied what remained of their magazines and began to race back to the boat.

Again, Kiertzner shouted, "Peter, move it."

Lox nodded, to no real effect, then emptied his own magazine and joined the race. Bullets struck the trees around him and tore up the dirt at his feet. He felt a bullet strike his back plate on his body armor, which threw off his balance. Almost immediately thereafter he felt a hot burning pain flash through his right thigh. *I don't think I want to look at that.* His run quickly turned into a very fast moving fall.

"Oh, shit!" Kiertzner cursed, still in his RP accent. Rushing, himself, he reached Lox about a quarter of a second after he'd nosed into the ground.

No time for a fireman's carry, thought the Brit, before grabbing Lox by his combat harness and simply dragging him along the ground. Kiertzner ran with his own torso almost horizontal. This was a good thing, as bullets still cracked the air around both of them, even as others brought down a shower of vegetable matter from the trees, above.

If I get shot in the ass, I'll never hear the, no pun intended, end of it.

Reaching the boat, Kiertzner cut left to bring Lox's body perpendicular to the edge of the ramp. Then he just rolled him over and in, before practically diving in himself.

The informal command, "Unass the bloody AO," sounds funnier in received pronunciation.

Kirkpatrick, head above the wheelhouse, had his own crew push and prod the freed slaves forward, toward the ramp. Besides his own, lightly armored, station, it was the best protected, the thickest, steel aboard. Moreover, its height provided more cover for more of the well deck, while pulling straight away, than any other part of the boat.

The machine gun on his starboard side spoke, with its ponderous, heavy, *thunk-thunk-thunk-thunk-thunk.* Half a second later its twin to port joined in.

"We just might make this," he said to no one in particular. "It does a body good when you can do some good in the world. Even when it's not really your job."

Enraged beyond measure, but not beyond reason, Janail crept on his belly up to the crest of the steep slope from which his property had been stolen. A few of his men, the stouter hearts, joined him to either side. The rest, more demoralized at the loss of the slave women than frightened of the machine guns, hung back. *What's the use? Allah has turned his face from us.*

Being an atheist, Janail was quite unimpressed with the notion of divine favor or disfavor. It was a superstition to be used by the clever, no more.

From some bushes which had, so far, kept him out of the machine gunners' view, he pushed his rifle out, seating it against his shoulder. He couldn't be sure what chain of events had led him to this, not in any detail. He thought, though, that the man who steered the boat with his head stuck about the little square in back was as much to blame as anyone he could find right now. He lined up his sights on the head, for the moment turned away from him and shielded by a helmet that, Janail suspected, his bullet would not penetrate.

The head turned; Janail fired.

It came to Kiertzner on the boat ride back, while sitting to one side of the wheelhouse. He was looking at Mahmood. He was sure he'd seen him before, but where . . . ?

He'd helped the crew remove Kirkpatrick's body from the wheelhouse and lay it out in the well deck, to make room for one of the other crew to steer. They'd been careful to leave the coxswain's helmet on to keep his brains from flowing onto the deck. Some Filipino women had gathered there, in a loose oval around the body, weeping and keening. No, they hadn't known even so much as Kirkpatrick's name. But they were a gracious and grateful people, in the main, and felt that no man who had had a part in delivering them from slavery should go unmourned.

He'd heard similar sounds before, of course, at other

men's funerals, in all corners of the former British Empire, wherever Great Britain still felt it had an interest. Among those places was Pakistan.

Kiertzner looked very intently at Mahmood's face. *Aha! Gotcha, ya bastard.*

Come on in, thought Simon, waiting hidden in the bushes as the Harrikat probed cautiously forward. *Come on in, you bastards; the water's fine.*

The RPV, before it left to refuel, had told him they were coming. A quick look at the map . . . a little intuition for just how the lay of the land would direct them . . . *and here I am, with a full platoon, in a shallow C, two dozen claymores, three Pechenegs, and them not having a clue.*

The claymores had been daisy chained on site, using det cord, with only the end mines primed with wire. Simon held both clackers, one in each hand. If one failed; the other would work.

Firing burst out in the distance well behind Simon, a combination, he thought, of small arms and heavier machine guns. Someone among the Harrikat to his front shouted something, which shout was repeated up and down the line. Whatever caused it, they threw caution to the winds, and surged forward, maybe fifty-five or sixty of them.

Smiling, Simon squeezed the clackers. A tsunami wave of pellets rolled outward, propelled on the blast wave of the explosives. Like light trees and buildings caught at the front of a tsunami, the leading—and more than a few of the following—Harrikat were simply bowled over and washed under.

And then the machine guns and rifles kicked in.

★ CHAPTER FORTY-FOUR ★

"I'm Spartacus!"
—Tony Curtis, in *Spartacus*

MV *Richard Bland*, east of Caban Island

Mr. Ayala was still unconscious. Even so, under the care of TIC Chick and one of the humanitarian doctors, he was improving. Whether he'd make it or not was still on the iffy side, but that iffy needle was slowly edging over toward, "Yes."

"I'll better my previous offer," Paloma Ayala said. "Half a million for every one of the filthy, butchering swine you bring me over sixty."

Welch shook his head. "No, Ma'am. That's very generous, of course"—*and I am so going to take a massive amount of shit back at regiment for losing one of our only two helicopter gunships, at about fifteen or twenty million a copy to replace*—"but a deal's a deal. We'll bring you all we can capture for the price you previously offered. Matter of fact, Captains Stocker and Warrington are still on the island, aided and guided by the aircraft, hunting down the last of them now. I'm afraid we've killed most of them already."

Mrs. Ayala tsked with disappointment, then brushed that aside, saying, "I've sent for some of my own people to join me by boat to help me deal with the ones you present me."

"Your people?" Terry asked.

"Well . . . not technically," Mrs. Ayala admitted with a scrunch of her aged, but still nigh perfect, nose. "Technically, they're a company of Philippine Marines. But their colonel has been on my . . . our payroll for many, many years. They'll do what I want done."

Terry shrugged. "That's up to you, ma'am. There is one thing, though."

"Yes?" She couldn't help sounding suspicious. She'd never had a good reason to trust anyone but her husband, not even her own children.

"How are your connections with the Philippine government and general staff?"

Madame laughed.

A video camera recorded as Daoud screamed from the electricity coursing through his body. Before the current jolt, he'd simply moaned, from the set of vice grips tightened around his left testicle.

Lox, seated, leg heavily bandaged over his sewn-up wound, supervised some of the Marehan in the process. None of them, barring Adam and Labaan, had ever so much as seen a science fiction book. But, by God, they knew how to inflict pain. Moreover, they'd all asked to join. After all, they'd lost their old homes and needed a new one. This was part of the price of joining.

"I won't tire of this, Daoud," Lox said, once the electricity cut off and the Pakistani slumped, quivering, to the bare mesh of the naval bunk to which he'd been tied. "And the pain won't end, for either you or Mahmood, until I have the name of that ship and the name of its owner. And both stories *match*."

"You'll kill me either way," the assistant wept.

"Not necessarily," Lox lied. "But, tell you what; if you don't tell us, not only will your agony go on indefinitely, but when we do kill you, we'll change you into a woman, first. You've seen our medical department, haven't you?"

God, that hack was an evil, evil *man. Hmmm . . . maybe I shouldn't have loaned that book to Madame.*

Caban Island, Pilas Group, Basilan Province, Republic of the Philippines

Eighty-three surviving Harrikat sat, wrists and feet bound, in the sand. A bit over half of them were wounded, some more or less seriously. Nobody from the detachment had bothered with giving them any medical care. This wasn't, or at least not directly, because of what they'd done to Mr. Ayala. No, it was that, given what they'd done to their prisoner, what Mrs. Ayala was probably going to do to the survivors would be such a nightmare that dying of untreated wounds would be a mercy.

Mrs. Ayala was already on the beach when the Philippine Navy landing craft, bearing both the number

296 and a considerable resemblance to the U.S. Army's Runnymede Class, dropped its ramp to disgorge Captain Ramos and his hundred and eighty-odd Philippine Marines. A Philippine Air Force helicopter would be along shortly to pick up and transport Mr. Ayala to St. Luke's, in Quezon City. The rescued women and children would be transferred by the LCM to the Philippine craft later on.

The Army's Scout Ranger Regiment would be credited with the actual rescue, even though they weren't sending anybody at all until sometime next week. The Filipino Armed Forces had more in common with the U.S. Armed Forces than a bit of history prior to and during the Second World War. Wouldn't do not to let every service branch have its share in the glory, after all. M Day, on the other hand, didn't care who got the credit, so long as it wasn't them. At least for the time being.

The captain reported in to Madame, saluting very formally even though she was a civilian in no official capacity. Ramos had been told by his colonel to do *whatever* she said, which sounded fairly official to him. He'd also gotten the message to bring an engineering kit, some heavy duty lumber, and a lot of rather large nails.

The captain didn't know, but strongly suspected, that he and his company had been chosen because of his vitriolic hatred not just for Moro separatists, but Moros, in general. Ramos had had also been told that, whatever the facts on the ground, he and his men were going to get credit for rescuing over a hundred Christian women and children from Harrikat slavery . . . provided, of course, that he and they kept his mouth shut about what really happened

I can do that easy, thought Ramos. *My men? Well, for a while, anyway. Maybe longer. The big lie works best, they say.*

The *Bland*'s own LCM was waiting, and had been from a couple of hours before, when the Filipino LCU dropped ramp. The body bags holding Feeney and Hallinan, the helicopter crew, and nine of Stocker's men were already aboard. Semmerlin, still better than half deaf, had been found sitting over the corpses of the two who'd gone looking for him. Psychologically, he seemed in a pretty bad way. He, too, was already aboard the LCM along with several hundred weapons, both M Day's, now gone redundant, plus a large stockpile from the Harrikat. They were kept very separate.

Stocker told his acting first sergeant, Moore, to, "get the men out of the tree line and onto the boat. Don't pull the guards out, though, until the Filipinos take over, formally."

"Yes, sir," Moore had answered.

While Moore trotted off to take care of that, Stocker, wet, filthy, and stinking from hunting the Harrikat, walked over to make any final arrangements with the Filipino captain.

Madame waited to speak until the last of the Kanos had sailed off in their boat. *So nice it was of Peter to lend me that book,* she thought. *It was so full of such wonderful ideas. Even if the author is apparently some kind of communist.*

Her speech to the surviving Harrikat was partially borrowed, partially her own. She said, in effect, "You all know what you did to my husband. You all know that you're going to die. But, since I am a Christian, I am very solicitous of your souls. So before you die you are all going to be thoroughly Christianized." Her hand went to the gold cross at her neck.

"I don't suppose any of you would care to save your lives by identifying your leader?"

Janail, tied like the rest and mixed in with the rest, his face half hidden by a dirty bandage and some blood borrowed from one of the dead, stiffened for a moment, until he realized that none of his men were going to turn traitor. *Fools. I'd have sold you out in a heartbeat.*

Seeing not one of the prisoners was going to take her up on her offer, she said, "Good. I wouldn't have spared you anyway."

Then, turning to Ramos, she said, "Crucify them. Here. In the sun. Start with their wounded. I don't want any of them to die before they feel the nails."

At about the time the fifth of the Moro prisoners was being nailed to one of the crosses assembled by the Philippine Marines, a small and very young girl walked out of the jungle and toward Paloma. The inside of the girl's thighs were bloodstained. She carried a knife in her hand. The old woman seemed to be in charge. Maria walked right up to her and asked, "Can I watch?"

Camp Aguinaldo, Quezon City, Metro Manila, Republic of the Philippines

The sign out front read:

General Headquarters
Armed Forces of the Philippines

The sign fronted an almost full length shelter from the rain out in front of the broad, mainly two story headquarters of the Philippine Armed Forces. Terry and Aida didn't see that, though. After Jake landed them in a nearby field, they were picked up by a long limousine with dark glass, whisked around the building, and shunted in through a side door. There a lieutenant colonel of the Philippine Air Force met them, then led them to the mahogany-paneled office of the Chief of Staff, a khaki clad General Delfin Santos.

Welch towered over Santos almost as much as he did over Aida. Still, the general didn't seem overly impressed, and was certainly unintimidated. Welch, himself, was at least mildly impressed at that.

After shaking hands, and giving a slight bow to Aida, Santos waved his hand at a couch and several chairs surrounding a coffee table set in an alcove to one side of his massive desk.

"Before we get to whatever it is the Ayala Clan asked me to discuss with you," Santos said, "I want to extend my personal appreciation to you and your organization . . . Maj . . . Mr. Welch, for freeing our people."

The general's English was, predictably, excellent, and his thanks seemed sincere. Even so, he seemed embarrassed. *It should have been our own, freeing our own,* Santos thought. *What is wrong with our country that we have to rely on foreigners?*

Terry nodded, saying, "We were glad to do it." *Though, in retrospect, I probably wouldn't—no, I wouldn't—have traded Kirkpatrick for them, if I'd known in advance that that was the price.*

"I understand you took losses," Santos said.

"A few," Welch admitted. Reticence was habit; in the organizations in his military background, casualties were never admitted to in any detail. Santos didn't press for names or numbers. His special operations forces were about the same, admission of casualties-wise.

"My condolences, again. Now, what was it you wanted?" *And didn't Mrs. Ayala say to give you whatever it was?*

Welch pulled out from a satchel a report from Lox concerning the interrogation of Mahmood and Daoud. This he handed over to Santos.

"The important part is the first paragraph," Terry said.

Santos read, his eyes widening in fury as he did. "They . . . those fucking animals . . . in *Manila*? How can I believe this? I can't; it's beyond belief."

Terry passed over the videos made of the interrogation, one for each of the prisoners. "Here's proof," he said.

Aida added, "General, I was there for part of the interrogation." Lox had deliberately kept her out of the more painful parts. "I've read the report and I've reviewed the tapes. It's all true. The Harrikat was going to use the money from Lucio Ayala's ransom to buy two nuclear weapons from the Russian, Prokopchenko. One of those was going to be used on a smaller city here on Luzon. The other was going to be hidden in Manila and used if we didn't accede to the Harrikat's demands to withdraw from Mindanao.

"They would have killed tens, hundreds of thousands. Possibly millions."

"So far as we know," Welch said, "Prokopchenko still has the weapons aboard his yacht, the *Resurrection*. Since he really doesn't need the money, we think he has some other political objective in selling them. You may still be a target."

His normally olive face gone pale, Santos said, "We'll find that yacht."

"And take it?" Welch supplied. "Recommend against. There's no necessary outside limit to what the Russians will do to keep news of this out of the press. And they have an interest in recovering their weapons."

"So?"

"Inform them and let them handle it," Welch advised. "They're not barbarians. And they're not incompetent or, at least, their own special operations forces are not. Bloody minded and ruthless? Yes. Incompetent? No. And they have a reach, even close to here, that you cannot match. They can find the yacht in a matter of minutes to hours, and be on it in mere hours after that. You'll still be looking for it a month from now."

Uncertainly, Santos said, "I will consider it, Mr. Welch. And, one thousand times more than before, you and your people have our thanks. What about the men who gave you this information?"

"We can turn them over to you, if you want them," Welch said. "If not, they'll be shot this evening and their bodies will be dumped at sea."

Aida flinched. She'd known that it was coming but . . . it was so contrary to the law she'd devoted her life to upholding that it grated on her soul.

"Yes, just go ahead and shoot them," Santos said. He looked intently at Welch's face. "There's more?"

"Yes, General," Terry admitted. "I have a problem with one of your local gangs, TCS. I would like your permission to handle it myself, and your guarantee that the Philippine Armed Forces will take a hands off approach while we settle matters."

Santos's gaze turned to Aida.

"He doesn't want to admit it," she said, "because it's painful. TCS grabbed four of his men, killing another one in the taking. One of the four they've already hanged like a dog and sent a video. They're demanding ransom. Mr. Welch intends to recover his own men and destroy the gang in Tondo. When he says, "destroy," he doesn't mean hurt. He means *destroy*." *God, haven't I seen that already?*

"You want to launch an attack on our people on our soil?" Santos sounded somewhere between incredulous and infuriated.

"Are they your people?" Welch asked. "Are they really yours when they deny any respect for or obligation to your own laws, your own citizenship, and your own country? Is it your soil, when your police have no authority there and TCS rules it like a private fiefdom?"

"I've thought about it a lot, General," Aida added. "I've been with the police most of my life, now, either active or semi-retired with special duties. I've thought about it even more since Mr. Welch and his people arrived.

"General . . . civilization requires police. But equally police require civilization. If there is no civilization, if there is only barbarism, with no law that is widely respected, the police are powerless. And you *know* the politicos won't let your people do anything about it."

"Soldiers can't build civilization, either," Welch said. "But, when allowed, we can destroy barbarism so that civilization can grow, or at least survive. That's what I'm asking, General. Let me and my men destroy some of the barbarism that's grown up here.

"And then we'll get out of your hair."

"But this . . . ? It's sure to come out," Santos objected.

"Actually," said Aida, "we have a trick for that."

MV *Richard Bland* east of Caban Island

"So what are we going to do with the hooker?" asked Graft. "Terry said it was up to us."

"I say we string the cunt up," Malone replied, "just like Zimmerman."

There was a general chorus of agreement on that, not least from Zimmerman's closest comrades.

"She's not entitled to a trial, at least?" asked Lox.

The men of A Company generally ignored that, except to boo it down. What was a trial to them?

"What are you bitching about, Lox?" Malone asked. "You had the bitch spread-eagled on a table, naked, with electrodes to her tits and clit."

"Yeah, I did," Lox agreed. "Wish to hell I hadn't. Going to be a long time before I forget about that. Going to be a long time before I sleep easy again, if I ever do."

Lox focused on Malone, intently. "So . . . Malone," he asked, "you going to put the rope around her neck? She's tall but she doesn't weigh much; you going to haul her up? I'm not going to help you. You want to watch her kick? Watch her face turn blue while she gags and tries to puke through the rope? You going to get under her once you tie the rope off so you can enjoy the smell of her shit when she lets loose her bowels?

"Or are you just trying to divert attention from the fact that you fucked up, hmmm?"

Caban Island, Pilas Group, Basilan Province, Republic of the Philippines

The Philippine Navy landing craft was gone for the time being, bringing the freed slaves back home. It would return in a day or two to extract the Marines, as well.

Paloma Ayala ran fingers through her long hair, culling from it some of the grains of sand the wind had blown up. She sat under an awning put up by her Marines, a defense against the fierce sun overhead. Beside her, in the sand, sat a young girl, apparently much abused. She seemed to be enjoying the spectacle even more than Paloma, herself, was.

Mrs. Ayala's eyes gazed with satisfaction on the small forest in front of her. There was no trace of pity in them, any more than the Harrikat had shown pity or mercy to her husband. Paloma has asked Maria if she could identify the leader, but the girl answered, no, that she'd never really gotten a good look at him.

When one of the Marines approached to disarm the girl of her knife, Paloma ordered him away. She was quite sure the girl would never harm her with the blade. What she was going to do with the girl she wasn't nearly as certain of.

But I think maybe I can make good use of someone who hates the Moros as badly as she does.

There were eighty-three crosses fixed upright on the beach. From each, by nails through wrists and heels, hung a man or a corpse. Most still lived, only those badly wounded previously having passed on.

The screaming and the begging were over now. If any man still had energy left, it was only to moan, to weep, and to extend his own life at the cost of much pain.

Janail wasn't so much a man any more as a thing of pain. Pain was everywhere. It was where his wrists had been penetrated by the nails. It was in every nerve that passed by those wounds, extending from his fingers to his shoulders. It was in the bones of his heels where the nails held him fast to the post, the *stirpes*. It ran from his toes to his thighs. It was every cramped muscle in between, as well. It was an agony in his lungs, struggling to breathe under the strain on his chest.

It was in Janail's mind, because he knew there would be no relief from the agony until he died. Perhaps worst of all, it was an agony both mental and moral, arising from a kind of moral confusion, as he prayed for death, to a god in which he did not believe, even as his cramped and aching legs pushed up against the piercing nails to relieve his chest and extend his life.

And it had only been six hours. Janail had at least another sixty to endure.

★ CHAPTER FORTY-FIVE ★

One of the tests of the civilization of people
is the treatment of its criminals.
—Rutherford B. Hayes

TCS Headquarters, Tondo, Manila, Republic of the Philippines

Diwata was already mentally selecting the next candidate for hanging, later in the day, when she got the call. "I have the money," said the voice she associated with Terry.

"I'll call you back in two hours," she answered, then hung up. Picking up her own phone, she called Lucas, telling him to report to her. He arrived at her office door in a matter of minutes.

"The Kanos are going to pay," she said. "Set it up."

"You going to call them for their initial instructions?" Lucas asked.

"Yes," Diwata said. "I'll tell them one car and one car only, no more than two men, and demand the make, model, color, and license plate. No weapons. I'll also send them first to the Rizal monument, at the Luneta; make sure you outpost it to see if they're trying to cheat. If they're clean when they get to Rizal, you contact them directly afterwards for further instructions."

Lucas nodded. It was a good choice for the purpose, open enough to see and crowded enough that his scout wouldn't be noticed. "How long do you want me to run them ragged?" he asked.

"Until after dark. We've done too many exchanges in the daytime. Time to vary things a bit, I think."

"You think maybe they involved the police?" Lucas asked.

"Nah! Least of our worries."

"You sure you want to give the three back?"

"Sure," Diwata replied. "It's just sound business practice to keep our word. We start acting like the Moros and people will stop paying and take their chances with something else."

"Okay," Lucas agreed. "I need a couple of hours to get security out."

Safe House Alpha, Hagonoy, Bulacan, Luzon, Republic of the Philippines

Terry had never really expected to lay eyes on the place again. But it was there. It *was* safe. And it still had a couple of vehicles, now reinforced by several more, that Lox hadn't felt obliged to burn. The whole area still stank of smoke and gasoline where Lox had torched two of the vehicles and three of the outbuildings.

Welch and Graft stood side by side. Around them, to their front, were another sixteen men of Alpha Company, in four teams of four. All wore mufti, though there was, in the semicircle of vehicles behind the teams, enough equipment for a small army.

Welch and Graft weren't obviously armed, though each had a pistol under his light suit jacket. Graft's weapon was in a shoulder holster. Welch had his in a high waist holster, from which he'd been practicing an initially awkward quick draw for quite some time.

The others sported a mix of weapons, though each team had one .510 caliber Whisper rifle, a .338 Lapua, a light machine gun—because, as Graft had said, "Ya never know, boss, when you might need one"—and a suppressed submachine gun. The light machine guns, Whispers, and Lapuas were equipped with thermal scopes, while the team leaders, carrying the submachine guns, wore goggles. Under their mufti, Welch and Graft wore body armor of the highest quality. The others did not, given that their mission would require a certain lightness on their feet.

Each vehicle also contained a laptop with an integral GPS, wireless and with a brand new sim card. Welch and Graft were wired for sound, with a long range radio, earpiece, and button mike. The others were similarly equipped, except that their microphones were of the boom variety.

Welch's and Graft's car had a leather satchel on the floor of the passenger seat. The satchel had been stuffed nearly to bursting with cash. What they hadn't been able to do with their own bank draft had become easy, though too late for Zimmerman, once the Ayala payment was released from escrow. The back also contained weapons and ammunition for Graft and Welch, plus enough to rearm Benson, Perez, and Washington, should that prove necessary.

The phone rang, the panel showing Benson's number as the caller. Welch held up a single fist for absolute silence, then answered it. "This is Terry."

Diwata relayed her instructions.

Terry answered with, "Late model Suzuki Jimny, silver. License plate is TIM three nine eight."

She then asked, "Do you have any questions?"

"No, none," Terry replied.

"Good." The cell went dead.

"Lox, can you hear me?" Welch asked.

"Got you, Terry," answered Lox, sitting in the RPV's control station with his injured leg propped up on a cabinet. Aida was with him.

"My destination is Rizal Monument."

"That's on the coast, just southwest of Central Old Manila," Aida said. "You'll be passing within a couple of miles of where your men are likely being held."

"Will they make the exchange there?" Welch asked.

"Not a chance," Aida said.

"Okay. Lox, take control of the teams and get them somewhere not too far, and not too obvious."

"I'm sending them roughly to the four curves of Santa Ana Racetrack," Lox sent. "Gentlemen, if you'll check your laptops you will see your four destinations."

"Good luck, everybody. Remember, weapons free is if I throw them the bag and our people are known present, or when I draw. If I pass it to them or place it on the ground? Hold your fire.

"Let's go."

Rizal Monument, Manila, Republic of the Philippines

One hour and four minutes later, Graft turned the silver Suzuki onto Roxas Boulevard, passing the obvious obelisk of the Rizal Monument on his left. Past the obelisk, he turned left on Kalaw Street, and then left again to head northwest on Roxas. When the phone didn't immediately ring, Welch directed him to circle the park. The Suzuki went right on Burgos, right again on Orosa, then took another right back onto Kalaw. Graft was just about to head northwest on Roxas again when the phone rang.

"My name is not important," said a male voice. "Nagpayong Ferry Station. You have half an hour."

MV *Richard Bland,* Twenty-two miles Southwest of Corregidor, Manila Bay

The cranes, all three of them, were whining as Pearson reconfigured the containers aboard his ship for maximum feasible innocence of appearance. The CH-750's were folded up, containerized, and struck below. The remaining MI-28, likewise, was partially disassembled and containerized. All the grunts were down below anyplace a customs official might look, except for a half dozen in merchant sailor dress.

He'd been careful, though, to leave the control station for the RPV up on the partial top level of shipping containers.

"Pity we can't track the cell phones from here with the RPV," said the pilot.

Lox responded, "Maybe No-Such-Agency can do that shit. Maybe. But it's out of our league."

"Yeah," the pilot agreed. "Still a pity."

Lox looked over at Aida, intently following the map displayed on the monitor. "Why the ferry, Aida?"

She shook her head. "Doubt it has anything to do with the ferry. It has to do with the lake?"

"Huh?"

Aida traced with her finger just above the screen. "Only two ways around it from there, south and east. South there are two roads for part of the way, but only one continues on past Los Baños. They'll watch that one. The other's a single road all the way. They'll be watching that, too, in case a convoy follows, even at a distance."

"Kinda clever," Lox said.

"They didn't get where they are by being stupid."

"It's maybe even more clever than they know." Lox called Welch. "Boss, we have a problem. Rather, we've got two of them." After explaining what Aida had seen, Lox added, "But they could try to make the trade on either the south of the lake, or the east of it. We need to split the teams up to cover both."

"That's pushing our margin of safety down pretty low," Welch sent back.

"No shit, but I don't see a lot of choice."

"Any sign they've moved our people from their head-quarters?" Terry asked.

The pilot shook his head. "I've been watching closely. Nothing like that on screen."

"No, boss," Lox replied.

"Yeah . . . crap. Okay, split them up, two each way."

Los Baños, Laguna, Republic of the Philippines

"Go to the mahogany farm a mile west of Saint Anne College, Lucena," said the man at the other end of the phone.

Terry was about to answer, "Okay," when Aida piped in, in his earpiece, "You're too calm. That's suspicious. Act frustrated."

Terry was about to answer her with a "Roger" when he remembered just who was still listening on the other end of the cell phone. He extemporized, "Will you fucking people make up your minds?"

"You ever want to see your people alive again, Kano," said the voice, "you shut the fuck up and do what you're told. The mahogany farm, one hour."

MV *Richard Bland,* Twenty-two miles Southwest of Corregidor, Manila Bay

"Are they going to make the switch at the mahogany farm?" Lox asked Aida.

"No way," she said. "It's much too soon."

"Besides," said the pilot, "they can't make the switch until they take our people from their headquarters. As near as I can tell, they haven't."

"Aida," Lox asked, "are you sure, absolutely sure,

they'll have been keeping our people at their headquarters in Tondo?"

"Absolutely?" She shook her head. "No. But everyone they've ever kidnapped before—that would talk to us, I mean; not all of them would—had the same story, a place—sometimes in the basement, sometimes on a different floor—with five or six mesh cages, and guards, that they were never moved from except to go to the bathroom and then right before the exchange. Every one of those that we've been able to track the route of, before they were exchanged, that route led back to Tondo, to their building.

"They're not political, except in the sense that they've got de facto political control of Tondo. They're not on the run. They don't have people ready to betray them at a moment's notice and, in Tondo, for sure, they don't have our police looking for them or their victims.

"They're their own country, at war with everyone else. That basement's just a POW camp. And you don't move POW's just for the hell of it."

MV *Richard Bland,* Five miles West of Tondo, Manila Bay

"I think I've got something," said the pilot.

The only way to tell it was night outside was by the green screen on the pilot's control board. Once the sun had set he'd switched out from his day camera to the nighttime version. In all that time, none of the three had moved from the container. Welch and Graft were now on the seventh leg of their ride to nowhere.

Lox and Aida rushed to the screen. A van was parked

at one corner of the building, TCS headquarters, that took up an entire block of the subdivision. It was impossible to tell the color, given that the camera turned everything light colored a sort of pale green. White was Lox's guess.

"That's the first time I've seen something park that close to their headquarters all day," the pilot said. "Nobody else had even tried."

"They've got their enemies," Aida said. "So they're touchy about car bombs."

"Where did the van come from?" Lox asked.

"No clue. One minute it wasn't there and the next it was. And . . . oh, oh."

Lox looked intently at the screen. A half a dozen of the locals, armed, were helping then prodding three much taller men into the back of a van. It was impossible to make out any detail, of course; the RPV was patrolling at a sufficient height to make hearing it impossible and seeing it almost so. Still . . .

"They're walking like their hands are bound. And I'm pretty sure the short one is Benson. Also . . . two light skinned, one dark. That's them."

He called Terry. "Boss, they're moving our people. Light van, possibly white. We're going to follow with the RPV."

"Roger."

When they came aboard, having climbed a ladder from a harbor patrol boat that had taken station alongside, Pearson noticed that both the pilot and the customs officials were heavily tattooed. It wasn't a surprise; Aida had briefed him already.

"Captain," she'd said, "how do you suppose TCS grew as much as it did and is as well armed as it is? They *took* control of that part of the port long ago."

The pilot did his job competently enough, guiding the ship to a smooth docking at the wharf next to Barangay One Twenty-nine. The customs men turned their tattooed faces to the totally fraudulent ship's manifests presented by the captain. They'd figure their cut as the containers were unloaded. For now, they just needed to get a handle on what was there to take their cut from.

And what's bizarre, thought Pearson, as the pilot and customs agents left the bridge, *is that, while they're at some level corrupt, and members of a criminal gang, they were more polite and honest than half the customs agents in half the ports in the world.* He mentally sighed. *I am reminded of the Roman merchant who joined the gang of Attila the Hun.*

★ CHAPTER FORTY-SIX ★

So when you are requested to pay up or be molested
You will find it better policy to say:
"We never pay any one Dane-geld . . ."
—Rudyard Kipling, "Danegeld"

TCS Headquarters, Tondo, Manila, Republic of the Philippines

Lucas said, "Out of your cages, Kanos, you're going to get redeemed." He motioned for Crisanto to open the cages holding the filthy and stinking prisoners. This, the ex-Philippine Marine did, being careful to only open one at a time. As each of the Americans was dragged out, a group of Crisanto's men flipped them over to their bellies and lashed their wrists together.

"Now, no fucking talking, assholes."

Benson kept his face carefully blank. At this point, they'd been confined, and tightly, long enough that they were almost incapable of walking under their own power. There was nothing wrong with the sergeant's mind, however. *Terry and the regiment might pay or they might not. They might try a rescue. On balance, I think that's more likely.*

"Where are we going?" Benson asked.

He was rewarded with a kick to his side, from Crisanto, just above the hip. It landed close enough to his kidney to be staggeringly painful. Benson gasped from it, biting his lip against crying out. Nor did the pain go away right away.

"'No talking,' the man said. That means no questions."

When the pain faded enough to allow a measure of thought, Benson tried to concentrate on what he and the other two might be able to do to help, in the event of a rescue. Nothing came immediately to mind. The best he could think to do was whistle a couple of bars from Tom Lehrer's "Be Prepared."

At first, TCS made the Americans walk under their own power. When Washington fell over, though, Lucas ordered Crisanto to help them. Two of the latter's men, one on each side, grabbed the Americans' bound arms, holding them up. Their shuffling steps remained uncertain.

There was a van, white painted, with short curtains hung around the rear windows, outside one of the headquarters' broad double doors. The back doors were open already; Crisanto's men helped the Americans stuff themselves into the back. Those back doors were then locked from the outside. After that, Lucas, Crisanto, and four of Crisanto's men piled in the seats in front. The Americans didn't see it, but two of the captors waved hands under their own noses at the stench.

"Keep your head and eyes to the rear," Crisanto said,

pulling out a Philippine Marines issue combat knife and rapping Searle's head with the butt to add an exclamation point.

Benson said nothing, Instead, once the passenger doors closed, and the van started moving, he leaned his shoulders into, first, Washington and, then, Perez, seated to either side of him, and began flexing and exercising his legs, at least insofar as the cramped space permitted. Again he whistled a bar from "Be Prepared:" *Don't solicit for your sister; that's not nice.*

Overhead, the RPV descended to about twelve hundred feet, its stabilized camera controlled by an image contrasting computer back on the *Bland*. At that range, the license plate could be read. The computer could also analyze the color of the van, presented green to the viewers on the screen but not to it, to differentiate the target van from every other.

The aircraft was still quiet enough not to be heard below, at least by anyone inside a vehicle, with the sound of the engine running and of the road vibrations. Unfortunately, the stall speed of a fixed wing RPV is somewhat greater than that of a van at a red light.

MV *Richard Bland*, Wharf at Barangay 129, Tondo, Manila, Republic of the Philippines

"Fuck!" cursed the pilot, "I lost them."

Lox, who had almost begun to nod off, jerked alert, heart pounding. "Wha . . . what? What happened?"

"They stopped at a light"—the pilot's finger tapped the map display—"right here at Capulong and Juan Luna. I had to do a three-sixty. The camera lost them behind a building, which fucked up the stabilization. By the time I did the turn and reacquired the same spot, the light had changed and they were gone. I guess I was following too close but I wanted the license plate."

"Shit. Shitshitshit. Aida?"

"What lane were they in?" the policewoman asked.

"Ummm . . . left lane."

"Follow Capulong, east," she said. "It will become Tayuman. Then it will link with Arsenio H. Lacson Avenue. Lacson goes south which is, I *think* where they're heading."

"Do it," said Lox. "And once you reacquire them, if you do, get some altitude so you don't lose them again."

"What if we don't find it?" Aida asked.

Lox shook his head. "I don't know. Things get a lot harder, anyway."

Long minutes passed, with the image of the ground passing underneath the RPV flashing across the screen. There were other vans, even white ones. The paint, however, didn't quite match. There were variables in manufacture, variables caused by exposure to the sun. There were even variables caused by a none-too-skillful job of repainting a stolen van.

The pilot set his curser on one likely candidate. It *looked* the same but then so had another that the computer had rejected. He clicked to mark the van for analysis, then moved the curser to a different box and clicked to begin the analysis.

The answer came flashing back on the screen: "Match."

Lox reached over and squeezed the pilot's shoulder. In another context, and with a different tone of voice, his next words might have been friendly. "Now *don't* lose them again."

Then he went back to directing the four shooter teams to keep them in as close as possible to Welch and Graft, without arousing suspicions.

Los Baños, Laguna, Republic of the Philippines

Ferd Franceschi drove as fast as road conditions would permit. Given that the National Highway hadn't been all that well maintained in some years, ever since shortly after the current depression had begun, this wasn't all that fast and was, in any case, well below the posted speed limit.

He, Malone, and two of the last four remaining and available men from Graft's team rumbled along the National Highway, heading west. They'd been among the two cars sent east of the big lake, the Laguna de Bay, and now having to race back to get into supporting distance.

Lox sent a message, "One mile north of Tagaytay City." At the same time, their laptop's screen changed to show a new route. Malone, with the laptop seated, in fact, on his lap, said, "Shit, that takes us way out of our way, all the way to Santo Rosa City. What say we—"

"Shut up, Malone" every man said, simultaneously. Malone would be a long time in regaining his street cred after the Maricel debacle.

"Just a thought," he said, apologetically.

MV *Richard Bland*, Wharf at Barangay 129, Tondo, Manila

Lox stared at the map. To Aida he said, "The last three stops have been all around Taal Lake: Lemery, Lipa City, and Tanauan City. And Welch is being sent now to Tagaytay. Does that mean the switch point is going to be around the lake?"

"Tell you in about twenty minutes," Aida replied. "Rather, I *may* be able to tell you. But not before they commit to either Aguinaldo Highway or to the National Highway."

"Fair enough," Lox said. "Though even there, that's assuming . . ."

"That's assuming TCS isn't being devious with their route. But why should they? Oh, sure," she conceded, "it might have made sense to lose a possible tail right after leaving Tondo. But they didn't even try. They're not going to try to lose a tail now that never had a chance to attach itself to them. And . . ."

"Yes?" Lox prodded.

Aida spoke perhaps a bit tentatively. "I think they've maybe gotten a little complacent, maybe even arrogant. That happens even to pretty smart people."

Lox, thinking of Malone and the hooker, thought but did not say, *no shit*.

"There are three or four things," Aida continued, "that I'd have expected them to do that they haven't done. They haven't done them before, either, mind you, at least not that I know of. But by now, if they were real pros, they'd have refined their procedures."

"Like how?" Lox asked.

"Well, for starters," Aida offered, "why no tail car or lead car for themselves? For another, if I were in the business of kidnapping people for fun and profit, I'd have interrogated the people I kidnapped rigorously—maybe not as rigorously as you, but then I'm more experienced and don't need as much coercion. If they'd done that, they'd have a better idea—yeah, no bullshit between us; anyone can be broken . . . anyone—of what they were facing. If I were them and I had your people, and I knew what you were, I'd have given your people back at the speed of light and tossed in the heads of the people who kidnapped them in the hope you'd call it even. They didn't do that last, so I doubt they did much of the first, either. That's arrogance."

Lox mulled that for a bit. "It's also possible they've got an ace in the hole we don't know about, either."

"Yeah . . . maybe. What, though?"

"I dunno," he said, "but I'm sure thinking hard on it."

Silang Crossing, Tagaytay, Cavite, Republic of the Philippines

There was a monument of some kind to the right of the Suzuki. It was too far away to read the plaque, though the bronze statue atop the thing suggested it had something to do with the liberation. A high sign nearby, sitting on a pole higher than the monument, was altogether too close to be in very good taste. The sign called upon somebody or other to, "Make Tagaytay . . . A City of Character."

Welch and Graft waited . . . and waited . . . and waited.

Mixed between anticipation and boredom, Graft asked, "What the fuck is a 'city of character,' boss?"

"I dunno. I suspect it's a little like the Homer Simpson Award for Excellence. Means nothing, in other words."

"Oh."

Lox came up on the net. "Boss, just a heads up. We've got teams all around you, mostly at a distance of about a mile. We're still tracking the people who have our people. Their van's probably going to pass either very close to you or right past you, in about an hour . . . maybe an hour and fifteen minutes. Aida and I are pretty sure that the exchange is going to take place somewhere within a few miles, ten at the outside, of your current location. There are a dozen prime spots for an exchange within that radius. There are hundreds, maybe thousands, of at least mildly possibles, all told."

"Roger," Welch replied. *I feel that old sinking feeling coming on.*

"This is a gamble," Lox said, "but I'm vectoring two of the teams to cover the two we think most likely, and the other two to get in position where they can, with a little luck, get in position to cover ten more."

★ CHAPTER FORTY-SEVEN ★

It is certain that stealing nourishes courage,
strength, skill, tact, in a word, all the virtues useful to
a republican system and consequently to our own.
Lay partiality aside, and answer me: is theft, whose
effect is to distribute wealth more evenly, to be
branded as a wrong in our day, under our government
which aims at equality? Plainly, the answer is no.
—Marquis de Sade

**MV *Richard Bland*, Wharf at Barangay 129, Tondo,
Manila, Republic of the Philippines**

"Oops, I was wrong," said Aida, at the van turned left on
Tagaytay-Calamba, heading east.

"Shit!" Lox exclaimed. "All teams, back in your vehicles.
Prepare to move to God-knows-where."

Aida held up a hand, saying, "Wait a second. Oh, yes,
get them mounted up again. But there's another possibility
than that they're heading east." She hesitated a moment,
then asked Lox, "Do you trust my hunches?"

He thought about it for an equal moment and found, "Yes, I do."

"Okay . . . two teams along Payapa Road, one at the Evercrest Golf Club and the other about three fourths of a mile south of it. The other two along the Tagaytay-Nusugbu road, one north of Splendido Golf Course, the other three fourths of a mile east of that."

"Okay." Lox sent the orders. "Now, can you explain why?"

"No, I can't. Maybe in a few minutes I'll know."

Lox let it pass for now. At least Aida had an idea, which was more than he could say at the moment.

Silang Crossing, Tagaytay, Cavite, Republic of the Philippines

Welch's phone rang. "Southeastern tip of the Splendido Golf Course. Then get out of your car. Keep your cell handy. I don't suppose you have a compass?"

"No," Welch lied.

"No matter. I'll direct you from there."

Graft restarted the vehicle, then pulled out onto the road, leaving the monument to whatever it was behind.

Lucas pointed out to the driver the road he was to take, an exceedingly sharp right. A half-bent over pole bore the sign, "Ligaya Drive," in faded white letters.

In back, Benson looked at Washington and gave him an elbow. They'd all heard that last command, "Then get out of your car." That was a pretty fair indicator that the maze they'd been running Terry through had just about come to an end. But did Washington understand that? A slow nod, almost but not exactly in time with the thumping of the van, said he did. Benson then repeated the elbowing with Perez. He, too, understood, returning Benson's elbowing with two of his own.

At least, I hope that's what that means.

MV *Richard Bland*, Wharf at Barangay 129, Tondo, Manila, Republic of the Philippines

"Bingo!" Aida exclaimed. To the pilot she said, "Leave off the van. I know where it's going."

"Wait," Lox told the pilot. To Aida he said, "That one you're going to have to explain."

"They wouldn't have told Mr. Welch to leave the car unless one or both of two things were true. Either there's somebody waiting at the tip of Splendida Golf Course, maybe to search him for arms, or he's going to be sent walking into the woods to the east, where the van will be waiting. I want the pilot to sweep that area."

"Why?"

"That hunch of *yours*. Whatcha wanna bet that TCS already has security teams on the ground around the area where they're going to do the exchange?"

Lox considered, *Even if we can't reacquire the van, and based on the light traffic and limited roads, we just might be able to, big, big advantage to be gained by taking out their security. Especially if they don't know we did.*

"Yeah," he agreed. "Yeah, that makes fair sense." He told the RPV pilot, "Do it."

★ ★ ★

"Ya know," said the pilot, watching his screens and puffing a cigarette held in his left hand, "while it's not necessarily impossible that three gay couples, all carrying rifles, decided to go out into the woods in the middle of the night to fuck each other, the facts that a) they're not fucking each other, and b) they've formed an almost perfect equilateral triangle on the ground, strongly suggests, at least to me, that they're not gay, that they are there for security, that their positions frame the center point where the exchange is supposed to take place, and, finally, that our little lady here is a genius."

Aida felt her face blush. She also felt a moment's gratitude that the subdued light in the container couldn't show it.

"Lemme tell Terry. And then we're going to start vectoring teams into position to cover the likely exchange point, and to kill those motherfuckers deader than chivalry."

"I'm gonna sweep a little wider," said the pilot.

Tagaytay-Nusugbu Highway, Cavite, Republic of the Philippines

Ferd first killed his headlights and then eased his car into the jungle just off the road to the south. With a twist of the key the engine died. It was inherently suspicious, but the pilot hadn't found any TCS security teams lying farther out than the three who formed the triangle. A risk? Yes, and they knew it. Still, it was an unavoidable one and a small one.

All four were mufti-clad. Their civilian clothing, at least the upper half of it, disappeared under battle dress taken from the trunk, along with their weapons. Floppy, broad-brimmed hats of the same material went on their heads. It was at least within the realm of possibility that the TCS security folks had acquired night vision equipment, since, according to Aida, they weren't a particularly poor organization. The fact that none had been recovered from the safe house in Muntinlupa said they had what had been there, to a certainty.

The dye in their battle dress would, if not outright defeat that, at least reduce its effectiveness. They'd debated taping IR chemlights, the tiny, 4.5mm versions, to their hats for mutual identification and control, but decided against it precisely because of that high likelihood of night vision equipment in the hands of their present enemies.

Ferd, as junior man, took over the Pecheneg. Malone, for all that he was on the collective doo-doo list, was still considered one of the better shots in the company. He got the Lapua .338. The team leader, Sergeant Trimble, pulled NVGs over his face and took the submachine gun, one of the Sterlings they'd gotten from Ben and that was now part of the Second Battalion's very esoteric armory. The .510 Whisper went into the hand of the best shot on the team, Sergeant Yamada, who despite his name and partial ancestry, stood about six-two once he'd unfolded himself from the cramped interior of the subcompact. The weapons were already locked and loaded; no need to make a racket with jerking bolts if it could be avoided.

Lox had vectored them to a spot off the road where began a long, winding, north-south ridge line. Quietly, they moved off from their car and formed in a single column on the east side of that ridge. Then, as quckly as the need for silence would permit, they began moving south.

MV *Richard Bland*, Wharf at Barangay 129, Tondo, Manila, Republic of the Philippines

Aida watched the progress of the teams on the pilot's screen. He'd done something or other to mark them, one through four, with Graft's vehicle as five and six, for himself and Terry.

"What would you have done," she asked Lox, "if TCS had had four or five security teams out? How would you have handled that?"

"What looks like four of our teams," he replied, "is actually eight. If we'd had to, we'd have held the longer-ranged guns, supported by a light machine gun, in place as soon as they spotted a target. Then we'd have had the shorter-range .510 caliber rifles with the team leaders move in close. Being down to two men at that point, they'd have been quieter and could have gotten in closer. We could have handled eight, presupposing that we'd gotten away with getting ours in position. It's called 'Factor P,' for plenty, and is the basis of all sound military planning, in every area from administration to intelligence to operations to logistics."

"But how did you know how many to send?"

"You never do," he said, his voice ripe with cynicism, "which is where the other basis of all sound military planning—make it up, make do, or do without—comes in. That, and be prepared to pay the price. That's another important factor."

"Oh. Police don't really think that way."

"Different missions," Lox said, "for different circumstances. So, different attitudes, different patterns of thought."

"What happens if you can't get them all with the first volley?"

"Then we fight in closer."

"Until they're all dead?"

"Until they're all dead," Lox confirmed.

"Yeah . . . like you said, 'different patterns of thought.' What if you can't get enough in position to engage them all at once?"

"Then Welch pays, we get our people safe . . . and *then* we kill 'em all. Oh, and take our money back."

"You sure you'll be able to do that?" she asked.

"No."

Splendida Golf Course, Taal, Republic of the Philippines

"Are we being watched?" Welch asked Lox, over the radio.

His earpiece answered back, "I doubt anyone in the clubhouse can see you, but it's just barely possible that their northwestern security team can. So, if you're thinking of having Graft tail you in, I'd recommend against until the shooting starts, at which point it won't matter."

"Roger."

Welch waited, sometimes pacing around the Suzuki,

for the phone to ring. The satchel full of cash he'd placed atop the car, not really for ease of retrieval but just to have something to fill up a few seconds with activity while he waited.

Making small talk, Graft said, "I'll bet this is a gorgeous course. I'd like to play it some time."

Welch who, after quite a few years watching U.S. Army officers waste their time—he considered it a waste—on golf courses, would have disagreed. At the moment though, he just didn't really care. "So take leave after the mission. Assuming, of course."

"Yeah," Graft grunted, "assuming. Funny, isn't it?"

"Isn't what?"

"With the whole world in depression, the government here can't keep the streetlights lit and the roads patched. But someone is paying for golf courses like this one."

"This is for the rich," Welch said. "The clever ones of those don't lose money in a depression; they profit from it."

"I never took you for a Marxist, boss," Graft said.

"I'm not. You don't have to be a Marxist to see that the very rich, the ones with no citizenship that means anything to them, especially, are different. You don't have to be a Marxist to despise them either."

The phone rang.

MV *Richard Bland,* Wharf at Barangay 129, Tondo, Manila, Republic of the Philippines

Lox ordered, "All teams, Welch is walking forward. SITREP on targeting."

"Team One, two hundred and fifty meters from the western security team. Targets engageable with the Whisper."

"Team Two. Tracking the eastern security team. Don't think we can get any closer than we are. Long shot for the Whisper. Probably have to use the Lapua, too. There's a drop off ahead of us. If we go into it we'll lose them. As far as I can see, we won't pick them up again until we're within thirty to fifty meters. That's pretty close."

"Team Three"—that was the grouping of Trimble, Yamada, Franceschi, and Malone—"at the southern tip of the ridge. We've got the northern team dead to rights."

"Team Four, covering the presumed exchange point. There's a van . . . I'd guess *the* van, rolling up a trail. It's going slow. We can't always track Welch as he walks forward."

"Terry," Lox sent, "unless you say 'no,' I'm going to have One and Three fire now."

"Why? Why without Two?"

"We can't get Two forward enough for a sure quiet shot without making more noise getting there than is safe," Lox explained.

Lox could hear Welch gulp. "Okay." He gulped again, the button mike picking it up faintly. "Do it."

Laural, Batangas, Republic of the Philippines

Yamada heard the command in his earpiece. He took a single breath, then half let it out. He had both targets within his field of view. They stood about fifteen feet apart, one facing out, one in. The range was three hundred, meaning the accuracy of the rifle was sufficient to place a bullet within just about three inches of his aim point. That was enough for a head shot but, *Why take a chance I don't have to? Still, wish I had some damned frangible. Ah, but with this low a velocity, frangible might not work. Nothing's perfect, I suppose.*

He'd already decided which one to go for first, the one facing outward who had a chance, a slim one but still a chance, of seeing the Whisper's very minimal muzzle flash.

He let that last half breath out, took another, and then began squeezing his trigger.

★ CHAPTER FORTY-EIGHT ★

No enterprise is more likely to succeed than one
concealed from the enemy until it is ripe for execution.
—Niccolo Machiavelli, *The Prince*

Laurel, Batangas, Republic of the Philippines

Seven hundred and fifty grain bullet. Velocity at the muzzle
of one thousand and fifty feet per second. Kick like a
freaking *mule*.

That was the other reason Yamada was the one carrying
the Whisper .510; he had the mass to absorb it. That recoil
was a more or less gradual phenomenon, of course,
helped immeasurably.

His target didn't have that saving grace. The half-inch
bullet impacted about two inches above, and half an inch
to the right, of his absolute center of his sternum. The
sternum shattered *instantly*, driving fragments of bone
into heart and lungs. The bullet, itself, precision cast
bronze, dumped most of its energy into that, and most of
the rest into meat and spine. It exited the body with very

little energy left, barely enough to travel another hundred meters and bury itself partway into a tree. *That* made a sound where the killing had not. But it wasn't the kind of sound a barely trained security goon was likely to recognize.

In Yamada's scope, the second, still living, guard turned towards something, the sniper knew not what. He didn't really care, either, so long as the guard remained visible. Still tracking in his eyepiece, the sergeant carefully and rather slowly turned the bolt, withdrew it, then slid it forward before locking it home. The brass casing made a very soft sound as it was ejected, and none at all when it hit the soft floor of the jungle. The hand went to the stock and the finger to the trigger. Squeeze . . .

As a practical matter, the next shot had to be quick, before the target stumbled over the body or went to investigate what Yamada suspected was an odd sound coming from behind him. Need for speed or not, though, *Calm yourself, shooter. Calm. You are the . . .*

Click. Phhhhttt.

Again, that mule's kick drove into the prone sniper's shoulder. Again there was a tiny report from the muzzle, too faint really for anyone to hear who wasn't just about right next to it. This time, though, when Yamada looked at the target it was still plainly and obviously standing. *Oh, shit, I . . .*

Yamada realized that Trimble was thumping him lightly on the shoulder. Nobody did that unless the shot was a success. The sniper looked again, more carefully, as the body crumpled to the ground. Yes, it had been standing, just as might a chicken with its head cut off.

The head was simply *gone*. Unseen, Yamada smiled with satisfaction. *Heh, heh; "quality is job one."*

Trimble sent to Lox, "Team Three. Two tangos down. Moving up to make sure."

"Make sure" was code for "cut their fucking throats, if any."

MV *Richard Bland*, Wharf at Barangay 129, Tondo, Manila, Republic of the Philippines

"Team one; tangos eliminated."

"*Bland*, Team Four. The van's stopped. But they're getting out. They didn't hear shit."

"Team Two. Ditto, my targets didn't react. Don't think they heard even a 'whisper,' either."

"Roger . . . roger." Lox breathed a heavy sigh of relief. Even Aida, whose area of expertise this was far from, breathed more easily.

The pilot, on the other hand, shouted, "Yee haw!"

Lox looked over the pilot's screen and picked a spot approximately equidistant from the still slowly walking Welch to the van. The van's headlights, which had been dimmed, suddenly flared.

Lox thought about how to control the movement of the shooter teams forward. *Grid coordinates? No way; they either have to break out the hand-held GPS, or the maps. Maps mean light, since NVG's aren't worth a damn for reading them. We'll go polar, then.*

He sent a direction and distance to move from where they were, a polar coordinate, to Team One, and another to Three. That, they could do with a compass, which gave off less light than an anemic firefly, and a pace count, which gave off none. Then he ordered, "Okay, Teams One and Three. Move on those directions, then find a position from which you can cover Terry. You should be able to scope him when you get there."

"Roger . . . Roger, already moving."

Laurel, Batangas, Republic of the Philippines

Welch walked slowly, about as slowly as he thought was credible in someone TCS believed to be a pure civilian. Whether it was slow enough, slow enough for a couple or three shooter teams to get in position, he didn't know.

He was nervous; only a fool wouldn't have been. That nervousness may have lessened when his earpiece told him that four of the TCS's six outlying security people were down. It didn't go away. He didn't try to make it go away either. *I'm not that good an actor, no kind of actor at all, as a matter of fact. If I don't sound nervous they'll get suspicious.*

Terry had spent most of his life lonely. In this, he was probably a match for ninety percent or more of the men and women of M Day. He, and they, had found a route out of loneliness with the Army, or whatever their original service had been. And, after their official service, they'd found a better than fair substitute with the corporation . . . the regiment.

He hadn't defeated it, however, not entirely, until he'd met his wife, Ayanna. For a brief moment, before forcing his mind back to the job at hand, he thought of her. At that, "thought" was probably not precisely the right term; it was more a rush of feelings and well-remembered images.

Stop it, Welch. That's for later. With a mental sigh, he pushed her, reluctantly, out of his mind.

Ahead, and a little to his left, two bright lights flared. They were far enough away not to blind, but they certainly diminished his night vision.

Assholes.

Again the cell rang.

"You see our headlights?" asked the now familiar male voice.

"I see them," Terry answered.

"Follow them. I'll keep on the line and tell you when to stop."

Crap. No more two-way conversations with Lox. I wonder if that's part of their plan or just serendipity.

"I heard, Terry," Lox whispered in his earpiece. "I'll keep you posted."

You would think, thought the leader of Team One, *that after owning this place for forty-five years, then fighting two campaigns here against the Japanese, that somebody would have made a decent map of the area. But nooo; that didn't happen.*

He sent the whisper to the *Bland,* "We're in a patch of low ground. It wasn't on the map we studied before coming here. We do not have, and probably won't get, a good shot. We're cutting left to find a better spot, but don't count on our finding one."

MV *Richard Bland*, Wharf at Barangay 129, Tondo, Manila, Republic of the Philippines

"Shit," said Lox. He looked over at the pilot's control board, counted the numbers from TCS—again, and really unnecessarily—and made a decision.

"Terry, we've only got two teams in position to cover you, Three and Four. And Four also needs to take out the van. That's not enough. Give them the money and get our people back. I repeat, give them the money and get our people back. Abort the rescue."

"No," answered Welch. "I don't think so." *Maybe we get our people back that way. But maybe we don't. And that much money in criminal hands will go a long way toward rebuilding their organization. Maybe if we'd been able to ambush the roads out. But we couldn't. So, no, we take our chances. And if I don't make it, Ayanna, honey, you're the best thing that ever happened to me.*

Laurel, Batangas, Republic of the Philippines

"What was that you said?" asked the ripe-with-suspicion voice on the cell phone.

"I was talking to myself," Terry replied. The nervousness in his own voice came naturally. "Almost stepped into a gully. Just avoided it. Barely."

"Okay. Come forward another hundred and fifty feet and stop. We'll come to you the rest of the way."

"I hear you."

Welch heard a continuous stream of reports in his earpiece. "Three . . . tracking two tangos northernmost . . . Four . . . we've got targets on Terry's right . . . Two . . . still have shots, relatively long range, on their OP . . . tracking . . . tracking . . . good targets . . . ready . . . ready . . ."

Terry stopped. His pace count told him he'd gone the distance TCS had demanded. The lights from the van were much brighter now. His night vision was shot. On the other hand, the approaching nine silhouettes—six TCS and three of his own, he figured—were plainly outlined by those same lights.

But I can't tell yet who's who. Shit.

As the people from TCS and their captives got closer, however, Terry was able to make out who was who. This prompted the thought, *Double shit,* since Benson, Perez, and Washington were pushed out in front of their guards.

"Three . . . clear shots . . . Four . . . clear shots . . ."

Lox said, "Four, concentrate on the people close to Terry. Switch to the van after that."

"Roger."

"Boss," Lox whispered, "we've got everyone but the middle three. They're gonna be yours. And I still think you should abort."

Will they respond? Welch wondered. *Will our people get out of the way? They've certainly been some dumbasses to date. Maybe Lox is right; give them the money. But . . .*

At a range of under fifteen feet the approaching party stopped. That same voice—Lucas's, though Welch didn't know that—demanded, "Where's the money?"

"Where's my guarantee?" Terry asked.

"I don't have time for this bullshit," Lucas replied. "If we were going to keep them we wouldn't have brought them here. And if I wanted you dead I could have given the order any time."

"Send one of them to me," Terry demanded. "One of them and I'll toss you the bag. Four million dollars. Just send one to me . . . as a gesture of good faith."

Lucas hesitated. It really wasn't unreasonable, what the Kano was demanding. He put his hand in the small of the big black's back and pushed. The Kano—Lucas vaguely remembered he'd given his name as "Washington"— stumbled forward, then tripped on his cramped legs, falling to his knees.

"Come on, Washington," Terry said, gently. The black stood a whole head taller than either of the other two prisoners. "Just come this way and get past me."

Lucas reached down, grabbing Washington by his collar, and tried lifting him up. All he really managed to do was half choke him. Slowly, with difficulty, and gagging, the black arose on unsteady legs. Once up, his captor gave him a gentler shove, propelling him forward toward Welch.

"Start walking uphill," Welch repeated. "In the direction I came from." Once Washington was abreast of him, Terry pulled his left arm—the one holding the satchel—backwards.

Benson whistled "Be Prepared."

Terry threw the satchel as hard as he could, directly at Lucas' face. Even as it was in the air, he carried the motion through, his right hand sweeping back, pushing the light coat away and exposing the pistol he kept in a high holster at his belt.

As soon as he saw Terry's right hand move, Benson threw himself into Perez. Both began to keel over in a heap.

As Terry's hand folded around the exposed grip of his .45, three shots rang out, the sound of the bullets' passing splitting the air. Only two of those three sonic cracks passed close by.

On Welch's left one of the people from TCS was flung back, his weapon flying, his legs picked up bodily from the ground, and his arms being driven inward by inertia. The one to *his* right simply exploded at the torso, the spray of blood, bone, and guts visible in the van's headlights as it flew out his back.

Welch didn't see that. Neither did he see the very similar fates of the two TCSers on his right. With his pistol coming out, his brain and the narrowed vision of his eyes were focused entirely on the silhouettes of the three armed men in the middle.

There was another shot. The light from the headlights had been fierce. The newly flaring light, though most of it didn't come from the headlights, grew fiercer still as the van, parked about fifty meters away, suddenly blossomed into a fireball. Team Four, or one of their snipers, at least, had gone for the gas tank.

Except as a glow on the edges of his consciousness, Terry didn't see any detail. The two snipers from the team, however, could. They laughed inwardly, in the couple of moments before the flash caused their scopes to temporarily overload, as the fireball engulfed the driver of the van, flashing his hair to a crisp, and then began burning him alive. His mouth was opened in a scream of pure agony, though if any sound came through it was overwhelmed by the roar of the gas-driven flames.

Crisanto, disgraced ex-Philippine Marine, was possibly the only one present, besides the captives and their ransomer, who immediately understood what the shots meant. If anyone else had, it was the six victims, two each to either side, and two back at the van. For all but one of those, though, their understanding, if any, was probably cut rather short by nearly instantaneous death.

With that instant understanding, Crisanto began bringing his rifle down at the big Kano standing in front of him. He was a touch younger, hence a touch faster, than the Kano. He also had the advantage that he didn't have to reach for and draw his weapon. He got the first aimed—or at least reasonably well-pointed—shot off.

Unfortunately for Crisanto, that shot was a little too well-pointed and too close range. The bullet left the muzzle spinning and yawing. It never had time to stabilize in straight and level flight before impacting at a poor angle on the ceramic plate mounted on the front of the Kano's body armor. It staggered the Kano back about half a foot, to be sure. But he was simply too big to be knocked off his feet without the bullet getting through to send ripples through his flesh and his nerves utterly haywire from shock and pain.

The Kano fired. His shot wasn't particularly well aimed, more of an automatic reaction to being struck on the chest plate. The .45 muzzle flashed with a bright yellow streak of flame, sending its bullet, much slower and larger, but also yawing, into Crisanto's abdomen. What had been a disadvantage when hitting an armor plate was a large advantage when hitting soft flesh and hard bone: the .45 caliber bronze-jacketed lead dumped all its energy into the TCSer's body, and that in a particularly sensitive area. The Filipino bent at the waist, losing his grip on his rifle, as his body was flung backwards.

Terry didn't mean to shoot when he had; he'd intended to go for a chest shot. Even so, when he reviewed it later, he had no cause for dissatisfaction. That one was down and wouldn't be getting up soon.

He rotated his entire torso to his left, passing by the man to whom he'd thrown the satchel to fire at the guard to his left. That one wasn't nearly as quick on the draw as the groin-shot one had been; Terry put two quick shots into his torso then fired for the head and missed.

That didn't matter; target two was down. Terry lined his pistol up on the one with the satchel, the leader, he thought.

Lucas had been surprised by the force of the throw. He'd been even more surprised at the volley of shots that had rung out from almost all sides. The dim awareness that his guards had mostly been thrown to the ground didn't help any. And just as bad had been the sudden bursting into flames of the van, and the wave of heat that had assaulted his back from those flames.

Even so, he caught the satchel and fumbled with it for long moments as realization set in that he was in serious trouble. The couple of shots that sang out between Crisanto and the Kano, and especially the muzzle blast from the Kano, had been shocked him even more. It really was *not* supposed to go like this.

Lucas dropped the satchel and began putting both hands up. *Surely they won't . . .*

"Fuck you, asshole," the Kano said, and fired.

Welch sat on the ground, armor undone on one side, and the hand on that same side massaging his sorely aggrieved chest. His tunnel vision, while still acute, was slowly expanding back out to normal The shakes hadn't quite started yet, though he was distantly expecting them. A few meters in front of where he sat, Sergeant Benson, his arms now unbound, searched over the bodies. He didn't bother with the ones near the van; they were toast.

Terry had the late Lucas's cell phone in his other hand. He'd scrolled through the contact list until he'd found a likely name, likely from the file Aida had provided and the information that had been twisted out of the hooker— "Diwata." He tapped the phone to form the text massage. "All's okay. Got the money. Taking the boys for a drink. Back later."

Overhead, the RPV still searched on the principle that, "you never really know." The four shooter teams had shifted positions, but remained in the same general areas, on much the same principle. Graft had taken all the arms in the back of the Suzuki—though that was on a general, not a specific, principle—and come trotting down as soon as the first shots were fired.

"What are you looking for, Benson?" Welch asked.

The sergeant was on two knees and one hand, bent over the first of Welch's targets, the one Benson had heard addressed as "Crisanto."

"This," Benson said, with great satisfaction, holding up a wicked looking combat knife he'd just taken from the still breathing, and possibly conscious, body. The knife's blade glowed cruelly, reflecting the flames of the van.

Benson shifted to straddle the chest and lock Crisanto's arms on the inside of his knees. Then he arched up. One hand grabbed Crisanto's hair and tugged it towards him, pulling the head to near vertical. The ex-Marine's eyes opened in confusion. Benson tossed the knife lightly into the air, catching it in a stabbing grip.

"Go to Hell *blind*, mothahfuckah," the sergeant cursed. Then the knife dove once, followed by a twist. Crisanto screamed. His hands struggled to find his face but were stopped by the body straddling his chest and the knees pinioning his arms. The knife dove again. Again Benson twisted it. Another scream arose; the hands became more frantic still in search of the bloody face.

"When you get to the waiting room, tell Zimmerman I said, 'Hi.'"

Then Benson spit once, before letting go Crisanto's hair and rising to his feet. He left behind two bloody orbs, resting on the TCS criminal's chest.

Welch had only one comment. "Make sure you cut his throat before we leave the area." Then he hit the send button on the cell.

★ CHAPTER FORTY-NINE ★

If an injury has to be done to a man it should be so
severe that his vengeance need not be feared.
—Niccolo Machiavelli, *The Prince*

**MV *Richard Bland*, Wharf at Barangay 129, Tondo,
Manila, Republic of the Philippines**

The bridge and the control station for the RPV erupted in
cheers when Welch reported, "We've got our people. No
losses. All tangos dead." Precisely to avoid cheering that
somebody might hear, coming from several hundred
throats, Pearson kept the news to himself and those few
who already knew, for the nonce. What he passed on
instead was Welch's order, "Have the RPV pilot bring his
aircraft back to cover Tondo. And tell Warrington that, as
soon after it gets there as he's comfortable with, he's to
execute *Schrecklichkeit*."

Lox waited for the RPV to return to overhead and for
Warrington to start moving his men and Stocker's up
before he said, "Aida, do your stuff."

The policewoman had been waiting for the command. Her cell phone was already set to the number she intended to call first. There were four more in a queue, waiting their turn.

She nodded and pressed the dial button. It took six rings before the deep-voiced answer came, in English, "And what can I do for you tonight, sexy? You finally decide to take me up on that employment offer?"

Aida smiled. There were criminals you just hated, and then there were criminals you couldn't help liking, even as you tried your best to bust their asses into hard time.

"Sorry, Nicasio," she answered, "you got the wrong girl for that one. If I didn't think you were joking, I'd be insulted."

"I'm joking and I'm not," came the answer. Coming from a known cutthroat, the voice was surprisingly warm, Lox thought.

"Yes, the offer's always open—you know that—but, no, if I thought for a minute you'd take me up on it, I'd go immediately to church and make the priest hear my confession if I had to make him hear it at gunpoint. See, I'd know then that the world was about to end.

"What can I do for you, Aida?"

"Nothing," she replied. "I'm calling to do you a favor."

"Oh?" The voice turned immediately suspicious.

"Oh, yeah. See, in about an hour TCS is going down hard. You'll know it's happening by a level of gunfire like you've never heard in your life. Wait until the shooting's over, then go in and stake your claim."

"How do I know it's true?" he asked. "Take on TCS? That's not a light decision."

"Well . . . old friend, that's up to you. You can always sit on your haunches and let Balingit, Honey, Manuel and Javier stake out all the territory. Though that would drop your gang from what? Maybe number two of six now? To about fifth of five?"

"How are they going to know, Aida?"

"Why, sweetheart, because I'm calling them as soon as I get off the phone with you"

"Bitch!"

"That's me" Aida replied cheerily. "Oh, one word of warning: If your boys go in before the gunfire pretty much clears, or if they try to take on some folks who look and act a lot like Kanos? Fifth out of five would probably be more than you could reasonably hope for. I'm telling you that as an old friend, Nicasio."

"Still, shit, Aida, even all of us together don't have the guns to take on even a quarter of TCS."

"Oh, that's the other favor I'm doing you, Nicasio. If you wait about an hour and fifty minutes and go to the intersection of Marcos Highway and Bonifacio? There should be sixty or so rifles and enough ammunition for . . . well, for a while, waiting there for you. They're Moro rifles but the Moros don't need them anymore. Some friends of mine will be dropping them off. Don't let your people fuck with my friends. Think: Not even fifth out of five."

"Why now?" Nicasio asked.

"Good question," Aida said. "Not sure I understand completely but a friend did mention to me that, when you have a problem and the law *can't* work, then you have to make war instead."

Aida hung up and asked Lox, "What was that tribe of Frenchies you said Julius Caesar called in all the neighboring tribes to exterminate?"

"Belgians, actually," Lox corrected. "Labaan told me they were called the 'Eburones.'"

Welch had taken most of the Whispers for the rescue, leaving only two for Warrington and the rump of the A Company left aboard ship.

Which is actually plenty for what I have to do, thought Warrington. *Kill a couple of tattoo-faced motherfuckers on the wharf, to let two columns of Stocker's men debark and move up the street, offing any security on the way, silently. And, with the cooks, I have just enough people left for that, to deliver five packages of small arms to five different locations, and to take down the grid.*

Sergeant Major Pierantoni, head still wrapped, stood on the bridge facing the operations maps. He was mostly recovered, at least for something like this, which allowed Kiertzner to resume duties as C Company's first sergeant.

From his perch on the bridge Warrington watched his two sniper teams do a bent-over walk to the gunwale nearest the wharf. One went to a point roughly amidships, the other went to the rear deck. On the way that latter one passed by five two-wheeled gurneys borrowed from TIC Chick, loaded with arms and ammunition, sitting on a pallet hooked to the aft crane. The snipers took seats at the gunwale, backs flush against it and rifles held across their laps. Their suppressors looked like nothing so much as four Fosters Lager cans, taped end to end and pained black. Atop the rifles were thermal scopes.

While the snipers hid themselves, the mufti-clad spotters stood upright and marked the positions of TCS's "Customs agents." One of them waved and a spotter waved back.

One of the snipers put a hand to his headphone and looked up at the bridge, directly at Warrington, as if to say, "Anytime this eon, boss."

Warrington used his own radio to send, "Stocker? Warrington. Your boys ready?"

"In ranks on the mess deck, ready to come up and rumble on your command."

"Yeah, fine. Just remember, no rumble until you get to the target area."

"Well, duh?"

"Lox," Warrington asked, "what have we got on the RPV?"

"Same three 'customs' dudes walking the wharf," Lox replied. "Two two-man patrols around the target. There are scattered armed men all around the town, but they seem to be moving in a sort of Brownian motion. No guard plan or schedule I can discern. I suspect a lot of them are just bored and looking for trouble. We'll have to call it case by case as Stocker moves up."

Looking for trouble? Warrington mused. *I wonder if they'll just luck out this very early morning and find some.*

"Skipper, you ready to pull out?"

"At a moment's notice, Major," Pearson replied.

Warrington nodded again. The ship wouldn't have to leave anything like that quickly, but it was nice knowing she could.

"Okay . . . snipers; on one. Four . . . three . . . two . . . one."

★ ★ ★

All three of the pseudo customs men lay sprawled and dead on the wharf. Warrington had watched the killing from his perch on the bridge. He didn't have any feelings for the dead men, one way or the other. His hate was entirely reserved for the masters of the gang. And it *was* pure hate; he, the rest of A Company, the ship's company, the aviation people, and Stocker's boys, had all watched the video of Zimmerman's hanging.

On the other hand, however many minions we can kill is all to the good, since our objective is to make the gang functionally extinct. When the law ceases to function, the only recourse is to make war.

"Stocker?"

"Here."

"The wharf's clear. Move out."

Pearson and Warrington exchanged a glance. *Shall we? By all means.*

"Crane Three?" the captain queried.

"Ready."

"Hoist the rifles over the side and set them down on the wharf."

"Aye, aye, Skipper."

"Crane One?"

"Standing by."

"Get those Elands down to the wharf."

C Company's Gurkhas really didn't have the right build to blend in, being much stockier than the local norm. But they had the right height, approximately the right skin tone, and the epicanthic fold. That would have to do. The Gurkhas, each bearing a suppressed submachine gun, and several hundred rounds of subsonic ammunition, with holstered pistols under their mufti, led off.

Also in mufti, and trailing the Gurkhas quite closely, was one team from A Company. They were similarly armed and had the mission of shutting down that part of the electric grid that served Tondo. The main transmission lines that served this part of the metro area ran north to south, from Paco to Doña Imelda to Quezon, on a line well east of the target. Only a single line ran into Tondo because, despite having a large population, its people, barring the gangs, were dirt poor and couldn't afford the expensive light bulbs caring and sensitive westerners and Japanese insisted upon and barred anyone else from making. There were plans for improving electric access, and for running new lines from Pinas in the south to Marilao in the north, but none for reducing the cost of a light bulb back to what it had been in those less caring and sensitive days of incandescents. Even the existing plans, pending the money coming available, would remain nothing more than high hopes.

Hopes in Tondo, regarding electric or any other utility service, or pretty much anything, weren't particularly high. It had been a big day way back when, when the government had caused the garbage dump *cum* landfill just east of Barangay 129 to stop burning. Any progress beyond that was just about inconceivable, and certainly too much to ask for.

For that matter, deep down, the Tondoese expected Smokey Mountain, as it had been known, to start burning again any second.

"What's that bloody stench?" whispered one of the Gurkhas, his given name was Nawang, to Sergeant Balbahadur, as the team stopped momentarily at the corner of Magellanes and Marcos Highway.

"Which one?" Balbahadur asked. "I smell rotten fish on the one side and rotten . . . well . . . I don't know what it is, on the other. It's pretty fucking awful though."

"Yeah, it is." Nawang got down on his belly, sticking his head around a corner. He scuttled back, rather like a very confused snake, and said, "I see nothing on the other side of the bridge. You would think . . . but." The Gurkha shrugged eloquently.

"Okay," Balbahadur said. "You and Thapa, go. Gurung and I will cover."

Smiling, Nawang took off at a sprint, with Thapa close on his heels. At the bridge that spanned the Binuangan River that separated the northwest corner of Tondo, proper, from Navotas, to the north. A few meters short of the bridge, the two Gurkhas stopped and proceeded to walk across, calmly, chatting in Nepali. They figured, not unreasonably, that with a hundred and seventy-odd native languages in the Philippines, there was a fair chance for anyone to take Nepali as just another language they didn't know.

On the far side they stopped and waved. What could look more innocent?

Then, with Balbahadur and Gurung following close, themselves followed by the two Whisper-armed snipers and their spotters, plus the antielectricity team, that followed by the mass of C Company, and C company trailed by three of the five gurneys loaded down with rifles and ammunition,

Nawang and Thapa walked calmly forward, toward TCS headquarters. They stopped only once, when a drunk sporting a face full of tattoos stopped them, demanding something they didn't understand.

He didn't understand, either, when Nawang shot him down like a dog on the streets of Navotas.

★ CHAPTER FIFTY ★

For the low, red glare to southward
when the raided coast-towns burn?
(Light ye shall have on that lesson,
    but little time to learn.)
—Rudyard Kipling, "The Islanders"

Navotas, Republic of the Philippines

There was a long, long trail of dead men with tattooed faces all along Marcos Highway and Lapu-Lapu Avenue. The Gurkhas didn't actually keep count; they just weren't that kind of people.

The route was right at a mile, a twenty-minute walk. Taking a bit of care about it, though, had driven the time up to over an hour. Setting up, again with considerable care, had taken the better part of another hour and a few more tattooed faces rapidly turning pale.

Finally, everything was ready. Overhead the RPV circled, silent and, if not itself deadly, conveying information that would turn into sheer deadliness in just a minute or two. The two sniper teams from A Company were stationed in a multi-story parking garage just east of the Marcos-Lapu-Lapu intersection. A Company's antielectricity team—"Team Juice"—was just off Circumferential Road three and the Binuangan River, ready to cut service.

Stocker's First Platoon was tucked in against some warehouses, southwest of Marcos. Second had moved up almost to North Bay and Lapu-Lapu. Third and Weapons, the latter having left their mortars and reconfigured as infantry, were stretched out in little knots along Lapu-Lapu, between Bangus and North Bay. The two Elands, freshly, even ostentatiously, painted in Philippine Army colors, idled for the nonce to the northeast side of Marcos. Farther out, three of the "Arms Distribution Teams"—at the bridges by the Navotas bus terminal, at Lapu-Lapu, and at Circumferential three—waited, guarding the presents.

This is going to be so much fun. Stocker inwardly giggled. He had a loudspeaker borrowed from the *Bland* clutched in one hand. He wanted TCS to know, there at the very end, why they were being destroyed.

"Team Juice?"

"Juice," reported the antielectricity team.

"Cut power."

There were more or less subtle ways to take down an electric transfer station. Juice wasn't big on subtlety. They'd just wired the thing "for sound."

Boom. The explosion was, no doubt, loud. It still wasn't really all that much louder than when a transformer blows on its own.

Ah, music to me ears, thought Stocker, from about half a mile away. *Eh?*

All the lights in the area went dead. Now only A and C

companies could see a bloody thing. *Yeah . . . fighting fair is stupid.*

"Sniper teams?"

"Standing by," came the answer.

"Be some good lads, if you would, and start taking out any TCSers on the grounds around their headquarters, eh?"

Stocker could neither see nor hear either the suppressed shots or the subsonic bullets. Enough time passed for him to ask, "Are we quite finished yet?"

"One sec . . . aha, gotcha, motherfucker. We're finished now, sir."

"Very good. Now, First Platoon, move forward to North Bay. Get in position for the assault. And remember, boys, no prisoners and no survivors."

It was the dogs that awakened Diwata, dogs howling in the slums to the west. She immediately reached for the light on the night table by her bed. Several taps on the controlling base produced nothing.

"Funny," she said, softly and sleepily, "I wonder what's killed the power. I wonder what set those dogs to howling. Might be the electric outage, I guess. Stupid dogs . . . ought to be shot . . . "

At that point two ninety millimeter explosions shook the building, throwing Diwata from her bed to the rug below.

MV *Richard Bland,* Wharf at Barangay 129, Tondo, Manila, Republic of the Philippines

Maricel nearly fainted when the light came on and the

door to the container holding her cage opened. She'd been sure she was for death, and had been dreading every minute since she'd been taken aboard. When she saw the man who'd so brutally tortured her, she didn't faint, quite, but her legs, refusing to hold her up, collapsed under her, letting her fall to the corrugated metal deck.

Cringing, looking around clasped hands held in front of her face, she begged, "Please, no. I have a baby. Please . . . I'm so sorry. Please don't. Please, please, *please*?"

A small woman, Filipina, Maricel thought, entered the container after her tormentor, closing the door gently behind herself. That woman made a subtle *get to your feet* gesture.

Cringing back even more, Maricel couldn't form words. Her head shook back and forth violently. *Nonononononono!*

"It'll be all right, girl," Aida said. "Come with us."

That promise meant nothing. *But what can I do? They can just kill me here and then carry my body and dump it. And they might make it hurt more if I don't go easy. Yes . . . they'll hurt me more to punish me for making them clean up the mess. I can't take any more pain.* Quietly except for some hopeless sniffling, Maricel forced herself to stand.

Lox and Aida guided the unsteady, swaying girl out of her cell, through an open area with a bunch of tables and the smell of food, then through a hatch and up several flights of stairs. The hopeless and helpless weeping never quite stopped. Indeed, it grew louder and still more hopeless, the closer she came to deck.

Once on deck, Maricel heard gunfire. A girl couldn't grow up and work in or around Tondo and not recognize the sound. This, though, was way out of line with anything she'd ever heard in her life. And she had no clue what those bright green lines arcing across the sky were.

Suddenly, the green lines all disappeared as great flames began billowing up to the sky. It hadn't quite registered before then that she was very close to home. It took a moment or two more to realize the flames were coming from TCS headquarters.

"Oh, God," she whispered, "all my friends."

They led her to the gunwale. *This is where they put a bullet in my head*, she thought. *God, please let it be over quickly. I don't want to be shot then drown.*

They stopped her just before she reached the ship's edge. The woman spoke then.

"Do you know why we band together into nations, girl?"

The question seemed so totally out of the blue that Maricel didn't really even comprehend it. She shook her head, a gesture that meant, in this case, *I don't understand*.

Aida took it wrongly, assuming the girl meant she didn't know why. She answered the question herself. Pointing towards the flames, she said, "We band into nations for just that reason. In the real world, little tribes like TCS are destroyed. They can't compete against determined bands of raiders. It takes more power than that to defend yourself against people like yourself, people with no law above themselves."

Ah, *now* Maricel understood the question. She wasn't

sure she understood the answer and, given that she was going to die, the answer didn't really matter anyway.

"It's the flaw in some utopian schemes," the woman continued. She looked at Maricel's uncomprehending face and said, "You don't understand that word, do you?"

"No." Sniffle. *Just get on with it, will you?*

"Never mind; here's the truth, a truth I've been trying to find for the last . . . well, for the last good long while. People band into nations, real nations—not travesties like TCS, gangs that fancy themselves nations—to defend themselves. It requires an emotional commitment. The limits of nations are not how far their borders can reach, but how far their hearts can. People with tiny hearts, people like TCS, can never reach very far, can never gather enough similar hearts together to defend themselves. Only real people, and real countries or causes, can do that. That's why TCS is going to die tonight."

Maricel lifted her chin. As death came closer, and her own resignation to it grew, she found a little spark of pride in herself. *If I couldn't live well, at least I can die well.*

"Are you telling me this so I'll know why you're going to kill me? I already know why."

"Nobody's going to kill you, girl," Aida said.

"I got the story from Malone. They took a vote, Zimmerman's closest friends. At first they were going to do to you what was done to him."

"Peter asked them," Aida said, her head inclining towards Lox, "which one was going to haul on the rope. None of them would volunteer. Then they thought about it some and took another vote."

Lox spoke then, softly and gently. Aida suspected he was ashamed.

"What it came down to, Maricel," Lox said, "was that when we thought about it, we really couldn't blame you. We—all of us—prostitute ourselves. And after . . . questioning you . . . I was pretty confident you didn't expect anyone to be killed, certainly not the way Zimmerman was."

The girl broke down again. Chin on her chest, she cried, "I didn't. I *really* didn't. I'm so sorry."

"We know," Lox said. "I'm sorry, too. About . . . well . . . you know."

Lox reached a hand into his pocket, pulling out a thick envelope. "We were all given a few thousand dollars worth of Philippine pesos before we came here. That's pretty routine in our work; never know when you might need some getaway money, after all. One way or another, we never give the getaway money back. It's *always* 'expended.'

"Anyway, the boys kicked in what was left and asked me to give it to you.

"It's about seven hundred thousand pesos," he said. "It's not a huge amount but . . . maybe it's enough for you to start over. I dunno . . . go to school . . . start a business . . . Or you can just waste it. Get drunk and forget about what we . . . what I . . . had to do to you. Your choice."

He handed the envelope over. Maricel took it wonderingly, her grip loose as if not believing it was real. She'd never even seen that much money in one place at one time. Even so, it didn't seem right to look in the envelope. Instead she asked, "You're not going to kill me? You *forgive* me?"

"No and yes," Lox answered. "Well . . . almost yes. We don't 'forgive' you so much as we can't find it in our hearts to blame you, not entirely. And, yes, you're free to go. We only held you this long so you couldn't warn TCS.

"We're really . . . " Whatever Lox was about to say was lost as the *girl* really started to cry.

Lox asked, "When I was . . . questioning you, and just now, you said you had a baby. Where is he, or she?"

Through her sniffles, Maricel answered, "He. I always leave him with my mother when I have to work. My mom lives well north of Tondo. My baby's safe."

Navotas, Republic of the Philippines

"All rounds expended," said the leader of the Eland Section. The dozens of holes in the walls of TCS headquarters sat as smoking testimony to that.

"Roger," said Stocker. He crouched behind a wall about a hundred meters up Lapu-Lapu from North Bay, enjoying the spectacle thoroughly. "Still need your machine guns for a few minutes. Break. Platoons, commence your assault."

There was hardly any fire coming back at the troops. At first there had been, as TCS's several hundred armed "soldiers" in the building rushed to the windows. They, however, couldn't see in the dark. Stocker's machine guns, RPG-29 Vampires, machine guns, some rifles, snipers, etc. *could.* It had been a matter of only a few minutes work to beat down the TCS's attempt at defense, leaving the windows clear and a not inconsiderable number of bodies on the inside floors. Whatever TCS was doing inside— and Stocker suspected that was mostly praying for deliverance—it wasn't inconveniencing their attackers in the slightest.

A new machine gun—or perhaps two of them, it was hard to tell with Pechenegs—joined in the shooting some-where on the other side of the building.

"Captain," transmitted Moore, now back with his own platoon since Kiertzner was back with company, "They're trying to get out the back." Moore chuckled. "We've demonstrated what a bad idea that is."

"No prisoners, no survivors," Stocker repeated.

"Well, duh, sir."

In Stocker's field of view, three teams of four raced forward to the building's walls. Two of the teams ran toward the southern wall, One disappeared around the corner where the wall turned north. He wasn't worried about them; steady machine gun fire directed at that wall gave testimony that they were well supported.

In each team two men were riflemen. One carried a double satchel charge, twenty pounds of C-4 in two bags, tied together, with a length of fuse and a friction igniter hanging out. A fourth man humped one of the Russian flamethrowers that had been drawn from *Bland*'s well-you-never-know-what-might-turn-out-to-be-useful stocks. Stored empty, they'd been in behind the little toe-popping mines.

Focusing on the nearer team lunging at the southern wall, Stocker saw the riflemen lash at the windows as they ran. Short bursts, but enough to frighten anyone from peeking out. When they reach the wall, all flattened their backs against it. The riflemen, one after the other, took out grenades, armed them, released the spoons, and—after a brief delay—tossed them through the nearest windows. Smoke, dirt, and the remnant shards of glass flew out, pelting the asphalt. There were also a couple of screams. Then the flamethrower man stepped back a few paces. A long tongue of bright orange flame, mixed in with blackish streaks, lanced out and through the window. Some of the liquid fire splashed against the window frame, but most landed inside. The screaming coming through the windows grew very loud. More flames lanced out, before the tank petered out, leaving the nozzle dripping a mere few drops of liquid agony. The continuing, and apparently growing, flames suggested there was plenty more burnable material inside than the flamethrower had sent there.

Fuel exhausted, the flamethrower man raced back across Lapu-Lapu to his initial assault position, a smoldering building on the TCS side of the road.

Now it was the turn of the trooper carrying the satchel charge. Before moving to throw, he pulled the ring on the friction igniter, then stopped and watched for emerging smoke and bubbling plastic on the fuse. Yes, it was lit.

The demo man only moved away from the sheltering wall a few feet, and that at an angle, before cutting in again to stand right next to the window. He took the satchel's straps in both hands, then twisted his torso away from the window. Centrifugal force lifted the satchel to about waist level. As it started to fall, the man whipped his torso in the other direction. The satchel charge swung wide, then entered the window. The straps bent at the window frame. Where the satchel was going now—except that it was definitely inside—was anyone's guess.

Even across the sound and fury of battle-approaching-massacre, Stocker heard, "Let's get us de fuck outa here!"

Then, in the few seconds before the blasts began, Stocker lifted his loudspeaker to his lips and spoke the message that was the point—or at least the exclamation point—of the exercise. The words, electronically amplified, echoed across the scene of carnage. "Before you cock-suckers decide to hang somebody, you really need to find out first just exactly who his friends are."

Everywhere Diwata turned was fire and death. The concrete of the floor was nearly covered with blood. If she hadn't been asleep, if she hadn't gotten up with bare feet, she'd have slipped in it.

She could see now, despite the lack of electricity, but that was far more curse than blessing. Everywhere were the dead and the dying. Some, caught by some kind of liquid fire, burned alive before her eyes, screaming and clawing at the fire that would not go out.

Flames were licking up the walls and across the roof. A stuffed chair in the open storage area to the west suddenly flashed into flame, disappearing in a cloud of smoke almost completely. The smoke reached her and she began to choke. Covering her mouth and nose with both hands, she turned and fled back toward her own chambers.

She opened a door, then passed through.

She heard someone speaking in English in an electronic

voice: "Before you cocksuckers decide to hang somebody, you really need to find out first just exactly who his friends are."

Oh, God, no. For that? They did this for that? What kind of monsters . . .

She never quite completed that thought. Faster than her mind could register it, there was a blast and a shock-wave that collapsed a wall upon her, pinning her down. The wall was already on fire. Flame touched her hair crisping it in an instant. Her face began to char. Down below, she could feel the fire eating into the flesh of her legs and torso.

No, no . . . not burning...no, not burning . . . not that . . . don't let me die like that . . . don't . . . "Aiiaiaiaiaiai!"

MV *Richard Bland,* Wharf at Barangay 129, Tondo, Manila, Republic of the Philippines

All kinds of boats and ships were pulling out, streaming away from Manila, Tondo, Navotas, and anything to do with battles in what had been a peaceful, if gang-controlled, port.

Neither police nor fire department had come to help yet. They probably wouldn't. This was unsurprising; after all, Tondo and the rest of the area held by TCS had been a "nation," a no-go area. The fire burned merrily and probably would until long after sunrise.

There were still firefights going on all over the area as the five remaining gangs, armed by M Day with captured Moro weapons, duked it out for dominance. Every gang member dead had to be counted as a plus. And every gang member with a tattooed face was soon going to be dead.

"Everyone aboard, Sergeant Major?" Warrington asked Pierantoni.

"Yessir. And the Elands back aboard and stowed in containers."

"Casualties?"

"Light," the sergeant major answered. "Lots to be said for surprise, you know."

"Not even any really badly wounded from this go-round," said Cagle. "There *is* a lot to be said for surprise."

Kiertzner, also standing by, quoted, "Americans; they'll cross an icy river, in the middle of the winter, in the dark, to kill you in your sleep. On Christmas."

"Well," Warrington countered, "in this case, Her Majesty's subjects got to do the killing."

"I'd better be going," Aida said. "If you folks are leaving now I . . . well, the truth is I hate the sea."

"You won't take us up on that job offer?" Pearson asked. "Lox says you'd be a boon to the regiment. And you wouldn't be on Third World pay scales, you know; you'd be on ours."

"I've got to think about it," she replied. "Yeah, it's a lot of money compared to my pension. Still, it's not a light decision. And I have to consult my children and grand-children. And, too, this is my *home*."

"I understand," the captain said.

"What about Welch and the rest of the company?" Pierantoni asked.

"We'll be sending the LCM in to pick them up at Calatagan. Shouldn't be a problem."

"Okay."

"What about the fucking tranzis?" Stocker asked.

"Already ordered their tickets, at our expense," Pearson said. "In gratitude for the help they gave—maybe not too willingly but they still gave—with our wounded. We'll drop them at Singapore and they can fly out from there."

"Singapore?" Stocker sneered. He was still on an adrenaline high from dealing with TCS. "Ho Chi Minh City would be more appropriate. And I still think walking the . . . "

"Andrew!"

"Oh, all right. Let the shits go."

Warrington chuckled. "Anyway, let's give Aida time to debark and then let's get the hell out of here and head for home."

★ EPILOGUE ★

I

Camp Crame, Quezon City, Republic of the Philippines

Aida wasn't really all that sentimental about the desk she'd been given and allowed to keep even after her semi-retirement from the police. Even so, cleaning it out was a break with the past. That was hard.

One of the younger men in the office stopped by, leaning on the door. "You're not leaving us, are you, Inspector?"

Aida shrugged. "Got a good offer elsewhere," she said. "And you people don't give me enough useful work to keep even a grandmother occupied."

"Where you going?"

"Guyana," she said. "That's over in South America."

"You speak the language?"

"They speak English. I can speak that."

"Well, we'll all miss you. And don't forget, 'Home is where the heart is.'"

"I never will forget," she said, heart beginning to break. "But sometimes you have to go away to protect what matters to your heart.

"*Magpakailanman dito sa puso ko.*" Forever in my heart. "Now go away before I start going all sentimental."

II

Caban Island, Pilas Group, Basilan Province, Republic of the Philippines

Janail hung now only by the nails. His cramped legs had no more strength to support him. Suffocation and death would follow soon.

The funny thing was that it didn't hurt anymore. He was past pain and past cares. He only wanted to get it over with. He was almost bored.

The funnier thing was that the pain had gone away sometime in the night, about the time he'd decided—surely a devout atheist would have called it a delusion—that he'd been wrong, all these years, that there was a God, that Mohammad was his prophet. After all, hadn't a vision of God, sitting in judgment over him, come as clear as revelation in the night?

He still had that vision engraved on the synapses of his brain, the stern-faced Allah, in boundless glory, surrounded by all the beings of the universe, his slaves, saying in a beautiful voice, "You have greatly sinned, Janail."

Then the Moro had wept, not with the pain but with the shame. *How could I have been so wrong? How could I have been such a fool. My God, forgive me.*

He felt death hovering near. Janail had been waiting for this moment. Using up the last of his strength, he lifted his head high, then rested it against the stirpes of his cross. "I . . . testify," he tried to shout, though it came out as little more than an inarticulate croak. "I testify that . . . there is . . . no god but Allah . . . I..I . . . tes . . . tes . . . I . . . Mohammad . . . is . . . messenger . . . of . . . ALLAH!"

"And there went the last one," thought Paloma Ayala, with vast satisfaction. Her Marines were already taking down the other crosses. Indeed they were mostly already down. The wood formed a great pyre, assembled nearer to what used to be the Harrikat camp. The pyre was covered already with the bodies of men who had died, oh, *very* hard. Beside it was a great, hand dug ditch. The Moros would be burned in a few hours, and their ashes dumped, scrambled, and then buried. The other two hundred and twenty or so, the ones killed in action, would be left out for the vultures of the press to feast upon.

As vast as was her satisfaction, Madame still fumed. *I offered to spare one of them, if he'd tell me who in my family set up my husband. None would, the filthy swine. I suppose that was my mistake for admitting that I wouldn't spare them anyway, earlier. Silly me.*

But it doesn't really matter. I've had the girl my husband was with questioned. It was a lovely little book Peter loaned me. Pity the tramp didn't survive. So I know it was Junior. And Pedro and his partner should be dealing with that little tumor from my own womb very shortly.

III

Yacht *Resurrection*, Gulf of Thailand

All the money in the world, thought Valentin Prokopchenko, *will not save me from this.*

Even down here, down in the lead-lined compartment over the pool, Prokopchenko could hear the fighting ranging below decks. And that sound grew closer by the minute. Daria, seated on the deck, whimpered with fright, occasionally crying out at particular explosions.

I wonder how Vympel defeated my yacht's radar? It must be Vympel; it's their job. That they could do so I never doubted. I'd like to know exactly how, though.

Who betrayed me? he wondered. *Who even knew, besides prospective customers? And there were few of those. I doubt it was the Harrikat. Maybe Shedova from Kazakhstan. He, certainly, still had close ties with the FSB.*

Not that it will change anything, the knowledge. They're going to capture me, and then I'm going to envy the ones who died in Beria's prisons and camps.

I still remember throwing up as a boy at what my father told me his grandfather told him: The days on end without sleep, the beatings. And those were only the start, the old man said. After that they went to work on the fingernails. Then the whippings . . . the burning . . . the hanging by the wrists with the arms tied behinduntilyour-shoudersdislocate . . .

Daria present or not, Prokopchenko leaned over and vomited on the floor.

"I can't let that happen," he said. "No . . . not to me. That can't be allowed."

Why did I come down here? What was I thinking? In his terror, Prokopchenko's mind went fuzzy and confused. For a moment he could barely remember what was going on above him. A hand grenade that shook the ship served as a reminder.

"Oh, yes," he said. "I remember now." He looked down at the control box he'd brought from a safe in his quarters. "Yes, I remember."

Control box in hand, Prokopchenko walked to the hatchway that led into the bombs. Twisting the latch he eased it open, then walked through.

"Valentin," Daria cried, "don't leave me!"

IV

Lawyers, Guns, and Money (SCIF), Camp Fulton, Guyana

Boxer was white faced as he reported to Stauer, the commander, which was to say the CEO, of M Day, Incorporated. They were both at least fairly good sized men, but Stauer topped Boxer by several inches.

"There's been a nuclear detonation in the Gulf of Thailand," Boxer said. "Nobody's claiming responsibility."

"Your contacts?"

"Won't say a word. Not a word. And I think they know who's responsible. This is . . . worrisome, Wes. I mean really worrisome. I'm scared. I knew things were bad, but . . ."

"Yeah, whole other order of bad. Can we do anything about it?"

Boxer shook his head, saying, "Nothing I can think of."

"Then we worry about what we *can* fix."

The sound of hammer and saw was everywhere, a symphony of buzzing and banging, with accompaniment from the cement mixer chorus and the jackhammer percussion section. The natural sounds of bird, insect, and reptile had little chance to be heard, even had those creatures elected to stick around. Barring only the mosquitoes, they generally had not.

Little by little—aided by labor from Venezuelan prisoners of war; at least until the final reparations payments were made—Camp Fulton was rising from the ashes left in the wake of weeks of air strikes. Even down in the concrete-shrouded depths of Lawyers, Guns, and Money, sometimes one could feel the vibrations through the ground and air.

Rising, however, wasn't quite the same thing as risen. The place was still largely a ruin, and would remain so for some months. Most of the troops were in tents, plus a few shacks and shanties. It said something of the corporation's degree of organization and discipline, that those temporary shelters were at least dressed right and covered down, close by their ruined former barracks and offices.

The corporation, which is to say, "the regiment," was in better shape, but by no means in good shape. Casualties had been severe, and in the worst hit units, crippling. They'd ended up by losing almost all their air assets, most of their little combat and amphibious flotilla, a frightful number of armored vehicles, and—between killed and seriously wounded—almost fifteen hundred men; which was more than a quarter of their starting strength.

One does not take on a major regional power with a single regiment and not pay for it . . . exorbitantly.

And yet the boys are happier than I've ever seen them, thought the Regimental Sergeant Major, RSM Joshua, as his boots clicked and clacked up the corridor's bare concrete floor, between the bunker's entrance and the major conference room. He spent most of his time in among the troops, after all—judging, gauging. Except for First Battalion—the regiment's mechanized force, still hurt and bitter over the loss of their commander—everywhere he'd gone since the end of the war it had been nothing but bright white smiles shining from faces either tanned or naturally dark. *Then again, why shouldn't they be happy, and proud, too? We won, after all.*

Joshua found himself smiling, as well, not least with pride, as he turned the knob to the conference room, opened the door, and stepped in. As he did, he could *feel* the pride, right in there with no little fatigue, bordering on exhaustion.

About half the required people were there already. Among these very prompt ones were Lana Reilly, nee

Mendes, born a Jewish South African and late of Tel Aviv and *Tzahal*. Great with child and nearing her term, Lana was, by popular acclaim, commanding her late husband's First Battalion. She was no more comfortable with the one than she was with the other, but at this point had little real choice about either.

Lana glanced down and put protective hands over her distended belly.

Joshua caught the movement and the glance. When Lana raised her head and lowered her hands, he gave her a confident, co-conspirator wink. *You'll do fine*, the RSM thought. *The men worshipped your husband and, bitter and hurt or not, would die supporting you rather than let down the memory of him. And, if you're younger than most of your privates . . . so what? Received divinity counts for more than age. And, sister, you have done been* injected *with it.*

Joshua, himself, steel hair topping black, leathery skin, was well into his sixties. Indeed, most of the regiment, or at least that portion of it made up of Americans and Europeans, were pretty long in the tooth.

Joshua's eyes left Lana Reilly and swept the room. There was Chavez—no relation to the late and unlamented Hugo Chavez—head of the regimental recruiting detachment, looking grimly and intently over some spreadsheet or other. Chavez's normally highly intelligent face was drawn and weary.

Yeah, thought the RSM, *I don't know for sure where we're going to make good our losses from either, let alone expand to the almost ten thousand men Stauer and Boxer are thinking of.*

On one side of Chavez sat the Adjutant, DeWitt, while the other flank was held by Dr. Scott Joseph, the chief medico of the regiment. Both stared just as intently at Chavez's spreadsheet as he did, himself. Lahela Corrigan, Comptroller's office, "she whose smile lights up the jungle," looked over Chavez's shoulder at the same information.

"No, sir; we can't afford anything like that," she said, definitively. "Not long term; not even with Venezuela's reparations payments."

Chavez scowled, even as Joseph deflated and DeWitt turned away.

"What's the problem, gentlemen," Joshua asked, taking a seat at the long mahogany conference table, opposite the other four.

"We need to add about six thousand, five hundred people to the rolls," Chavez explained as his fingers absently drummed the spreadsheet. "Guyana just doesn't have them; it's neither that populous, nor does their culture turn out huge numbers of prime military material. And if we actually found whatever Guyana does have, and tried to recruit them, this place wouldn't even run in the half-assed fashion it does. Not after the divergence of all that human capital."

DeWitt shook his head. "And we can't recruit any substantial numbers of Latins. They're not bad soldiers, properly trained, but we're talking *highly* incompatible cultures, and that's even worse because we just stomped the shit out of one of their sister countries."

"Even worse than that, Sergeant Major," said Lahela, "by our own rules we'd end up paying more for the Latins than we pay the locals, as long as the cost of living increment of pay is indexed to home country. That would be *bad* internal politics.

"And if we tried to fill the new table of organization with Americans and Euros, we'd just go broke, because their pay is *also* indexed to the cost of living in their home countries."

Joshua thought, with exasperation, *Officers! And the bloody warrants are not better.*

"Look north," he said. "There are a bunch of islands out in the Caribbean with economies that aren't a lot better off than Guyana's, and have similar cultures. Maybe even look as far as Belize, which is dirt poor, or along the Carib coast of Panama and Costa Rica which, just like the islands and here, are mostly descended from English-speaking slaves. Just like me," the RSM added with a smile.

"I have it on very good authority," said Doc Joseph, "that you are descended from some African who wandered north to Egypt and enlisted in the legions, eventually rising to senior centurion."

"Both sides, I suspect," the RSM said, agreeably, "since my mother was even more of a hardass than my father."

"The other Caribbeans; they decent military material?" Doc Joseph asked.

"Some are; some aren't," Joshua replied, with a shrug. "But I'll tell you, one of the finest soldiers I ever met in my life was a black, English-speaking, *Colonense* from Panama. And, if that fails, look to South Africa for Zulus or Zimbabwe for Matabeles. Or both. And most of them speak English, too."

He turned his attention back to Chavez, gesturing with a waving finger. "Between the Caribbean coastal areas, the poorer islands, and some Latins, plus—if we have to go that far—Zulus and Matabele, you can find your six and a half thousand. And our prestige in the Carib has grown to amazing heights. I don't know if it has in southern Africa but it wouldn't surprise me.

"Failing all that, the Indian Army discharges on the order of three thousand or so Gurkhas a year. Be willing to bet some of those would like to sign on, given the chance, and we don't have to pay them like we do the ex-British Army Gurkhas we have."

"As for some Latins, Colombia's internal war is winding down, while their per capita income isn't huge, so it wouldn't upset the pay index much. And I'd be very surprised if they weren't just tickled pink that we stomped the shit out of the Venezuelans."

"That means a major split of my recruiting organization," Chavez said doubtfully. "I'll need more people. Do you think the boss will buy it?"

"Count on it," the RSM answered, with utter certainty. Then, smiling as if at a secret, he told Lahela, "And we can afford more than you might think. Why do we need so many by the way?"

Warrant Officer Marc Tyrrell—from Marketing, which mean, in effect, Future Threats—spoke up then, from one of the chairs lining the wall. "Well . . . Sergeant Major, there's been some trouble for some time, down in Mexico. Now it seems to be spreading north fast."

★AFTERWORD★

Usual disclaimers: Read this at your own risk. If you trend left—or libertarian, for that matter—and you read this, and your head explodes, it's on you; you have been warned. Note that you didn't pay anything extra for it and you don't have to read it. Admit, in advance, that if you whine about it you can only be whining because it's here for others to read. And then go look in the mirror and ask yourself if you're quite as committed to free thought and inquiry as you thought you were.

Further note that, unlike some, I have no interest in doing your heavy thinking for you. This little piece isn't dispositive, nor do I intend that it be. It is mostly a set of hints, clues, and directions of places to look. Taking the hints and running with them? Following the direction to some place in the conceptual universe? Reading the clues? That's all on you. At most, this is a loose framework around which you may, perhaps, build something useful for yourself, once you start looking at and past the hints and clues.

Finally, remember the difference between a true believer and a true disbeliever. Rejecting someone else's fantasy makes you the latter, not the former. And you should be proud of yourself if you are.

Intellectually Challenged, Part I

So, you wanted to know if I *really* think the world's going to be as bad as I present it in the COUNTDOWN series? Short answer: Hell, no; I think it's going to get much, much worse than that. I'm just showing the early stages, when fighting the descent into barbarism is still possible, and brave men and women are still trying. They may not win, and the odds, frankly, are stacked against them. At some point in time, even the bravest get tired of slamming their heads into brick walls. That, or they die.

Moreover, most of the dismal and depressing background in this series is already visible, in proto form, at least, in the world we live in, today. Give it a little time. Or you can just relax, because we probably don't have that much time.

But why are we crumbling? Read on.

> Anyone else could have told me this in advance,
> but I was blinded by theory.
> —Bertrand Russell

I'm often accused of being anti-intellectual, a charge to which I can only reply, "Guilty! And why are you saying that as if it were a *bad* thing?"

I make that reply, of course, largely for the outrage it causes.

Even so, we are where we are, and we're going where we're going, because of where we've been over the last couple of centuries. And where we are and we've been is in the age of the intellectual: Rousseau, Kant, Marx, Shelley, Sartre, and even Nussbaum, for example, on the one hand, and Lenin, Mussolini, Stalin, Hitler, Mao, and Pol Pot, on the other. ("What? Hitler? Stalin? Mussolini? Intellectuals?" Oh, *absolutely*. The only real difference between the last six and the first is that the last were simply more effective at bringing their dreams to life, at remaking the world in their image, than the first six were or are.)

In any case, that outraged charge of anti-intellectualism seems to me to be a bit confused and misguided. You see, it springs from the notion that intellectuals are, and intellectualism is, inherently and always intelligent and that to be against either is to be pro-stupidity.

Are intellectuals intelligent? Always? Reliably? Enough to bet your future and your children's on? I'd suggest not.

One example: Jean Paul Sartre once—in 1935, I think it was—visited Nazi Germany. Upon his return he pronounced that he could see no difference between Nazi Germany and Republican France. Sartre also famously said, "We were never so free as under the German occupation." Now, while I'm not a strong Francophile, it seems to me that there were a few nontrivial differences there to be seen between Nazi Germany and Republican France, as well as between France under its own rule and under Nazi rule, by anyone with eyes to see and a brain to process the information. How bright did one have to be to see them?

And yet Sartre—an intellectual darling of the twentieth century—could not see them. This was intelligence?

Nonsense. While there are intelligent intellectuals, surely, this *kind* of intellectualism is the opposite of intelligent. It is profoundly unintelligent, as any mode of thought must be considered unintelligent that reasons only within the brainpan, that rejects objective truth for things the thinker desperately wants to believe are true.

Rather than burden the reader with more examples, let me suggest a couple of lines of inquiry you can take for yourself. Go think hard upon Marx's insistence on there being a progressive income tax, and match that against what control over the means of production actually means. See how intelligent you find that disconnect. Similarly, turn to Rousseau's *A Discourse on Inequality* and ask yourself how probable it was that the first to declare ownership over property merely bluffed his neighbors, as opposed to credibly *threatening* them.

In any case, when you get through those little exercises, you might come to agree with me that the case for granting a presumption of intelligence to go with the title of intellectual is, perhaps, something less than airtight.

Let's be charitable, though. Anyone can be wrong, on occasion; it's only human. But how about a studied unwillingness to learn?

> I remember very vividly, a few months after the famous pacifist resolution at the Oxford Union, visiting Germany and having a talk with a prominent leader of the young Nazis. He was asking about this pacifist motion and I tried to

explain it to him. There was an ugly gleam in his eye when he said, "The fact is that you English are soft." Then I realized that the world enemies of peace might be the pacifists.

—Robert Bernays, Liberal MP,
House of Commons, 1934

Another part of intelligence is ability to learn, to include learning the things that are unpleasant. Contemplate the phenomenon of pacifism, clearly an intellectual doctrine, though, of course, there are strong pacifist streams in a number of religions, too, as well as religions—Jainism, say—that are entirely pacifistic.

I'm here to talk about intellectualism, though, not religions. I'll leave them aside with the observation that, to the extent they're unworldly, that they expect their judgment and reward in the hereafter, and scorn the material world of the day, they are, at least, internally consistent and have nothing of major principle that they really can learn. It's already set in stone for them, graven articles of faith, and contrary temporal facts are irrelevant.

But what about the intellectual and secular pacifist?

Pacifism's been around about as far back as we can see in history. Even so, it really got its start, in any big way, as a result of the Great War. You can understand—it's not at all hard to understand—how pacifism got that big shot in the arm: Millions dead, millions more disabled and disfigured for life, entire landscapes ruined, cities blasted and crumbled, the Earth poisoned—in places it's still poisoned—the economies essentially bankrupt, and over four years of waste almost beyond imagining, and all of that for a lousy cause and a poor resolution, with subsequent revelations that most of the wartime propaganda was lies, thus adding insult to injury.

I'm not a pacifist, not even a little bit, but, you know, I could almost see myself becoming a pacifist, if I'd been through that and had no contrary factors to weigh. Sadly, however, and I do mean sadly, there are now, and have been since at least 1939, contrary factors to weigh.

We may doubt just how much the Oxford Pledge, that "In no circumstances will this house fight for its King and country," really swayed Nazi Germany or Fascist Italy. One suspects very little. It didn't have to. It was not primarily a cause, but a symptom of the pacifism that swept the United Kingdom and France—to a degree the United States, too—following the Great War.

It was that pacifism that caused France to acquiesce in Nazi Germany's reoccupation of the Rhineland. It was that that caused Britain and France to acquiesce in the Anschluss between Germany and Austria. Pacifism saw the Sudetenland occupied, and then the rest of Czechoslovakia gobbled up or severed away. One suspects that the cultivated unaggressive, nonbelligerent, nonviolent attitude was at least in good part responsible for the most welcome break Germany got, during and after the invasion of Poland, up until the invasion of Denmark and Norway, and their assault on the west, in 1940. Too, it was at least a factor in American isolationism.

Sixty million or so dead later, most of the world had learned. Yet the pacifist intellectual never did. Though Bertrand Russell bounced around quite a bit after the war, he ultimately ended up pretty much where he'd started, having apparently learned nothing he could accept from the events of 1939-1945. Perhaps . . . even probably, he never could have learned, because learning would have meant for him, and for the intellectual pacifist, generally, profound personal unhappiness at having to give up his fantasy. The pacifist still believes, despite the vast and compelling historic evidence to the contrary, that pacifism—though it can only be locally, hence dangerously, applied—is inherently and universally moral.

Of course, the Second World War was not the only refutation of pacifism out there. Contemplate the Moriori people who inhabited the Chatham Islands. Total pacifists by the command of their (dare I say it? I dare; I dare.) intellectual king; when eight- or nine-hundred Maori showed up in 1835, the Moriori were conquered, killed, enslaved and *eaten*. The few survivors were forbidden by their conquerors to have children together and thus was their existence as a people effectively extinguished.

In their defense, the Moriori really weren't given a lot of time to learn, so rapid was their destruction. But the modern, intellectual, secular pacifist? What's his or her excuse? Why haven't they learned? How can that failure to learn be considered intelligent? And if the rest of us haven't learned or won't learn from pacifism's grotesque and murderous misdiagnosis prior to 1939, and its continuing fraud *cum* idiocy after 1945, how unintelligent would we be?

For those who subscribe to this view, the "manufacture of consent" metaphor gives them a clear conscience to undertake the wholesale reeducation of the deluded masses in order to get them to see their true good, which—no surprise—can be secured only by following the dictates of their intellectual superiors, whose capacity to think independently is proven by their rejection of all traditional and local values and their adoption of the ideal of rational cosmopolitanism.

—Lee Harris, *The Cosmopolitan Illusion*

I've dumped on Martha Nussbaum's "Patriotism and Cosmopolitanism" before, in *Carnifex*. Perhaps I owe her an apology. (If so, it would be a debt that rested very lightly on my shoulders, to be sure.) Not that I think I pegged it precisely wrongly, mind you, but—*mea culpa*—I don't think I really understood what was going on there, at the core of the thing, at the time I wrote. I think I do now. And here it is, perhaps in somewhat convoluted form. (But then, we're talking about some convoluted minds and trains of thought, so you'll have that.)

First, a question: What is happiness? (Oh, stop the Genghis Khan quotes. That's, at most, how to get it, if you're a fairly odd sort, not what it is.) The pshrinks and philosophers seem to differ. Some say it's an emotion. Others disagree. No one seems to disagree, however, that, as a minimum, happiness is a derivative of emotions, an emotional state. Just shunt that off to one side of your mind for a bit, but we will get back to it. I presented it here, early, just to give you a little time to re-assimilate the concept.

On to "Patriotism and Cosmopolitanism"! More specifically, what I intend to do is show how Nussbaum's thesis is objective nonsense and then postulate how it came to be that a well educated and eloquent woman could put forth and maintain such nonsense with a straight face.

At the center of Nussbaum's idea, I think, is the notion that logic demands that, once we've drawn the circles of nationality around ourselves, we must—having been exclusive, the once—continue to draw ever narrower circles. This is false, as I alluded to in *Carnifex*. Whatever the logic might be in a closed system, one with no external threat, we don't live in that system. The system is, indeed, a fantasy. It would be intensely illogical—if survival and freedom have any value—to draw circles so narrow that successful collective defense becomes impossible. Just ask the Arabs, who usually have weak nations, but who have perhaps the most closely drawn circles in the world, how well they've been doing against the Israelis for the last six decades.

Yes, that means that, in the real, the non-intellectual, world, we do not necessarily draw those circles narrowly because, logically, factually, objectively, and *intelligently*, we might well end up being kicked out of our homes if we did.

Also, as I mentioned, in *Carnifex*, what does actually happen when national boundaries are erased, or at least weakened, in a theoretically closed system without an actual, admitted or perceived external threat, is that, *contra* Nussbaum, *then* people start drawing narrower circles. Scots and Welsh, for example, start ceasing to be Britons and begin to revert to much narrower identities, as the EU becomes more powerful and the nation states of

Europe weaken. It is very unclear that the European identity the EU would like to foster will ever get out of the starting gate, except among a very few.

Similarly, no useful pan-African identity has come from sub-Saharan Africa's weak states. Less still does a pan-human identity develop, in a place without those nationalist circles. No, no, there the narrow circle of the tribe matters.

So if logic demands it, why doesn't it happen? Why, indeed, does the opposite happen? It's really quite simple: Logic has little to do with it. Rather, the driving force, the one Nussbaum is loathe to admit to, is not logic, it is emotion. And reason's part in this is only to realize, accept, analyze, and deal with the fact that emotion rules, not a distant logic, and especially not one with false premises, *ab initio*. Anything else would be illogical.

It is obvious. It is intelligently applied emotion—not cold logic, except for the logic of defense against a threat—that makes people draw the largest circles to which they can feel an emotional tie.

So why can't a woman as well educated, eloquent, and apparently logically reasoning as Martha Nussbaum see that? I can't be certain, of course, but I can offer a suggestion as to what I think was going on. I think it was a multistep process: 1) she was projecting her logic on to the rest of mankind, despite copious evidence that mankind is not logical, 2) she was simultaneously denying our right to be, and our existence as, primarily emotionally driven beings, 3) despite the probability approaching certainty that a people which loses its sense of nationhood will fragment into weak and possibly warring factions, and high likelihood that such a people will become, thereafter, subjects, or perhaps slaves, of those who did not lose their sense of nationhood, she would still have us do it, because, 4) the attempt would make her happy, which is to say, it would engage her emotions in a personally satisfying way.

In other words, a) I doubt that even she, herself, realizes that she is as emotionally driven as the rest of us poor, ignorant 'eathens, and that that drives everything she says beyond the merely trivial, while b) though she does so differently from the way some other noted and notable intellectuals use others—financially and sexually—she has no more care than they do for what would happen to the rest of us, in the real world, should we be so silly as to follow her advice, so long as our doing so makes her happy.

That, friends, is sociopathy. We do not exist as independent, morally significant, individual beings to Nussbaum anymore that we would to Sartre, Shelley, or Marx. Our function is merely to make them happy.

If I am right in this—and I frankly do not see any other way for a clever person like Nussbaum to put forth such a factually fraudulent argument—can we reasonably call making that kind of misprediction, maintaining it in the face of copious evidence to the contrary, and that kind of lack of personal insight, truly intelligent? Again, glib and eloquent I readily concede, but intelligence is more than these.

> One has to belong to the intelligentsia to believe things like that: no ordinary man could be such a fool.
>
> —George Orwell

★ ★ ★

One of the ways to tell if a philosophy is inherently illegitimate is to ask and answer certain questions, the answers to which either must be historically and universally valid, or must postulate some profound change in the human condition such as to allow them to be valid in the future even if not in the past. These include: "Would the philosophy depend for its continued existence and prosperity on a particular kind of society, which society is its antithesis? Would it undermine the defense of the very kind of society it requires to continue to exist and prosper? Having undermined its home society, would it need universality to continue to exist and prosper while having no credible way of attaining that universality?"

My typical reader will probably understand fully how those three apply to both pacifism and cosmopolitanism. But let me give one that that some of my readers are likely to choke on: Ayn Rand's objectivism, coupled with her rejection of altruism.

How would objectivism have dealt with Nazism or Stalinism, in the past? It would self-evidently have failed; only the *intensely* stupid could imagine Rand's self-centered egotists dealing effectively with either the altruistically motivated Wehrmacht or the Red Army. And don't bother with, "Well, that just shows that altruism is inherently evil." That's simply nonsense; like a firearm, altruism is morally neutral, neither good nor evil except in respect to the uses to which it is put. (Yes, this does mean that generally pro-gun objectivists who make the claim have latched on to the moral and intellectual equivalent of the gun grabbers' argument for gun control and confiscation.)

In any case, what Rand was doing there was something profoundly intellectual, and profoundly unintelligent, fully equal to the stupidities inherent in pacifism and cosmopolitanism. She forgot that there was a real world outside her brainpan and beyond the limits of her fantasy, which world contained people whose emotions, whose altruism, could be harnessed for purposes inimical to Rand's own, and which she could neither convert, defend against, nor conquer.

You can call this intelligent intellectualism if you want. But why would you?

I'll be continuing the conversation in the next volume of the Countdown series, *Criminal Enterprise*.

★GLOSSARY★

APERS—Anti-personnel

AT—Anti-tank

Barangay—Tagalog word meaning an administrative
district, a neighborhood, or a village,
similar to Barrio.

C-4—An RDX based plastic explosive. Among other
uses it forms the filling of a claymore mine.
It has a very distinctive, plastic cum solvent,
smell to it.

Camp Fulton—A military installation in Guyana,
main base of M Day, Inc, though there are a
number of smaller satellite bases for the
constituent battalions and squadrons. Named
for Master Sergeant (retired) Robert "Buckwheat"
Fulton, who was killed in action in Africa during
the initial operation.

CH-750A—sport plane with very short take off
and landing abilities

Chemlight—Also Lightstick. A plastic tube with two chemicals inside, one in a glass vial, which, when broken, produces cool light for a limited period of time. Some produce light beyond the human visual spectrum

Clacker—The detonating device for a claymore directional anti-personnel mine

Claymore—A directional anti-personnel mine. There are many broadly similar versions made around the world.

Daisy Chain—A series of explosive charges or claymores, connected by det cord, such that the explosion of one will set off all the others. Not a good place to be down range of. Oh, and curb your thoughts.

Datu—A traditional Moro title of nobility and authority.

Det Cord—Also "detonating cord." An explosive, formed inside a thin plastic covering, that is about the size of, and sometimes strung like, clothesline. Useful for having one explosion set off another.

Dustoff—Aeromedical evacuation.

Eland—A light armored car, French designed, South African built. Different models have different armaments. M Day's are all either

90mm cannon armed, or have had the turrets removed to clear space to load up infantry.

FSB—Federal Security Service; the successor to the Soviet Era's KGB.

Gun Pod—Also minigun-pod. A self contained, generally aerodynamically sound, container, meant for attaching to an aircraft, and holding a machine gun or multi-barreled minigun. Some gun pods carry light cannon.

Gurkha—Also Gorkha. Nepalese-born or descended mercenaries serving in the British Army, in small numbers, the Indian Army, in huge numbers, and as sundry security detachments around Asia. Amazingly brave, tough, resilient, and aggressive soldiers, especially considering that they spring from a Hindu culture loaded with charming and inoffensive people.

HEAT—High Explosive Anti Tank; a shaped charge warhead.

Kalis—A kris, a (usually) wavy knife or sword, traditional among the peoples of Indonesia, Brunei, southern Thailand, and the Moros of the Philippines.

Kano—Filipino slang for American. No necessary prejudice involved.

LCM—Landing Craft Mechanized. The Regiment has obsolescent LCM-6s.

Lightstick—See Chemlight

M Day, Inc.—AKA, "The regiment." A private military corporation, begun as a single use, ad hoc grouping, to effect a particular hostage rescue, the members mostly decided to stay together and keep in the business. Besides hostage rescues, they engage in various other military and quasi military actions, around the globe, along with running a jungle training school at their main base in Guyana.

Marsden Matting—See PSP

MI-28—A highly capable Russian-built helicopter gunship, analogous to an American AH-64 Apache.

Minigun Pod—See Gun Pod

Mufti—Civilian dress

No-Such-Agency—NSA, the National Security Agency. They don't really deny that they exist anymore.

NVG—Night Vision Goggles

ODA—Operational Detachment Alpha, an "A Team," a twelve man grouping of special operations soldiers

Out—When speaking over the radio, a term
    indicating the conversation is finished.
    "I have nothing else to say."

Over—When speaking over the radio, a term
    meaning, "I'm done talking now; your turn."

PASGT—Personal Armor System, Ground Troops;
    the American military body armor that
    started the modern trend toward heavily
    armored soldiers.

Pecheneg—A Russian light machine gun, modified from
    an earlier model, the PKM. It is M Day's standard
    light and general purpose machine gun.

PFM-1—A small, lightweight, scatterable anti-personnel
    mine. Very politically incorrect. The PFM-1S is
    slightly more PC, since it has a roughly timed, and
    somewhat unreliable, self destruct feature.

POW—Prisoner of War. Sometimes EPW,
    for enemy prisoner of war.

PSP Perforated Steel Planking. A material, the
    sections of which are designed to be hooked
    together, to form a temporary runway.

PSYOP—Psychological Operations. Think leaflets and
    loudspeakers, printers, presses, and propaganda.

PT—Physical training.

Push—When discussing radios, either the specific frequency being used or the coded sequence of frequency hops, if using frequency hopping.

Roger—Normally, when speaking over a radio, a term meaning, "I understand." As a practical matter, military sorts use the expression all the time, in normal, face to face, conversation to convey the same meaning. A general affirmative, often heard in the form of "Roger that shit."

RP—Received Pronunciation. An upper crust British accent, largely unknown in working class circles and increasingly rare even among the upper middle class.

RPG—Pocket Propelled Grenade or the launcher that fires one.

RPV—Remotely Piloted Vehicle, often called UAV, for unmanned aerial vehicle.

SAPI Plates—Bulletproof, more or less, usually ceramic, inserts that go in special pockets in body armor.

Schrecklichkeit—A German word meaning terror or frightfulness.

Searcher—An Israeli-built Remotely Piloted Vehicle

SITREP—Situation Report. If given over the radio, in the form of, "SITREP, over," it means, "Tell me what the hell is going on, succinctly."

Spec Ops/Special Operations—(Author's definition) Typically small unit actions, the operational, strategic, propaganda, or geo-political importance of which, and the price of failure in which, are sufficiently high as to justify the early commitment and organization, of extraordinary human, financial, and material resources, and special training of the individuals and organizations concerned.

Strela—Any of a number of different models of Russian-made, shoulder launched, anti-aircraft missiles.

Tagalog—With English, an official language of the Philippines.

Thermal—Also "Thermal Imager." A night or limited visibility vision device which, instead of amplifying ambient light, picks up differentials in heat.

Thermobaric—An explosive that takes its oxygen from the surrounding air. This not only gives more explosive power for a given weight, it tends to suffocate whoever the blast, heat, and lung-destroying post-explosion vacuum do not kill. FAE, Fuel Air Explosive, is a form of thermobaric.

Tore—Filipino for tower; in the case of rum, a tall round bottle.

Tranzi—Transnational Progressive(s). The shortened version is believes to have been coined by one David Carr, a lawyer in the United Kingdom. Think: UN and EU bureaucrats, do-gooders who do quite well for themselves, left wing academics, and very spoiled two and three year olds, never quite weaned from mother's breasts.

Tzahal—The Israeli Army

Unass the AO—Move away from the area of operations. Similar to, "Get the Hell out of Dodge."

Vampire—Also RPG-29. Also Vampir. A Russian-made, shoulder fired, anti tank weapon. It is arguable whether the Vampire is a rocket launcher or a recoilless smoothbore, since the propelling charge burns out completely while still in the tube. Very nice.

Vympel—A Russian special operations unit, under the FSB and charged with anti-terrorism and nuclear safety operations.

Whisper—Where a weapon is indicated, a rifle, generally suppressed, firing a large heavy bullet over a weak charge to drive it at less than the speed of sound. About as quiet as one can get, while still killing someone at a range of six hundred meters or more.

Wilco—When speaking over a radio, a term meaning, "I will comply."

Zodiac—An inflatable boat.

★★★
Acknowledgements,
in no particular order:
★★★

Yolanda, who puts up with me, Toni Weisskopf, the late Jim Baen, John Ringo, Dr. Scott Joseph, Dr. Rob Hampson, Ken Uecker, Dr. Alfredo Figueredo, Mike Rollin, Neil Frandsen, Michael Gilson, Tim Arthur, Charlie Prael, Chris French, Ori Pomerantz, Leo Ross (RIP), Arun, Ron Friedman, Tom Wallis, Tim Lindell, John Raines, the Kriegsmarine contingent of the Bar (you know who you are), Buz Ozburn, David Burkhead, Alen Ostanek, Mike Sayer, Barry Lowe, Steve St. Onge, Dave Helma, Mark van Groll, Peter Gold, Sergeant Major (Ret.) Henrik Kiertzner, Doc (who's in the Rockpile by now and doesn't need the OPSEC issue), Ben-David Singleton, Dan Kemp, Wendy Stewart, Cpt Andrew Stocker, Mrs. Tootie Poulter, and the cover artist, the great Kurt Miller.

If I missed anybody, chalk it up to premature senility.

The Following is an excerpt from:

MONSTER HUNTER LEGION

LARRY CORREIA

Available from Baen Books
September 2012
hardcover

❧Chapter 1❧

Most of the things Las Vegas has to offer to its hordes of tourists don't hold much appeal for me. Having been an accountant, I am way too good at math to enjoy gambling. As a former bouncer, I'm not big on the party scene. Strip clubs? Happily married to a total babe who could kill me from a mile away with her sniper rifle, so no thanks. Sure, there were plenty of other things to do in Vegas, like over-priced shows, taking your picture with Elvis, and that sort of thing, but as a professional Monster Hunter, I'm pretty jaded when it comes to what constitutes *excitement*.

However, there is one thing in Las Vegas' extensive, sparkling arsenal of tourist-from-their-dollars-separating weapons that I'm absolutely powerless to resist, and that is a kick ass buffet.

The flight in had taken forever and I was starving. So first thing upon arrival at our hotel, I had called up every other hungry member of Monster Hunter International that I could find and we'd set out to conquer the unsuspecting hotel buffet.

This was a business trip. Normally *business* for us meant that there was some horrible supernatural thing in dire need of a good killing, but not this time. Las Vegas was the site of the first annual *International Conference of Monster Hunting Professionals*.

The conference was a big deal. Sponsored by a wealthy organizer, the ultra-secret ICMHP 1 had been billed as an opportunity to network with other informed individuals, check out the latest gear and equipment, and listen to experts. There had never been an event like this before. Every member of MHI that could get away from work had come, and though we were the biggest company in the business, we were still outnumbered five to one by representatives of every other rival Monster Hunting company in the world. In addition there were representatives from all of the legitimate supernaturally-attuned organization and government agencies, all come together here to learn from each other. Despite just oozing with all of that professionalism, we had all taken to calling it *ick-mip* for short.

The conference started tomorrow morning, which for most of the Hunters meant a chance to party or gamble the night away, but for me, it was buffet time. As a very large, high-intensity lifestyle kind of guy, I burn a lot of calories. I may lose at the gambling table, but I never lose at the dinner table. Plus the food at the upscale establishments tended to be above average, and since Hunters made good money, my days of eating at the dumpy places were over. Besides, all of the ICMHP guests were staying at the new, ultra-swanky, not even totally open to the public yet, Last Dragon hotel. The Last

Dragon's buffet had actual master chefs from around the world, and was supposed to be one of the best new places to eat in town. The internet had said so, and who was I to argue with the Zagat survey?

My team had just gotten back from a grueling mission and most had simply wanted to crash. I'd only been able to coerce Trip Jones and Holly Newcastle into coming, though Holly had complained about watching her figure and said that she was going to *take it easy*. When it came to food I had no concept of easy. Despite his aversion to being around humans, Edward had been tempted by my wild tales of hundreds of yards of glorious meats, none of which needed to be chased down and stabbed to death first. However, his older brother and chieftain, Skippy, had forbidden it. Turns out that it is really difficult to eat in public with a face mask on. It is tough being an orc.

There had been an incoming flight due shortly with a couple of Newbies onboard, and Milo Anderson had volunteered to stay and be their ride to the hotel. Earl Harbinger had said these particular recruits were especially talented, so they'd earned the field trip. Lucky them. My Newbie field trip had been storming the *Antoine-Henri* and fighting wights.

Last but not least for my team, my lovely wife Julie had said she was tired, encouraged me not to hurt myself at dinner—she knows how I can sometimes be over-enthusiastic for things that come in serving sizes larger than my head—and then went to bed early. She had been feeling a little under the weather during the trip.

After ditching our luggage, which mostly consisted of

armor and guns, we'd snagged a few of the other Hunters staying on our floor. Most of the floors of the Last Dragon hotel was still in the finishing stages of construction so the place hadn't even had its grand opening yet. Officially, the hotel wasn't ready yet, but since ICMHP was supposed to be secret anyway, it was a perfect place for several hundred Hunters to stay, and the ICMHP organizers had even gotten us a killer discount. ICMHP would be the first ever event for its conference center, but luckily, the casino, shops, and—most important—restaurants were already open to the public.

"Wow . . ." Trip whistled as he looked down the endless food trays of the top-rated all-you-can-eat place on Earth. "That's one impressive spread." It really was. Lots of everything, cuisine from every culture, all of it beautiful, and the smells . . . They were absolutely mouth watering, and that wasn't just because I'd spent most of the day squeezed into a helicopter smelling avgas fumes and gun smoke, this place was awesome. "This is how Vikings eat in Viking heaven."

"Valhalla," Holly pointed out. "Viking heaven is called Valhalla."

"I know that," Trip answered. "Surprised you do though." It was a lame attempt at teasing her, since everyone present knew that Holly just worked the dumb blonde angle to manipulate people who didn't know her well enough to know that she was an encyclopedia of crafty monster eradication.

"Sure I do. I had this really sexy valkyrie costume one Halloween," Holly answered, completely deadpan. "The chainmail bikini was *so* hot . . . Though it did chafe." And then she started to describe it in graphic detail. Watching the always gentlemanly and borderline prudish Trip get too embarrassed to respond coherently was always fun for the whole team, but luckily for him the hostess called for Owen Pitt and party of ten, and seated us before it got too bad.

I'd managed to gather several other Hunters who hadn't been too distracted by the pretty flashing lights and promises of loose slots to forget dinner. The Haight brothers were from Team Haven out of Colorado, and though Sam was dead and Priest had been promoted to be their leader, they would always be called Team Haven. Cooper and my brother-in-law, Nate Shackleford, were from Paxton's team out of Seattle. Gregorius was from Atlanta and since the last time I'd seen him he'd decided to ditch his old military grooming standards and I had to compliment him on the quality of his lumberjack beard. My old buddy Albert Lee was stationed at headquarters in Alabama and he was always fun to hang out with. VanZant was a team lead out of California and Green was one of his guys. I'd worked with all of them at one point or another, either from Newbie training, battling Lord Machado's minions at DeSoya caverns, or fighting under the alien insect branches of the Arbmunep.

The Last Dragon's buffet was in a large, circular, glass enclosure inside the casino's shopping mall. The whole place slowly rotated so that the view out the windows was constantly changing murals, gardens, and fountains. The diners got to watch as one story below us hundreds of consumers blew all their money on overpriced merchandise. It was kind of neat if you liked people-watching as much as I did. Inside the restaurant there were even ice sculptures and five different kinds of chocolate fountains.

After heaping food on our plates we took our seats. It had been a while since I'd seen most of these particular coworkers, and in short order my arm had been twisted into talking about the case we had wrapped up just that morning. In fact, my team hadn't even thought we'd be able to attend ICMHP at all, because we'd spent two fruitless weeks trolling the crappiest parts of Jackson, Mississippi looking for our monster. It was January, and we'd gotten rained on the whole time. Bagging that aswang at the last minute had been a stroke of luck, giving us an excuse to pack right up and hightail it to Las Vegas where we could be much warmer and dry for a bit. I like telling stories, but whenever I started exaggerating to make the monster even more disgusting Trip would correct me. He always was good at keeping me honest. Besides, since the damned thing had been an imported mutant Filipino vampire with a *proboscis*, you didn't need much hyperbole to make it gross. This was not the sort of dinner conversation that you would have with polite company.

MHI tended to be a noisy, boisterous, fun-loving bunch, and as you filled them with good food and drinks they just got louder. Soon, everyone else was cracking jokes and telling stories too, interrupted only by the constant trips back for more food. Green was skinny, and VanZant's nickname was "the hobbit" because he was maybe a stocky five foot four, but even our small Hunters had appetites, not to mention that Gregorius was about my size, so we were putting a hurting on the place.

However, as Nate pointed out, at seventy bucks a head, we were darn well going to get our money's worth. Luckily, they had seated us far enough to the side that we weren't bugging the other, more normal, patrons.

They had stuck together a few tables into a long rectangle for us. I was sitting at one end across from Green and next to VanZant. Green was bald, hyperactive, and had been a San Diego police officer before MHI had recruited him. I'd accidentally broken his collarbone back in Newbie training, but he'd never seemed to hold a grudge about it. Green was a scrapper, one of those men that wasn't scared of anything, so getting severely injured in training was no biggie. I'd lost count of how many beers he had drunk, and apparently he'd already hit the mini bar in his room before coming down. The waitress just kept the refills coming, because since we had to walk past slot machines to get out of this place, the management probably wanted their guests as incapable of making good decisions as possible. His boss, VanZant, just frowned as Green got into a noisy argument with bomb expert Cooper over the proper use of hand grenades.

VanZant was a courteous man, so he waited until there were several different conversations going on before leaning in to ask me quietly, "So how's Julie doing?"

The question was understandable. VanZant had been with Julie when she'd been injured during Hood's attack on our compound. He was one of the few who knew something about how she had survived, her lacerations sealed by the lingering magic of the Guardian, leaving only black lines where there had once been mortal wounds. "Pretty good. Mostly we don't think about it." Which wasn't true at all. The thought that she had been physically changed by magic from the Old Ones was always there, gnawing away at our peace of mind, but there wasn't much we could do about it.

VanZant's concern was evident. "Has there been any... change?"

He meant to the supernatural marks on my wife's neck and abdomen, reminders of things that should have killed her. "Still the same as before." The marks had saved Julie's life three times, from Koriniha's knife, a flying undead's claws, and even the fangs of her vampire mother, but there was no such thing as *gifts* when the Old Ones were concerned. Everything from them came with a price. We just didn't know what that price was going to be yet. "We've been trying to find more information about the Guardian, who he was, where the magic comes from, maybe even how to get rid of it, but no luck yet."

One of the Haights was telling a story about parking his truck on a blood fiend when the hostess led another big group into our section of the restaurant. There was a dozen of them, they were all male and all dressed the same, in matching tan cargo pants and tight black polo shirts that showed off that they all really liked to lift weights. Every last one of the newcomers was casually scanning the room for threats. It was obvious that the half of them that couldn't sit with their backs to the wall were made slightly uncomfortable by that fact.

They were Monster Hunters. A Hunter gives off a certain vibe, and these men had it. Wary, cocky, and tough, they were Hunters all right, they just weren't as *cool* as we were. VanZant scowled at the gold *PT Consulting* embroidered on the breast of every polo shirt. "Oh no…" he muttered. "Not these assholes."

"Friends of yours?" I whispered as the hostess seated them a few feet away. I noticed that most of them were studying us the same way we were studying them. Apparently my table gave off that Hunter vibe too. There was a little bit of professional curiosity and sizing up going on from both sides.

VanZant wasn't happy to see them. "They're a startup company headquartered in L.A. They've been around about a year. Loads of money, all the newest toys. They're professional, but…"

From the look on Green's face, he didn't like PT Consulting much either. He spoke a little louder than he probably should have. "Their boss is a real prick and they've been weaseling in on some of our contracts. They'll swipe your PUFF right out from under your nose if you aren't careful."

A few of them seemed to have overheard that, and there was some hushed conversation from the other table as they placed their drink orders. "Easy, Green," VanZant cautioned his hotheaded friend before turning back to me. "PT Consulting is prickly. They've got this *modern bushido*, code of the warrior culture going on. They take themselves real seriously. Their owner is a retired colonel who got rich doing contract security in Iraq. When he learned the real money was in PUFF, his company switched industries, lured away a bunch of MCB with better pay, and set up shop in my backyard."

"You don't sound like a fan…"

"He gives mercenaries a bad name, and MHI is mercenary and proud. I'd call him a pirate, but that's an insult to pirates."

"Prick works," Green supplied again. "Thieving pricks, the bunch of them."

I noticed a couple of angry scowls in our direction. They recognized us too. It probably didn't help that I was wearing a t-shirt with a big MHI Happy Face on it. *Oh well, not my problem.* I just wanted to enjoy my second plate of steak, sushi, and six species of shrimp.

The oldest of the PT men got up and approached my end of the table. He was probably in his early fifties, but built like a marathoner, sporting a blond buzz cut, and suntan lines from wearing shades. His mouth smiled, but his eyes didn't. "Well, if it isn't Monster Hunter International. What an unexpected pleasure to run into you gentlemen here. Evening, John."

VanZant nodded politely. "Armstrong."

Armstrong scanned down our table, sizing us up. Unlike his company, my guys were dressed randomly and casual, except for Cooper and Nate being dressed fancy so that the single young guys could try to pick up girls later, and the Haights looking like they were on their way to a rodeo. Armstrong saw Gregorius sitting toward the middle and gave a curt nod. "Hey, I know you from Bragg . . . Sergeant Gregorius, right? I didn't know you'd joined this bunch."

We had recruited Gregorius after the battle for DeSoya Caverns, where he'd been attached to the National Guard unit manning the roadblock. Apparently he knew Armstrong in a different professional capacity, but judging from the uncomfortable expression on Gregorius' face, he shared VanZant's opinion of the man. "Evening, Colonel . . . Wife didn't want me sitting around the house retired and bored. This sounded like fun."

Armstrong's chuckle was completely patronizing. "I didn't recognize you with that beard. You look like Barry White. Staying busy I hope," he said as he scanned over the rest of us. He paused when he got to me. I was pretty sure I'd never met him before, but I am rather distinctive looking and had developed a bit of a reputation in professional Monster Hunting circles, some of which was even factual. So it wasn't surprising to be recognized. "You're Owen Zastava Pitt, aren't you?"

"In the flesh."

"I'm Rick Armstrong." He said that like it should mean something. *Rick Armstrong.* Now that was a proper super hero secret identity name. "I'm CEO of PT Consulting." I stared at him blankly. I looked to Trip, but my friend shrugged. "PT Consulting…"

"Potato Tasting?" I guessed helpfully.

"No. It's—"

"Platypus Trampoline?"

"Paranormal Tactical," he corrected before I could come up with another.

"Nope." I shrugged. Armstrong seemed let down, but tried not to let it show. What did he expect? I was too busy battling the forces of evil to pay attention to every new competitor on the block. Julie took care of the marketing, I was the accountant. "Doesn't ring any bells."

"Oh, it will." He smiled that fake little smile again. "I'm sure we'll have some teaming opportunities in the future."

I didn't know this Armstrong character, but something about him simply rubbed me the wrong way. Plus, VanZant's opinion was trusted, and if one of our team leads said that they were assholes, that was good enough for me. "You should leave me your card, you know, in case we're too busy doing something big and important and a little case pops up that we don't have time to pay attention to." I can be a fairly rude person when I just don't give a crap.

"Well, MHI is *established* . . ." Armstrong said, meaning *old*. So that was how it was going to be. "But we're the fastest growing Hunting company in the world. We've got experienced men, a solid business plan, financial backing, the best equipment, and top leadership."

"Nifty. I should buy some stock."

"Speaking of leadership, there's a rumor going around about MHI's." The way he said that sounded particularly snide.

"Oh?" I raised a single eyebrow. This conversation was cutting into my precious shrimp time. "What about our leadership?"

"Word is that Earl Harbinger's been off his game lately. I heard he disappeared for a few months, came back depressed and missing a finger. Rumor is that he had something to do with that incident up in Michigan. You know, that *mine fire,*" he made quote marks with his fingers, "that killed half a town in their sleep, or so the MCB said. I'd hate to think that was one of his cases that went bad."

Sure, Earl hadn't been the same since Copper Lake, but that was none of Armstrong's business. I didn't know all the details about what had happened in Michigan, but I knew enough to know that Earl wasn't *off his game,* he was *angry.* A government agency that he didn't want to name had put his girlfriend into indentured servitude.

"Maybe Harbinger's thinking about hanging it up? That would be *such* a shame. A real loss for our whole industry."

"I'll be sure to pass along your concern. Because, wow, if Earl Harbinger were to retire, who would men like you look to for inspiration?" I gave him a polite nod that I intended to say *shove off dirt bag.* "See you at the conference."

"Tomorrow then. Looking forward to it. I've got work to do. You boys have a nice supper." He went back to his table to say goodbye to his men. I swear half of them had to resist the urge to salute.

"I *hate* him so much," Gregorius said softly, but didn't elaborate further.

"Well, you do sorta look like Barry White," Cooper told him. He flinched when Gregorius thumped him in the arm.

Soon enough our conversations had picked back up, and if anything, were even louder than before. Milo called my cell to tell me that he would be here soon, and that he and some of the Newbies he'd picked up at the airport would be joining us for dinner. I'd met the crazy elf girl, Tanya, when she'd impersonated an elven tracker to tag along on one of our jobs. She and Edward had saved some kids that had blundered into a pocket dimension filled with telepathic fey monsters. She was the first elf MHI had ever hired, which I still wasn't convinced was entirely a smart move, but Milo assured me that she would easily be able to pass for human in public. The other Newbie was named Jason Lacoco, a name I recognized as the Briarwood Hunter Earl had recruited during the Copper Lake incident, but who I hadn't met yet. I told Milo I'd have the hostess pull up another table.

By the time I put my phone away, Green was telling a very animated and inappropriate story, and using a cream puff for special effects purposes. Most of my group was laughing loudly at him. The PT men were all stoically chewing, glaring his way occasionally. Apparently the modern warrior code meant you weren't supposed to carry on in such a manner in public.

I was filling plate number three with nachos, pot-stickers, and mozzarella sticks when Nate came up beside me. He had been sitting at the far end of the table, so had missed my chat with the PT leader. "Hey, Z. I need your help with the black shirt dudes."

"What do you mean?"

"They keep eyeballing us."

"It's because we're so damned handsome, Nate. They just can't help themselves."

"You say so, but they seem *angry*."

I looked over as Green downed another beer, belched loudly, and then wiped his mouth with the back of his hand. I couldn't hear what he was saying, but Trip seemed distressed and everyone else was amused. Trip, ever the voice of reason, seemed to be trying to get Green to quiet down. VanZant's seat was empty. He'd probably gone to the bathroom and left our drunken vice cop momentarily unsupervised. A few of the PT consultants were looking fairly belligerent at this point. "Is Green trying to pick a fight?"

Nate sighed. "He's still mad about a job his team did all the dangerous work for, but PT swooped in and claimed the PUFF at the last minute. Green was personally out twenty grand and one of their team almost got drowned by a giant squid in the process."

"So you don't need my help with Pontoon Tactical, or whatever their name is, you need help controlling some of our men. Look, why don't you go tell Green to chill out? You are a Shackleford. This is your family's company." I know Earl was expecting a lot from Nate, as he was the one expected to carry on the Shackleford family name. That was a lot of pressure, especially since his big sister pretty much ran the nuts and bolts of the operation already. Nate was tough and enthusiastic, but still trying to figure out his place in the company. The tall young man looked sheepishly at his shoes. "But you won't . . . Because you don't want to come off as the boss's grandson and annoying wet blanket on everyone's good time . . ."

"Reverse nepotism is a hell of a thing. I'm still low man on the totem pole. I say anything and I'll just come off as a whiner trying to throw Julie's weight around."

"If you imply Julie is heavy, she will shoot you." I knew that wasn't what he meant. Besides, Julie was in great shape. My wife was a 5'11" Amazon warrior southern belle art-chick sniper. "And you know she doesn't miss much."

"You know what I mean," Nate pleaded.

"Ask Holly. Nobody will mess with her."

"Are you kidding? I think she finds the whole thing

amusing. Please, Z, I don't know all these guys very well, but they respect you."

"I'm no team leader." Some of us had headquarters' duties above and beyond being on Hunter teams, but as far as the actual MHI org chart went, I was only the finance manager. Which put me at about the same level as our receptionist, only Dorcas had been around longer and was scarier.

"You're also the God Slayer."

Valid point. Travelling to another dimension and blowing up a Great Old One did earn you some cool points with this bunch. "Leadership sucks sometimes, Nate. You're going to have to get used to it." His older sister would have simply kicked everyone into line, but the youngest Shackleford hadn't found his groove yet. He'd been a Hunter longer than I had, but it was tough to grow up in the shadow of legends. "Alright, fine. Just let me grab some more fish sticks."

By the time I'd plopped back down in my seat, I could tell that Green had clearly egged the two nearest PT Hunters on to the point that they were itching for a confrontation. The man certainly had a gift. I could sense there was ugly in the air. Normally that wouldn't bother me too much, but we were supposed to be professionals, we were outnumbered, and I was pretty sure that I recognized one of the PT men from watching Ultimate Fighting on TV.

"Z, that one dude keeps looking at me!" Green exclaimed, voice slurred. "He must think I'm sexy!" Then he looked over at the Ultimate Fighter and licked a cream puff suggestively.

The Ultimate Fighter got up quickly, and Green, being stupidly fearless at this point, did too. Trip intercepted Green and one of the PT Hunters grabbed the Ultimate Fighter's arm. Me and my tray of goodies stepped between the two sides as I tried to play peacemaker. "Whoa! Easy, man." He bumped me and I got Thai peanut sauce on my shirt and most of my food landed on the floor. It says something about how much I've matured over the last couple of years that I didn't knock him the hell out for wasting such precious cargo. About half of the PT Hunters got up quickly. On my side the Haights and Gregorius jumped up, looking eager, while the rest of my side had that inevitable resignation look of *I'd better help my idiot friends* on their faces. Say what you will about Hunters, they always have your back. "Everybody, relax. No harm meant. My friend's just had a few too many."

Trip dragged the sputtering Green back into his chair. Luckily, Trip was the stronger of the two.

I tried to defuse the situation. "I've seen you on TV, right? Light heavyweight. You were great. I love that stuff—"

"Keep your idiot on a leash," Ultimate Fighter snarled as he was guided to his seat. "Uncivilized Alabama rednecks."

I thought that Green was a Californian, but saying so probably wouldn't have helped matters. In fact, I think Nate was the only native Alabaman at the table and he was well spoken and wearing a tie. I sat down. "Green, you dumbass. Chill the hell out already or I swear I'll break *another* one of your bones."

"Sorry, Z. It isn't my fault they're such jackasses. I was

just telling everybody about how PT is a bunch of no-good, backstabbing, lying, cheats, and Armstrong is a thieving sack of—"

"Dude, use your *inside* voice," Trip suggested as he studied the table of muscle and testosterone growling at us. "I don't want to get beat up."

Green giggled. "I'm not worried. We got Z. Just hide behind him. That was my plan. He's *huge*."

"Thanks," I muttered. "I'll remember that when I'm getting my teeth kicked in."

A server came by, and I quickly apologized for the mess and slipped her a twenty. Luckily nobody had called security, and it looked like everything was going to be cool. VanZant got back, saw that some of the staff was cleaning up my spillage and everyone looked tense, and asked what he'd missed. I jerked a thumb at Green. "I think he needs to sleep it off."

VanZant shook his head sadly. "He gets spun up sometimes. I've got him. Come on, man. Why don't you go splash some water on your face or something." He dragged Green up by his collar.

"But, I didn't finish my creampuffs!"

"My apologies, Z. He is a really good Hunter when he's sober."

Crisis averted, I went back for replacement food as VanZant led our most inebriated Hunter away. I caught sight of a small man with a gigantic red beard waving at me from the entrance, and so I pointed Milo in the direction of our table. The last of the MHI dinner party had arrived.

Plate partially reloaded, I was preoccupied with using

tongs to pick up some crab legs when somebody bumped into my arm. Another solid fellow had been reaching under the sneeze guard at the same time. "Pardon me," he said politely.

"Sorry about that," I answered as I moved a bit to the side. "Didn't see you. Easily distracted by crab legs, you know."

"Thanks." He scooped up several pounds of crustacean and dumped them onto his plate. Crouched, he still barely fit under the sneeze guard. He straightened his back and towered over me. I'm 6'5", was wearing thick-soled combat boots, and he still had me beat by a few inches.

"If you've seen that show about how hard these are to catch, that just makes them taste even better . . ." I trailed off. The man seemed strangely familiar. Probably thirty, he was thickset, with biceps like hams stuffed under his black t-shirt. His enormous head was stubbly with short dark hair, and there was a crease running down the middle where he'd had a severe skull injury or maybe brain surgery. Beady eyes narrowed as he got a better look at me. One of his eyes wasn't pointing in quite the same direction as the other one. A look of confusion crossed his wide, flat face.

Where did I know this man from?

Of course I hadn't recognized him at first. He'd aged. After all, it had been several years, and he hadn't had that scar on his head nor the bad eye. Plus the last time I'd seen him I'd been kneeling on his chest and dropping elbows against his bloody and unconscious face until his eye had popped out and his skull had broken in half.

"*You!*" we exclaimed at the same time.

His tray hit the floor with a clatter. The other patrons around the seafood area were suddenly quiet. The giant's mouth turned into a snarl and his hands curled into a fist. "Son of a bitch!"

The final illegal, underground, money fight I'd ever participated in had been against this monster. All I'd known going in was that he was a killer, a prison hardened, brutal machine of a fighter, and then he'd beaten the living hell out of me until I'd finally taken him down, lost control, and nearly beaten him to death. I'd never even known his name.

I took a step back. He was right to be mad. I'd lost it. It was the worst thing I'd ever done. "It was an ac—"

"Accident?" Veins were popping out in his neck. "I was out, and you didn't stop hitting me until they dragged you off! You put out my eye!"

"Sorry." *Man, that sounded pathetic.*

"You ruined my life!" And with a roar, the giant charged.

I lifted the metal serving tray like a shield just in time for his fist to bend it in half. The tray went flying and a waitress screamed. Dodging back, I thumped hard into the table with the ice swan. An instinctive duck kept my head attached to my body as the giant threw a massive left hook that decapitated the swan. Then he lowered his shoulder and rammed into me, taking us both onto the table. The ice swan toppled, hit the floor, and exploded, sending bits everywhere. The table collapsed beneath us and we went rolling off in separate directions.

There were a few seconds of shocked silence and then fight or flight kicked in for everyone in the buffet. For the regular people, it was flight from the two very large men crashing about. Sadly, flight wasn't the normal first reaction for a Hunter. There was a battle cry from near the exit. "That PT guy hit Z!" Green shouted as he shoved his way through the people . *The man that had attacked me was wearing a black shirt* . . . Green sprinted across the restaurant yelling, "Fight! Fight!" Then he dove and tackled a random PT employee who was getting a piece of pie from the desert bar.

"No! It's not them." I got up, but the giant was already coming my way again, and then I was too busy protecting my vital organs from his sledge hammer fists to communicate.

The occupants of the MHI table had all stood up to see what was going on, and so had the Paranormal Tactical crew. The two sides looked at each for just a moment . . . and then it was *on*. The last thing I saw was one of the Haight brothers clubbing a PT Hunter in the jaw, because then I had to concentrate on my own problems.

The giant was coming my way, hands up and loose, protecting his face. Even enraged, he was moving like a pro. The last time we'd squared off had been a close one. This was the toughest human being I'd ever fought, at least now that I knew Franks didn't count as human.

"I don't want to fight you," I warned.

"Should'a thought of that before you tried to murder me."

He came in quick, but this wasn't a ring, and I wasn't fighting fair. I kicked a chunk of ice and he instinctively flinched aside as it zipped past him. I yanked a cloth off a table and threw it over his head like a net. I'd like to say that I did it dramatically and all the plates and pitchers stayed in place, but they didn't and most of them shattered on the ground. Temporarily entangled in the tablecloth, he couldn't defend himself very well, so I charged in swinging. I slugged him twice in the stomach, and when his hands went down, I reached up and tagged him with a shot to the mouth.

But then he threw the tablecloth back over me, and I think it was an elbow that got me in the side of the head. I was seeing stars when he slung me around and put me into the meat area. Ham broke my fall. The meat-slicing buffet employees ran for their lives. Getting up, I hurled a pot roast at the giant and he smacked it across the room.

We clashed. There wasn't any finesse at all; it was just a slug fest. We went back and forth, trading blows. Too busy trying to protect my face, I got hit in the ribs, which sucked, and then he nailed me in the stomach, which really sucked, and suddenly I was regretting the several pounds of food I'd just consumed. His shoe landed on a piece of ice, and as he slid off balance, I snap kicked him hard in the thigh of his grounded leg.

He went to his hands and knees. "Stay down!" I ordered.

The restaurant patrons were evacuating. Green had someone in a choke hold and another PT man on his back. I'd forgotten that VanZant had used to be a champion welter-weight, and he was knocking the snot out of a PT man twice his size. The Haights seemed to be having a jolly time, until one of them got hit with a chair. Gregorius was wrestling a PT Hunter next to the soda machines. Ultimate Fighter had Cooper in an arm bar. Albert, despite the cane and leg brace, was a shockingly tenacious fighter, and he was facing two PT Hunters at once, which apparently Trip didn't think was very sporting, because he slammed one of them *through* a corner booth. Even Holly had gotten into it. A PT man hesitated, not wanting to strike a girl, until she groin kicked him like she was punting a football.

Turning back to the giant, I didn't see that my opponent's hands had landed on another serving tray, which he promptly swung and clipped me in the temple. That one rocked my world. I landed flat on my back. The giant came over to stomp me, but Nate body checked him into the soft serve ice cream machine. Too bad the Shacklefords were from Alabama, because the kid showed a lot of promise as a hockey player.

The vanilla spigot had broken off and soft serve came spooling out. "Got no problem with you," the giant said through gritted teeth. "Just him. Get out of my way."

"You mess with MHI, you mess with all of us!"

The giant cocked his misshapen head to one side. "What? *MHI?*"

Nate tried to punch him, and though he was fast and relatively skilled, the giant was simply out of his league. He effortlessly slapped Nate's hands aside, grabbed my brother in law's tie to hold him in place, then slugged him. One, two, three solid hits before Nate's brain had even recorded the first impact. Nate went down, out cold.

That really pissed me off, and I came off the floor, ready to kick some ass.

Hotel security guards were pushing their way inside. Since the restaurant rotated on a platform, the whole place was shaking badly under the stampede. The other ice sculpture fell and broke, and somehow somebody had managed to throw something hard enough to break one of the chandeliers. There was some screaming as Green got pepper sprayed and more screaming as Lee shoved a rival Hunter into the chocolate fountain.

One of the PT men got in my way and I dismantled him. I didn't have time to dick around with these chumps when there was a real enemy to fight. I stepped into the clumsy swing and drove my forearm and all my mass into him so hard that he went spiraling over a table. Another of the black polo-shirted Hunters had gotten between us, so the giant simply picked him up and tossed him over the sushi bar, not even bothering to slow his pace. We met in the middle and proceeded to beat the crap out of each other.

He was fast for a big man, and so was I, but he had a reach advantage, so I had to keep moving to stay ahead of him. I wasn't used to being the smaller and lighter fighter. We locked up on each other as we hit the far end of the buffet, both of us throwing knees and elbows. Between the two of us we probably weighed close to seven hundred pounds, and the furniture broke around us like someone had turned loose a herd of enraged wildebeests. I didn't realize we'd gone too far until my shoulder hit the cold glass of the restaurant's bubble. The glass cracked.

I caught my boot against the railing, heaved the giant back, and managed to hit him with a staggering overhand right. That slowed him down.

"Lacoco! Stop! Z! Owen! What the heck? Quit hitting that Newbie!" Milo was running our way, just ahead of a bunch of casino security and a Las Vegas police officer. "You're on the same team!"

The giant must not have heard Milo's words, because he bellowed, launched himself into me, caught me around the waist, and we hit the interior window. The glass shattered around us and then we were falling, *briefly*. We hit water, but it wasn't particularly deep, because right after the water came tile. And the tile was *very* hard.

Groaning, I lay there, flat on my back in half a foot of water, covered in sparkling shards, the wind knocked out of me, staring up at the hole in the buffet's glass wall one story above, as cold water from a dragon headed fountain spit on us. The giant was on his side next to me. He had a few nasty cuts on his face and arms from the glass. I probably didn't look much better. I realized then that his not-quite-in-the-same-direction eye was fake, because it had popped out and was sitting at the bottom of the pool between us.

A huge crowd of gamblers and shoppers were standing there, gaping at us. Many of them started taking pictures.

At least the fall had finally knocked the fight out of him. The giant looked over at the MHI Happy Face on my tattered shirt with his good eye and groaned.

"Jason Lacoco?" I gasped.

"Uh huh…"

"Owen Zastava Pitt." I coughed. "Nice to meet you. Welcome to Monster Hunter International."

Then several police officers converged on the fountain to arrest us.

— end excerpt —